A HUNDRED
HONEYMOONS

A Hundred Honeymoons

A Novel

J.S. Wilson

Rev. date: 10/12/2020

To order additional copies of this book, contact:
Xlibris
844-714-8691
www.Xlibris.com
Orders@Xlibris.com
803461

CONTENTS

BOOK 1: HOPSCOTCH

BOOK 2: CARNAL

BOOK 3: LETTERS

BOOK 4: TEN YEARS LATER

To Cheryl.
Also to all the wonderful people of San Luis Obispo County, California,
who live in the garden spot of the world.

Women are predators too.
It's just that the prey is different.
—A. J. Strindberg

BOOK I

Hopscotch

CHAPTER 1

Mitchell Drive

Mitchell Drive was six blocks long, lined on both sides with trees and modest one-story, stucco homes of muted pastel colors, vintage 1930s- and '40s-style. Cars were parked in almost every driveway, and the lawns were trim and freshly mowed. Families in Sunday dress-up were in many yards and porches. Middle-class America lived in this self-proclaimed "small-town safe" neighborhood in San Luis Obispo, California. The warm, lazy day under an azure sky was just as it should be in the late summer of 1960.

The Southern Pacific Railroad tracks ran north and south, and this morning a slow freight chugged its way toward the yard. It would pick up more engines, then head north up Cuesta Grade and the Salinas Valley beyond. The train clickety-clacking mixed with church bells for a rhythm as four girls played hopscotch on a cracked sidewalk in front of 651.

Sally, fourteen years old and about to enter high school, was playing with Zoe, Gail, and Cecilia. Sally was just over five feet tall and radiated nervous energy. She had sparkling blue eyes, velvety skin, a slender waist, and perfectly formed legs. Her honey-blond hair was pulled back into a French braid and held in place with red ribbons. Her skirt swayed over well-formed hips, and a white sleeveless top accentuated her developing figure. These qualities made her seem older than her years. Grandma had taken her to buy a training bra a few months earlier, but it was already too small—and it showed. Sally's appearance was a blend of the little girl's clothes her grandma chose for her and the young woman who reluctantly wore them. She exuded confidence and had a coquettish smile that masked her increasing sense of rebellion and womanly feelings. Her curiosity and fantasies about high school, boys, and dating grew and grew.

Sally's sisters, Zoe and Gail, were different from her and each other. Zoe, the youngest, was a bit chubby and flighty. Wearing a flowered pink jumper, she had a hand-me-down look about her. She talked constantly, because to Zoe, life was a frolic.

Gail, two years older than Sally, was the responsible one. She wore wire-rimmed glasses and had a motherly quality. In her shorts and oversized top, she seemed bored with the game.

Cecilia, Sally's sometime friend, lived across the street with her sister, Maria.

Julia Anderson, better known as Grandma, had raised Sally, Zoe, and Gail since their parents had been killed in an auto accident some years earlier. In her house, rules were strict and church attendance was a must. Gail and Zoe followed the rules, but not Sally. The increasingly confining nature of her home life had her kicking at the edges.

The day's scene was set by Mrs. Claussen and her spaniel, Clyde, who waddled at the same pace. Two doors down, Mr. Parsons proudly washed his new Ford, and two shouting boys cavorting in the car wash runoff were covered in mud. These engineers of the future blocked the runoff with leaves and dirt to make a lake to float their boats. Next door, Brian, Sally's friend, threw a baseball against a fence with the periodic *wham-clump* of throw and catch.

Families were preparing for church as the girls primped and the boys resisted. Men were talking sports and women family. Backyard barbecues were being prepped for dinner.

Number 651 was a gray-blue one-story with a gable roof and brick porch. A bay window with bric-a-brac perched on the sill faced the street. A big chestnut tree grew in the grass parking strip. A long sloped driveway with a grass middle strip ran to the garage and a backyard filled with trees.

Faded lines from long-ago hopscotch games were still visible where the girls played. Games had been played there forever, it seemed. Music could be heard coming from up the street.

> I'm gonna sit right down and write myself a letter (pau-pa-ya … pau-pa-ya)
> And make believe it came from you. (pau-pa-ya … pau-pa-ya)
> I'm gonna write words, oh, so sweet, they're gonna knock me off my feet.
> A lotta kisses on the bottom, I'll be glad ya gotta 'em.
> I'm gonna smile and say, "I hope you're feelin' better" (pau-pa-ya … pau-pa-ya)
> And sign "with love" the way you do.
> I'm gonna sit right down and write myself a letter!
> And I'm gonna make believe it came from you!

It was almost Sally's turn at the game she'd once enjoyed but now found childish. The sound of the ball hitting the fence and Brian's exclamations on catching it distracted her. Feeling impatient, she said, "Will you get a move on, Zoe?"

Zoe missed her throw at the eight, saying, "Oh poo!"

Sally gave her disappointed sister a dismissive look and tossed the token at the seven. As it landed with a clink in the square, she jumped up and gave a squeal of success. She hopped up the squares with practiced grace: "One, two, buckle your shoe; three, four, shut the door; five, six, pick up sticks; seven, eight, lay them straight; nine, ten, a big, fat hen." She then picked up her token and came back down the squares, jumping at the cross-tree and back to the start.

Sally aimed her token confidently but then heard Cecilia behind her cry out, "Wait!" Pointing at the scuffed chalk line at the top end of the eight square, Cecilia quickly took a piece of chalk from her pocket and straightened the line.

Zoe said, "No fair. You didn't do that for me. No fair! I'm telling. Oh poo!" She looked to see if Grandma had heard the forbidden word.

Sally tossed the token, which landed in the middle. "Yes, yes," she said triumphantly, repeating the cadence as she moved forward. As she bent to pick up her token, she heard a car approach from down the street. She began, "One, two, buckle my shoe; three, four, sh—"

Hearing the car draw near, she and the other girls turned and looked east. Zoe pointed down the block, and Brian stopped throwing the ball.

The older black convertible had its top down, white sidewall tires, and "flicker" hubcaps that winked in the sun. The occupants pointed at the house across the street from the girls.

Boys! Two in the front and two in the back! The devil-may-care teenagers caught the attention of the girls, who craned their necks to see. The driver was large and blond, and in the passenger seat was a tall, thin boy with black hair. One of the boys in the back was short, powerful, and poorly groomed, and the boy behind the driver was singing along with the same song on the car radio: "A lotta kisses on the bottom, I'll be glad I got 'em."

The car slowed as the driver checked each house number and then pulled up and stopped just opposite the hopscotch game. Sally's heart beat faster, and she could tell it was the same with the other girls. She inspected the driver, who had bad teeth. He looked up inquisitively and asked, "Hey, ah, girls, where's 654 on this street? We could use a little help."

Sally felt a tingle and straightened her skirt, looking away and then back toward the boys. The game forgotten, the boys enjoyed their full attention. The girls were now as focused as they could be, and each preened subconsciously.

Before Sally could speak, Cecilia jumped forward and sang out, "It's over there! Maria told me to look out for you. She's waiting at home." She pointed at her house across the street, then dropped her token, sprang over the curb and around the front of the car, and ran toward her house across the street.

The short boy in the back seat laughed and pointed. "See, I told you she was for real. It's not the next street. This is it!"

"What's your note say?" the driver asked his companions.

"I didn't write it down," Phil said. "I thought you did. Shit! But it was this one or the one we passed before, um, Caudill or up farther on Lawrence."

Sally giggled as the boys taunted each other back and forth in a good-natured way.

In the passenger seat, the boy with the black hair said, "Don't matter now. That's it."

Sally noticed that the second boy in the back seat, who was reading something, seemed indifferent. He had soft, almost transparent, hooded gray eyes and high cheekbones over a full sensual mouth. Barely glancing up, he said, "We're way off. You've got no idea. She was BS'ing you."

"Screw you, Todd!" snapped the driver, who seemed focused on Sally. "Let's figure this out so we can get some. Let's see her note." He grabbed the address note and read, 'Fourth street on the right. Lots of flowers.' We'll see what these girls have to say."

Sally was surprised to hear Cecilia shout from across the street, "Remember me? It's Cecilia. I was with Maria yesterday. You gave her the doll you won at the carnival, remember?"

They all nodded in agreement, and then looked across the street to Cecilia and Maria's house. Maria was sixteen, skinny, and not pretty, but she was popular with boys. Sally, Zoe, and Gail looked at one another knowingly. Maria had a reputation for being easy.

Frank, the driver, turned off the engine and then casually flipped the keys in the air and caught them. He yelled at the big blond boy with the bad teeth, "Get a move on, Kit!"

Sally started to speak, but just then Cecilia, standing provocatively with her hands on her hips, yelled, "Maria's home, too."

Kit said, "Oh yeah, we remember!" He exited the car by swinging his legs over the driver's side door and hopping out. "You're not coming, Todd?" he asked.

Todd said disparagingly, "Nah, not for the likes of *her*."

Then his eyes landed on Sally, and the message in his eyes forced her to back up against a tree. A newborn awareness of self—hair, makeup, legs, bustline—stirred her down, down, down into her tummy. She looked back and their eyes lingered. Surprise, longing, fear, and lust mixed in her as never before. What was it? She whispered to herself, "Todd. His name is Todd!"

His friends' raucous laughter drew Todd's attention back to the street, but his eyes didn't leave Sally. He said, "No, you guys go on. I didn't actually meet her anyway."

Kit swung his blond head around and, flashing his broken teeth, said, "See ya in a while, Todd. You'll wish you'd come along—ya know what I mean? Ya got to grow up sometime, and now's a good time. If it's no, take care of Blackie!"

Sally could feel Todd's eyes sizing her up in a way that she instinctively understood for the first time. Self-consciously aware that she was glowing, she wanted his eyes to stay on her. She felt a self-awareness she'd never experienced before.

Todd shrugged and said to Sally, "Blackie's the name of his car."

Cecilia and the other three boys crossed the street to the house, where Sally could just barely see Maria's slender profile inside. Cecilia and Maria's parents worked Sundays at the inn across town. The boys' reason for visiting Maria was well known but only hinted at around the neighborhood.

Zoe shuffled nervously at the base of the hopscotch tree, for she was more interested in Todd and Sally flashing eyes at each other. The resumption of the game was secondary now.

Todd unlatched the door and got out of the car with slow, deliberate motions, then leaned against the passenger side door. Sally got a full view of him. He was tall, just shy of six feet, with broad shoulders, muscular forearms, dirty-blond hair that fell down over his forehead—and those soft gray eyes! He was almost, but not quite, skinny. Sally's inner voice decided on *wiry*. And he had a relaxed confidence about him that she liked a lot. He wore jeans, a very white T-shirt, and sneakers, and his shirt stretched over his washboard stomach muscles. Casually, his left elbow on the door and his legs crossed in front of him, he turned to face her. He carefully took in the scene, standing pensively at the starting point of the game.

Sally glanced at Zoe, silently asking, *Will you do anything? What will he do?* Todd's maleness permeated the scene, and her awareness of him was overwhelming. Part of her wanted his complete attention, but the other part was scared of the warmth inside her. His eyes were so brave that she felt like he was undressing her. Should she take her turn while he watched?

She picked up her hopscotch token and put it in the nine. The new womanliness in her wanted to show off. She felt as if she knew where each and every part of her body and spirit were, and he was *seeing it all*. He slouched against the car door, radiating masculinity.

Sensing that she was about to take a big step in life, Sally began. One, two, three, then split at the five and six. Each hop, each number, each bend felt like it was in slow motion. A little breeze pushed her skirt up, and she felt her new bust bounce up and down. And then the seven, and turning, picking up her barrette at eight. His eyes were intent on her, and the edges of his soft mouth turned up a little. Was it a smile of expectation? Back down the squares at seven, six, five, four, three, two, one, and end. She felt both relieved and self-conscious.

All her hopping flexed her strong legs, the skirt riding up on her tights. Her bust stretched her blouse, and one button gave way to reveal her small but growing snow-white cleavage.

Todd sucked in a breath of admiration and said with a laugh, "Not bad, not bad."

Now confident, she challenged him, "Do *you* want to play?"

"No, not me. I'm not a hopscotcher. It's a girls' game." He laughed fully and deeply.

From the house, Sally heard a bustle of activity and voices. Grandma emerged from the front door with a pitcher of lemonade and cookies, saying, "Oh girls, it's time for refreshments! Come to the porch and sit down." Her eyes registered the boy's presence.

"Hello there. Will you join us for an early snack?" Grandma gestured in Todd's direction, and then hesitated upon noticing that Todd and Sally were staring at each other. Looking at them, she said, "You've met Sally, I see."

Todd started and a little sheepishly said, "Ah, no ... Well, yes!"

"Well, I'm Mrs. Anderson—Grandma—and these are my granddaughters, Zoe, Gail, and that's Sally. She's fourteen."

Sally almost jumped out of her shoes when Grandma mentioned her age. She went pink in the cheeks, which Todd didn't seem to notice with his attention diverted to the refreshments.

"My friends Kit, Phil, and Frank are visiting ... across the street," he said.

Grandma said, "Oh! Those in the car? I guess that must be—"

He replied, "Yeah! Kit's the big blond dude with the bad teeth. Phil's the short guy, and Frank's the, the wingman, I guess you'd say."

Grandma gave a disapproving smile, knowing the reason for their visit. "And you aren't a friend of Maria?"

"Nah, not me. I'm ... Nah, not me."

By now, everybody was aware of a little tension in the air.

Grandma gestured at the lemonade. "Would you like some lemonade and cookies? Quite refreshing on this hot day."

"Yeah ... Okay, thanks." Todd walked to the brick porch and the tray of refreshments.

Sally looked hard at Grandma and moved toward the porch. New feelings stirred in her, but what message were they conveying? These new feelings took over as Todd neared the porch. Her heart leaped when he drew close and their arms brushed against each other. It was electric.

He reached out and said, "My name's Todd. Nice to meet you, uh ... Sally."

Should she take it? Part of her said no, but the warm spot in her tummy said yes. She took his hand, replying gently, "It's nice to meet you, too, uh ... Todd."

Their eyes met as their hands touched. Grandma's stare said no, but Sally's feelings were way past a retreat from *him* now. Her posture became more adult, and the voice coming from the warm spot swept up and said, *He touched me.*

His mouth opened slightly but made no sound.

Sally smiled and looked away, her cheeks glowing with this new feeling. Her eyes gestured toward the lemonade and cookies. As Todd reached down for a mason jar, his upper arm brushed across the front of Sally's top, and an electric current again swept over her.

Grandma eyed Sally and Todd as they drank their lemonade in unison. There was a long, poignant silence.

Then Todd said, "Hot day, huh?"

Sally picked up the conversation and replied, "Um, yeah, it's a little too warm. Well, the weather, I mean." Her entire body was glowing now, and her heart beat faster. She licked her lips and shuffled her feet. The champagne bubbles in her eyes were really working now. This new feeling of want curled around the place where he'd brushed against her body.

The cookies were eaten, and the day drew on. The wind picked up, blowing Todd's hair and ruffling Sally's skirt. They made small talk while Gail and Zoe just sat and took in this unfolding boy/girl adventure. Grandma asked Todd, "Are you from around here?"

"No, I'm from over the hill, out in the Carrizo Plain. The Wyrum ranch, the Rocking W, out toward Bakersfield. Nowheresville kinda. Around Simler Station."

"Oh, the Rocking W. Your family are ranchers?" asked Grandma.

"No, I'm working on the ranch. The boss, Mr. Wyrum, is my uncle. I'm there over the summer. It's thirty-five thousand acres, cattle mostly, some horses and crops."

"And the rest?" Grandma asked. "Not much out that way as I recall. What's your school, and where's your dad?"

"Oh, the rest. Hogs, chickens—ya know." Todd hesitated, and then went on. "I used to study along with the Wyrum girls, but they're off to a fancy school back east. I'm off myself to a new high school in the fall. A senior, I hope, 'cause I'm a little ahead in my studies. Not quite sure where yet. Who knows?"

"Oh my! A little ahead are you? Is that because you're older?"

"No, no ... I'm actually younger—sixteen. I just got ahead in my studies, that's all."

"I see! Good for you. So you live way out there with your folks?" Grandma rephrased her question.

"No, I live up in San Bruno, near the city—San Francisco, I mean. School's there. Capuchino High School. That's where our team's from— our boxing team. Mr. Johnson's our coach. I just met the others here 'cause I'm out on the ranch for the summer. I'll be a sophomore next year, someplace. Might be around here. Who knows? Kind of complicated. We've moved around a lot. My mom's an army nurse." Todd gave a nervous shrug. He didn't answer Grandma's question about his father.

"Do you work on the ranch? I mean, like part-time, weekends?" Sally asked.

"Oh yeah, for darn sure. All that. Chores in the morning, wrangle in the afternoon. Like all this summer—six days a week, and more at roundup. The Boss, he works us pretty hard."

"Oh my, do you like that? To be pushed so hard, I mean?" asked Grandma.

"That's ranchin'. Got a great foreman—Cruz. Knows about all there is to know about wrangling. Fun around the bunkhouse, too, with the wranglers—uh, cowboys, I mean—ya know? My Spanish is getting better ... I mean, with Cruz speaking only Spanish when we work."

Grandma and Sally looked on with amazement as he continued.

Todd looked down at the porch with that sheepish look that women find so disarming. "Miss Lady—Mrs. Wyrum, I mean—she treats us good, ya know? And her cooking is the best."

Commotion erupted across the street as Todd's friends came tumbling out of the house and ran happily back to the car, sounding off as they went.

"Hey, let's go, Todd. Time to hit it, guy. We've gotta get to the match."

"Match? What match?" Sally asked.

The big blond boy said, "Oh, we're in a boxing tournament over at the high school. The tournament, ya know, this weekend."

"Oh, at *my* high school?" Sally asked, noticing a mouse under his right eye. Looking at the other boys, she saw a split lip, a swollen cheek, and bruises here and there.

"Yours? Yeah, nice school. Good gym!" the blond boy answered.

"Oh, the gym," said Sally. "Yeah, the gym's fine." With all that was going on here, she could scarcely believe he was interested in the gym. She and the blond boy looked at each other again.

Phil said, "Hey, it's time to hit it. We got forty minutes."

Todd drained the last of his lemonade and put the mason jar down on the tray. "Well, Sally, we've got to head out and, and … I mean …" He and Sally stood there in an adolescent stupor as the other boys motioned toward the car.

"Uh, great! And thanks to you, Mrs. …" Todd seemed embarrassed.

"Grandma. Just Grandma."

"Uh, thanks," said Todd. "Well, gotta go now. And uh, I'll see you later, Sally uh … Hope I'll see you—well—again. I'll see you later, huh?"

Sally's eyes darted around at the other girls nervously. "Will I see you?"

The blond boy shouted, "Come on, Todd. Come on! Forty minutes. Let's get out of here."

"Gotta go now, Sally. Will I … see you later?" He vaulted over the car door and settled in. Kit got behind the wheel as the others piled in. He gunned the engine, and pulled away from the curb.

Sally put her hand up to wave before she could think to ask, *Where? When? How?* This long morning before church, which had seemed so boring a moment ago, was over in a flash of black and chrome headed down the quiet street. Sally watched the car make a right at Broad Street and head downtown. She tried to stop it with her eyes, but it just kept going.

She saw Todd look back a couple of times, as if he felt the same way, but the car kept moving, and she knew he wouldn't stop. In a moment, the car and Todd were out of sight, but not out of her thoughts. She sat down abruptly on the porch.

Grandma picked up the tray and said, "There will be other boys."

Sally looked up at Grandma with angry, disappointed eyes. "No, Grandma, he's important. He's the boy I want."

Grandma shook her head. "My, my, my, that's quite a thought. My word!"

Then Sally noticed the mason jar he'd touched with his lips. She reached into her pocket and pulled out her handkerchief. Then she took the jar that he'd drunk from and pressed it against her stomach, just below her slowly heaving bust. She looked at it, then up the street. The other girls noticed her do this but held quiet. Holding the jar in both hands, she walked across the grass and leaned against the tree, again looking off down the street.

When Sally said Todd's name to herself, Grandma saw her lips move. She also noticed Sally's adjusted posture and recognized the challenge that Sally's growing maturity would bring.

"Sally's got a boyfriend! Sally's got a boyfriend!" Zoe teased, pointing down the street.

Grandma scolded Zoe. "Now shush. We'll see about that."

Zoe stopped, but she stuck her tongue out at Sally and said, "Nanny nanny, boo boo."

Sally glanced at the hopscotch game and wondered if she'd ever play it again. She walked back to the porch, looking up the street. Brian was still throwing the ball against the fence in the yard next door. Keeping his eyes on Sally, he nodded toward the back of the house.

She knew what he meant, but with more important thoughts on her mind now, she just ignored him. He looked slightly disappointed and just kept on with the ball.

Grandma came back out and asked, "Well, what did you think of that? About that boy? What do you think of him?"

Sally looked up boldly, the mason jar in her hand. "Someday, someday I'll marry that boy, that Todd. I'll marry him." She pushed her chin up and walked into the house.

Grandma's jaw dropped. "My, my, my."

CHAPTER 2

Desired

Sally walked through the entry and down the hall to her room. Glancing at the mason jar in her hands, where her memory of him was imprinted, she could see the look in his eye and hear the lilt of his voice. There was something in that voice, those eyes—something more, some little hurt or tenderness she wanted to hold and help, heal, treasure, and make her own. She shut the door and leaned against it. A slight smudge from his lips was on the edge of the glass, and there was a chip in the rim. She held it close to her face and realized that just like the mason jar, Todd had a flaw that she could soothe.

Pulling open her dresser drawer, Sally folded back her socks and tops. Then she raised the glass to her lips, softly kissed it once more, and tucked it in the back, right-hand corner behind her underwear. Looking at the drawer's contents derisively, Sally realized she now felt a need for lingerie—not underwear. Somehow that change went along with the warm feeling.

To look in the mirror was to thrill at her own blossoming. Sally's developing figure had attracted the attention of boys and the jealousy of some of her girlfriends. She'd begun not just to show up, but show *off* in class, and the eyes on her felt good.

"Church! You've got about an hour to get ready," Grandma yelled down the hall.

"Okay, okay," Sally called back. She noticed the window was open and the curtains moved gently in the breeze. Next door, Brian's bedroom window was open. She chose a white sleeveless top with buttons down the front and a pink skirt, which would match the new low-heeled shoes she'd gotten as a gift from an aunt. She put on her underwear and training bra, disliking both intensely.

Grandma came in without knocking, slamming the door behind her. She looked at Sally's selected outfit and said, "No, that won't do. Won't do at all." She glared at Sally, then reached into the closet and selected a flower-print dress with a small collar and buttons down the back. The skirt was long, as were the sleeves. She then set out a pair of brown lace-up shoes.

Eyeing the earrings, lipstick, and rouge on the nightstand, Grandma shook a finger at Sally and said, "That won't do, either. You are a pious young lady on her way to church. Not a ... party girl! Didn't I tell you to get rid of those things last week? What, oh, what am I going to do with you, young lady? Do you want me to talk to Deacon Jennings about this?"

Sally quietly steamed until Grandma got to the line about telling Deacon Jennings, but then she turned away and smirked just a little. She'd noticed how the deacon seemed to be watching her more and had a different look in his eyes when she kneeled during service.

Grandma left the room, glaring at Sally and slamming the door shut.

Sally picked up the things Grandma had selected, put them neatly on the bed, and walked to the window. A breeze ruffled the curtain. She took off her skirt and unbuttoned her blouse. Her breasts overflowed the cups of her training bra, which now barely covered her nipples. Remembering Brian's nod while playing ball, she reached over and parted the curtains just a little. She could see his profile back in the shadows. They'd done this before.

She and Brian had been conversing across these two windows since they were little. When she'd first noticed him watching her like this, she'd shied away without letting him know she'd seen him. But his looks grew more and more bold as time went on, and gradually she'd let him see more of her. Last week she'd opened her blouse for him. It had excited her to do so.

Now as she stood at the window, the morning's events and thoughts of Todd immersed her in erotic fantasies that she unsuccessfully tried to push away. Ever since she and Grandma had had "the talk," mixed feelings had competed inside Sally. Grandma had bluntly described the evils of "self-touching," the intentions of "bad boys," and the dangers of "lewd dressing." She had also made it quite clear which girls Sally was *not* to associate with, and Maria was at the top of the list. Salvation—Grandma had actually used that word—was found through the church.

Sally ran her hands up and over her growing bust. For months now, this warmth had been exciting and frustrating her. It was not something she willed—it just happened. The more she stewed over Grandma's warnings and her own fantasies, the more she thought, *How can something described as so wonderful be bad?* She wished Todd was there, but at least the warm feeling was.

Sally looked over at the pile of little girl clothes Grandma had selected. *Can she force me to be that little girl again?* Her inner voice, thoughts of Todd, and warm spot said, *No.*

She opened her blouse and adjusted the curtain so the sun shone through. As the slight breeze blew the curtains across her pale-pink roses, the sensation thrilled her. She licked her lips, pouted, and took a deep breath. Dropping her eyes to look at herself, she then raised them slowly, knowing Brian was only a short distance away.

The boy she'd befriended when they were kids had been replaced by a young man. Brian leaned back against his bed and stared at her—his shirt open, belt undone, and jeans hanging loosely around his hips. Even in the shadow of the room, Sally could see his intensity. He was rubbing his hands across his tense lower abdomen, and the lump in his Levi's was just barely discernible.

"Hi, Sally. Ah, warm isn't it ... ?"

A shiver ran through Sally, and she sucked in a breath as she showed him her silhouette. "Hi, Brian. I see you. Can you see me?" She gave him a little finger wave, then pulled the cord and raised the blinds slowly, allowing rays of sunlight to slant in and across her body. She unstrapped her bra so that it hung loosely off her breasts. As she slowly let it slip off, fully revealing her bust, she sensed Brian's anticipation.

Now the sheer curtain barely concealed Sally's nakedness. She leaned forward, pressing her body against the curtain. Running her right hand up her tummy and across her mounds, she cupped a breast and squeezed just a little. Without realizing it, she let out a loud whimper. She could see Brian's mouth open as he drew in a breath. He leaned his head back, and the veins of his neck stood out.

She listened to hear if Grandma or her sisters were nearby. My God, if they caught her doing this! *But the thrill is worth it,* her inner voice said, and that overcame her fear. She ran her hands over her hips and thighs.

She wanted to touch herself as she'd almost done many times before. The fabric rubbing her pinkness had made the warm spot wet.

Even though she looked into Brian's room, Sally saw Todd. The hands that touched her were his hands, and she was transported into a fantasy about him. As she squeezed herself, it was really Todd fondling her. She swooned but kept control. She felt power over Brian, which felt good in every way. She knew she was seductive and womanly. Could she retreat into a little girl self now? *No!*

Brian's dim figure lay back on the bed, and she could see he was naked from the waist down. When he began to move his hands, his face grew tense and his body arched forward. She could just barely hear his breathing, which became labored. His loins tensed in and out.

Pushing even farther into the window, Sally looked out with hooded eyes, posing for him. The fabric fell away, exposing her bosom as she cupped her breasts. They tingled, and she said, "Do you want to touch them, Brian?" She wondered about the girlie magazines she'd seen in his room.

"Oh, Sally, ah!" Brian's composure began to dissolve, and he gasped for breath.

Sally kept fondling herself while giving Brian little glimpses to further excite him. It was going to happen. Her eyes wanted it, and she leaned out the window to give him a full view. He could see all of her above her hips now. A moan escaped his open mouth, his head thrown back. She could see him, and her heart raced in anticipation of what was about to happen.

"Oh, Brian!" escaped her lips. It was so erotic, and she felt the warmth all over. She drew in a breath and saw him tense up again, then twice more. It was so exciting. She knew, but she didn't really know.

Sally felt as if she could have reached out and touched his want. What was it like? How did it feel? Was it warm or hot? Her own body craved something, something. What would it feel like to have that something? She had ensnared him completely, yet in doing so she'd addicted herself to wanting, needing it. The sensuality of having such power over a boy thrilled her.

Images of the carnal pleasures of men and women filled her imagination. She sensed, knew, she wanted it all—the looks, touching, being felt, him in her hand, stroking. Thoughts and images of Todd filled her mind and made her wet. She touched herself slowly, then faster, then frantically, and finally an exquisite feeling surged throughout her body. Nothing in her life, even her most erotic fantasies, could begin to describe how wonderful it felt. Her orgasm didn't just take her beyond good; it captured and addicted her right from that first moment. She wanted—had to have—more, much more, of this.

Sally slumped to the floor and curled up around her heaving tummy. Her mind drifted across the street to Maria and what she was known for. Now Sally understood the fun, the feel of *it*! Oh yes! "Oh Todd," she moaned.

~

Abruptly Grandma's voice interrupted her thoughts. "Ready yet, young lady? Church at noon."

The words rang out, halting Sally's fun in its tracks. "Almost," she called out with the disappointed tone of someone awakened from a dream.

Brian's convulsions swam into her mind, but Todd was in his place. "Oh, Todd," she whispered. It wasn't just him, was it? That other self, the woman, wanted more—and not just soothing love, but the thrill of the lust she'd just experienced.

Unfolding herself from her cocoon of joy at the window, she crossed to the bed and surveyed the motley collection of "church clothes." She didn't want these little girl dresses. The white sleeveless blouse, pleated pink skirt, white heels, and makeup was what she needed. And the underwear—yuck! The training bra—double yuck!

Sally sat on the edge of the bed, still half dressed. She didn't wonder what had become of Brian, because Todd filled that space. But she did wonder, now that she'd watched Brian, how something that big could fit in her small place. She made sure the door was shut, then listened to make sure the others were way down the hall. From her dresser, she got a small hand mirror and sat on the edge of the bed. Pulling down her panties, she held the mirror up between her legs and wondered. Would it hurt—something so big going into such a small place? But the thrill of just thinking about what was next made her heart beat faster, and she could hardly wait.

Activity down the hall made Sally stop her inquiry abruptly and put the mirror back. She dressed quickly, applied some makeup she'd hidden, then looked in the mirror again. The reflection wasn't quite what she wanted, so she hiked up her dress a couple of inches and pinched her nipples. *A little better*, she thought. Slipping on the ugly brown shoes completed the outfit.

Grandma, Zoe, and Gail were waiting at the full-length mirror in the front hall. After adjusting her own simple print dress, Grandma turned and faced Sally. With a surprised and cross look on her face, she said, "Oh my, no! That just won't do, now, will it, young lady? I've told you about this before."

Zoe and Gail smirked and giggled. "You're in trouble now, Little Miss Fancy," said Zoe.

"Well, what—?" Sally retorted.

Grandma took a step toward her, gripped her by the arm, and marched her to the bathroom. Opening the door, she flipped the light switch and placed Sally squarely in front of the mirror at the sink. She turned on the cold water, put a washcloth in Sally's hand, and asked, "Is this the way you want the deacon to see you, looking like a ... floozy?"

Sally balked and said, "What? I look the way you want, don't I?" Imagining the deacon's gaze on her developing figure when they got to church, she smiled a little to herself. She knew what the deacon wanted her to look like.

Grandma grimaced. "Lipstick on a child is the devil's work. Off with it."

Reluctantly Sally scrubbed at her lips and face while shooting dagger looks at Grandma.

"Now, don't you feel better, Sally? You look like a sweet young Christian girl again." After she dried Sally's face, Grandma marched her back down the hall to the entry. When Zoe and Gail giggled again, she said, "Enough of that, girls. Sally looks just fine."

Grandma's outfit was topped with a wide-brimmed hat and large flower-covered handbag. Gail had a similar church look, while Zoe had a bonnet, and she and Sally carried small handbags more suitable for children. After checking themselves out in the hall mirror, they all walked out the door, across the porch, and down the steps. In spite of their hats, each raised a hand to shade her eyes, for the sun was higher and hotter now.

Mitchell Drive still looked its Sunday best. Many more people were out in their yards now or getting ready to leave for church. The little boys still played in the street with their make-believe dam and lake—all smiles, fun, and laughter. They were also wet and muddy, and Gail scolded them, "Your mom's gonna be mad at the mess," but the boys ignored her.

Maria and Cecilia came from across the street, and they all piled into the car, shoving and complaining. Grandma got in behind the wheel, and they all finally settled in with Sally squeezed into the back seat between Gail and Maria. This forced her to confront Maria's outfit, perfume, and behavior—yuck!—so she sulked as they drove up Broad Street on the way to church.

On the ten-minute drive, they passed friends walking along and waved greetings to some of them. When they passed some boys, Maria leaned out the window to let them see more of her. Grandma, in the front seat, couldn't see to admonish her. It just made Sally even more resolved to be more womanly.

Sally wondered where she could get some of that bust-enhancement cream she'd read about in magazines at the beauty parlor Grandma went to. Maria didn't have much in the way of boobs, but she showed off what she had. Sally wanted much bigger ones. All that cute, colorful lingerie she'd seen advertised would be nice, too. Todd would like that, she was sure. *My Todd*, she thought. She imagined Todd in Brian's place, and her tummy curled up around that image.

~

Parking at the church was the usual mess, so they had to park far from the entry. Sally had to walk self-consciously through the crowd, feeling like a little girl. She thought she was one of the prettiest girls in town, but she didn't feel that way dressed as she was today.

Deacon Jennings was a foppish, peering-into-you kind of man. He wore an old but carefully cared-for suit under his black robe, including a bow tie with a high-collar shirt. He gave Sally the once-over as he took her hands and then kind of slid them away, which made her uncomfortable. Maria was walking just a little behind her. When the deacon noticed Maria, his eyes instantly fell on her cleavage before he quickly averted them. Sally felt a bit jealous that she wasn't the first noticed. She knew that the deacon's brother was the principal at the high school she'd be attending this fall and wondered if he'd be the same cloying type.

In the foyer, each woman picked up a little wood-stemmed fan from a wicker basket, and the large congregation filed in and sat in the wooden pews. As the women waved their little fans, it sounded like hundreds of butterfly wings.

The sermon was about avoiding temptation, of all things. The deacon peered down from the elevated pulpit and seemed to direct his speech right at Sally. Toward the end, he mentioned something about "being your own judge," which made Sally ask herself, *Could something that feels so good be bad? I mean, if God gave us the ability to have that feeling, could it be a sin?*

Afterward, everyone partook of a potluck lunch served in the church basement. The half hour they were down there was filled with the usual chitchat, gossip, and plans for the afternoon.

Sally's mind was filled with Todd as they walked out of the church. The deacon's eyes replayed his earlier taking-in of Sally's blossoming figure. Grandma gave each girl an envelope with one dollar in it, which they dropped in a box in the foyer.

Mrs. Sondheim, who had befriended Grandma and her girls, was in a conversation with some of her club friends on the patio. She had a slender figure, dressed beautifully, and had fashionable hair. Her hemline and blouse were not what most of the other ladies would consider proper attire for church, but of course, that didn't matter to Mrs. Sondheim since she was married to one of the leaders of the county. She also had her own small accounting firm and served as a county commissioner and head of its finance committee, so she could do as she pleased—and usually did.

Hanging back as she passed Mrs. Sondheim, Sally said, "Hi! I love your dress."

"Oh, this old thing? I've had it for years. But sometimes fashions come back, and you've got to take advantage." She posed as the other matrons looked on a bit disapprovingly, though the men obviously felt differently. Looking at Sally, Mrs. Sondheim continued, "You know, Sally, with your figure, a dress like this would suit you to a tee. You've grown up a lot since I last saw you. You're a beautiful young lady now, and you should dress and behave that way."

Sally blushed a little and said, "Well, Grandma doesn't agree."

Mrs. Sondheim glanced at Grandma, farther away in the crowd, and giggled. "For all her good qualities, Sally, Grandma's not exactly a fashion luminary, is she?" They both laughed at their private joke, and Mrs. Sondheim continued, "When you'd like some advice on a new look, I could help out, you know. Lingerie, too!" With that, she turned back to her hoity-toity friends.

Sally's imagination took in these words and also those from the sermon:

be oneself. The self she wanted to be like was Mrs. Sondheim, only even more sexy.

The congregation dispersed and went to their cars, happy conversations continuing. Grandma gathered the girls, but Maria was across the lot talking with some older boys. When Grandma yelled at her to get in the car, Maria came back reluctantly.

An older girl watching said, with an edge to her voice, "So long, GB."

"What's that mean?" Zoe asked.

Sally chimed in, "Yeah, what's that mean, Grandma?"

"We know," a couple of boys standing nearby said, with knowing laughs.

Cecilia said, "I know, too."

Grandma, shaking her head, abruptly cut Cecilia off. "Oh my, that girl. Now hush, Cecilia, right now. Get in the car, girls."

Sally knew better than to ask again what *GB* meant, but she resolved to find out on her own.

The boys were talking about boxing as they walked away. They yelled across the parking lot at some friends, "See you at three! We'll pick you up."

Sally's ears perked up. *Boxing? Todd, oh my!* And then she realized— Todd was in the boxing tournament at the high school that afternoon.

A plan started to form in her head. What time? How to get there? What to wear? And most important, what story to make up to deceive Grandma? Who could help her make up a good excuse?

Then she knew. Only Maria was experienced and devious enough to help her.

CHAPTER 3

Boxing

After church Sally changed into a skirt and blouse, and then found Grandma on the back porch cleaning the barbecue grill. "Grandma, can I go over to—"

But Grandma broke in and said, "This is awful, just awful, Sally. Look at my hands. Oh, this old wire brush! Didn't I ask you to do this last week?"

Sally hated cleaning the grill, and her thoughts raced to find an excuse, any excuse, for not having done it. "Grandma, remember you wanted me to finish up that bazaar stuff?"

Grandma's expression turned from cross to questioning, which told Sally she was on to something. "Hmm, I'm not sure I meant for you not to clean the grill, Sally. Can you help me now?"

This called for creative thinking from Sally. "I promised Maria's mom, remember?"

Again the questioning look from Grandma. Altering Maria's clothing to be more modest was one of the few ways she could think of to get the girl to be more ladylike. Sally knew she'd hit on a good excuse to go across the street.

"Well, okay," said Grandma. "But remember, dinner's at six."

"Okay. Thanks, Grandma!" Almost too enthusiastically, Sally sprang up and went inside, slamming the screen door. Then she hesitated, remembering the sewing basket she needed if she was to pull off this ruse. She got it from the linen closet in the hall, then went out the front door, where she confronted her sisters still playing hopscotch.

Looking up in surprise, Gail said, "Where ya goin', Sally?"

"I'm gonna help out with Maria's dress redo that Grandma wants done. It will take all afternoon, though, so *don't* disturb us," she said, giving the girls a rather stern look. They paid only passing attention, then went on with the game.

Sally gave the boys on the street, still playing in the mud, a wide berth. Just as she started around them, they raised their hands as if they were going to throw mud balls at her. She shouted at them threateningly, "Don't you dare! I'll tell your mother."

Gail and Zoe yelled, "Do it! Do it!"

The boys feigned as if to throw the mud balls, but didn't. After Sally got to the other side of the street, they went back to throwing mud at each other.

Sally's next dilemma was how to get Maria to buy into her plan, and Grandma too.

She'd known him only a few minutes, but it didn't matter. She imagined Todd sitting close and softly, romantically talking to her. Would he kiss her? Would she let him? What if Maria tried to cozy up to Todd? Sally sure wouldn't put it past her. Neither that floozy Maria nor any other girls were ever getting near him. Todd was hers!

On Maria's porch, Sally noticed the door was ajar and shouted, "Anybody home?"

A moment later Maria appeared and said, "Mom's not home. Do ya need something?"

"Not really, but I know you were thinking of going over to the boxing match to meet friends and stuff this afternoon," Sally said with a nervous smile.

With a questioning look on her face, Maria replied, "Uh, yeah?" Just then Cecilia appeared in the hall, and Maria half turned to her and said knowingly, "You're not going."

Cecilia eyed them and exclaimed, "I'll tell! Mom knows what you want to do."

Maria's eyes got hard and her voice had an edge to it. "You won't tell, because if you do, I'll tell her about the Hummels you broke. That wasn't an accident like you told her."

Cecilia turned and sulked back down the hall.

After a triumphant moment, Maria smiled slyly. "It's that other boy who stayed in the car that you want, isn't it? I mean, this morning. He's in the boxing, isn't he?" She raised her chin and said, "I only let them have a little fun, you know? But I'll let them go further tonight, maybe. They really like me, because I'm a party girl. I put out, not like those prissy girls, those PTs." She stood up straight and preened proudly.

Sally's jaw dropped a little at what she'd just heard.

Maria noticed this and said, "Yeah, I'm right, aren't I? You want him, I can tell. I know boys—I know what they want. I saw him in the car across the street. He's cute. Will you let him? You can come with me. I'll let you use my lipstick and other makeup."

Sally's heart was pounding. "How do we get to the gym at school to see the boxing?"

Maria was way ahead of her. "I know some older boys who'll drive us. They have a really cool car. You'll see! We'll go out the back gate. What's in the basket?"

Sally said, "I told Grandma I was going to help modify your dress."

Maria nodded. "That *thing*! We'll fool with it and make it look changed, okay?"

Sally took out the sewing kit, and Maria got the dress. As they modified it a little, Maria asked, "Your granny is strict, isn't she? My mom too. She wants me to rejoin the Girl Scouts. Can you believe that? Those prissy little girls."

After a short discussion, they decided on a plan to fool both Grandma and Maria's mom. As they dressed and did their makeup, Sally could tell that Maria was jealous of her more developed figure. *Too bad*, Sally thought.

After looking in the mirror—and obviously wanting a compliment, Maria asked, "How's this?"

"Oh yeah, the boys will like that look," Sally told her. Then she remembered something. "One other thing. What does PT mean?"

Maria cast her eyes down and gave Sally a prideful smile. "I take care of them, you know? I help the boys relax, sometimes with a gang bang. The high school boys mostly, but at the college, too. They really like me, not those PTs from up in Aquila Alta. They love me. They got needs and they depend on me, because I put out."

Sally's shock must have been obvious, because she knew what "put out" meant. But what about *PT?* she wondered.

After a few last-minute adjustments, they left and met the boys at the car on Broad Street. At school, Maria and two boys headed to an area behind the maintenance building, while the others walked toward the gym.

Sally could now fully focus on finding Todd, but where, how, and when? She looked around the building, where she'd been a couple of times, though not lately. Did it look familiar? The entry was old, not well lit but clean. The floor was polished wood, just scrubbed. Off to the left were the restrooms. Sloping down to another area was a long hall with a "Locker Rooms" sign hanging overhead. Against one wall stood a well-lit trophy case filled with old photos, trophies, pennants, hats, and other souvenirs.

Adults and kids milled around, a few of whom Sally recognized. Up ahead she could hear the voices of the crowd, amplified by the open space of the gym, and every few minutes a shout or groan would break out. There was excitement in the air, but Sally's own excitement had nothing to do with boxing.

She suddenly realized that she was alone. This was unusual, because she always had someone to go places with—Grandma, her sisters, a friend, someone! It made her feel a little vulnerable, but that soon passed. She was there to meet Todd, and that was all that mattered. And she didn't want to share Todd with anyone, especially any other *girl*.

The noise from the gym made it obvious to Sally that the boxing was underway. Was Todd in a match yet? Oh no, had he finished already? Was he there at all? Questions raced through her mind, and panic crept in. *No, no, no, don't get upset. Calm down,* she said to herself.

She walked into the gym and looked for a seat. She was still apprehensive, but her desire to see Todd pulled her forward. She stood at the top of an aisle leading down to the ring. The crowd of about two hundred fans, mostly men, surrounded the ring, which was set up about four feet above the main floor. The dank smell of sweat and smoke filled the air. The gym was dimly lit except for the ring itself, which was bathed in a harsh light from directly above. No one except the referee was in the ring.

On the other side of the gym, Sally could see a group of girls in cheerleader uniforms. She paid them special attention, because she wanted to be a cheerleader when she started high school. Their outfits were short green skirts and white tops trimmed in gold. Even from across the gym, she could tell how pretty and statuesque the girls were, and every eye was on them.

Walking down the aisle, she saw a seat at the end of the fourth row. She sat down and said hello to the man next to her. Some commotion behind her drew her attention, so she turned to look. To her amazement, Todd came walking down the same aisle toward the ring. He wore a hooded white robe with "San Luis Obispo HS Boxing" across the back.

Sally's heart leaped, and she gave him a little finger wave. "Hi, Todd. Remember me ...?" Her words trailed off, as though spoken in a whisper. Among the noise of the crowd, her voice was barely audible even to herself. Todd didn't even look up—just kept up a steady pace to the ring.

At the edge of the ring, a big man in a sports jacket and slacks helped Todd up and through the ropes. On the back of the man's jacket was the school's name and "Coach" in big block letters. As he helped Todd out of his robe, the coach looked back and surveyed the crowd, and his eyes briefly lingered on Sally. She looked back at this big, athletic, handsome man—tall with wide shoulders, a rugged face, and big hands. He exuded a confident masculinity and looked every inch an accomplished athlete. For just an instant, Todd faded from her thoughts.

Another boy and his coach entered the boxing ring from the opposite corner and began the same sparring routine Todd had done. After a few minutes of this, the referee called both boxers to the center of the ring and gave them instructions, and then each went back to his own corner.

Todd wore green and white, his school colors. As Sally focused on his tall, wiry form standing in his corner of the ring, the boy she'd fallen for that morning became the man of her dreams. He looked so sensual. Her heart pounded, and she grew more excited with each passing moment.

A loud bell rang, and the boxers quickly moved to the center of the ring. Sally definitely was not prepared for what happened next. They began hitting each other—gloves smacking, voices groaning, and bodies crouching through the first round. Todd used a series of straight left-handed punches interspersed with hits from his right, and each punch snapped his opponent's head back. The other boy swung more wildly and with less effect. At the end of the round, Todd threw a body shot that buckled the other boxer.

Sally screamed at Todd, at everyone, as obvious pain showed in both boys' faces. *Oh, my God!* It was awful and yet stimulating in a ruthless kind of way, and she couldn't stop watching. The crowd roared around her. She was mesmerized, but at the same time, she didn't like it. She wanted Todd to win, and she wanted the other boy to stop hitting him. *Oh my, please stop,* her inner voice cried. She tried to get Todd's attention, but he didn't notice her.

The bell rang again, and the boxers went to their respective corners. Todd's coach climbed into the ring and splashed water on him, removed his mouthpiece, and spoke to him in a very determined way. The coach looked angry, gesturing with his fists clenched, but Todd did nothing. Another man from outside the ropes gave Todd a drink from a bottle, which Todd then spit into a bucket. *Oh yuck,* Sally thought.

Then the coach put the mouthpiece back in Todd's mouth, the bell rang again, and the boxers were back at it. Now there was more action but less movement. Every time Todd hit the other boy in the midsection, a *whoosh* sound came from the boy. After a minute or so, the crowd—and even Sally—could tell Todd was winning. The other boy backed up after almost every punch, and blood ran from his lower lip. Todd's face was a red mask of determination. His hair whipped around, sending sweat flying across the ring and even into the front rows. Some of it landed on Sally's leg. Without hesitation she touched it. It felt like him. *Is this what wanting him means?*

The bell rang again, and the boys went back to their corners. Todd's coach climbed into the ring again and talked to him, and this time a devilish smile turned up the corners of the man's mouth. He nodded, patted Todd on the shoulder, and gave him some instructions illustrated with mock punches.

Sally noticed an empty chair in the second row on the aisle, so she moved up and sat down. Just then a stir rippled through the throng around her, and most eyes turned to the left. The man to her left stood up to look at whatever was causing the stir, and even Todd's coach looked around. Sally craned her neck to see what was up.

What was up was a stunning girl walking by the ring apron. Wearing the cheerleaders' uniform with the short skirt, she moved with a sexual, confident grace into Sally's view. She had smooth buttermilk skin, big, brown gypsy eyes, and a luxurious pile of raven-black hair. Her legs were well formed, and her hips swung along as she walked by only a few feet in front of Sally.

But what most attracted the attention of the crowd weren't the girl's eyes or hair. It was her cheerleader top pulled tightly around her perfectly formed bust, which jiggled in rhythm with her walk. Pride in her appearance shone in her eyes as she surveyed the spectators' attention, and Sally's desire to be on the cheerleading team grew. Men's eyes filled with lust, and women's eyes snapped with condemnation and jealousy. The girl's every move indicated that this was exactly the impression she sought to make on people.

A few seats over from Sally, a girl shouted, "Hi, Brenda!" Brenda looked up for the briefest moment, acknowledging the girl with a flick of her eyes.

At the corner of the ring, Brenda turned to go down the other side, hesitated, and then bent over as if to pick up something. Just for an instant, her eyes met Sally's. Then, as quickly as she'd entered Sally's world, Brenda's cleavage and firm, heart-shaped tush were around the corner and out of sight in the crowd.

Sally immediately didn't like Brenda, but she envied the attention she got. It was a form, a look, that Sally wished she had—or would someday. She lowered her eyes to her own maturing self in the awful training bra, hoping.

The bell rang again, and Todd sprang up and went back to boxing. Almost immediately the other boy delivered a hard blow to his head, and Todd staggered back and onto the ropes just above Sally. He looked dazed, and blood ran from his nose. Slumped against the ropes, he took several more punches. But as the other boxer moved in, Todd spun to his right, away from the flurry of blows, and then hit back at the solar plexus of the other boy. The boy's knees buckled, and he went to the canvas on all fours. Gasping for breath, Todd walked to the neutral corner just above Sally, and their eyes met briefly. Sally smiled, but Todd just turned away and leaned back against the corner ring post.

The referee counted to seven and then waved his hand back and forth across the face of the prostrate boy. He motioned for the other boxer's corner coach, and with that, the match was over. Todd walked to the center of the ring, where his coach lifted him up like a feather. Todd's mouth was open, and there was blood on his mouthpiece. With happy relief on his face, he waved at the crowd.

Sally was relieved too, perhaps even more than Todd. She wanted him to look at her, but he didn't.

Some people groaned, while others, including Todd's teammates, cheered. After a few minutes, both boxers and coaches were called to the center of the ring. The referee took both boys' hands and raised Todd's gloved hand as the victor. Then the boxers spoke to each other in friendly camaraderie, which surprised Sally after so much violence.

Soon the boxers and coaches left the ring and disappeared into the locker room area. Other matches followed, but none that Sally was interested in. After a while she became bored, so she went into the foyer where a crowd milled around the refreshment stand discussing the various matches.

As Sally stood near the gym entry, the cheerleaders filed out—the same girls she'd seen from across the ring before Todd's match. They were pretty and carried themselves in a haughty manner. They were the social elite of the high school, and it showed—especially on Brenda, who had straightened her blouse to look a little less like a hussy. She and Sally glanced at each other as she passed.

Immediately following the cheerleaders was a tall, austere woman in a tight black skirt, white blouse, and low heels. She had an athletic figure, her hair was pulled back in a bun, and her heavy makeup was perfect. Her eyes were blue, and she had an aura of tough discipline about her. Her cold blue eyes briefly met Sally's in an almost predatory way.

At the front of the exit aisle, the file of cheerleaders stopped. One of the girls asked the tall woman, "Shall we go out to the bus now, Mrs. V?"

"Yes, and don't dally with those boys. Understood?" Mrs. V barked coldly. She and Brenda, exchanging smiles and a few words, looked back down the aisle at Sally. As the girls walked out, they were greeted by their many fans, though still obviously under the authoritarian eye of Mrs. V.

Sally's attention was still on the cheer team as she stood almost alone in the foyer at the top of the locker tunnel. She wondered about the name and demeanor of that woman. Would she play a part in Sally's desire to be on the cheer squad? After seeing that line of beautiful, popular girls, Sally really wanted to be included.

She didn't feel very confident as she waited in the bare, cold corridor. The space was lit only by a few light bulbs hanging from the ceiling in tilted wire cages, and the musty smell of the corridor was even worse than the big gym.

Down the hall, a door slammed, echoing around the building. A moment later, Todd stood under the harsh hall light. Seeing him, Sally thrust the knuckle of her left index finger in her mouth and whimpered. He was still in his bloodied boxer trunks, but without the tank top. Standing with his arms at his sides and his hands still taped, Todd looked triumphant. His tall, sinewy body glistened with sweat. He wasn't muscled like a football player. His tendons were etched on him, especially his chest and trapezius muscles. The chiseled chest descended to a six-pack stomach. His gray-green eyes were set confidently. His chest heaved and fell with each breath, and blood dripped from his nose, which made him look even more desirable to her.

Everything about him said that he was *her* man. He looked back at Sally with an upturned chin and that lock of hair fell across his forehead, which was so sexy. As another boxer passed by, Todd spoke with him briefly, and then started up the corridor toward Sally. His walk was measured and smooth. He came close, gave her a half smile, and said jokingly, "Hi, Sally, long time no see. Glad you could make it. You like the match?"

She smiled and turned her face up to his, only inches away. "Hi, Todd. Surprised? Yeah, I'm glad that you won." They laughed a bit nervously.

Then Todd gave Sally the thrill of her young womanhood by taking her hand and saying, "I've gotta change, so can you wait? I won't be too long."

Sally replied, "What about your friends, the other boys? Will they be cross at having to wait?"

"Let 'em wait. I'll be back in a jiffy." He turned and walked back to the locker room door, where he paused and gave her that little upturned chin gesture again.

A minute later, the foyer doors slammed open with a loud bang. Standing there with her arms crossed and an angry expression on her face was Grandma. Both Sally's sisters were there too, obviously happy to witness this scene. One look at them told her who had tattled.

Grandma said, "You, young lady, are coming home right now. You are grounded for the rest of this month, plus all the chores you said you'd do but didn't. I am so disappointed in you. It's that boy from the car, isn't it? And boxing, my word, of all things! Wait till the deacon hears about this. Temptations like that boy are the devil's work. You'll have some explaining to do on that score also, I'm sure. My, what a day this has been!" Then she took Sally by the arm and led her outside.

Sally looked back and made a show of resistance. "Grandma, please let me stay just a few more minutes. Please?" But it was no use.

As Grandma pulled Sally along, Gail said, "He's no good, is he, Grandma?"

Grandma nodded in agreement and said, "At least for Sally he's not!"

Sally looked back with tears in her eyes and whimpered, "Oh, Todd!"

CHAPTER 4

Todd

When Todd came out of the locker room, he ran up the tunnel to the entry as fast as the crowd would let him, hoping Sally was still there. He bumped into other boxers and coaches several times in his hurry, but Sally was gone.

One coach said, "Where's the fire, kid? She'll wait, Todd. Don't worry."

When he got to the foyer, Todd dropped his gym bag and looked around anxiously, but Sally was nowhere in sight. He thought she might have gone into the ladies' room, but when she didn't emerge within a few minutes, he asked a girl standing nearby to check and see if Sally was inside. He described her as a short, cute blonde, but the girl came back out a minute later and gave him a shrug.

Then he checked at the snack bar, but Sally wasn't there, either. By then the building was almost empty, so Todd went out to the big porch that overlooked the ball fields and parking lot. Nothing!

The team bus back to Atascadero would leave in a few minutes, so Todd couldn't wait much longer. He thought about calling her, but then remembered he didn't know her last name or phone number. And because he hadn't paid much attention on the drive over to her neighborhood, he didn't even know where she lived. The friends with whom he'd come to San Luis Obispo were long gone back to San Bruno, so he couldn't ask them. Wow, what a girl, and he couldn't even get in touch with her.

Or maybe Sally had left because she didn't want to see him again? "Holy shit, what a mess. I finally meet a cute, hot-looking chick—and lose her in ten minutes? Did I screw up or what? Shit, shit, shit!" He didn't care who heard.

Todd saw the old yellow dog of a school bus in the parking area, where a few team members were waiting. After all, it was late Sunday, and most everyone would be off to do family stuff. Getting back to the ranch so late, he was going to miss the Sunday barbecue. Leftovers for dinner, if he even got that, and he was mighty hungry already. Was a girl even worth all this? Then the image of super-cute Sally appeared in his mind. *Well, maybe.*

Despondently, Todd sat down on the stairs leading to the parking lot. Coach saw him and gave a "come on" wave, then pointed north toward the highway and Questa Grade. Todd waved back, picked up his gym bag, and walked to the bus. It was a disappointing walk.

The half-hour ride back to Atascadero produced the usual round of jokes and discussions about boxing, future bouts, and, of course, girls. By the time they reached Santa Margarita, all the boys and the coach were sleeping the sleep of the dead.

When they arrived at the school parking lot, where they'd agreed to meet, it was getting late. Most boys were picked up by their parents, but some, like Todd, still had a long way to go to get home. The Wyrums' ranch, the Rocking W, was still more than an hour away, back through Santa Margarita and out Highway 58 toward Bakersfield. Todd hoped it was Miss Lady who picked him up and not his uncle, the Boss.

A tall moose of a man with a permanent scowl, the Boss was a hard driver and a heavy drinker with little patience. His buddies called him a bottle-a-day man, and by this time of day, he would be two-thirds into a bottle of Jim Beam. Because he was always either drunk or hungover, his disposition was generally sour or worse. He carried a rifle, shotgun, pistol, and bullwhip in his truck. He used the whip on any animal (and a few people) that didn't meet his standards, which changed in relation to his degree of sobriety. He had been a rodeo cowboy as a young man and suffered lots of injuries, which contributed to his demeanor. He seemed not to like Todd, but it was hard to tell, because he was cross with most everyone. He had been this way for as long as Todd had been spending summers there, since he was seven.

Within minutes, Todd—hot, hungry, and tired—was the only one still waiting in the parking lot. Having won felt good, but missing Sally frustrated him. It would be dark at the ranch, and he'd get leftovers for dinner. Finally he saw the GMC headlights coming toward him. *Wow,* he thought, *it's just Miss Lady. What a relief!* Riding back home on that winding road, in the dark, with the Boss driving while three sheets to the wind would have been dangerous.

When the truck pulled up, Todd was greeted with a big smile. "Hi, Todd," said Miss Lady.

"Glad to see you, Miss Lady," Todd replied. "I could eat that bale of hay you have in the back."

As she pulled out of the lot, Miss Lady said, "The hay is out. The steak sandwich, potato salad, and quart of milk in the bag will have to do."

"Oh yeah!" Todd wasn't surprised, because Miss Lady was just as nice as the Boss was mean.

Mrs. Bonnie Wyrum—or Miss Lady, as she was called by most folks—was in her late thirties, but it was hard to tell because she was so pretty, with big hazel eyes set off by a nice tan. She was about five feet five with long blond hair that she let swing freely, long legs, and a good figure that she didn't try to hide. Somehow she kept her hands and nails impeccable. Most of the time she wore jeans, a western shirt, and cowboy boots. She, too, had been in the rodeo, as a barrel racer with the call name of Miss Lady, in addition to working part-time as a preschool teacher. In fact, it was at a rodeo where she'd met the Boss long ago. Everyone knew it was the big ranch that had originally attracted her. She was altogether a classy lady.

Miss Lady was isolated at the ranch, an hour's drive from town and at least ten miles from any other ranch. And how much tender attention could a drunk give her? *None* would be a short but adequate answer. Indeed, her husband's lack of tender attention was at the root of Miss Lady's frustration. She did love the ranch, but what about the woman herself?

Not only was the Boss cold and into the bottle, but now her two daughters were gone to boarding school and riding academy most of the year. In any case, they'd been Daddy's girls most of their lives anyway. For all his neglect of his wife, the Boss was close to Joan and Jackie, and they had always returned the feeling. In fact, the older they got, the more distant they grew from their mother. Miss Lady was alone with her ranch, and that was exactly how she thought of it—*her* ranch.

The drive home was all about eating and Sally. Todd described Sally—talking on and on about her hair, figure, clothes, eyes, mouth, and laugh—in glowing, rapturous terms.

Miss Lady could get only perfunctory information from Todd about the boxing match, pretty much amounting to "Not bad. I won." Finally, needing a subject change, she asked, "Well, what about school next year?"

"Oh yeah! It's not completely set up yet, but a couple of things I want to take are available. I really like chemistry and French, and both are on the curriculum."

"Why French, Todd?" asked Miss Lady. "It seems odd, a kind of different subject, don't you think? How did you ever get interested in that, of all things?"

Todd replied, "Bonjour, madam! That's 'Good day, madam' in French. I got it from a lady friend of Mom's. Sounds neat, doesn't it? Anyway, I'm gonna take it."

"Well, that's up to you, so good luck with that," said Miss Lady.

This boy who sat next to her had been at the ranch for more than eight years, always interesting and full of surprises, but the tall muscular man he'd turned into was a shock. Some things—his warmth, easy laugh, affectionate hug, and familiarity—were the same, but ... And that same lock of hair still fell across his boyish forehead.

~

Highway 58 out to the Carrizo Plain was winding and in disrepair. As their conversation dropped off, Todd dozed, and his head fell against Miss Lady's shoulder. He awoke as they turned onto the winding, rutted ranch entry road of packed dirt. He apologized, and she answered with a smile.

The Rocking W sprawled across 35,000 acres of rolling hills in east San Luis Obispo County. Forty miles west was Santa Margarita, and fifty miles east was Bakersfield. The nearest recognizable point of interest was Syncline Hill. Cattle and horses used most of the land, but there were some crops too. Vistas were long, and the area had an isolated, timeless feel. It was not a place that invited you in, but once you were there, it held you tight. Water was scarce and carefully husbanded.

The Wyrums lived in the "big house"—one story, about three thousand square feet, in the Spanish style with three bedrooms and a wide, covered porch all around. Two big California live oak trees shaded the west and uphill sides. It sat just below the brow of a hill, looking south over the outbuilding of the working part of the ranch. Just west of the big house was an ice house where the ranch's meat and produce were stored, along with the emergency generator. Behind all this was an old orchard of apple, apricot, cherry, and walnut trees.

The access road came up behind the house under one of the big trees. An old hitching rail and watering trough sat back from the entry porch. A separate carport was on the east side. A windmill up the hill fed water to the house, clinking and clanking as it filled the trough with gurgling water. These sounds set the tone of the place—isolated, beautiful, inviting, home.

Down the hill were six other buildings: the "old house" from homestead times (still used occasionally), two barns, a tool shed, the bunkhouse, and the Cruz Shack. They all sat around a common pasture area about the size of a football field. At the north end was a paddock, and south of that was the corral.

Seldom used, the old barn was run-down, with a repair pit and tool room. Behind it sat an array of abandoned plows, trucks, and other old farm implements. The new barn held most of the equipment, tools, and supplies needed on a daily basis.

The bunkhouse was long, with eight bunks plus a washroom/toilet out back. Along one side was a shed roof where all the cowboys' gear was stored: boots, tack, saddles, ropes, and so on. Years back, Todd had hung a heavy and a light bag that he used often. Weather tight and cozy was the best one could say of the bunkhouse. There were usually three or four wranglers, though it was full during roundup. It was a happy place of laughter, jokes, stories (some even true), and lessons for Todd.

The Cruz Shack was down the hill to the west. Mr. and Mrs. Cruz, a Mexican couple, worked the ranch year-round. Cruz, as he was always referred to, managed the stock and was considered the best hand anywhere. Short, wiry, and dark, he could outwork anyone. He spoke only Spanish with a heavy barrio accent. Mrs. Cruz worked the house and garden with Miss Lady. The Cruzes were stoic and kept to themselves. They had a child, but not on the ranch.

When Todd first came to the ranch as an eight-year-old, he was pretty lonely staying in the old house. Soon he asked to bunk with the cowboys, and he'd spent the summers there ever since. He learned Spanish and a wide range of stuff about wrangling from Cruz, and Miss Lady's tutoring gave him a leg up in his regular schoolwork. The only bad part was the Boss, who made every chore hard—even when it wasn't.

Over the past couple of years, Todd had become the go-to guy for fences, which was exhausting, dirty, and often dangerous work. Barbed wire could hurt if you weren't careful, or even if you were. But mostly it was *hot*, and the dry, windless furnace with little shade was exhausting. Todd did get time to practice, though, and boxing was the only thing he and the Boss shared an interest in.

~

When they got to the house, Todd sat up attentively, and Miss Lady asked, "You got homework?"

"Not yet. Not until school starts."

"You know, Todd, when I was in Bakersfield High, I never did a lick of homework my entire four years. Rodeo and parties and—well, you know—was all I was interested in. That's why I admire your study habits and ambition so much."

"That's all? Just rodeo and parties?" Todd asked.

"Well, I was a cheerleader for a short while, but that didn't work out."

"I admire you, too, Miss Lady. I do. You're the best woman I've ever known, for sure."

Her feelings went deeper, and on impulse, she reached out and stroked his left arm. The feel of him made her draw in a breath. He reacted briefly with questioning eyes, and then the moment was gone.

As she turned off the truck, the engine rattled and Todd said, "That's not good. Needs a tuning. Want me to do it tomorrow morning?"

She hesitated and said, "Well—"

"No," he interrupted, "I'll get it fixed tomorrow." Then they both got out of the truck, and Todd said, "Bye, and thanks for the ride home."

Without acknowledging Todd's thank-you, Miss Lady strode briskly into the house, slamming the door and then leaning against the jamb. She was back in the domain of the Boss of short temper, foul language, and booze. He had once been dependable, even fun, as a husband and ranch partner, but he'd turned into a useless, rodeo-broken, alcoholic lout without feelings. She imagined a fleeting image of Todd as she heard the heavy tread of the Boss's big boots.

His hulking frame filling the hallway, he slurred, "Where ya been? Oh yeah, the kid. The boxing. He's back? How'd he do? Win?"

"Yes, he won, and now he's back." She pushed past him and went down the hall to *her* bedroom. They no longer shared a room or a bed.

The Boss called after her, "What the hell? Goddamn it, what's the matter? Damn women!" He threw up his hands and returned to the living room and Jim Beam.

As she entered her bedroom, Miss Lady told herself, *Oh my, crazy lady, what are you doing? And who's this cutie slut Sally anyway? This is ridiculous. Get a grip—he's just a boy, a little boy. We are just going to forget about this whole thing.*

~

Todd could hear a little of the exchange between Miss Lady and the Boss as he walked off toward the bunkhouse. He shook his head knowingly. He rounded the big house and went down through the paddock.

When Cruz and two cowboys asked about the boxing, Todd gave them a brief recap: "I won—TKO. The team won. A good day—most of it, anyway." But he didn't say anything about what was *really* on his mind—Sally. He just grabbed a chair, his tack, and saddle soap and started cleaning. They all spent the evening talking about Todd's year away and what the summer had in store. It was fun.

All this made Todd feel right at home. Because he had moved around so much, the ranch and the Carrizo Plain had become his one constant home. He could count on it to always be there, if only for the summer.

It never seemed to occur to anyone that Todd wasn't paid for his work. He got an "allowance" of five dollars a week, usually on Friday.

The mile-long road connecting the highway to the ranch crossed two gullies, referred to as *barranca* since most places in the region had retained their original Spanish names. One gully, forty feet wide, could be crossed on an old railroad flatcar from which the wheel trucks had been removed. The flatcar still had the faded words "Southern Pacific Railroad" painted on it. The other gully was more shallow, just twenty feet wide, and was spanned with wood beams. During heavy rain, which was rare, it often got washed out.

A continuous line of barbed-wire fencing stretched around and through the whole ranch, and it needed constant repair and replacement. The cowboys didn't mind riding and checking fences, but they hated replacing them, so that had become Todd's responsibility.

Six days a week, the breakfast bell—actually a rusty triangle hanging on a rope—rang at the big house at six, signaling the beginning of the day. Twenty minutes later, Mrs. Cruz or Miss Lady would serve breakfast at a big table in the bunkhouse. Each hand also got a brown-bag lunch to take with them.

The breakfast bell was just one of many sounds that made up ranch life. Others included the thud and ring from the horseshoe pit, clinking of spurs, boots on the porch, checkers, the swish of lariats from the barrel-roping area, horses whinnying, hoots and minor arguments, plus the sounds of odd cowboy things being made, such as beating a fifty-cent piece into a ring. In contrast to all that noise, the day ended with the quiet calm of winking stars after a long dusk.

Mornings were for chores. After lunch came the wrangling—being a cowboy—which was what coming here was all about. Todd's horse was Splash, a big black mare with the markings of spilled paint on her right foreleg and down her left haunch. White, brown, and tan intermingled from hip to hoof in both places. Splash could handle cattle, fence riding, pulling up stumps, and most anything else. Every time Todd rode, he had a sugar cube ready in his left breast pocket. He and Splash were a great team, and each summer they renewed their friendship.

With breakfast finished, the hands gathered on the porch and assembled their gear. Each person received instruction from Cruz or the Boss—in Spanish from Cruz, while the Boss barked his orders in hungover English. Todd saw Miss Lady only on Tuesdays and Thursdays for his lessons.

~

The Monday after the boxing match was not unusual except for one thing. Mrs. Cruz gave Todd a note from Miss Lady telling him that there would be no lesson this week, only a homework assignment. This was curious, but he chalked it up to a town trip or rodeo club.

The following week, Todd took his homework and rode Splash up to the big house for his lesson. But before he could dismount at the hitch rail, Miss Lady came out the front door all dressed up with makeup, hair, and all. Todd leaned on his saddle pommel, shirt open and a relaxed smile on his face. As he nodded and pushed back his hat brim, that lock of hair fell over his forehead. He looked down at Miss Lady and said, "Well, here I am, ready to go. I got my stuff done, all of it."

Sitting on Splash, Todd was the picture of a confident cowboy, not the boy of yesteryear. Miss Lady moaned softly and looked away, crying, "Oh, Todd, it's no good. I can't, I just can't!"

As she backed away, Todd asked, "What's the matter? Did I do something wrong?"

She motioned him into the house, but didn't offer him any refreshments as she usually did. Miss Lady was not her usual warm, helpful self. She simply told him to redo his homework for the session. Even the algebra assignment drew no comment as it normally would've. Then she handed him a typed sheet of instructions for Thursday and said, "That's all for today, Todd."

Miss Lady walked to the door, then turned to him and said, "The phone is out until we get a lineman to fix it, so you won't be able to call out for a while. You can't contact anyone, not even what's-her-name—you know, that girl."

"Uh, what girl? Oh, *that* girl? You mean Sally?" Todd asked.

There was an odd look on Miss Lady's face, and her eyes were heavy. "Well, I guess. You can't expect me to remember her name. Anyway, no calls out—or in, either."

Todd said excitedly, "Did she call? I mean, wow, did she? What about my mom?"

"No, there were no calls. When the phone's back working, it's okay for your mom to call in, but no others. Now you can leave. I have lots to do. Bye!" She walked off toward the kitchen without looking back.

Todd could tell Miss Lady was irritated. He said to himself, *My homework must have been really bad.* Or was it something else? He remembered something one of the cowboys had said about a rude girl at the roadhouse a while back: "I guess she's on the rag. He'd never asked what that meant, but considering what had just transpired, he probably should have.

For the next two weeks, Todd did his work and studies as usual, and Miss Lady remained cool the whole time. One other thing changed, however. The normally hot Carrizo weather got even hotter.

One morning the Boss showed up at the bunkhouse. After sending away the ranch hands, he asked Todd, in a friendly way, about his boxing. Todd filled him in in a matter-of-fact way because he was leery of the motives behind the Boss's unusual demeanor. When he finished, the Boss nodded in tacit agreement, then reached in his vest pocket.

Taking out a set of keys, the Boss handed them to Todd and said in a slurred voice, "You're sixteen right? You got a learner's permit, don't you? Hope these fit, but don't know for sure."

Todd looked down at the keys in his hand and nodded. "Yeah, I do."

"Well, kid, we've got a big fence project coming up, and you can't do it without wheels. In the old barn, as you know, is a 1940, flat head V-8, pinhead Ford pickup. It's been sittin' there in bad shape for goin' on twelve years. You're gonna fix it and use it for haulin' fence material. Do you think you know enough from the hands and Cruz to fix it?"

Todd had heard about needing this fence for a couple of years now, but it seemed like one of those things that, like so many other ranch improvements, was all talk and no action. Happily surprised, he replied, "Yes, sir! I know fence, and I know trucks. No problem."

The Boss half grunted. "Well, that's good. Yeah, good. Start today. All the tools are in the barn. If you need anything else, just tell Miss Lady, and she'll get them in town." He started to walk off, but then turned back and asked, "How long to finish the fence?"

Todd's past experiences with the Boss had taught him that to give a definite deadline and then miss it was bad news. He said, "Can't tell yet."

The Boss gave another grunt and walked off.

The new fence would go from the top of the third hill, across the second barranca, and up the next hill. That was more than three hundred yards through boulders and thick brush.

Todd took several days just to clean up the old barn, including the walls, doors, and double-hung windows. The dusty truck, covered with owl droppings and cobwebs, sat over the pit. A long bench along a wall was piled with tools and parts, and other tools hung over patterns on the wall. A parts and supplies room was just inside the main door, but it was disorganized and stacked with supplies. Worst of all, the sky could be seen through holes in the wood-shingled roof in places. *That's the first item of repair,* Todd thought.

By the end of the week, the barn was cleaned and organized. Now it was time for the truck repairs. With help from the cowboys, he hauled the pickup out of the barn, washed it, and pushed it back over the repair pit. Then he drew up a list of needed parts and supplies—tires, brake pads, oil, grease, points, plugs, distributer cap and wires, belts, battery, coil, condensers, light bulbs, and so on—and gave it to Miss Lady.

~

The cowboys were very respectful of Todd's study time. None of them had much education, and they were proud of Todd's ambition to be a doctor. The ranch routine was broken on Saturday nights by high times at Mary's saloon/general store/gas station on Highway 58, and then there was church on Sundays, at least for some.

Miss Lady had not warmed up much. She seemed to avoid Todd, and he wondered if he had offended her. She'd also alluded to Sally again in a dismissive way. Maybe she wanted to meet Sally, but what was up with that? Hell, he didn't even know Sally's full name or where she lived. Maybe he should tell Miss Lady that. As far as Miss Lady was concerned, confusion reigned.

One morning, on impulse, Todd picked some wildflowers from the only fertile ground in that desert-like place. He thought maybe that would cheer up Miss Lady and end her funky mood.

When he arrived at the house, she had her back to him as he entered. When she heard him, she said coldly, "Sit down."

In the friendliest voice he could muster, Todd said, "I got something for you, Miss Lady. Here are some pretty flowers for a pretty lady. Hope you like 'em."

She turned to face him with that hard look of late. When he reached out and offered the flowers, her jaw set for just a moment. But then her face dissolved and a little sob escaped her lips. "Oh, Todd. Oh my ... I just don't know how I'm going to ... Thank you so much, you sweet, adorable boy. How wonderful. Oh, what am I going to do with you, Todd?"

Totally nonplussed, Todd said, "I'm sorry if it wasn't the right thing to do. It's just that lately you've been kind of ... Well, I just wanted to cheer you up. If I misfired on this gesture, I'm really sorry."

She regained her composure. "It's very thoughtful, Todd, and I'm so appreciative. You're the only one around here who ... I love them. I'll put them in water, and they'll cheer me up. My sweet Todd!" Walking past him, she reached out and stroked his cheek briefly.

After that, they did his lessons. Nothing more was said about the flowers, but Todd left mighty confused. On the next lesson day, the flowers were on the worktable in a fancy vase. He still didn't know what was going on. Some days she was happy, other days standoffish. The way she'd touched his cheek after he'd given her the flowers had seemed odd. What was going on? It had felt more like a caress or ... Wait, could she like him that way? *No, don't be a jerk, Todd. That's impossible*, he told himself.

~

The Boss hadn't come around to check the truck repairs, so on that score, all was well. The parts would take a while, so the painting, upholstery, and wood bed would have to come later. In the meantime, Todd surveyed the property line fences for alignment using an old surveyors transit he'd found almost hidden in the back of the barn. It must have been left behind and forgotten long ago by some surveyor. Recent disputes about power line easements across the Carrizo made this work a priority

This big new job had one saving grace. Last summer, a visiting surveyor had left an old transit on the ranch and taught Todd how to use it. This work was fun. He was in charge of how, when, and where to do each fence. Each morning he'd saddle up Splash and the packhorse and ride out to the area he needed to check that day.

First he'd set up the transit at the day's corner brass cap. So far he hadn't found any misalignment. He'd check the alignment, record it in a logbook, and then make sure the posts were secure along the length between corners. Anytime he found an insecure or broken post, he'd fix it. New wire had to be strung in some places, but most of the work involved tightening the wire at the cross-braced posts every hundred feet or so. A few posts had to be replaced, and for that he had a spoon and rotary digger, plus a come-along—and, of course, wire cutters, hammers, and other necessary tools.

Todd had stored posts and wire in several places before he'd begun, so he didn't have to go back to the ranch for supplies during the day. Splash and the packhorse grazed while he worked. Todd would take a break every hour or two at a salt lick or water trough. The work sure did keep him in shape. He always wore his cowboy hat and drank lots of water. Almost every day, he saw Cruz or the cowboys working the cattle and horses. They never stopped to help, though—just gave him a wave and howdy.

Two weeks passed while Todd waited for parts for the pickup. Late one Saturday morning while he was washing the underside of the truck from the pit, he thought he heard a voice, so he turned off the noisy machine. Dressed in cutoff jeans, he was barefoot and completely drenched, with water dripping from his hair.

Standing just outside the garage doors was Miss Lady. After a moment of surprised hesitation, Todd stammered, "Oh hi, I didn't expect you. I mean, I would've been ... Anyway, welcome to Todd's Garage and— Shower Room, I guess." He smiled and reached for a towel hanging on the door near her.

"Hi, Todd. I have the parts—for the truck, I mean. Where do you want them?"

Standing only a step or two from her, Todd smiled self-consciously as he toweled himself off and said, "Well, Miss Lady, I guess you kind of caught me by surprise."

Her face grew intense, and she reached out and touched his cheek, just like she'd done when he gave her the flowers. After a brief hesitation, her hand slipped down his neck and along his shoulder. Quickly she regained control, turned away, put her hands on her hips, and shook her head. "This is just impossible. The parts ... I mean, the *stuff* is in the back of my truck by the big house. You can come anytime ... I mean, come *get* them from the back of the truck. Oh, whenever! Goodbye!" She turned and briskly walked off around the end of the barn.

Todd was now really perplexed. He called out after her, "Yeah, I'll come up and get them right away. I mean, like right now if you want. Jeez!"

He finished drying, slipped on his jeans, boots, and a shirt, and went to get the parts. He figured it would take a week or so more to finish the truck, and then he'd be working full-time on the fence.

~

Late Saturday, Todd was finishing up the last section of fence on a low hill overlooking a side road off Highway 58, about two miles west of Mary's saloon/garage. He and Splash were hot and tired. Pulled over on the shoulder, facing east, was a big, new yellow convertible half in the ditch. Todd patted Splash on the neck and said, "Looks like those folks got some trouble." He rode down carefully to the car, still on the other side of the barbed-wire fence.

Near the front of the car stood a woman and a short, heavyset man. The dude, in porkpie hat, plaid sports coat, and wing tip shoes looked to be about fifty. He was stooped over and looking at the right front tire while the woman watched.

Probably in her mid-twenties, wearing shorts and a low-cut blouse, she was a knockout and totally foreign to the Carrizo. She gave Todd a big smile as she stepped from behind the car and said, "Hi, cowboy. Can you give me—us—a hand?"

Todd averted his gaze and said, "Ah, good day to you too. You got a problem there?"

The man shook his head, then looked at the flat. "Know anything about fixing this, kid?"

As Todd sat on Splash on the pasture side of the fence, he could see that the tire was flat and partly off its rim. Ignoring the man, he tipped his hat and said, "Ma'am, I might. Looks bad, off the rim like that. Bent, too. You must have driven a ways on the flat to deform it and all."

The man looked up the highway with exasperation. "Well, yeah, I thought it wasn't bad, so I just went along from that rise. Got a spare in the trunk. Give you ten bucks to help me."

Todd said, "No pay necessary for help 'round these parts. I'll see what I can do." The woman kept moving around, which distracted Todd mightily. He walked Splash up to the fence and let the horse get a good look at it, then turned around and rode back about sixty feet. Turning to face the fence again, Todd stood up in the stirrups and looked both ways down the highway. With a "Haayyyaaa," he put his spurs into Splash's flanks and sprinted for the fence. The smooth jump ended on the roadway with the horse's shoes clanking on the asphalt.

Clutching her arms across her chest, the woman squealed, "Oh my!"

The man said, "I'll be damned—a real cowboy. That was some jump, kid."

Todd walked Splash over to the car and dismounted. He now got a full view of the woman. She was maybe five two, with short blond hair and big hazel eyes. Well made up, she had full red lips formed in a little pout, and she was wearing Bermuda shorts and a halter top full to the brim. She averted her eyes to let Todd get a full view of her proudest asset—and just as she intended, he couldn't tear his gaze away.

The man, half smiling, interrupted the scene. "I'm Joe Berg, and this is Bea, my—uh—niece. How about it, cowboy? There's ten in it for you. Yes sir, that was some jump."

Still unable to avert his eyes, Todd replied, "I'm Todd. How the dickens did you get way out here off the highway? Spare's in the trunk?"

"Don't matter how anyway. Never mind about that," Joe said.

Bea bent over as Todd looked at the flat. Her breasts were in his face now. She just smiled.

Todd pulled his eyes away, walked to the rear of the late-model Oldsmobile, and stood over the open trunk. The spare was partway out and leaning on an old suitcase. He took it out and bounced it on the asphalt, but it was flat too.

They walked back to the front of the car and stood a moment looking at the front tire. On closer inspection, Todd noticed the fender jack had tipped and partly fallen, lodging itself up in the wheel well. He took off his hat, undid his neckerchief, and mopped his brow. Bea's closeness was distracting.

Just then they heard a truck coming fast from the other direction and turned to look. It was Miss Lady's GMC. As she came closer, Todd waved, but she drove right on by, a scowl on her face. He said, "That's odd. She could see me—us. What could she be angry about? I work for her up on the ranch."

Bea smirked and said, "She sure didn't look happy."

"Something for sure," said Todd. "Darn odd, that. Well, what the heck. Let's get on with it. Flat tire, no spare, broken rim and jack. Sure can't fix this here, so gotta get to a garage. Mary's is up the highway about two miles. Could take it there."

"Damn, how the hell we gonna get there? I'm not walkin' in this heat," Joe said.

A minute passed, and finally Todd said, "Well, I could ride up and get them to send the tow truck. Take a while, but I'm sure Luke, the mechanic, could fix it."

Joe took off his hat, shaded his eyes, and mopped his brow with a handkerchief. Looking up at the late-afternoon sun, he said, "Can't fix it, huh? No, I guess not, so we need a tow truck. How long would that take to get here?"

"If the truck is even available, being it's Saturday and all, about an hour," Todd replied.

"Well, kid, I don't want to seem ungrateful, but waiting an hour in this heat?"

Bea looked at Todd helplessly, and then piped up. "I've got to get out of this sun. The top on the car won't go up. What am I to do? Can I go with you, on the back, I mean? The horse can carry two, can't he? Joe's got to stay and guard the car. Don't you, Joe?"

Todd said, "Horse's name is Splash, and he's a she. Two can ride that far. No problem with that."

Obviously not pleased with Bea's plan, Joe said, "If there was any other way, I'd do it, but I guess there isn't. Go on, Bea, but hurry up. I could get a stroke in this sun."

Bea looked *very* pleased.

Todd took a moment to consider this, and then said, "Well, okay, it's a plan. Tow truck will be here asap, but like I said, could be an hour or so. Bea can wait in Mary's saloon for you. In fact, things should start partying down in a couple hours or so. The place is go-to-hell—I mean, heck—wild on Saturday night. Every cowboy in the Carrizo and then some will be there. You might enjoy it. A band from Bakersfield is on for tonight."

Looking at him with drooping eyes, Bea asked, "You'll be there too, won't you, Todd?"

"Yes, of course. I've got a pool game to shoot with Zeke. Oh yeah, I'll be there."

CHAPTER 5

Rheingold

Todd reached down, clasped Bea's little hand in his, and swung her up behind him in the saddle. "Ya all set there, Bea?"

She settled against his back and cooed, "Oh, you bet. Ride 'em, cowboy."

The ride to Mary's took about twenty minutes. He walked Splash along for a while, but after a few minutes of this, Bea asked, "Can't we go a little faster? This is fun, isn't it?"

"Well … Okay there, Bea? Off we go." Todd spurred Splash into a trot and then a canter. Bea did feel good against him, and he began to get an erection. Splash knew the way, so he just relaxed into the ride, and she made sure they both enjoyed it all the way.

Mary's came into view as they crested a low hill. It was three buildings set back about a hundred feet from the highway. Out front along the road was a tall sign that said "Mary's Store," which included the saloon, liquor/ general store, and garage. Absent the cars, gas pumps, and neon sign, it could have been a scene from the old West, complete with horses, cowboys, and windmill.

The saloon/store/roadhouse part was clapboard with a wide canopy over the wooden, elevated boardwalk. The saloon had a long bar on one side, and tables and chairs filled the rest of the floor. Through an arched doorway on the far side was a pool room with two tables that were pristine compared with the rest of the run-down place. Cue racks, stools, and a jukebox lined the walls. Todd's personal cue was in a special rack, along with several others.

Connecting the liquor/general store to the saloon was a breezeway, lined with benches along one side, that ran the length of both buildings. At the end sat a Coke machine that dispensed bottles from a hand-operated dispenser filled with ice water. Insert a dime, and heaven was yours.

To the west was the garage/gas station, also of clapboard and hip roof, with a lean-to on the east side. There was a repair bay with a pit, plus an office and restrooms. The two tilting pumps out front were the old type, showing fuel flowing in big round glass containers on top. A "Signal Gas" sign hung from a wooden pole, and everything was dirty, smelled of grease, and needed repair and paint. Two hitch rails stood out front, along with a water trough.

About a hundred feet behind the garage, three huge oak trees hung over Mary's house, which matched the other buildings in style. Between the saloon and the house was a corral and small hay shed, and behind that were several junked cars and six motel-like cabins linked together with carports. The cabins were mostly in use only during roundup time.

The whole complex sat on the north side of Highway 58, in the middle of a wide-open plain that stretched as far as the eye could see, until the dim outline of the mountains that separated Mary's from Kern County broke up the view. It could have been 1850 or 1950.

When they got to Mary's, Todd pulled up Splash, then reached around and helped Bea down. They walked to the garage to arrange for a tow for the Oldsmobile.

"Howdy, Todd. What can I do for you?" Luke, the attendant, surveyed Bea pretty hard.

"Well, Luke, there's an Olds with a flat out west. The owner needs it towed in and fixed."

"Sure thing. I'll grab the truck and head out right away."

Bea asked Todd, "Will I see you tonight at the music and dancing?"

"Yes, I'll be there ... Well, Bea, this is just about it, I guess. You can wait in Mary's while I get the tow set up." Todd pointed out the saloon entry.

"Okay, Todd. So ... I'll see you tonight, then?"

Todd replied, "Oh yes, unless the Boss says no, which is unlikely. I *do want* to come, though."

Todd's choice of words inspired Bea. "I hope you can come, Todd, and I hope you'll *come with me*."

Todd, however, was oblivious. "Bye for now, Bea."

Luke went in the office, then came back out a minute later and said, "I just got a call from the Rocking W. Miss Lady said you need to get back. Something's come up. Didn't say what."

Todd's first thought was *How did Miss Lady know I was going to the garage?* Mysteries abounded with her, it seemed.

Bea swung off to Mary's, and Todd was at the ranch fifteen minutes later.

~

The GMC and the Boss's truck were parked in front. Down the hill, he saw the cowboys barrel roping in front of the bunkhouse. They'd be off to Mary's soon, so he'd have to hurry if he wanted a ride. He dismounted, pulled a sugar cube from his shirt pocket, and gave it to Splash.

The front door of the house was open, so Todd leaned in and called out, "Boss? Miss Lady? Anybody home? It's Todd. I came back on the double. What's up?" Hearing angry voices from down the hall, he waited a minute and then called again, "It's Todd. I'm back." Still no answer.

Then he heard Miss Lady's voice rise. "You're letting the rest of the perimeter fences go to hell while you've got Todd working on that new one that we don't really need. You're so into Jim Beam that you can't do any—"

"Watch your mouth, lady!"

Looking down the hall toward the living room, Todd could see that the Boss had his two-thirds-into-the-bottle look.

Miss Lady stood in front of him and yelled, "You're an ass sometimes, Mr. Wyrum!"

Enraged, the Boss stepped closer to Miss Lady with raised arm and closed fist. He yelled, *"You ungrateful cunt, I'll make you—"*

At that exact moment, Miss Lady flinched and the Boss glimpsed Todd down the hall. Lowering his fist, he glared at Todd and asked, "Hey, kid, what're you doing up here? The cowboys are getting ready to head off to Mary's. Better get a move on if you want a ride in."

Shocked, Todd wasn't sure what he'd just witnessed. He stammered, "Miss Lady, uh, called down to the garage. Said I was needed back here quick ... So, uh, I'm here."

Miss Lady said in a high, choked voice, "Clean these windows. I've got my rodeo club meeting on Monday."

The Boss exclaimed, "Shit, what'd you say? Mrs. Cruz just finished cleaning them, like ... yesterday, didn't you?" He swung around and looked into the kitchen at Mrs. Cruz.

"Oh yes, I did what Miss Lady said. Cleaned them all yesterday," Mrs. Cruz replied.

Tension filled the house, and fear was etched on Miss Lady's face. Walking over to the sliding glass door, she pointed at a dog's paw prints and said, "Well ... this doesn't look clean to me."

Almost before Miss Lady finished the sentence, Mrs. Cruz was vigorously cleaning the glass door again.

"Shit, Todd," exclaimed the Boss, "get the hell outta here. I don't want to see you around here until Monday. I got one hell of a job for you, and you'll need all the energy you got to finish it. Not like this last one, which you lollygagged around on. Hell, it took you goddamn near three weeks when it should have been a week. Back in my day, I'd have had it done in a week—no more, for sure. A damn week!"

Miss Lady said, in a rather uncertain tone, "He shouldn't be going to Mary's. He's just a boy, after all. We're supposed to be setting a good example and steering him in the right direction."

"What?" said the Boss. "I'll be damned! He's been visiting Mary's going on ten ... Well, since he first came here, and he's been tipping back beers most all that time. You want to stop him *now*? What's got into you, anyway? First the windows, then no Mary's on Saturday night? It isn't that time of the month, is it?"

Mrs. Cruz retreated to the kitchen, and the Boss and Todd just stood there, wondering what was going on. Finally the Boss said, "Get on down to the bunkhouse, Todd. They'll wait for you. And I meant what I said about this new fence project. No more screwing around."

Todd said, "I'm ready to go repair that old fence as soon as the supplies get here. How about that power posthole digger you said we'd get?"

"Too expensive, and you don't need it," the Boss replied. "The stuff we got will do fine. You just got to work harder. I saw you out on the fence line a couple days ago. You was sitting by the salt lick, just talking to Splash and scratching your ass. Now get the hell outta here before I have you do them windows, which for damn's sake we don't need ... Can't figure that woman out."

Todd knew better than to argue with the Boss in this mood. He tipped his hat and started to back out of the room, but then remembered one last question. "Uh, Boss, what time of the month were you asking Miss Lady about?"

The Boss gave a short laugh. "Ain't nothin' for you to worry about, Todd. Now get the hell outta here."

When Todd got to the bunkhouse, it turned out the cowboys weren't ready. He sat on the porch for a few minutes and pondered recent events— the Boss's raised fist, Miss Lady caressing his cheek, her odd moods, how she looked at him. Excitement rose in him as he wondered, *Could it be?*

Carnal thoughts invaded him as he showered and got ready to go out. He imagined himself with her. Doubts began to overpower his hesitation. *Does she want me?* Ever since he'd come back from the boxing match in San Luis Obispo, she'd been acting different. Her previous warmth and friendly help had given way to an attitude he'd never seen before.

~

Todd recalled last Tuesday morning's lesson. He'd arrived about seven thirty with all his homework done. The front door had been open, so he'd stepped inside and announced his arrival: "I'm here and ready."

Miss Lady had called out, "Come in!" so Todd had put his stuff on the dining table as usual. A few minutes later, she'd showed up in her robe, not the usual ranch outfit. In fact, she'd looked even more like a queen, as she was often described.

When she'd leaned over to review his work, her bosom had touched his shoulder and her fingers stroked his neck. Minutes later, when she'd sat down opposite him and reached for his lesson sheets, her robe had fallen open, revealing her cleavage.

Todd had tried unsuccessfully to avert his eyes, and he'd gotten hard. So he had stood up—reluctantly, because of his excited condition—and faced away from Miss Lady.

At that moment, the Boss had walked into the room, noticed Todd's condition, and blurted out, "What the fuck? You getting ideas about my wife? You'd better the hell not be, 'cause I'll kick the shit outta you, kid. Get the hell outta here, unless you want a beating."

Miss Lady had exclaimed, "Boss, it's nothing like that! We're doing Todd's lessons, just like every day. Now just calm down. Todd, I think we're finished here, so you can go back to the bunkhouse." Then she'd pulled her robe back around her and walked toward the hall.

The Boss said, "Goddamn it, Miss Lady, you ... You'd better be more careful about—"

Interrupting him, she said, "You're such a jerk, seeing everything as a conspiracy. We were just ... Oh, what's the use of explaining anything to you when you're half sloshed?"

"Screw you, Miss Lady, I'm not drunk. And I meant what I said, Todd. I'll kick the crap outta you!" The Boss walked past Todd, shoving him aside, and went outside, slamming the door behind him.

Todd and Miss Lady averted their eyes and didn't say anything, then left the room. She was shocked at her own behavior and afraid for Todd.

Todd was totally discombobulated. He had seen the Boss's face, but more importantly, Miss Lady's body.

~

In the truck with the others, there were enough distractions for Todd to put aside the cross currents pulling at him. His buddies knew how to relax and have fun on a Saturday night. They were the old breed of cowboys, and nothing would ever convince them that they didn't have the best of all possible lives—wrangling on the open range with the sky, grass, dust, and friends. Oh yes, and some wild Saturday nights, too.

Each cowboy was different, but when it came to the work, they were interchangeable—and good at it, too. Anyone who came to the ranch had to prove himself to the others, and they were as strict as any college professor in their judgment. This applied to Todd also. He'd endured many a humiliating lesson before being admitted to the bunkhouse as an equal, and he was very proud of that. The rules, though unwritten, were strictly adhered to:

- Never back down in a fight.
- Do your work without complaint.
- Admit to a mistake and move on.
- The Boss *is* the boss.
- Never lie to a friend.
- Your horse is your best friend.
- Women are separate, except ladies of the night.

The Rocking W cowboys were all veterans of World War II, a subject rarely spoken of. Todd was closest to Zeke, who was short and wiry, with a wild crop of blond hair that sat on his head like a hat. In fact, without his hat Zeke looked undressed. When he took off his hat, a broad white band stretched across his forehead, in sharp contrast to his otherwise tan face. Zeke was Todd's pool partner and a good pool shark, as Todd was beginning to be. They had games most weekends at Mary's.

Todd had gotten to know Zeke by accident, after having been at the Rocking W for a year or two. Over Zeke's bunk hung a tired old photo, askew in its frame, and one day Todd had asked about it. Zeke had explained that the picture was of the ten guys in his B-17 bomber crew during the war. They'd flown in the 390th Bomb Group out of Framlingham, England.

Todd really enjoyed history, especially about World War II, and he had asked if Zeke kept in touch with the guys. A funny, faraway look had come over Zeke's face as he answered in a forlorn voice, "No."

"Oh, sorry, Zeke. I didn't mean to pry," Todd had said, noticing the look on Zeke's face.

Zeke had slowly said, "No matter, it's okay. I was the only one who got out. That's all. I was the right waist gunner and kind of fell out and, and ..."

"Got out?" Todd asked.

Again there was a pause, and then Zeke explained, "Over Gelsenkirchen, April of '44. We caught some flak, and I was the only who got out before she went down. *Chile Lady* was her name. Good bird, and great guys!" He looked at the photo again and said, "Long story, Todd. Sad story."

Todd remembered that moment for a long time. It was the first time he was addressed by name, rather than simply as "kid." He knew then that he was part of the bunkhouse gang and a real cowboy.

The ride to Mary's was filled with the usual jokes and BS'ing, though someone did ask, "What's up with Miss Lady? She's off her game lately. Even the lunches aren't so good."

The parking lot at Mary's was half full when they arrived, including Joe and Bea's yellow convertible. A few folks had come on horses, which were tied up at the hitching rail. Todd knew most of the ranch families, cowboys, and assorted locals who were there. Everyone was shooting the breeze, just waiting for the band to start. Kids ran around in the crowd, and teenagers mostly hung out in the parking lot. Boots, cowboy hats, and jeans were standard for everyone.

Mary's had a long mahogany bar with a brass foot rail and a mirrored back filled with rows of bottles and glasses. Neon beer signs were scattered around the place, and there were lots of tables with red-checkered tablecloths spread around a central dance floor. At the back, on the right, was a two-step-high bandstand with an upright piano sitting next to the back door and a big window. An open doorway on the east wall led to a pool room where chairs and cue racks lined the walls. The pool room was used for occasional community meetings, and when the doctor came by on his monthly visits, it served as an informal exam room.

Now and then some well-known entertainer played Mary's. Little Willie Littlefield, who wrote "Kansas City," came over from San Luis Obispo's El Morocco Club occasionally. One time a young Buck Owens stopped in before an engagement at the Bliken Owl in Grover City.

The big neon Rheingold Beer sign hanging in the front window had special significance for Mary, because Rheingold was her surname—besides being a brand of beer out of Los Angeles. Mary, who had immigrated to the United States from Germany after World War II, was probably in her mid-fifties and not to be messed with and carried a blackjack. Occasionally she'd dress up in a Bavarian outfit—dirndl and all—and impress folks with her bowling-ball-size tits. Cowboys came from miles around to see her dance the polka, which was like watching two watermelons arguing in a gunnysack.

On these occasions, customers sang the Rheingold Beer theme song. The tune—not the words—was borrowed from the German opera *The Red Cavalier*, and the jingle went like this:

> My beer is Rheingold, the dry beer.
> Think of Rheingold whenever you buy beer.
> Not bitter, not sweet,
> Extra dry, flavored treat.
> Won't you try extra dry Rheingold beer?

The bartender, who was also the bouncer, was a big Indian named—of course—Chief. On any Saturday night, he'd be much needed in both capacities. And a group of whores from Bakersfield often hung around. All these things made Mary's feel like a home on the Carrizo.

Todd got a Coke at the bar. Things hadn't really gotten started yet, so he went into the pool room. A cowboy he knew asked, "Want to get in the game, Todd? You might earn some dough." And indeed he might. Thanks to following his mom's military moves for many years, Todd had picked up the game in many an NCO club, and he was really good.

One of the guys at the table was a minor pool hustler from out of town. Todd knew the type. The guy said, "Yeah, kid, wanna try your luck?"

Todd piped up, "Sure thing. What's up?"

"Five a game. How about it?"

A crowd gathered, including the rest of the ranch crew, and several guys made side bets. They knew how good Todd was, and they wanted to see the out-of-town dude taken down.

As the newcomer, Todd was allowed to break—and he ran the table. A big cheer went up from the crowd, and Todd broke again. This time the game went on awhile with the dude winning. Todd won the third game, his opponent the fourth. By then, the pool room was crowded with guys spilling out the door.

The last game came down to the last ball, and Todd had the shot. It was a hard one, so he missed in a way that forced his opponent to take an even harder shot. The other guy made the shot but scratched the cue ball, which gave Todd the final shot. He made it, to the cheers of the partisan crowd.

Bea pushed through the crowd and gave him a hug. "Are you my cowboy, Todd?"

Todd picked up his money, gave the dude a sly nod, and walked to the bar area a hero.

After a while the band came in, set up, and began to play. Dancing started and the waitresses began to serve, arriving at Todd's table after a few minutes. One of the cowboys at the table made a pass at their waitress, but she just brushed him off and took the table's order. This got a laugh out of everyone, and the guy said, obviously a little embarrassed, "I guess she's on the rag."

There's that phrase again, thought Todd. "Hey guys, what the dickens does 'the rag' mean?" he asked.

There was a moment's hesitation on craggy faces, and then a huge peal of laughter and guffawing broke out. Zeke nearly fell out of his chair. A working girl at another table turned and said, "My word, *this kid* needs to learn a thing or two. That's no way to talk with ladies present."

"You gonna teach him, Bunny?" asked another cowboy.

She put an arm around Todd's shoulder, saying coyly, "Well, I might at that. How about it, young man? You ready for some adult schooling?"

Another cowboy at Todd's table said, "You'll get better than a college education from Bunny here on that score, Todd. Right, Bunny?"

To make sure he understood, Bunny loosened a couple of buttons on her blouse and leaned close to Todd. "Oh my, it would be my pleasure to school this young, innocent, clean-cut stallion."

But that was as far as she got, because Bea had left Joe at the bar, came over, and broke in, "Hold your horses there, city girl. Todd and I are about to dance. Come on, Todd. Like you promised, remember?" She put an arm under Todd's elbow and coaxed him toward the dance floor.

Bunny yelled, "Bitch! Cradle robber! Are you his mommy or something?"

"Slut!" exclaimed Bea. "He's got better taste than the likes of you."

A fight would have started right then if Zeke and the others hadn't separated them. Bea and Todd went out on the dance floor, and Bunny began trying to hustle other cowboys.

Bea began to apply herself to Todd in aggressive ways that made him uncomfortable. As the band struck up "Honky-Tonk Angels," by Kitty Wells, a cowboy asked to cut in. This gave Todd a chance to walk away. "I'm hot. I think I'll go outside," he said.

Unfortunately for him, Bea replied, "Good idea," and grabbed his hand. She led him out into the refreshing evening air and said, "Let's put one of these empty cars to good use. This one right here will do, see?"

Realizing that he was in over his head, Todd said hesitantly, "No, I'm okay right here. You go."

Bea pushed her boobs out at him, still hoping.

At that moment, Bunny came out the door, pointed at them, and said, "She's got that boy—that kid—trying to screw him."

Right behind her came the Chief, who stood over them and said to Bea, "Now, you know better than to hustle a young man like this. You'll find lots of action inside, I promise you."

Just then Todd noticed Miss Lady standing over by her GMC, and he wondered what she'd seen.

In the midst of all this, a brawling group of cowboys came crashing out the door, followed by a crowd of cursing, kicking, swinging drunks. They spilled into the parking area and flailed about among the cars. One guy swung a pool cue so hard that it smashed a headlight on the yellow Oldsmobile.

"Holy shit! That's Zeke and the guys. I gotta help!" Todd yelled. He sprang up, pushed Bea aside, and lunged into the mêlée. The crowd now milled and fought around the cars, crashing into the windows and yelling obscenities. More patrons poured outside, and the brawl continued. Todd and another cowboy flailed around in the dust amid a lot of swinging and cursing.

Mary herself came out and began to use her blackjack. Chief pried the drunks apart, sending several flying like pinballs. Within a minute or two, it was all over but the shouting. Black eyes, skinned knuckles, and split lips was about all the damage done. Like any place with a shortage of women, the fight had started over girls. Zeke and a couple of the Rocking W cowboys started singing the Rheingold song, but Mary quickly said, "Not tonight, boys. Show's over!"

The other guys in the fight were from the Bar J, and it wasn't unusual for the two ranch crews to mix it up. There was long-standing bad blood between the Rocking W and the Bar J.

Everyone went back inside. Chief gave Todd an approving nod and a Rheingold instead of a Coke, saying, "On the house." The evening continued. Drunks, whores, fights, and fun—pretty standard stuff for a Saturday night at Mary's, though the Rheingold Beer jingle never got sung.

Todd looked around for Bea and Miss Lady, but he didn't see either of them. Joe told him that he'd found Bea curled up under a table, crying after the Bakersfield girls had worked her over. Then Joe took Bea and drove off in the damaged Olds.

When the Rocking-W gang got home, everything was back to normal. The same crowd would be back at Mary's next week with the same results.

CHAPTER 6

The Fence

As good as his word, or threat or whatever it was, the Boss got Todd going on the new fence the Monday after the fight at Mary's. It was lucky for Todd that he'd finished repairing the Ford. He was sure the Boss would have started the new project anyway, and it would have been ten times the work lugging the materials and tools around by hand or even horse and wagon.

The fence posts, barbed wire, fasteners, and tools were stored in the big barn. Todd spent Monday cleaning all the tools and sharpening the posthole diggers and saw. He wouldn't know exactly how much material was needed until the Boss laid out the job.

The first order of business on any Tuesday was his lesson. Todd had completed his homework and was ready for his new assignment, and then he'd see the Boss right after that. He drove the truck up to the big house—the first time he'd driven it except just around the barn. He anticipated compliments, at least from Miss Lady. The Boss's reaction was a question mark.

Todd parked in front and walked up to the front door, which was open, as usual. He walked in and called out, "I'm here, Miss Lady, and I've got a surprise to show you."

She walked down the hall with an odd look on her face, though not angry or disapproving.

He pointed out the door at the truck and said, "Surprise—she's done! What do you think? Pretty nice, huh?"

Miss Lady stepped by Todd, rubbing against him in the narrow doorway. "Oh my, a truck! Your specialty, it seems. It's coming along, or are you finished with it?" She still had that odd look on her face.

Todd replied, "Yes, I'm finished. Well, unless the Boss gets picky and throws a few minor complaints at me."

"Well, cowboy, you going to give a pretty girl a thrill? Like a ride, maybe?"

"Why, yes, ma'am. Where would you like to go? Remember, I've got a learner's permit."

"Just down the hill and anywhere you'd like, but not on the highway," said Miss Lady.

"What about my lessons for today?" asked Todd. "Like I said, my homework is done."

"Not to worry. I know you're ahead, so why don't you just give it to me?"

Todd escorted her to the truck, opened the passenger side door, and ushered her in with a bow. He then went around to the front of the truck, got in behind the wheel, and said, "Well, we're off. Ta-da!"

They drove around for half an hour. Todd talked about the truck and his plans for it, describing every part, even the carburetor. Not once did he mention Sally.

During the ride, with all the turns and bumps, Miss Lady slid across the seat and jostled against him several times. When that happened, he felt her push away. But each time she did, that feeling returned and he imagined her hands all over him. He liked this, but it made him nervous too. Finally he said, "This road is just too much. We'd better get back. We've still got a lesson today."

Miss Lady said, "You're a whiz at it all, Todd, just a whiz. We can skip the lesson for today."

"See you Thursday, Miss Lady, okay?" Todd said when they got back to the house. Miss Lady just nodded, got out of the truck, and went in the front door. Then Todd waited in the hot sun for the Boss to come out and get him started on the fence.

Finally the Boss showed up, looking hungover, and got in the Ford. "Top of the hill," he said.

"Yes, sir! How about the truck? Cool, huh?" Todd gestured at the dashboard.

The Boss looked around with bloodshot eyes. "Never thought you'd get it going. Been in there for ten years or more. Heard you guys mixed it up Saturday night. This seat is for shit!"

"Yeah, I hope you'll spring for it to be reupholstered. But sure, we mixed it up with the Bar J gang. Zeke led the way, and we came out on top, for sure."

"How about you?" asked the Boss.

"I put down that guy with the bad teeth—Remember him?—and another guy who I don't know."

The Boss actually laughed. "Damn right I remember, bad teeth and all."

Todd didn't mention the other stuff as they drove to the top of the fence job site. The hundred yards of the new fence would stretch across a barranca and up the next hill. It was the rocky nature of the hills and the barranca that would make it hard.

"I want it as straight as a string, Todd. Bird's-eye straight over the barranca, too. Hear me? I think a week should do it. You got all the tools you need, but what about materials?"

The Boss would enjoy him failing in the "bird's-eye straight" department, for sure. Todd could just picture the scene—him pointing at the fence, a good job but not perfectly straight. The Boss would most likely hold forth with a large helping of "in my day" bullshit and then tell him to tear it out so a professional fence company could do it right. He probably expected Todd to protest the "bird's-eye straight" instruction, because it was obvious a survey instrument was needed for that.

Todd replied most confidently. "Done deal, Boss. I'll get going right away." His confidence was high because the Boss didn't know about Todd's secret weapon, the surveyors transit he'd found.

"Okay, and I want it dead straight, you hear?" said the Boss. "It's gonna be another hot day, looks like."

After Todd dropped off the Boss, he collected the necessary materials and tools, and especially the survey transit. It took a couple of loads to get everything to the site. The tools included a rotary digger, clamshell digger, shovel, sledgehammer, carpenter's hammer, wire cutters, saw, wheelbarrow, creosote, and gloves. One other item was essential—Corn Husker Lotion for his hands, because the splinters and barbed-wire cuts always needed attention.

He started by walking the length of the fence line. He was lucky that it was an area with very few rocks, which he would have needed to remove, a hard job. Next he sighted the transit and set up the fence line. Crossing the barranca—the gully—was hardest, but the two hills were no picnic either. He moved to the top of each hill and sighted in on the stakes he'd set straight to the top of the next hill. All were set at equal intervals.

The survey layout and removal of stuff took three half-day sessions. Todd still had his regular work to do in the afternoon, which was easy compared with the fence drudgery. He guessed the Boss would eventually stop by to chew him out and give him the usual "in my day" baloney. Todd smiled to himself, thinking that he should ask, "What day was that, Boss?" That just might get his goat.

First he creosoted the bottom of each split-rail redwood post. Digging the postholes was hot work. He began with the rotary digger, then switched to the clamshell if he hit rocks. For big rocks, a long steel bar was needed. Each six-foot post was two feet in the ground and four feet up.

The critical thing was to dig the holes in the right place. The undulating ground, rocks, and side hill slant made it tricky. Digging a hole twice, or even more, was much more work. Todd over-dug each posthole, then used a little backfill to get the depth right before squaring the post in the hole. When height and location were right, a temporary brace held it. A heavy slurry of the backfill filled the hole in three lifts of eight inches, each with a little overfill at the end. He'd come back in a few days to check the alignment plus tamp down the backfill.

Todd drank lots of water and kept his head covered and wet, but he was soaked through with sweat in just half an hour. There were no trees around, so he just sat down in the shade of the truck every so often.

And wouldn't you know it? On just such a break, the Boss showed up. He surprised Todd, yelling, "Goddamn it, no wonder you're behind. Sitting on your ass and finger fuckin' gets you nowhere. I knew it, damn if I didn't. You lazy city kids are all the same."

Todd hadn't heard him coming, so he jumped up and yelled back. "Whoa! What the hell, Boss? You can't sneak up on someone like this."

Now it was the Boss's turn to be shocked, because Todd had never defied him before. He said, "I wasn't kidding about getting a move on, Todd."

As Todd watched the Boss drive off, he wondered if they had just crossed some kind of mutual respect line. The Boss hadn't said anything about "back in my day," and he'd used Todd's name instead of calling him "kid." *Holy cow!* he thought, but he'd just have to wait and see.

City kids, huh? Todd thought about all the shitty jobs he had had all through junior high and high school—unloading box cars, poaching fish, cutting firewood, retrieving golf balls at night. Then he looked the fence over and said to himself, *This is pretty damn good, Boss!*

~

The next week was the same—fencing in the morning, wrangling in the afternoon. By the third week, Todd was into the barbed-wire installation. He'd seen the Boss inspect his work from afar, and he was hoping that the old adage "No news is good news" would hold true.

Todd needed to string three strands of barbed wire, and at the end of each section, there was a cross beam to brace it. Todd used two braces, not just one, and he tied each brace cinched tight with barbed wire. Each brace was also notched into the end post.

He faced one unforeseen problem in laying up the barbed wire, and on the list of things that could go wrong, this seemingly little item loomed large. The big galvanized staples used to fasten the wire to the post had a looped, round head that when struck with a normal hammer slipped off unless hit just so. This was difficult on a vertical split-rail post. They would bend or more often slip off the hammer and ping off into the brush, gone forever.

His efforts to solve this problem with the staples failed, but he wondered if the old framing hammer he'd seen in the barn might work, since it had a serrated head. He found it and replaced the broken handle, then soaked it in water to make it snug. It worked! He then sighted in with the transit and made a few adjustments, and it was very close to straight.

On Wednesday, Todd worked extra hours on the barranca crossing to get it set just right and finished. But the heat climbed to at least 110 degrees, and finally he decided to quit for the day. He gathered the tools and transit and put them in the truck, but then it wouldn't start. He tried and tried, but had no luck. He figured it was vapor lock, but he was too hot and tired to fix it. More importantly, he was also out of water, and his only option was to walk back to the big house, get water, and then head for the bunkhouse.

At the house, he took one look at the cold water in the trough and knew what he had to do. He took off his boots, belt, and shirt and fell backward into the water. In all his young life, few things had felt that good. He just lay under the water for a while—mind blank, body in heaven.

~

From inside the house, Miss Lady watched this mini-drama unfold—Todd like a sheik coming out of the desert to an oasis. She watched his slow striptease with bated breath, her arms folded across her breasts and hands clutched up under her chin. That boyish face gave way to his rangy body with its broad shoulders and the rippling tendons of his chest, and his six-pack rippled with every motion. His arms looked like bundles of wound wire, stretching and relaxing as they moved. His sweaty, filthy jeans encased him like a kid glove, showing every manly part of him in exquisite detail.

When at last Todd opened his eyes and looked up, a shadow loomed over him through the water. The mirage shimmered and sparkled as he slowly raised his head. To his surprise, as his eyes cleared, he saw Miss Lady leaning over the trough, gazing down at him. Those eyes were intense with a new look he'd not seen before.

They were both startled when Todd's head broke the surface and he sat up, blew out some water, and took a deep breath. The water struck Miss Lady in the breasts and ran down her cleavage, revealing her bosom and nipples. Todd drew in a quick breath.

Miss Lady stood up straight and gave a short laugh. "My word, Todd, you must be very, very hot to dive into the water trough like that." She realized that it was now her turn to be revealed by her wet blouse.

Todd stood up in the water trough and combed his hair back with his fingers, but that one lock still fell across his forehead. His shy, boyish smile and slightly embarrassed, downturned eyes reached deep into her. His manly body called to her in every way a woman could hear. She couldn't fight the loneliness and neglect any longer. Her will drained away, and she let the feeling take her to him.

"Why, Todd, you're all wet—dirty, too. My, my! Why don't you come in the house and get cleaned up. I've got some clean things you can change into."

Todd stepped out of the water and started toward the front door, then paused and said, "Miss Lady, I can't go in dripping wet. I'll mess up the house."

"Oh my, yes, you're right," she replied. "I'll go in and get you a robe. Just leave your filthy clothes out here on the porch. I'll be right back."

Todd started to take off his jeans just as Miss Lady came back out on the porch. She looked at him, then turned her eyes away, as her tummy turned to Jell-O. Eyes averted, she reached out to hand him a towel and bathrobe. "Here, Todd. Just come inside when you're ready."

He toweled off and wrapped the robe around himself. It must have been the Boss's robe, because it was too big for Todd. He wondered where the Boss was, since his truck wasn't in the garage.

When Todd entered the house, he heard Miss Lady call out, "I'm down here in the bedroom. Come on and take a shower. Towels are on the shelf. I've got some clothes for you, and I'll need to change too."

In the master bath, which he'd never been in before, Todd took a hot, soothing shower.

~

Miss Lady looked in the mirror and saw droopy boobs and a little tummy fat. Just a few faint stretch marks too, but after two children, what could one expect? *My goodness, Todd probably has no idea what a stretch mark indicates.* The few lines on her face seemed deeper than they had that morning. She asked herself, *Was the floozy in the Oldsmobile or that Sally girl more to Todd's taste?* Was she making a mistake seducing Todd? The words *seducing Todd* stuck in her throat.

Miss Lady put on Chanel No. 5 and applied a touch of feminine spray, then changed into a full-length, white satin dressing gown. She did her hair up with a Spanish comb, and colorful Indian theme earrings and bracelet rounded out the look she wanted. Would the high heels be too much? She slipped them on anyway. *In for a penny, in for a pound.* Then, sucking in her tummy, she checked out her profile in the mirror.

She laid Todd's clothes on the bed and sat down next to them. The fact that they wouldn't fit him was irrelevant. Opening her robe at the shoulders and up her leg to the hip, she called out, her whole psyche at the ready, "Todd, are you okay in there?"

"Boy oh boy, did that feel good!" he exclaimed from the bathroom. "Thanks a million. I hope it hasn't inconvenienced you."

"No, Todd, it's quite all right." She whispered to herself, "The boy has no idea."

The door to the bathroom opened, and Todd stepped out. He was the epitome of sensuality with his boyish face, manly physique, tussled hair, half-open robe, and relaxed smile. His jaw dropped a bit when he saw Miss Lady sitting there, and a long "aaaaah" escaped his lips.

She patted the bed beside her, but he drew back a bit, so she stood and reached for him. "Take my hand, Todd, please?"

He did so, though hesitantly, and she drew him to her. Still holding hands, they sat beside each other on the bed. Miss Lady could see the mix of confusion, lust, and fear on Todd's handsome face as she moved closer.

Todd pulled back a bit as his eyes took in her body, and his lips moved but no sound came out.

Her sultry smile said it all, if only he'd known that language. "Don't be hesitant. Haven't you sensed this over these last weeks? Oh my, Todd, I have!"

Todd tried to speak. "Miss Lady, I ... I ..."

Seeing his resistance weaken, she said, "I've got something for you." Nodding at the clothes on the bed, she reached out and brushed the lock of hair from his forehead.

His sultry gray-green eyes lost their fear, leaving only lust.

"Oh, Todd, can we talk a little about our feelings? Can we? For so long, I've seen you look at me in *that way*."

"Miss Lady, you know ... Around the ranch, my feelings are ..."

She spread her legs a little wider, exposing her inner thigh as she slid even closer to him. He didn't pull back this time as she said softly, "This is our time, the time we've *both* fantasized about, I'm sure. When you've looked at me that way, haven't you wished for this moment, this touch?" As she closed the small gap between them and guided his hand to her leg, she could see his erection growing under his robe.

Todd sat still, leaning slightly toward her. He started to say something, but before he could utter a word, she moved her lips—slightly ajar—close to his. His effort to speak turned into the gentlest of kisses, and gradually their lips yielded to their fantasies.

Over the hurdle, Miss Lady thought, overjoyed to know he was hers. She stroked his hair as the kiss grew more intense. She moved his hand to her bust and slid her own hand inside his robe to his washboard abs. Their hands explored further until an impassioned embrace enveloped them.

She pushed his head down and helped his mouth find her bust, and then his tongue licked her nipples. Not grabby like a boy or demanding like a man, he let her desire come to him. She fell backward on the bed, pulling his face to her tummy and saying, "We're each other's now, aren't we?"

He nodded as they kissed. Boyish yet manly, his body was hard and his hands were strong and exploring. Their kissing, touching, and moaning continued as she guided his mouth and hands to every part of her body. Her dream fantasy was coming true.

She guided his hand to her inner, upper thigh. As she reached out and touched, ever so gently, his erection, he leaped like a startled stag. Then she relaxed so that her cleft slid down onto his probing fingers, which found the wet lips of her want.

He stood over her with his robe open and said, "My very own Miss Lady." He softly kissed her open mouth and sucked the glowing embers of her nipples, raising her ecstasy higher and higher. A long groan coursed through him, and he lifted her like a feather and devoured her mouth with his. His erection slid across her tummy as she rose. She wrapped her legs around him, clawed his back, and ran her fingers up into his still-wet hair.

A desperate passion possessed them now, and they intertwined in unrequited lust. All she had to do was release her hold on him, and he slid right up against her. She relaxed little by little as the feel of him, all of him, was delivered into her. *Oh yes*, her innermost self responded, as a tiny gasp of joy and triumph escaped her lips. All real and imagined inhibitions fell away, and she was overjoyed and ready. A glance in the mirror next to the bed showed her the scene in all its sensuous beauty. The doubts of moments earlier were gone. There was the blond, slender woman of her young self, reborn—and Todd, her very own Todd. *Oh my, oh my!* She let her desires run to him as she'd long fantasized, and his gentle power did not retreat from her challenge.

She had awakened the man in the boy she loved, and he gave her everything she desired. His love and passion were balanced on the fulcrum of her own. Her animated face was framed by disheveled blond hair, and her sparkling blue eyes were filled with the purest joy—and, oh yes, conquest. Their kisses fell on each other as though they'd found water in a parched desert. All control was abandoned, and love and lust consumed them.

A rhythm of lovemaking now took hold of them, and they slipped off the bed and to the floor as eruption followed eruption amid groans, screams, and slippery grasping. And yes, words of love were still interwoven among the blooming flowers. An empty space in Miss Lady's soul was being filled, and Todd's huge, pulsing erection overflowed her wet vagina. In turn, the warm ball of Jell-O in her tummy released around him, and she gradually introduced him to other possibilities and experiences. His young spirit and body met her every challenge, even beyond her expectations.

When they finally lay back and drew breath, Miss Lady could feel his seed roll around—huge, hot, and wondrous—in her honeyed place. "Oh, Todd, my Todd, I've waited so long. I wondered if ... I didn't know if you'd ... In my dreams, you've been in my arms so often. And now kiss me—and more!"

"Me, too. Oh Lady, I saw you at the lessons, in the truck, by the corral, and ... I never thought it could be this wonderful."

"Never before?" she asked. "I mean, with high school girls, never?"

He hesitated a moment, then shook his head and said, "No."

She cradled his head in her arms, rocked him gently, and said, "Oh my. Oh my."

When Todd's eyes looked deeply into hers, his look said it all. Miss Lady was a bit shocked at her own audacity, but Todd just kept looking at her with love in his eyes. They lay there and kissed and laughed and snuggled when they were physically spent, but the romance remained. Her instincts told her she could never let go of this feeling, because her emotional everything had finally found its sanctuary. Even her towering lust was a footnote compared with her feeling of fulfillment, and Miss Lady was happy for the first time in an eternity. She'd found what she hadn't known she was looking for. Her Todd—*hers*!

~

For Miss Lady, all the lessons of life fell away that afternoon with Todd. Discretion, avoiding excess, being careful, and a woman's place just disappeared as Todd consumed her every thought, feeling, and action.

And the man she'd awakened was an insatiable conqueror of her world. In what seemed like an instant, everything now revolved around him. Try as she might to integrate him smoothly into her daily life, her feelings and desire for him overpowered everything. Just as there was no space left inside when he made love to her, there was no room left in her feelings for anything else.

When she was able to step back a bit, the reality of it all came into focus. He was a teenage boy, a minor, and she was a woman in her late thirties. She asked herself. *Could this be statutory rape?* But at the same time she knew she could never let this feeling go, never, even at that extremity. The impulse in her said, *Why live if I can't feel like this?* And what of Todd? What would this do to his life.

The reality of the Boss, her husband, reverberated in her thoughts. What of the ranch, money, everything? If he found out, what then? Considering the things he carried in the cab of his truck—rifle, shotgun, bullwhip—was Todd safe?

When she didn't see Todd for a day, even a few hours, missing him made it impossible for her to do anything. His eyes, his touch, feeling him inside her was all she thought of. And it wasn't just making love that she thought about, for the question loomed: Were there other women? What about that Sally girl and others like the tarts at Mary's? Jealousy climbed into her throat like a serpent when these doubts arose. The only safe place for Todd was in plain sight on the ranch or inside her. The only way to guarantee he wasn't with some other conniving slut was to make sure there was *nothing* left. She pursued Todd everywhere on the ranch—big house, old house, barns, corral, pasture, even the bunkhouse—and he followed her every instruction or hint closely.

She seduced him in every position possible. This young stallion of a boy couldn't get enough of her. All her fantasies and erotic longings were fulfilled to overflowing—and he was huge, which always left her joyously sore the next morning. Should she introduce Todd to oral sex? she wondered. Would he be shocked, embarrassed, or put off? And could she take it?

Miss Lady felt Todd even when he wasn't there. Sometimes it was soothing and gentle, at other times powerful and overpowering, but he was always an aphrodisiac.

Their lovemaking grew in intensity, and it wasn't just Todd—she went wild, too. Their lovemaking, passion, and feelings grew, and all her desires were explored. Her own favorite was to sit on him and watch his face change as he erupted into her.

And it wasn't just carnal pleasures! Often they would lie together on a bed or blanket and hug, kiss, and talk. Sometimes they'd sit under a tree up on the high pasture and talk, and she treasured his companionship more and more. Todd became not only her lover, but her friend too.

Miss Lady had given up caring what other people in the valley thought. Only women would notice anyway, since they had a nose for "Todd" kinds of episodes. Her secret was safe with them, because they were keeping their own desires hidden. Did the cowboys know? She pushed that thought away. What about the Boss? Whores were as common to rodeo cowboys as horses, saddles, and bourbon. He'd probably had his own share of infidelities. Miss Lady did care about the ranch, but he couldn't take that away from her. He could beat her—he'd done it a couple of times when drunk—but that didn't worry her. Pregnancy was out because of the troubles after her second daughter.

Miss Lady and the Boss had gradually drifted further and further apart, and now they seldom spoke unless it was about business. Occasionally he rolled over to screw her, but without emotion. He was gone early and away all day, and by ten o'clock at night, he was blotto on the couch, watching some old movie. Within a few weeks, this seemed normal. No dream she'd ever had measured up to the reality of Todd. Even beyond the carnal heaven he'd become, her mind drifted to cooking, cleaning, ironing—domestic things. Without realizing it, she had started imagining wifely activities.

These thoughts didn't form until one day at the post office. A letter arrived for Todd, but it wasn't from his mother. It was from the San Luis Obispo school district, and the dominoes began to fall into place for Miss Lady. In a few weeks, he'd be gone away to high school. She drew in a breath in shock. How could she keep him at the ranch? Oh my God, she couldn't, could she? After all, Todd was a schoolboy!

Miss Lady took the mail back to the GMC, sat in the cab alone, and foresaw the dream world she'd built begin to crumble. As she drove back to the ranch, the many hurdles ahead started to pile up. Todd would be leaving in a few weeks, and her two daughters would be back soon, though now as young women. Could they possibly miss what was going on?

My God! He's sixteen and in high school, and I'm thirty-nine. When he's twenty-six, I'll be forty-nine. Oh, my God! And that Sally girl was not far away either; in fact, there'd be dozen of Sallys at his high school. Visions of Todd immersed in that sea of girls filled Miss Lady's fears. It didn't matter who or where or when. What mattered was that he wouldn't be with her, near her, in her. *Hell!*

As she sometimes did, Miss Lady sat on the bed where she and Todd had first been together, then looked in the mirror. But she didn't see the vivacious woman she'd been that morning. Looking back at her was an older woman with droopy tits, belly fat, crow's-feet, and graying hair.

Crazy schemes occurred to her: Run away to Mexico, someplace, any place. Could she tutor him on the ranch? Get a house in San Luis Obispo and live with him? *Would people think she was his mother? Oh my God! Am I molesting a minor?* But she wasn't, was she? No, he wanted this too, didn't he? She had never conceived of this kind of problem—who would?—when she'd married into the Wyrum clan. The Boss's sister's boy hadn't ever figured into anything back then. The old woman in the mirror had no answer for her.

Miss Lady recalled a case, a few years back, when a local teacher had gotten involved with a student. She had been convicted of child molesting and done a stretch in the Tehachapi women's prison. Miss Lady's psyche went wild, seeing herself in that place. The emotional stress, fear, frustration, and exhaustion overwhelmed her, and tomorrow he'd be here bright and early for his "lesson." She took a few sleeping pills, and the cloak of sleep quickly enveloped her.

CHAPTER 7

The Getaway

Miss Lady awoke early after sleeping almost thirteen hours, but the panic of the previous day hadn't faded. She thought if she could just get into her normal routine, she might make it through the day. *Then what?* She couldn't think that far ahead.

Careful not to wake the snoring hulk next to her, she got out of bed, showered, and dressed. *I'll start with coffee and the mail*, she thought, *since that's as normal as it gets. Then Todd will be here for his lesson—but no, I can't think about that.* The brown envelope from the school district sat on the kitchen table, along with the other mail. *Should I open it?* She made coffee and started thumbing through the other mail.

A flyer from the Bakersfield Rodeo Association was asking for entries in the county fairs. It had been years since she'd entered a barrel race, but she knew she could still ride. She paused to listen to the faint sound of a bell ringing in her head. What was it? Taking the flyer and her coffee, Miss Lady went outside and sat on the porch. These early mornings were her favorite time of day. The bell in her head kept ringing as slowly she formed a plan.

She'd sign up for barrel racing, and when she got to the fair, she'd get the Boss to let Todd take her the tack that she'd "forget" to take with her. This would be better than hanging around with the girls back home and in the way. She'd miss their homecoming, but lately they hadn't been getting along anyway. They were Daddy's girls and a couple of spoiled ranch princesses. Miss Lady calmed down and pushed aside thoughts of Todd departing.

Minutes later the Boss came plodding into the kitchen, hungover as usual. He grabbed his coffee, sat down in the bay window across from Miss Lady, and said, "Mail."

She pushed the pile across to him, and he began thumbing through it. When he came across the flyer from the rodeo association, he said, "Interesting!"

Miss Lady mustered up her courage. "Yes! I'm gonna enter the barrel races this weekend."

The Boss nodded and said, "No shit? Might work out, but you'll miss the girls coming home."

They didn't share much, but rodeo was of interest to them both. She said, "I'll take both horses. Be gone until the twenty-eighth. The girls? Well, as you know, we haven't been getting on very well since that prom thing in June."

He shook his head. "That stuff still bothers you? Boys will be boys. It was them that got it started. We've got good girls, and it wasn't their fault. They were just in the wrong place at the wrong time."

"Good girls?" said Miss Lady. "They lured those boys. We're lucky that Sheriff Big Earl was around." She knew the Boss just couldn't discipline them. Like lots of teenage girls, they rebelled against their mother's control and used Daddy as a foil.

"Well, I'm not lettin' you go there alone. You know the rodeo crowd. I'll get Zeke to go along." He went out to the patio and motioned Cruz and Zeke, who were nearby, to come over. When they got to the patio, the Boss said, "Listen up: Miss Lady's goin' to do some rodeo out Bakersfield way in a couple of days. I want one of you wranglers to tag along. She'll need some help. Oh yeah, and don't worry, 'cause you'll get extra pay."

Zeke said, "Can't spare even one. Roundup's about on us, and we don't have those boys from Manteca to help. You want to hire on those Bar J cowboys? I don't think so."

Cruz nodded his head and said, "*Sí!* Need more *vaqueros.*"

"Hell, Boss, we got more stock than last year, fewer hands, and prices are up. We got to get to market early to get that price," Zeke said.

"Yeah, yeah, I know. Damn!" said the Boss.

Miss Lady started to say something, but then she heard Todd say, "It's me. Homework's done."

They all turned to look at him and said collectively, "Morning!"

"Letter for you, Todd. It's not from your mom," Miss Lady said reluctantly.

Looking at Zeke, Todd, and Cruz, the Boss said, "Yeah, you gotta have help. I hate to do this, but the only one left is Todd. Sorry, but it's got to be him. He's the only wrangler we can spare."

In that instant, it all fell into place. *My God*, thought Miss Lady, *I'll be alone with Todd for close to a week.* Suppressing a whoop, she said, "Well, I guess we'll just have to muddle along. Somehow."

Sensing some hesitation on Todd's part, the Boss said, "Hope you're up for this, 'cause there ain't no other way. More pay in it for you. Twenty dollars—plus your allowance, of course. How about that, with a bonus if Miss Lady wins?"

Her good luck was just too much for Miss Lady, who said, "If you're not able to do this for me, Todd, I don't know what I'll do."

Suppressing a smile, Todd put his hat back on and said, "Well, I guess. Yeah, I'll go."

She gave him a hug and said, "Oh, Todd, thank you so much. I'll make it as easy on you as I can." Her double meaning was so obvious to Todd that he had to suppress a laugh.

The Boss didn't catch on.

When Miss Lady regained her composure, she began imagining a week with Todd—dirty horses, raunchy honky-tonks, seedy motels with swamp coolers, hot nights in old four-poster beds, drunk cowboys, horny ranch girls, red eye, bourbon, beer, and Todd. *Heaven!* She knew the ropes, for she'd been part of it long ago. But she'd have to watch the rodeo girl contingent, because Todd would be prime for them, sure enough.

While the others talked rodeo, Todd opened the letter, which contained a certificate of admission, housing voucher, bus pass, class schedule, medical forms, and sports sign-up sheet. He noticed that he could challenge prerequisites. The medical forms had to be signed by a doctor. He said, "I've got approval to go to school in San Luis Obispo. There's also a doctor's form that has to be completed. How am I going to do that if I'm at the rodeo?"

Miss Lady said, "We're in luck. That doctor from French Hospital in San Luis will be set up at Mary's tomorrow for his monthly visits. I'll take you by there on our way to Bakersfield ... Then it's a plan. Be ready early, Todd."

Everyone nodded in agreement.

Todd finished the last section of the fence, then packed Miss Lady's rodeo stuff. They would load Paint, her horse, into the trailer the next morning. Paint was a beautiful, rather small horse that was indeed a *paint*, similar to what an Indian might ride. There was a lot to do, but they all pitched in.

Bright and early the next morning, Todd and Miss Lady loaded the truck, hitched up the horse trailer, and were off to see the doctor at Mary's. Todd drove, and as soon as they were out of sight of the house, Miss Lady yelled, "Son of a gun, if we didn't luck out on this one. Yippee!"

~

The doctor knew the Rocking W crew, so Todd's visit with him was a breeze. Todd was cleared to play sports, plus he got a pre-ROTC exam, which was important because of the possibility of a scholarship if he did well.

They left Mary's and made it all the way through McKittrick and to the Kern County fairgrounds without stopping, though with lots of fun and kisses. Then they checked Miss Lady in for the barrel racing. As they stood in front of the office, Todd noticed a poster advertising amateur events, so they signed him up for the saddle bronc riding event.

Todd took Paint to the barn and parked the trailer in a secure lot. Miss Lady knew several motels in the immediate area, so they picked one up Highway 178 on the way to Lake Isabella. Just as she'd expected, the Lakeview Motel was seedy, secluded, and nowhere near a lake. It was set back from the highway behind droopy eucalyptus trees, with a broken sign out front blinking red and green. A covered porch, supported by leaning four-by-four posts, connected the front office to a long row of rooms that stretched out away from the highway. The dusty building, in desperate need of paint, was tan stucco in the Spanish style of the 1920s, with a roof of broken tiles.

A bored middle-aged woman in a shabby print dress checked them in. She gave them a condescending once-over and said, "It's four fifty a night in advance, and checkout's at eleven."

Their room was painted off-white and carpeted in tired green shag, frayed at the edges. A table and two chairs in front of the window looked out on the parking lot. A double bed with nightstands and lamps was against one wall, and the large gilded mirror over the headboard gave the whole scene an old-fashioned whorehouse appearance. An obnoxious fake rawhide-covered light fixture hung from the ceiling, and wooden venetian blinds hung off-kilter over the window, letting in dusty streaks of sunlight. All the bathroom fixtures needed repair in some way.

"Perfect!" Miss Lady said.

"Yippee, it's ours!" Todd said. He followed her into the room, then paused and asked, "But haven't we forgotten something?"

"And what could that be, lover?" she asked.

He picked her up in his sinewy arms, stepped back outside, and then carried her into the room and set her on the bed.

She nuzzled his neck and said, "Oh, Todd, you're so sweet. So very sweet!"

They folded into each other's arms and fell back across the squeaky old bed. After a luxurious few minutes, Miss Lady gave a start and said, "I almost forgot. I've got a surprise for you too, my lover boy."

She leaped up, retrieved a piece of cloth from the side table, and blindfolded him. After stripping him naked, she set up an old seventy-eight rpm record player that she'd brought. Then she slipped into a skimpy outfit that she'd had for a long time but never worn, started the music, and removed Todd's blindfold. "Happy birthday," she whispered.

Todd said, "But my birthday's not until October."

"I know," said Miss Lady. "This is *my* birthday that we're celebrating."

"But wasn't that in June?" asked Todd, laughing.

"I had my *little visitor*, you know?"

Todd's face showed only incomprehension.

Miss Lady explained, "I was having my period. You know—on the rag. I'm sure you've heard that term, haven't you?"

"*Holy cow!* So that's what that means?" Todd asked.

"Sometimes you surprise me, Todd. You really do. Don't the cowboys explain stuff to you?"

"What stuff?" Todd asked.

Oh, my God, he's really only in high school, isn't he? she thought. She looked in the mirror above the bed, then at him, then back at herself again. *I'm thirty-nine, and he's only ...* She ran a hand through her hair, turning to and fro, preening.

The voice inside persisted. *Oh my God!* But she and Todd were here, and he was hers for the *now* of it. *Let it go,* she told herself. *Let the questioning feeling die. He's mine!* The questions, however, rushed on anyway. He'd carried her over the threshold, and they both knew what that symbolized. *Oh my*, she thought, *he's a kid, sixteen, and I'm thirty-nine.* It was as if she'd inscribed their ages on the mirror. What might the Boss do? Todd's mom and teachers? And the cops? She understood. An image of Big Earl looking at her through iron bars flitted by. But then, before any more doubts could intrude, she heard the first fuzzy bars of "Smoke Gets in Your Eyes":

> They asked me how I knew
> My true love was true
> Oh, I of course replied
>> Something here inside, cannot be denied!
>> They said someday you'll find
> All who love are blind
> Oh, when your heart's on fire
> You must realize
>> Smoke gets in your eyes!

Todd's face kept shifting back and forth between sexy and serious. Watching Miss Lady's gyrations, Todd's mind drifted back to that morning on Mitchell Drive, Sally, and what the lyrics conveyed of young sparkling eyes, blond hair, and coquettish smile. For a few fleeting moments, smoke was in his eyes. But his hesitation was only momentary as the here and now of Miss Lady's sexy form captured him.

Her discarded clothing piled up, until she was down to a G-string and pasties. Then Miss Lady proceeded to fulfill her own longed-for dream, hoping it was his, too. "You got something for this poor stripper?"

"I've still got ten from a pool game at Mary's," Todd replied.

She asked, "Aren't I worth at least a fifty?"

"I don't even know what a fifty looks like," admitted Todd. "But how about a hundred—on credit, of course!"

Singing along with the record player, she danced around him until he was fully aroused. Through the window blinds, the blinking neon sign cast a pattern of irregular stripes across the musty room, as Miss Lady's erotic form swam among them. Amid gasps and whimpers, her fears crumpled and the moment took over. "I love you, Todd. My Todd!"

"I love you too, Miss Lady."

~

The next morning, Miss Lady awoke to a scene from an X-rated movie. Todd lay in a pile of bedding on the floor, clothes helter-skelter around the room and the mattress askew on the bed frame. Laughing, she said, "Oh my, we've been naughty, haven't we? What a scene."

Todd awoke to her laughing, looked around the room, and joined her. Their playful awaking led to more wild, noisy lovemaking and then a brief nap.

They awoke again, spent, and lay cuddling each other for several minutes, but then a sudden banging on the door roused them. Todd started to get up, but Miss Lady stopped him and said, "I'll get this. It might be … you know who." She untangled from Todd, put on her robe, and went to the door.

It was the desk clerk.

Miss Lady said, "What do you want? Can't you see we're busy?"

The clerk said, "You're making a racket and disturbing the other guests."

"Baloney! There are no other guests—or can't you find a man of your own? Get outta here!"

Looking shocked, the woman turned and walked back toward the office. After a few steps, she looked back and shouted in a high voice, "Cradle robber!"

Miss Lady smiled. "Jealous!"

As she slammed the door, Todd laughed and asked, "What did she say?"

She lied. "I don't know, Todd. Something about the noise. She's just a busybody." They broke into playful laughter, falling back onto the bed and into more lovemaking.

CHAPTER 8

Rodeo

After Miss Lady dealt with the clerk, she and Todd proved that two people *can* take a shower in a thirty-inch-square stall. On the way to the fairgrounds, they found a place for breakfast—a renovated Southern Pacific dining car, still looking much like the original. Appropriately named the Dining Car, it was clean and neat, with vintage World War II–era décor and old railroad photos.

The restaurant was empty except for a few truck drivers. Looking around, Miss Lady said, "Well, if the truckers like it, the food must be good."

A sign at the register said, "Wait to be seated." A well-dressed waitress greeted them with menus and said, "Good morning, and welcome to the Dining Car. Right this way."

Todd was fascinated, especially by the train photos and memorabilia. "Wow, Miss Lady, look at all this great stuff!"

With Todd's interest in the trains, the reality of his youth confronted Miss Lady again. His enthusiasm was more like that of a ten-year-old, and it brought her up short. She thought he might even take down one of the model trains, lay it out on the floor, and play with it—toot, toots, and all.

With some effort, she persuaded Todd to leave the trains and sit down. Then she ordered coffee and dry cereal, while Todd ordered orange juice, half a grapefruit, chicken-fried steak, hash brown potatoes, eggs over easy, and a short stack. Both orders came with toast, and Todd ate both servings with butter and marmalade. Miss Lady took in this feast with disbelief, and her inner voice said, *He's a growing boy.*

After breakfast Todd excused himself. He was always polite, a virtue Miss Lady really liked. He got up and examined all the photos and displays again, making many comments.

Collecting the dirty dishes, the waitress said, "Now, that's a growing boy you have there, ma'am! My son used to eat like that. What is he, sixteen? If your son wants any copies of our display, there's a list and costs in the brochure."

"Well he's ... Yes, he's my son," stammered Miss Lady.

When Todd came back to the booth, he leaned over to kiss her. But she brushed him away, hoping the waitress didn't notice. "I think we'd better get going, Todd," she said. "We have lots to do today."

Surprised, Todd asked, "Is everything okay? I'm not gonna bite you—really!"

"Oh, Todd, everything's fine." Miss Lady left money on the table to cover the cost of breakfast. In the truck, she scooted over to the far side so the waitress wouldn't get the wrong—*right*—impression. Then after they'd driven off, she moved close to Todd as he drove to the fairgrounds.

The place was packed, and there were the wannabe tagalongs, as usual, including the rodeo girls casing the cowboys. Miss Lady knew all about that, because she'd been an enthusiastic rodeo girl herself—and that brought up things she didn't want to think about. Her own rodeo girl career had started when she was about their age. She and Todd were bound to see people she knew, and she'd just have to deal with it as it came up. She'd have to clue Todd in. Would he take it as the boy he was or as the man he was becoming?

The carnival atmosphere of the fair enveloped them, but still Todd parked the truck and got Miss Lady's gear ready for the next day's events. The leather had to shine, as did all the tack. The custom-made, monogrammed chaps needed to be perfect.

Miss Lady spent time with the horses, working them around the practice area. Then she went to a nearby salon to get her hair, nails, and makeup done. After that, she went shopping for clothes. She had to look "cowgirl" with a perfect fit, and she reluctantly went to a bigger size after the first two outfits were too snug. Todd's recent attention had increased her bra size too.

Later in the day, Miss Lady saw her friend Gert, who had been a rodeo girl too. When she showed Gert the new outfits, her old friend noticed the change right off and asked, "Why, Miss Lady, what in the world have you been up to? Has the Boss finally gotten his macho back?"

"Oh my, I had no idea ... I guess he has." Miss Lady's reply probably didn't fly with Gert, but she thought, *So what?*

After lengthy discussion, since Miss Lady and Gert both had fuller figures, they decided it was no big deal. Miss Lady would have loved to share her joy at having Todd's attentions, but Gert being Gert, she decided their relationship might be too obvious. Having had her own adventures, Gert would immediately realize what was up.

Late in the day when the fairgrounds were cleared out, Miss Lady came back from the salon and found Todd sitting on the corral fence. Two girls, in the usual skintight jeans, were talking with him. Actually, *flirting* with him would be more accurate.

Miss Lady decided that having "the talk" with Todd couldn't wait, and it wasn't going to be easy to explain to him how some people might not see their age difference in a positive light. For just a moment, panic gripped her. She waved at him, and when he waved back, the girls turned to see who it was. A lump grew in Miss Lady's throat—a throat that on the previous night had felt him there.

Todd got the girl-giggle thing from his admirers. When one girl said, "See you tomorrow, Todd," he backed up to Miss Lady and replied, "I'll most likely be too busy. So long for now!"

But they wouldn't let it go. "We'll be at the barn dance tomorrow. Can you go? We want to dance with you. Mrs. Wyrum, can he go to the dance, please. We'll be good to him."

Miss Lady's inner voice spoke to her, and she had a vivid picture of their intent with Todd. Before he could give the wrong answer, she said, "No, Todd, we need to talk. We'll do it at dinner."

After they stowed their gear and took care of Paint, Miss Lady said, "It's late. We'd better grab a bite."

"More than a bite," Todd replied. "I'm starved. I just had those sandwiches, a bottle of milk, and potato salad for lunch. Aren't you hungry? I could eat that horse." He pointed at a mare in the far stall.

Miss Lady said, "Well, yes, but where?" Keeping their secret was now front and center for her.

Todd said, "It's your town, Miss Lady. You know this area. You pick it."

She thumbed through her memory for places where she wouldn't be recognized. A high-end hotel? No. Todd was a manure-covered mess, and she probably smelled the same. A fancy restaurant or the country club? No! She knew some hoity-toity ladies who were regulars there.

Then Todd's simple taste rescued her, when he said, "As far as I'm concerned, the Dining Car is fine."

"Well, lover," said Miss Lady, "the Dining Car it is. Lead on!"

As they drove up Highway 178, Miss Lady wondered if this was the right time to have the talk—sex, money, secrets, his mom, family, crime, the Boss, rodeo girls, and age. This last topic lingered, and she wondered, *Should I wait for the question to just go away?*

At dinner, Todd, the growing boy, answered the question. She had a salad. He ordered salad, soup, steak, baked potato, peas, garlic bread, and apple pie à la mode for dessert. His fascination with trains continued, and it now involved a truck driver and a new, younger waitress.

The waitress showed a lot more interest in Todd than in her job. When she brought the bill to Miss Lady, Todd was still looking at trains. The waitress said, "Your son's so cute. What's his name? Do you live here?"

"None of your business, we're not from around here, and it's best when serving customers to avoid getting personal. You're a waitress, not a personal guide, so mind your own business." Miss Lady was immediately embarrassed at what she had just said, which made her realize that the talk had to happen now.

The waitress said indignantly, "I'm only being friendly. He seems so nice, unlike you."

Miss Lady dropped the money on the table and called to Todd, "Time to go."

As they walked out, the waitress bent over a bit in their direction, which gave Todd a clear view of her assets. Then she called out in a very come-hither voice, "Bye, bye! Hope I see you again."

As they drove off, Todd asked, "What was that all about? Kind of dumb!"

"Definitely!" replied Miss Lady, but on the way back to the motel, she grew apprehensive. The talk could damage their relationship unless she handled it just right. The closer they got to the motel, the more she didn't want to get there.

Todd sensed something. "Is everything okay? You seem upset. Was it the dumb waitress?"

"Well, yes and no, I guess," said Miss Lady. "We'll talk when we get to the room."

It was twilight, and the blinking motel sign loomed in the distance. When they pulled up in front of the room, Todd said, "I'll get the gear. You can go on in."

Alone in their room for a moment, Miss Lady was glad for the time to think, even as her emotions whipsawed around. For the talk, she thought it best to leave her clothes on.

Todd came in and said, "A good day's start. Tack and Paint prepped and ready for tomorrow." His relaxed smile, with that lock of hair falling down over his forehead, made him look like a little boy about to be in trouble. It was a look that turned women's tummies into warm Jell-O.

Then he did something that was going to make the talk much harder for Miss Lady. He reached into a brown paper bag and took out a small package. Walking over to Miss Lady, he took her hand and said, "I want you to have this, no matter what."

She stared at him and said, "Todd ... what?"

"This is for you," he said, placing a small black velvet box in her hand.

She stammered because of what the box looked like. "Todd, I don't know what ..." She was both afraid and overjoyed at the same time. Her hands shook as she opened the lid. Sitting there on a black cushion was a small silver ring with a tiny turquoise stone set in it. She sucked in a surprised breath and said, "Oh my, Todd, it's beautiful. My favorite stone, too!"

He took the ring and slipped it on the ring finger on her right hand, where it fit perfectly.

She looked at this innocent, handsome boy/man who had now completely captured her heart. Then she threw her arms around him and half sobbed, "How did you know? I mean ..."

Todd held her gently, stroking her hair. "Why cry? Isn't this a good thing?"

"Oh yes, Todd, it's beautiful. I just didn't expect ... What am I—*we*—going to do?" The boy at the diner and the man in front of her now fought for position in her life, her heart. Her emotions gave way, and she stumbled to the bathroom, shut the door, and sat on the toilet.

He called in a confused voice, "What's wrong, Miss Lady? It's the right size, isn't it?"

With as much control as she could muster, she replied, "Oh, Todd, it's just right."

Todd asked, "Then why ...?"

"I'll be out in a minute." Miss Lady went to the sink, washed her face, and combed her hair. Her mind spinning, she thought, *I can't go through this again tomorrow. I've got to do this now.* She looked again at the ring and wondered, *How did he know?* Trying to put on a serious face, she opened the door and said, "Todd, this is wonderful of you. I love it. It was sweet of you."

"Miss Lady, you deserve it. With the advance the Boss gave me, I could actually afford to get you something nice—something from in here," he added, patting his heart.

Oh, this boy could sure touch a girl. She gritted her teeth and asked, "Can we talk now?"

Casually leaning on the doorjamb, he said, "Shoot! Is it about tomorrow's events?"

"No, Todd, it's about us, you and me—and all the other people. Well, I mean, all the cowboys, folks we meet, and ... just everyone. Come sit beside me here." She patted the bed.

"Sure, we meet lots of folks. Nothing wrong with that, right?" he asked.

Miss Lady couldn't seem to get around to the subject in a subtle way, so finally she just blurted it out. "That waitress this morning thought you were my son. The waitress this evening at dinner did too."

Todd was on his feet in front of her even before she'd gotten out the words. He stood there in indignation with his hands on his hips. "Son! I hope to hell you straightened them out on that. Holy shit! Sorry about the language, but jeez. What are we, Miss Lady? I mean … Jeez!"

She took his hands and swallowed hard. "We're lovers, Todd, aren't we?"

He nodded, then looked away. "Yeah, for sure. Did you straighten them out?"

"I didn't say anything," said Miss Lady. "It surprised me too." She could see the confusion on Todd's handsome face. "My darling, it's our age difference. It doesn't matter to us, but it does to other people. They think I'm, well, taking advantage of you. There are even laws about this sort of thing."

Todd said, "That's BS. I'm with you because ... Well, you're not taking advantage of me. What law? What a joke. The only thing is—well, there's the Boss. He'd most likely just kill me."

"Oh, Todd, don't even think that. No, that's not going to happen. No!"

"But he treats you like shit, Miss Lady, and even tried to hit you that time, didn't he? He's just a blob of Jim Beam on the couch. You, Cruz, and Zeke run the ranch. Pardon my language."

"I know, I know Todd. He's a brute."

Todd continued, "I mean, so what? Can't we just ignore them—him? Darn, who cares? And he'd better not do anything to hurt you, or I'll kill—"

"No, honey, you can't do that! My word! Let's figure out a way to, well, mask our love, just for now, okay? I mean, by being a little standoffish when we're in public."

"What do you mean by *standoffish*?" asked Todd. "I'm with you. We're together."

"When people ask, we could just say you're the ranch's stable boy," suggested Miss Lady.

The words were barely out of her mouth before Todd jumped up and exclaimed, "Stable boy! Shit, shit, shit! I'm a cowboy as good as any of them, except Cruz. Stable boy? Is that what you think of me?"

Miss Lady knew immediately that she'd made a mistake. All cowboys were proud to be cowboys, and any suggestion to the contrary were fighting words. "Todd, I didn't mean it. I shouldn't have said that, and I'm so sorry. You are, indeed, a very good wrangler—a real cowboy, as all the hands know. The whole valley knows you're good at it. Oh please, I'm so sorry.

You're my cowboy. Todd, you are my *only* cowboy. How clumsy of me. Hold me, Todd, please?"

He glanced away, then turned and embraced her, and they held each other for a long time. Finally Todd said, "You know, my friends wouldn't give a hoot for what we do. You're beautiful, and everyone knows it. I guess you may be right about some folks, though."

She thought it best to keep up lighter banter until he calmed down. "Well, I could tie you up and take you around with me like some kind of mascot that I make love to. How about that?"

He laughed and said, "Sold! Anything but ... How about we just tell folks that I'm your rodeo horse wrangler? Lots of competitive riders have them, you know? I just won't kiss you so much."

"Good idea, except the part about the kissing. That has got to continue, cowboy, just not in public." She gave him a big wet smack, and then they made tender, romantic love.

~

Next morning on the way to the fairgrounds, Todd wanted to stop at the Dining Car again, but Miss Lady, not wanting another run-in with the waitress, said, "Let's get there early so I can work out a little before the prelims. How about we grab a bite at the fairgrounds?"

"Okay," said Todd. "I can get some takeout and meet you back to the stables. Okay with that?"

Miss Lady said, "It's a plan."

After they'd eaten, they went about getting her ready to ride. Todd took care of the horse and tack while she dressed. When Miss Lady came out, she was really dazzling—even more beautiful than usual.

"Wow, oh wow," Todd exclaimed.

Miss Lady said, "At a rodeo, competitors are seen and judged from a distance, so everything is overdone."

"How's that? I thought it was a race, not a beauty contest." He said this half in jest.

"Where girl competitions are concerned," said Miss Lady, "it's always a beauty contest. So I look okay?"

Staring at her, Todd said, "More than okay. Hubba hubba! How about we visit the barn?"

Miss Lady laughed and said, "Why, Todd, people might get the wrong—I mean, the *right*—impression."

At the arena, she made a few practice runs, and Todd noticed something he'd taken for granted on her chaps. The monogram down by her boots said *Miss Lady* followed by a big *W*. A thought flashed across his mind: *She's married to the Boss, my uncle. She's his wife and my aunt. What does that make me?* He said, "I've got the camera. How about I take a picture of you?"

"And us together, too!" she insisted.

Todd took a few shots of her and then got a passerby to take one of them together.

The competition started with more than forty women. Todd sat on the fence to watch, and some of the riders were quite good—and very pretty. After the first dozen or so, Miss Lady rode over to him and said, "Now, don't look too hard at those other girls. You're my rodeo stable wrangler. Don't forget, I roped you first."

Miss Lady was the tenth rider. When the caller announced her and mentioned a few of her previous victories on the circuit, cheering and applause broke out as she rode up to the line and waited. She made a good start, but even at the first barrel, Todd could tell she wouldn't be the fastest, and at the second and third barrels, she got wider and wider. *But boy oh boy*, Todd thought, *she sure did look great, chaps flapping and hair flying!*

After talking with the officials, Miss Lady walked over to Todd and said, "I didn't qualify. Just not enough practice. But I've got you—and I'm going to present the colors tomorrow! How about that!"

"Wow, congratulations! You looked fabulous," said Todd.

She happily fluttered her eyelashes at him and said, "All for you, my cowboy. All for you."

At the end of the day, the contestants hung out in front of the judges' office. Todd hung back until he had to give Miss Lady some papers to be turned in. When he walked up to her, he addressed her coolly, remaining at arm's length. "Here are the papers, Miss Lady, all filled out."

The girls in the group gave Todd the once-over with short, teasing laughs. One of them asked Miss Lady, "Who's the young vaquero you've got wrangling for you? Oooh, he can wrangle for me anytime, day or night."

Miss Lady replied dismissively, "He's got a full-time job right now."

But they were rodeo girls, and they couldn't have cared less if Todd was in high school, college, or no school. They were in the beefcake business, and Todd was prime. They'd be on him like a duck on a june bug. An image of them seducing him formed in her mind, but she pushed it away and said as coolly as possible, "Get the truck, Todd. It's time to go."

Todd tipped his hat. "Horse is in the barn, and tack is all laid up and ready for tomorrow."

Even though Miss Lady tried to hide her love for Todd, the rodeo girls could sense something. One girl waved and called after him coyly, "Bye, Todd. See you tomorrow."

Todd and Miss Lady grabbed some food at a local place and took it back to the motel, where they ate on the porch. Todd unscrewed the porch light, so there was only the glow of the far-off neon. They were exhausted, so it was an evening of mostly talking and gentle lovemaking.

~

Todd awoke early, showered, and got dressed, then readied their things for the day ahead. Arriving at the fairgrounds, they had a quick meal. Today was all business.

While Miss Lady got ready, Todd saddled Paint. As he helped Miss Lady into the saddle, he noted that her bust stood out more prominently than usual. Then he sat on the fence and waited for her to present the colors.

The colors and the anthem were the first things up. Miss Lady would be carrying the rodeo association flag, accompanied by the United States and California flags. Junior rodeo girls rode on each side of the three flags and carried streamers on shorter poles.

From a covered platform, the caller announced the honorees who would carry the flags. "Today we have an honored guest to carry the rodeo association flag. She is a longtime member who has over fifty victories in barrel racing, our own Miss Lady, queen of the Carrizo."

The crowd applauded politely, but Todd yelled, "Yeah, Miss Lady. Go, go!"

She heard him and tipped her hat. Nobody could see her red face, but she wasn't embarrassed—just happy that he cared.

The girls on the fence also took note of Todd's yelling. In fact, he had yelled so loudly that it drew the attention of the caller, who announced, "Well, there's a Carrizo Plain fan of Miss Lady. And more power to you, Miss Lady."

Moment later, they were off around the arena. The flags flew, and Miss Lady bounced. After three circuits, they stopped at the grandstand where Old Glory was raised high and the other flags were lowered. Then the high school band struck up "The Star-Spangled Banner." After that, the riders took their mounts to the barn, and Miss Lady sat with Todd.

For reasons the caller didn't explain, Todd's saddle bronc ride got included in the pro events. He was eighth among a dozen riders from all over the Central Valley. Todd had done this before in the corral on the ranch, but never in a competition. The horses were not the best quality, he noticed. His horse was Cherokee, a smallish bay gelding. It was the opinion of the cowboys he asked that Cherokee was more of a bucking horse than a spinning horse.

Only one rider before Todd made the eight-second required time. The main danger in saddle bronc riding was getting a boot hung up in a stirrup, although unlike bull riding, it was unlikely that a horse would step on you. The main safety features were the rodeo clowns, who helped if you got in trouble, and the outrider, who rode alongside to take you off your bronc if you lasted eight seconds. Todd watched each rider for a hint of which technique worked best, but none looked especially good.

Just before his ride, he waved to Miss Lady, who was near his chute. The stall itself seemed narrow, but he thought maybe he was just nervous. Cherokee was kind of jumpy in the stall. Todd knew that a horse could tell if a rider was scared or nervous, so he tried hard to be calm. He gave one last hard pull on his hat, then settled in and yelled, "Outside!"

The gate opened, and Cherokee jumped out with a twist. This threw Todd up, forward, and sideways, but he kept his seat and regained a strictly fore-and-aft motion as the bucking brought them out in front of the grandstand where Miss Lady sat.

Miss Lady had been in rodeo from an early age, and the rough and tumble of it was just normal for her—that is, until Todd came out of the chute. At the first buck, she went into hysterics, standing in her seat and screaming, "Todd, be careful! Oh, no!"

A woman close by said, "Your boy out there? Nice-looking kid. Relax, he's doing fine."

Cherokee was throwing Todd around like a rag doll. Eight seconds seemed an eternity, but finally the buzzer went off and the clowns closed in to distract the horse. Quickly the outrider came alongside and tried to help Todd off, but just then the horse jerked to the right. Todd fell between Cherokee and the outrider, and all tangled up, he fell under the horses' hooves. The crowd gave a collective gasp and jumped to their feet. A second later, the horse moved away, and the clowns kneeled over Todd, prostrate on the ground.

Miss Lady screamed and leaped over the low rail in front of her. She fell to the dirt of the arena, stumbled over to Todd, and fell at his side, pushing one of the clowns away. Cradling his head in her lap, she said, "Oh, Todd, my darling. Oh God, get a doctor!"

Todd looked up into the tearful face of Miss Lady and said, "Wow, I guess I made the time."

Miss Lady replied, "Oh, the time? Who cares? Sweetheart, are you all right? You scared me so."

Todd stood up and waved at the crowd, who gave him a roaring round of applause. Then he walked with Miss Lady's help to the arena exit.

The last two riders didn't make the eight seconds, and one of the other riders who had made the eight seconds was disqualified, so Todd was the winner by a small margin.

After several more events, the chairman of the association handed out the awards. Miss Lady accompanied Todd to the podium, where he was given a big silver belt buckle. The chairman said, "You've got a mighty loyal fan in Miss Lady there, son. Mighty fine indeed!"

Miss Lady took a picture of Todd receiving the buckle. Then an assistant to the rodeo association asked Todd and Miss Lady to stand together so she could get their picture.

Exiting the arena, Miss Lady held Todd's hand, no longer caring what anyone thought.

~

They ate dinner at the Rodeo Cantina, a one-story, wood-frame restaurant with a bar, pool tables, and a jukebox blaring western songs. The parking lot out front was jammed with cars, and a crowd of cowboys and rodeo spectators filled the place.

Every table was occupied, but Miss Lady saw a rodeo friend and asked if she and Todd could share the table. They didn't actually want to be with anyone, but it was their only option. Miss Lady sat in the empty chair, and Todd—introduced as her rodeo wrangler—stood behind her. The crowd was young, but everyone shared an interest in rodeo, and the talk was of the day's events.

A waitress walked up and said to Todd, putting her hand on his shoulder, "Hi, Todd! We meet again. You won today. Nice ride. I was cheering for you." Recognizing her voice, Todd and Miss Lady looked up in surprise to find Bea standing there.

Miss Lady scowled at Bea and said, "I'll have a Rheingold and a cheeseburger."

Bea looked poison right back at her and asked, "What's this handsome *young* champion gonna have? And where's that belt buckle? He should be wearing it, don't you all think?"

The table agreed, and Todd said, "Okay, I've got it right here." He took off his belt, removed the old buckle, and snapped on the new one. Then he put on the belt, to the clapping and cheering of everyone. "Thank you! It's a real honor, yes sir, a real honor," Todd said. Bea still had her hand on his shoulder.

Miss Lady said pointedly, "That's all for now, *waitress*." She reached over and removed Bea's hand from Todd's shoulder. The other women at the table took note of the confrontation, and Bea disappeared into the crowd.

Several cowboys congratulated Todd, who responded graciously, and Miss Lady felt proud.

Soon Bea brought their beer and food, leaning in just enough to display her ample cleavage. Rudely dropping Miss Lady's order on the table, she leaned in and whispered loud enough for only Miss Lady to hear, "Enjoy it, cradle robber. Do these folks know what you're up to?" Then she walked off and talked to some cowboys, who glanced at Todd but said nothing.

Todd and Miss Lady dived into the food. The jukebox was playing just about every country artist—Hank Williams, Patsy Cline, Marty Robbins, Buck Owens, Bob Wills and the Texas Playboys, and more. Everyone was happy as the evening progressed with more drinks and dancing.

Todd went to the pool table, asked to play, and was admitted to the game. His opponent was a dude-looking guy who had a custom cue. Miss Lady came over to watch. The game was eight ball, and the dude said, "Name's Jimmy. Want to put ten on the game, *kid*?"

The emphasis wasn't wasted on Todd, who asked, "Why not make it twenty, *Jimmy*?"

"Okay by me, *kid*."

Todd turned to Miss Lady and said, "Will you get my stick out of the truck?"

"Right, boss!" Miss Lady's reply wasn't wasted on anybody either.

The game wasn't even close. "Want to go again, *Jimmy*?" asked Todd. "Another twenty—or maybe fifty?"

Jimmy gave him a dismissive look, picked up his cue, and walked off without a word.

As the crowd clapped, Miss Lady kissed Todd on the cheek and said, "My hero!" Then they went back to their table. Todd didn't dance, but after a while one of the girls at the table—young, pretty, and flirtatious—asked, "Will you dance with me, cowboy? I mean, to celebrate your win?"

Todd hesitated. "Well, I kind of, uh ... don't dance too well. Hardly at all, really."

Miss Lady butted in, trying not to show her jealousy. "He's right. He'd step all over you. Let me give it a try. I've been through this before, so I know how to avoid injury."

Todd and Miss Lady got to their feet and threaded their way through the dancers on the jammed dance floor. She was in her element. She loved to dance, and now, holding Todd, she was in heaven. The jukebox started playing a popular song, "Your Cheatin' Heart," by Hank Williams. Todd wasn't much of a dancer, but Miss Lady hardly cared as they twirled romantically.

Nobody cared except Bea, who was talking in a hushed tone to a cowboy named Stan. Between songs, Stan walked out on the dance floor and tried to cut in on Todd and Miss Lady. He was shorter than Todd, barrel chested and rugged looking. He kind of pulled Todd back and said, "This is man's work, kid. Let me cut in and help you out. Why don't you go polish your new belt buckle? I'll take over here."

Miss Lady said, "We're fine, and Todd's man enough for me—and more than you, anyway."

Todd stepped closer to Miss Lady and said, "She's right on that score, so butt out."

Stan pushed Todd again, grabbed Miss Lady, and said, "Scram, *kid*!"

Miss Lady tried to calm things down, but as usually happens when women interfere in a men's dispute, she just made it worse. She pushed Stan away, took Todd's hand, and tried to leave, but the cowboy held on to her.

Todd got in his face and said, "Do that again and you'll be on the floor!"

The dancers pulled back from them, and one guy exclaimed, "Oh no, not this shit again. Calm down. There are plenty of girls to go around. Knock it off!"

Bea shouted, "Kids shouldn't be in here. Run him out, Stan, and her too while you're at it!"

As Stan grabbed Todd by the shirt and pushed him away from Miss Lady, she gave a little scream. For Todd, that was the last straw. He hit Stan with two quick jabs, then a right straight into his solar plexus. Stan's knees buckled with a *whoosh* of breath, but he stayed on his feet and hit Todd in the head. Todd staggered, then hit Stan with a right cross that drew blood. Todd hesitated, as he should have done in a fair fight. But this was a brawl, and Stan used the moment to recover. He hit and kicked Todd several times, leaving Todd's nose bleeding.

Bea pointed at Miss Lady and yelled, "Get 'em both, Stan. Her too!"

Todd deflected another roundhouse right, then hit Stan with two quick jabs. Stan kept swinging, over and over, but with little effect. Blood was flying everywhere, even getting on the crowd.

Everyone was yelling at the combatants when the bouncer arrived. He quickly pulled them apart and said, "Goddamn, Stan, I told you about this shit. The door's that way. Get out!"

Miss Lady, almost hysterical, threw her arms around Todd and asked, "Are you all right? That brute! Oh, sweetheart, are you hurt?"

As Stan walked out, a friend of his said, "Goddamn, Stan, that kid almost took you."

Stan yelled back at the group, "Screw him! I could take him in a walk."

The crowd laughed and dispersed. There was nothing unusual about such scenes around rodeos.

Bea yelled, "Kid's under age. Kick him out, and her too!"

The bouncer replied, "Put a sock in it, Bea. He's only having a Coke."

Todd regained his composure and said, "A beer was ordered for me, but I didn't drink it."

The chief said, "Stan's mean! You held up pretty well, Todd. Done some boxing, have you?"

Miss Lady pointed at Bea and said, "She started this. You should fire her right now."

The crowd was watching, especially the women, as Bea pointed back at Miss Lady and said, "She's screwing, that, that kid, that *boy*! Cradle-robbing bitch. Arrest her!"

The bouncer scoffed, "Come on, Bea, get back to work. We got most of four hours left."

As Miss Lady and Todd watched Bea walk away, Todd said, "All in a day's work. Time to go."

They walked out arm in arm, and Miss Lady said, "My tush is telling me that I haven't barrel raced in a year."

In the truck, she snuggled up to her cowboy, who was a little bruised but proud. She said, "And another thing! Where in the world did you learn to play pool like that?"

"Well, when I was traveling hither and yon with Mom and the army, I hung out at the NCO clubs. Pool was always being played. I just joined in and got pretty good at it."

She snuggled up even closer. "My hero!"

CHAPTER 9

Picnic

When they parked at the motel and got out of the truck, the exertions of the day became apparent. They could barely move, much less unload the truck.

Todd said, "I'll get it. You go inside and get into bed."

"I'll take you up on that for sure," agreed Miss Lady. "My butt feels like it's in a vise! A hot shower should help."

"Ditto on that. See you in ten," said Todd, and he began unloading. When he had finished, he went in the room and found her sitting on the bed, wrapped in a towel and drying her hair.

Watching him hobble in, Miss Lady said, "You *really* look like a rodeo rider now. Lots of hot water."

She was right—the hot water was like a wonderful dream. He came out of the bathroom to find her curled up in bed, fast asleep. She hadn't even completely dried off, and her hair was flung across the pillow like blond seaweed. Her right leg hung partly off the bed, with a sheet covering her up to mid-thigh.

"My little mermaid," Todd whispered to himself.

He sat down in a ladderback chair and began thinking. Soon he would no longer be around her, the ranch, the Carrizo, wrangling, or Splash. He'd be studying at a new school and ... Suddenly Sally's image skittered across his mind. Only a few days more. Would she be there? The summer's events had profoundly changed Todd, without his young self realizing it. Even with the swamp cooler clinking along, he fell asleep in the chair. Later he got into bed.

The morning sun was streaking through the blinds when Miss Lady began to stir. Her eyes fluttered open, and then she gave Todd a kiss. "Good morning, darling," she said softly.

He awoke slowly and yawned. "Miss Lady, any suggestions for what I can do for you?"

"Oh yes, just love me as the true self you are right now—this day, this morning, this minute. That's quite enough. Oh, my Todd. That's enough, except for ... coffee!"

"You are so, so right!" agreed Todd. "Coffee is what we need, but we don't have any."

Miss Lady untangled their legs and stood up. After a moment of orientation, she grabbed the big old bedspread from the pile on the floor, wrapped it around herself, and said, "But I know where to get some."

Todd said, "Whatever works!"

She took her purse and said, "See you in a few."

Todd saw her pass by their dirty window as she headed toward the office.

Miss Lady walked barefoot to the cluttered lobby where the same woman was behind the counter. Miss Lady went to the coffeemaker on the sideboard and made two cups of coffee.

The clerk said snidely, "Think you're pretty hot stuff, don't you, *Mrs. Wyrum*? Yeah, I know who you are. Saw you in the sports section, about the rodeo. Paper's right over there on the counter. I know you're married—and not to that *boy* back there, either."

Holding her two coffee cups, Miss Lady stuck out her tongue at the woman. As she walked to the door, not being overly careful about how well the bedspread covered her, she smiled and said, "I'll bet it's been years—many, many years—since you got *it* into that dried-up old thing." Then she slammed the door behind her, knowing she'd had more orgasms this summer than most women have in a lifetime.

As she opened their motel room door, Todd yelled, "Ya got the black plasma?"

Miss Lady replied, "Right here, cowboy. Ah, black plasma coming up!"

He took the cup, stretched, and said, "Let's go out in the sun. How about it?"

"Fancy! Veranda, is it? I think some clothing might be in order, don't you?" She checked out his lean, wiry body. He'd filled out over the summer. He now had that lithe look, with ropes of tendons in his arms and legs. His washboard abs coursed in and out as he moved. He still had a boy's face, but his eyes had changed. There was sureness to them. He knew!

For the first time, Miss Lady projected forward. In a week, Todd would be gone. She pictured him in high school. My God, *her boy* was going to be let loose on those girls. With what he knew now, they wouldn't have a chance. As she thought back to her own high school days, images of waitresses, telephone operators, secretaries, bored housewives, teachers, ranch girls, and hairdressers danced through her jealous mind. But as quickly as such thoughts arose, they were banished by the joy of today, when Todd was hers and only hers.

They sat on the "veranda," a broken-down, covered wooden walkway. For them it might just as well have been the Ritz.

"What was that about black something?" Miss Lady asked.

"The coffee," said Todd. "That's what we call coffee on the boxing team."

"Black plasma? Okay, it fits. Hey, I think a picnic is in order. We'll drop by the Dining Car, pick up some food, soft drinks, and beer, and then head up toward the mountains. I know a place with a beautiful spring that flows year-round. You'll love it."

Todd lay on the warmth of the veranda and said, "Let's do it!"

By the time they got lunch and drove to the lake, it was eleven o'clock and hot. The place was picturesque, shaded, and secluded. Just right for them! Todd spread a blanket under a big tree growing over some rocks. They lounged around, drank beer, and ate lunch. After that, they got naked and went for a swim in a deep pool nearby, then took a nap. It was wonderful.

They didn't talk about the future. Before dessert, Miss Lady fell asleep.

~

After she awoke, they laughed and talked about the ranch and rodeo. But when the topic of Todd's summer studies and upcoming high school courses arose, the future interrupted Miss Lady's happy day like a smack across the face. The reality of Todd's departure and the end of the dream they'd been living—most especially these last few days—hit her all at once.

Todd didn't realize it the way Miss Lady did, because he *had* a future.

But without him, she had no future—no love, tenderness, or caring—and the abyss of her lonely tomorrows loomed. Just the thought of it made her lower lip quiver and tears stream down her face. She clutched him to her and cried, "Todd, I don't ..."

Then she heard him softly humming "Smoke Gets in Your Eyes." Tears filled his eyes, which just made it all worse. She tried to hold it back, but the inevitability of him leaving crushed her. She looked within herself for the courage to face this terrible reality, and finally the woman in her shone through just enough. She wiped her tears away and kissed him on the cheek, saying, "We'd better go. I'll call the ranch on the way and let them know when we'll arrive."

Then Todd's voice broke through her cloud of despair. "Can't we just hold each other for a while? There's as much time as we want, isn't there?"

They fell back onto the blanket and continued cuddling and talking. Trying to inject some good news into their conversation, Miss Lady said, "Your truck will be done soon, you know?"

"Yeah, the damn truck!" Todd exclaimed. "But it's nothing compared with you. I'm hardly the same person I was in June, don't you think? Still it'll be nice to start a new school year with a really cool truck."

Again the dreaded look into the future arose, but she threw her arms around him and said, "You've changed, but in some ways you're the same. All good, Todd! You are my man, and you'll live right here in my heart always and forever."

They had crossed the abyss on the bridge to their separate futures. What would be would be. The feelings, however? Oh yes, they'd stay the same.

They gathered everything, packed the truck, and drove off with Todd at the wheel. Miss Lady scooted close to him.

When they passed their motel on the way back to the ranch, Todd said, "It had a great view of the lake, didn't it?"

Miss Lady laughed. "A real luxury place with a classy staff. That busybody bitch can just ..."

In Bakersfield, they stopped and called the ranch, and reported that they'd be home in an hour or so. Then Miss Lady turned to Todd and said, "Boss says there's damage to the fences at high pasture and to get to it right away."

Todd replied, "Back to normal, it looks like. I'll get right on it in the morning.

~

Sure enough, Zeke told him about the fence damage right off. Todd got his tools together, saddled Splash, and rode up to the high pasture to get started. Telling the other hands about the rodeo would have to wait until later.

Todd rode along the whole length of the high pasture fence and found about a hundred yards of damage, but only one or two posts would need attention. None of the lateral bracing was damaged, which was good luck. Most of the wire was okay and usable. It looked to him like it had been damaged by cattle, not vandals or the Bar J crew.

Todd let Splash graze for a while, then got to work. Most of the wire was rusty, so his hands got chewed up. The splices were especially hard, and he wasn't finished until after five. As he and Splash rode along the fence for one last check, his thoughts were filled with leaving and Miss Lady.

Back at the barn, Todd put Splash in the barn and then walked over to talk with Zeke and the Boss, who were waiting for him.

The Boss asked, "Well, what do you think? Did the Bar J crew mess with my fence?"

Todd said, "I fixed it all, and only two posts were damaged. I couldn't tell for sure, but it was most likely cows. If it had been the Bar J crew, I expect the damage would have been much worse. Zeke, did you notice any cows with wire injuries over the past week or so?"

Zeke contemplated for a minute, then said, "As a matter of fact, we did see a couple of those three-year-olds with wire cuts. Could have been them. Could have been!"

The Boss glared, but with Zeke's backup, Todd was in the clear. He gave Todd a half-bottle-of-Jim-Beam look, with breath to match, and asked, "How did y'all do? And Miss Lady?"

Todd spoke up proudly. "Miss Lady didn't qualify in the barrel racing, but she presented the rodeo association colors the next day. She looked great and got a big hand."

"And you? Have fun?" Zeke inquired.

"Well, as a matter of fact, I entered the amateur bronc riding competition. I got thrown pretty hard, but nothing busted. I came in first after a Cal Poly rider got disqualified, and I've got the buckle to prove it." He gave them a big smile, lifted his shirttail, and showed them the buckle.

"Holy cow! That's great, just great. Can I see?" Zeke asked.

Todd's news drew a rare smile from the Boss, who said, "I'll be damned! We'll make a cowboy of you yet."

Zeke said, "Glad you got something for your trouble. Was it tons of work getting Miss Lady ready? Sorry about that. I'd have gone myself except for roundup, you understand?"

Todd could hardly contain himself, and he lowered his hat brim over his face to cover his huge smile. "Yeah, it was some work. But all in all pretty good, I'd say. I expect Miss Lady'd agree."

The Boss nodded, took out his wallet, and gave Todd a fifty-dollar bill.

"Jeez, Boss, that's mighty generous of you," Todd said. "I mean, I did my job is all."

"One more thing," the Boss said, appearing somewhat nervous. "Your mom's due here tomorrow. Got some big news or other she needs to talk with you—us—about."

Todd was quite surprised. After a long pause, he asked, "What's the big news?"

The Boss just shrugged. "Noon for lunch in the big house. Dress nice."

After Todd left, the Boss and Miss Lady reviewed some ranch business and her expenses from the rodeo trip. Just as they were concluding, he fingered a bill from the Lake View Motel. It was for one room. He asked Miss Lady, "What's this one room shit? Where'd Todd bunk? Was he in that damn room with you? That fuckin' kid! I swear, I'll kick—"

"Oh my God, Boss, you are so off base! He slept in the trailer, for God's sake, to save money. Are you losing it?" She turned her guilty face away when she said this.

He glared at the bill, then flipped it away and walked out.

~

Confused, Todd went down and leaned on the hitching rail in front of the bunkhouse. *What the hell does he mean by "dress nice"?* Clean jeans and a shirt was dress-up on the ranch.

When the cowboys came in to clean up, he gave a full description of the rodeo trip—fight and all. They took great interest and asked lots of questions. What stock was used, who were the other contestants, and where were they from? They wanted to know all about the rodeo girls and whores, clowns, outriders, judging, horses, and so on. Todd's story about falling between the two horses got the most interest, and each of the cowboys then had to relate their own experiences with broken bones, horse kicks, bull stomping, stirrup hang-ups, bad judging, drunk fights, and on and on.

Soon Mrs. Cruz brought dinner by. To Todd's surprise, on his bunk was a pile of clean clothes and a small envelope. He opened it and unfolded a note from Miss Lady that said, "Thank you so very much for your help during my rodeo trip. You were indispensable to both my success and my enjoyment." To his shock, inside was something he'd never seen before— two fifty-dollar bills.

Todd was tired, but he didn't sleep well that night. Leaving the ranch and Miss Lady filled his mind. The next morning, he worked on roundup until eleven o'clock and then stabled Splash. At the bunkhouse, he cleaned up and got dressed. Todd was nervous. Contact with his mother was rare and not always pleasant.

For a long time, he'd lived at boarding schools or on the ranch, which seemed so normal to him that he didn't think much about how different life was for other kids. He rarely saw his mother, and he had no memory of his father. Todd considered the ranch his home and the Boss and Miss Lady his family. *But I guess that's really changed now,* he thought.

Because she was seldom around, Todd and his mother, Major Wyrum, the Boss's sister, had an unusual connection. When they were together, she was cool and detached. Though she never admitted it, the army was her first love.

As Todd was leaving the bunkhouse, Zeke said, "Good luck," as if he knew something Todd didn't.

The front door was open when Todd got to the big house, but he knocked anyway. Joan came to the door and said coolly, "Hi, Todd. Your mom is in the living room waiting."

Todd said, "Hi, Joan. Welcome home. Bet you're glad to be back."

She only nodded. The Wyrum girls had always treated him like a hired hand, not family. He'd never figured that out, and for that reason he steered clear of them as much as possible.

Joan disappeared, and Miss Lady appeared in the hall. She placed her fingers on her lips and blew him an air kiss, then followed him toward the living room.

Todd adjusted his clean shirt and told her, "Thanks for the duds—and the other stuff, too."

In the living room, Todd's mother stood next to her brother, the Boss. She took a couple of steps toward Todd, extending her arms, and said, "Todd, you look wonderful. I so looked forward to seeing you again. How you've grown. Just look at you. You're such a handsome man now. Don't you think so, Bonnie"

With a little more enthusiasm than necessary, Miss Lady said, "Oh my, yes. He's a real cowboy now. He pulls his weight around here, I can tell you."

Major Wyrum was about forty, with dark-brown hair, flecked with a little gray and pulled back into a bun. She was wiry, like Todd, but with a severe cast to her. She wore little makeup and a plain print dress. She'd been an army nurse for her whole adult life.

Lunch was ready, and they all sat down to eat. At his mother's request, Todd told her about his life on the ranch as briefly as he could, while she listened with forced attention. Then she went into great detail about the Army Nurse Corps. She was in charge of all the nurses at Letterman Hospital on the Presidio in San Francisco.

After lunch the Boss got up, walked over to the sideboard, and picked up some papers. He sat down with a serious look on his face and nodded at the major. Tension grew in the room.

The major half turned to Todd and said, "I'm being transferred to Germany, so we'll have to make different arrangements for you. With your approval, I'm giving power of attorney to the Wyrums on your behalf while I'm away. It's a two-year posting, but it could be longer. I could take you with me, but considering the move, language barrier, and schooling, you'd be better here. Don't you agree?" She gave Todd a cold smile and continued, "It's best for you, especially since you're now enrolled in this new school, and the Wyrums are nearby. It's very convenient, don't you think?"

Todd could tell that his mother was really irritating Miss Lady. The major's words pleaded with Todd, but her eyes were cold and self-serving. Her disdain for Todd was obvious, and it drove Miss Lady up the wall. Without pretext, Miss Lady pushed back her chair noisily, abruptly got up, and left the room. Her face was contorted in barely controlled anger.

Todd hardly knew what to say. He looked at the Boss, who gave only a shrug of resignation. After a moment, Miss Lady came back in the room, still obviously angry.

The major continued, "Todd, I've set up a plan at the army bank that will cover your living expenses. If some emergency arises, my brother or perhaps Miss Lady *might* help."

My God, she's treating Todd's future like a business transaction, Miss Lady thought.

"And another thing," Todd's mother said. "I know you want to be a doctor and that you're planning to enroll in the army's JROTC program. This new school has that program if I'm not mistaken, right?"

"Yeah, you're right about that," Todd replied with resignation.

"There really are no other realistic options. I've talked it over with my brother, and he's on board. If you're in agreement, we can proceed," said the major.

Todd could tell that his mom's aloofness was making Miss Lady angrier by the minute. Also, the Boss was showing signs of Jim Beam as he slouched in his chair and asked, "Have we got a deal here, Todd? How about you, Miss Lady? Any objections?"

Miss Lady turned her seething face away and shook her head, seemingly afraid to speak. The major sat there with a pleased look on her face. There was a long pause as everyone waited for Todd to answer. Finally he asked, "Two years, you think?"

The major looked around for confirmation and said, "Then, Todd, it's settled."

"Works for me," Todd said flatly. Then he stood up and abruptly changed the subject. "Well, Boss, Miss Lady, what about the truck?" he asked. "You still going to let me have it when I turn seventeen next month?"

Todd's question didn't distract Miss Lady from her focus on the major. Facts, logic, practicality, even reality was out, and rules were forgotten. This was now a *girl fight* over a man—her man! She said to the major, "It's settled. I'll give the Ford to Todd when he's seventeen. You can go now."

Miss Lady's words caught everyone, especially the major, by surprise. The major looked at everyone and said, "Well, I guess ... Yes, I'll go."

Looking at Todd, Miss Lady realized she might have been a little too forceful. "What I meant was that you can leave, depart, go away knowing Todd is in good hands with us. Oh hell, it's settled then. Let's all sign these power of attorney papers and be done with it, okay?"

Now Todd could tell that his mother was angry too, and a heavy mood settled over the room.

The major gave him a perfunctory hug and said, "Well, my boy, I've a long drive ahead of me, so I'll say my goodbyes now. I'll miss you, but I know you'll be better off here than in Germany. I'll write as often as I can." She picked up the papers and her purse and asked, "You'll file these, Myron?"

The major then walked to the front door, shook Todd's hand, and said a stiff goodbye to the Boss and Miss Lady. As she got into her car and started to drive off, she rolled down the window and yelled sarcastically, "You will take good care of him, *won't you, Miss Lady*?"

Miss Lady yelled back, "Why, of course. Not to worry, *Mom*!"

Watching his mother's car disappear, Todd asked, "Holy Toledo, what was that all about?"

The Boss just gave a Jim-Beam shrug, and Miss Lady said, "Never mind, she's gone now."

In mild shock, Todd said goodbye and went down to the bunkhouse.

After he left, Miss Lady said pointedly, "That's some cold bitch of a sister you've got there, Boss. My God, we've sold cattle with a lot more empathy than she mustered for her own son. Germany isn't far enough as far as I'm concerned."

~

The next three days were filled with work for everyone at the Rocking W. Todd spent most of his time checking fences in the morning and wrangling in the afternoon. It was just about dark when they got back to the bunkhouse and dinner. Mrs. Cruz made an extra effort to have really good food for them, because the twelve-hour days took a toll on everyone. The food was a morale booster, and the tub of ice-cold beer when the day was done wasn't bad, either.

Todd got his gear cleaned up and ready at the end of the day, instead of doing it in the morning before work like the other cowboys. He didn't like to be rushed, especially during the morning stillness, and it gave him a chance to keep things in perspective. He had time to finish up his work on the periodic table. Would he be ready for a new high school and JROTC? he wondered.

Todd missed Miss Lady something awful. She was in his dreams constantly—at every stretch of fence, and with every stray he brought in. With all the work, plus Joan snooping around, Miss Lady had no opportunity to see or speak to Todd. She gave him a wave as he rode by the house each day, but that was about it.

One Friday morning as he rode out, Miss Lady came down from the house and waved him over. "Todd, I'm so sorry we've not been able to talk or meet these last few days. It's been ... frustrating, and I miss you so. Wasn't it wonderful, exquisite, at the creek? How are you?"

"I can't hardly sleep without you," Todd said "and I've got blue balls half the time. Try rounding up strays in the saddle all day like that. Not fun, I'll tell you!"

Miss Lady said, "I'm going to be driving you to the bus tomorrow about one o'clock. Does that fit?"

"Shoot, ask the Boss!" said Todd. "I don't know what he's got me doing or when. I haven't seen him since that meeting with Mom. Cruz and Zeke just keep hammering on me to get in all the strays, and there are a ton more out there than we ever had before. They're everywhere—not in bunches, either, so every one of them has to be run down. This is the most roping I've ever done, swear to God! It was past eight o'clock when I got in last night."

Miss Lady reached out to touch him, then wisely pulled back when she heard Joan behind her. She gave Todd a warm, loving smile and turned to go back to the house.

Todd heard Joan shout at Miss Lady, "Where's my riding habit? You didn't give it away or something, did you? Jackie will be here tomorrow or the day after, and I want to have it ready."

Miss Lady, obviously irritated, said, "Joan, everything is in your room *someplace*!"

Todd tipped his hat and nodded his head in that way she found so sensual. That lock of hair fell down over his forehead. She blew him a discreet kiss.

The rest of the day went as usual, but Cruz let Todd off a little early so he could get ready to leave the next afternoon. He spent several hours storing all his gear—saddle, tack, chaps, clothes, and some tools—and then went to say goodbye to Splash, which was sad and involved sugar cubes. Horses have a knack for sensing the emotions of their riders, and Splash was no exception. Sensing Todd's mood, his sadness at leaving, the horse put her head on Todd's shoulder as he cleaned the stall. Todd stroked her as a parting gesture.

He got back to the bunkhouse just as the other cowboys were coming in. As he was doing a few last-minute tasks before dinner, Cruz and his wife showed up. Oddly, she hadn't brought dinner with her. All the guys milled around the big table nervously until Zeke finally said, "Come over here, Todd." Then the guys removed their hats and crowded the table, and everyone shook Todd's hand, even Mrs. Cruz.

Zeke began, "Todd, we know you're off to a new school, ROTC, and all that. It might be a while before we see you again, so we wanted to kinda send you off with something to remember your old gang by. Of course, we hope you never really need it, except on the ranch and all."

Cruz reached under the table and brought out a long leather rifle scabbard. With a smile, which was unusual for Cruz, he handed it to Todd and said, "Open it."

Todd took it, pulled off the top cover, and looked down at a .306 lever-action saddle rifle—cleaned, oiled, and ready to use. It wasn't new, but it looked well cared for. "Holy moly, wow! I'm—I don't know what!" He ducked his head and said, with tears in his eyes, "I don't know what to say, guys. I'll treasure it always and take really good care of it. It actually looks like your old rifle, Zeke, the one you had before you got the varmint rifle with the scope."

They all laughed self-consciously, and Cruz said in heavily accented English, "It is a very good rifle, and sighted good too."

Zeke chimed in, "It's the best gun I ever had, dead-on accurate and rugged enough for any cowboy use. And you're a real cowboy, Todd—the real McCoy! You're one of us. Use it with pride, because you earned it. And we know you'll make a real fine doctor, too."

Todd knew that in their eyes, being a cowboy was the highest calling.

Not guys to stand on ceremony, they put their hats and left Todd to savor his rifle. A little while later, Mrs. Cruz brought down dinner. There was the usual talk of cows, fences, the heat, whores, and roundup. They all turned in early because the roundup was still the primary focus, and it was a real job getting ready for that.

Todd was up and finishing the last of his chores even before breakfast. Then the wranglers were off to the range, each guy shaking Todd's hand and wishing him all the best as they left. Todd cleaned and packed the gear he would leave on the ranch. He put his tack, chaps, lariat, and personal effects in his locker and secured it with a padlock. By noon he was done and packed, and he sat under the bunkhouse awning, just mulling everything over.

Before one o'clock, Miss Lady pulled up near the bunkhouse. Todd threw his gear in the back of the truck and leaned in the driver's side window, where Miss Lady sat behind the wheel, perfectly made up, hair coiffed, and smiling. Her blouse was open enough to see most of her cleavage, and her perfume wafted up to him.

Their faces close together, she said, "I don't dare kiss you, but I want to."

Todd just nodded and looked around to see if the girls were nearby. Then he reached in and touched the bare skin just under her blouse.

Miss Lady's mouth opened with a little breath of excitement. "Not here, Todd. I've got a lunch packed. We can go up on the high pasture. The roundup has cleared that area."

"Yes, it's been cleared by—guess who? Me! Lunch is a good idea." He went around to the passenger door and got in.

They drove to the exit road, and when they got to the first barranca, Miss Lady stopped the truck. Pointing at the fence he'd fixed so carefully, she said, "The Boss says it's the best fence on the ranch. I'll bet he didn't say anything to you, did he?"

"No, but I know it is," Todd replied.

They drove to the high pasture and parked. They got out, collected the lunch, and walked hand in hand the three hundred yards to their spot, amid giant boulders and overhung by huge live oak trees. It was quite warm but shaded, and the tiniest of breezes helped dissipate the heat.

Todd spread a big Indian blanket, and Miss Lady got out the food. "Hungry?" she asked.

"You're joking," Todd replied. "Me, a cowboy, hungry? Perish the thought."

She laughed and continued, "I was only asking, sweetheart."

"It's funny. All I've thought about is loving you, but now I just want to—"

"Shh! I feel the same," said Miss Lady.

They lay back against a big rock and cuddled, touched now and then, but said nothing.

Miss Lady had prepared well—roast beef rolled in tortillas, potato salad, hard-boiled eggs, apple pie, and homemade lemonade. They sat and ate with a relaxed happiness, and then Miss Lady said, "I've got a special treat. I'll bet you've never had champagne, right? Well, I sure hope you haven't, because I want your first time to be with me."

"You're right, I've never tasted champagne. Bring it on, Miss Lady, just for us."

While she got out the two glasses that she'd brought, Todd opened his first bottle of champagne. After a couple of tries and some instruction from her, with a huge pop and a geyser of bubbly, it was open. "Holy cow! What kind of stuff is this?" yelled Todd as the liquid drenched both of them.

Miss Lady laughed hysterically and said, "Oh, Todd, this is how it's supposed to be—a celebration!"

"I sure do like what it's done to you. Oh, babe!" he exclaimed, surveying her wet blouse.

"Why, you old lech. And look at you!" She turned away and toweled off a little.

Todd took off his shirt and clutched her to him. Their wet bodies squished as they kissed, but then they pulled back. Somehow sex didn't seem to fit in today.

They both had tears in their eyes, but then Miss Lady pulled back and said, "No, none of this sadness. We've got to make this a happy occasion. Now let's have a toast and drink up. You make the toast!"

"No, you do it, Miss Lady. I'm at a loss for words, truly I am."

She reached in her purse for a small bag, handed it to Todd, and said, "Open it, my darling."

Todd pulled the drawstring and out came a leather, horsehair, and silver bracelet set with a tiny turquoise stone. He looked at her and said, "It's beautiful, and I'll wear it forever." He slipped it on his left wrist and gazed at her with his, sexy, gray-green eyes.

"It's a Tejon Indian symbol of bravery, given to warriors to reward them for their heroism," Miss Lady explained. "The Tejon were the tribe here in the Carrizo before the Spanish and us."

Todd looked lovingly at her and started to reply, but she put two fingers up to his lips. He drew her back against the cooler, and they drank the champagne. "Well, Miss Lady," he said, "I've got lots to remember this summer by. There's my rodeo belt buckle, and the cowboys gave me Zeke's old Winchester, which it's a real honor to have."

She said, "Oh yes, Todd, that's a symbol of their respect for you. Really nice!" They sipped the champagne slowly, the specter of their parting looming among the rocks and trees.

Finally Miss Lady said, "I think it's getting on to four o'clock, so maybe we should …" She couldn't finish because the end was in sight, and the ball of fear she'd fended off for days now swelled up in her throat. Todd sensed it and held her even tighter as she began to sob. She clutched at him, and cries of anguish interrupted her tears. She called out his name over and over, and he just held her, rocking back and forth and humming.

Finally she regained control and said, "I'm like a big baby, aren't I? I knew this was coming."

"I feel pretty sad myself," said Todd. "I've got a lot out ahead of me, but I keep thinking of our yesterdays. Doesn't make much sense, does it?"

"Unfortunately it makes perfect sense." She let go of him and they both stood up.

Todd said, "This will always be our special place, for sure, like a honeymoon spot. We've had a hundred honeymoons this summer, haven't we?"

Miss Lady gave a quick last sob and said, "Oh yes, my Todd! Well, here we go."

It took only a few minutes to collect everything and start back to the truck. When they got to the edge of the clearing, before the oak tree and rocks disappeared behind the hill, they held hands and looked back at their little piece of paradise. Todd loaded everything in the back and got in. Miss Lady started the truck and drove back to the highway, turning west toward the bus and the future. For her, it was almost a road to the gallows. She was so upset that after a few miles, she slowed the truck to only twenty miles an hour. She couldn't make her foot press the gas pedal that was taking Todd away from her.

Todd scooted over next to her and turned on the radio. "Come on, cheer up," he said. "I'll be at the Houson House in San Luis Obispo, which is only two hours away. You can bring me the truck."

But Miss Lady knew it was much farther than that, a world away. Todd's was the world of high school, and hers was ... blank. Not blank in place or time, but in her heart. Being a young man kept him from understanding that. In his man's heart, there were no blanks. Yes, there was good and bad, success and failure, feast and famine, and all that, but no blank spots. In her woman's heart, *blank* was the feeling, and it was worse than nothing.

The radio began one of their favorite tunes, and Todd sang along, hoping to cheer her up: "You are my sunshine, my only sunshine. You make me happy when skies are gray. You'll never know, dear, how much I love you. Please don't take my sunshine away."

Miss Lady joined in, and pretty soon the truck sped up, too. This put a little more joy into the trip. A half hour later, they turned north on El Camino Real, and soon Atascadero came into view.

Right on time, they found the Greyhound bus depot on Palma Avenue and parked. The bus was waiting, but they sat for a moment, just looking at each other. She pulled him to her and gave him a long, sobbing kiss. Her wet face was a mask of melancholy.

"It's time, Miss Lady. The bus is about to leave," Todd said, gathering his stuff. They walked together across the parking lot to the office, where he bought a ticket.

Then they stood awkwardly, near the bus, and the old adage "Parting is such sweet sorrow" crossed both their minds. Finally Todd said, "Oh yeah, one more thing. Here's the key to my bunkhouse locker. Best you keep it. I might lose it, moving and all."

Her hand shook as she took the key. Softly and lovingly, Todd closed her fingers around it. Her lower lip quivered as she said, "I'll keep it until … until you come home."

Then the bus door opened with a hiss, and Miss Lady said, "Now, no more of that." Todd released her, and they walked the short distance to the bus, holding hands.

The driver stood at the foot of the entry steps. He took Todd's stuff and put it in the luggage locker, then climbed back up the steps, sat down, and said, "All aboard. Time to go. Say goodbye. She'll still be here when you get back, I'll bet. Come on now, you two. Time's wasting."

Miss Lady was barely composed as Todd gave her a kiss, then climbed on board the bus. At the top of the steps, he blew her one last kiss. The driver closed the door, and the bus pulled away.

Through the windows, Miss Lady could see Todd walk down the aisle of the bus. She walked in time with the slowly moving vehicle, each window framing him like a snapshot, until finally the bus pulled out of sight. She clutched his key, then slipped it into her bra. The image of him standing in the water trough—handsome, wet, dirty—lingered, never to fade from her heart.

Walking back to the truck, she recalled a quotation she'd heard long ago: *"I have a fire burning inside of me, but no one stops to warm themselves."*

Her inner voice said, *Well, Todd stopped, didn't he?*

Book II

Carnal

CHAPTER 10

School Days

It was a summer of preparing for high school, and Sally wondered, dreamed, and worried the whole time about every conceivable thing, including what had become of Todd.

Grandma's idea of what a high school girl should look like was not at all what Sally wanted, so they fought at every turn about makeup, hair, and especially clothes. Sally got lots of input from Maria from across the street, whose taste was the opposite of Grandma's. In fact, Grandma described Maria as *shocking*, *brazen*, *tramp*, and *slutty*, and Maria was forbidden to come to their home.

Grandma enlisted Sally's sisters to help influence her personal appearance choices, and nothing was beyond their nosy reach. Zoe and Gail teased Sally unmercifully about everything. Her nail polish, hair ribbons, jewelry, dresses, and especially her makeup elicited their scorn, and Grandma even confiscated certain items. On top of all this, Sally's figure continued to develop. She wanted lingerie, but Grandma bought underwear for her instead, and Sally's body overflowed these depressing articles selected by Grandma.

One Sunday after church, Sally got an idea after a conversation with Mrs. Sondheim, who had again volunteered to help Sally with her look. Given Mrs. Sondheim's position in the community, Grandma could hardly object openly to her assistance. Thus began a whirlwind of activity, at the insistence of Mrs. Sondheim. Sally got a totally new look, which Grandma could do nothing about, because in San Luis Obispo County, it wasn't wise to disagree with the queen bee, Mrs. Sondheim, in a social setting.

It was the beauty parlor one day, nails the next, plus a makeup specialist from a fancy store. This was all interspersed with advice on a routine to prepare for cheer team tryouts. Mrs. Sondheim and Sally chose everything, while Grandma's choices were ignored. And so Sally got a brand-new look and, best of all, more confidence. She also got tryout advice from Mrs. Sondheim, who had once been a cheerleader herself.

When dressing for church, Sally made sure to dress down to please Grandma, whose response was, "Oh, Sally, you look lovely, and I'm sure the deacon will agree."

Sally said to herself, *I'll bet! He won't be able to look down the front of this outfit.* Still, on the first day of school, she went to the bus stop on Broad Street dressed like a dumpy little girl.

That first day on the bus, Sally found out about the cliques. Boys in letter jackets and girls in new outfits stood out, but the most popular students were the cheerleaders, who made sure everyone knew it. At Triangle Park, the bus stopped, the door opened, and a crowd of kids got on. The last girl to get on was wearing a cheer squad outfit, and every eye was on her—with good reason. She had a voluptuous figure. It was the girl Sally had seen in the gym at the boxing match.

One of the boys in front said, in a respectful, almost awed tone, "Hi, Brenda!"

Brenda undid the top buttons of her already-too-tight blouse, gave him a dismissive look, and swung down the aisle, the center of attention. The areolas of her nipples showed ever so slightly as she bounced along.

As she passed Sally, their eyes met in a challenging way. Brenda sat right across from Sally and said, "Oh, you're that *girl* from the gym during the boxing match in June, aren't you?"

Shocked to be remembered, Sally could only stammer, "Y-y-yes."

Brenda replied, "Yes is right! I'm sure that Mrs. V noticed you too!" Then she turned and talked with other students, leaving Sally bewildered about what she had meant. Sally knew that she didn't like Brenda, but she was jealous of her figure and the attention it got.

At her new school, Sally's classes were easy, but getting socially involved was hard. The campus was a confusing maze of paths, buildings, and trees, plus two parking lots. There were six old two-story brick structures, and student lockers lined the halls. Sally's locker was in the gym, down a set of wooden stairs, in a corridor lined with frosted glass doors labeled "Coach," "Office," "Administration," and "Cheer Team." This last door got Sally's full attention.

Within a week, Sally had settled into her classes, but she found them boring. The school seemed to be focused on social life. In her dumpy clothes, Sally was mostly ignored, and she yearned to get into her new things. From the first day, her interest centered on making the cheer team. The jocks and cheerleaders were at the top of the social pyramid, along with the band and majorettes. Football, basketball, and boxing were the most popular sports. The cheer squad was separate, and there was a lot of competition between the cheerleaders and majorettes.

Among the adults, only two people stood out for Sally—Mrs. V, the cheer team coach, and a man respectfully referred to by everyone as Coach. Mrs. V strode the halls with self-importance. She was tall and always impeccably dressed, with hair drawn back in a bun and perfect makeup, and it was clear she was a disciplinarian.

Coach, who led the football and boxing teams, was quite different from Mrs. V. He was six foot three, broad shouldered, and ruggedly handsome. He had a crew cut, dressed in slacks and white shirt, and moved with athletic grace. Coach was reserved but friendly, and both men and women were drawn to him. Even Mrs. V deferred to him.

Within a week or two, Sally realized that Brenda was the center of attention among the students. In the halls, her voluptuous figure parted a crowd like a ship going through a narrow channel. Brenda's every move said *sexy*, and she carried herself as though every boy desired her and every girl envied her. Sally grew to both envy and hate her.

When the school newspaper advertised cheer squad tryouts for new girls, Sally was presented with a real challenge. She was determined to try out in her new clothes, stylish hair, and makeup, but she wasn't sure how to go about fooling Grandma. And under no circumstances could she let her sisters in on what she wanted to do, because they'd blabber for sure. Finally she decided to sneak her things from the house to her school locker, leaving enough things behind so that Grandma and her snoopy sisters wouldn't catch on.

Most girls sneaked stuff into the restrooms, so Sally didn't think that would be too difficult. She looked forward to the surprise her new look would generate, especially her lingerie and makeup. After her final class on the Friday of tryouts, she gathered her things and went to the restroom, which was filled with the commotion of girls getting ready and helping each other with their dresses, makeup, and hair.

Sally didn't know what to expect at the tryouts, but neither did the other girls who filed into the gym. As they waited, they all stood around and gossiped. Sally noticed that her new look was drawing attention. It wasn't just her new look either, because her figure had really developed over the summer.

Sally jumped when finally the double doors slammed open and Mrs. V strode in with another cheer team girl. Mrs. V blew a shrill whistle and shouted, "Quickly line up on the end line. This is Marylyn, head cheerleader. She's a judge and will help me today." Marylyn, who stared at them coldly, was tall and buxom with short black hair and heavy makeup.

Mrs. V said, "There are twenty of you, but only three will be selected—one on first team and two alternates. Now that we've had a look at you, go to the locker room and get into your gym clothes. Come back when you're ready. Now hurry!"

Within five minutes, they were all back and lined up.

Marylyn yelled, "Are you ready?"

The candidates mumbled, "Yes."

"Louder!"

"Yes!" the whole line answered.

"Yes what?" shouted Marylyn.

Furtive glances passed along the line, and then they answered, "Yes, sir!"

"What? Do I look like a sir? Sir, indeed! The correct answer is 'Yes, ma'am.' Now let's hear it!"

With shaky voices, they all yelled, "Yes, ma'am!"

Within ten minutes, Mrs. V and Marylyn had intimidated twelve girls into leaving. Then Mrs. V shouted, "Any more quitters? Because if there are, now's the time to go. Well?"

The remaining girls lined up, and Marylyn put them through some exercises. Mrs. V pulled three girls out of the line and dismissed them. Two cried as they left. That left five scared candidates.

Marylyn had them do high kicks, back bends, splits, and more. After fifteen minutes, they were all breathing hard and feeling more insecure—except Sally. The moves Mrs. Sondheim had shown her, plus her own exercises, had prepared her well, and she was confident that she was the best candidate for the first team. She was tired, but she felt good about how she'd performed.

At that point, the rest of the cheerleaders, including Brenda, entered the gym and filed up to the judges' table. They didn't look sympathetic at all.

Marylyn said, "Now I need a helper. Brenda, will you do some cartwheels for us?"

Brenda pranced forward, did a pirouette, preened, and stuck out her huge chest. She did three perfect cartwheels with a high bounce at the end that sent her boobs flying. With an edge in her voice, Mrs. V asked, "Can any of you five girls do *that*?" and they all raised their hand.

After putting the five remaining girls through more exercises, Mrs. V pulled two of them aside and said, "I'm sad to say that you've failed the basics. Better luck next year." Clearly disappointed, they left the gym.

About that time, Coach entered by a back door, and the aura in the room instantly changed.

Then Mrs. V took pom-poms from a bag and placed a pair in front of each of the three remaining girls. "These are as much a part of your costume as the outfits you'll be issued if you make the team. Understood?"

They all gave a weak, "Yes."

She said, "What? That was no answer. Once again, is that understood?"

The three girls jumped and said, "Yes, ma'am!"

"That's better," said Mrs. V. "I warn you, discipline is *very* important. There's punishment for misbehaving, and dismissal if it continues. Marylyn will keep me informed of any infractions. Understood?"

"Yes, ma'am!" they replied in unison, springing to attention. It was clear that this was going to be harder than they'd expected.

~

To the three remaining girls, Mrs. V announced, "You have all made the team. Now it's time to decide who are alternates and who is first team." The three girls and the judges eyed one another ominously.

The two other girls did their routines first, and then it was Sally's turn. Mrs. V said, "Aah yes, you're the girl from the boxing match last June, with the little rosebud mouth. Brenda told me you'd be here. My goodness, how you've developed."

This startled Sally—and it showed, because Brenda gave her another little finger wave.

Then Mrs. V said, "Okay, Sally Anderson, let's see what you can do. Begin."

"Yes, ma'am!" Sally did a cartwheel, and then stood waiting for comments.

"That was very good, Sally. Now another, back this way," said Mrs. V.

Sally did one more cartwheel and finished right next to Mrs. V, who patted her on the tush. Brenda nodded her approval as Sally came back to stand in front of the judges. The tryouts continued with pom-poms.

After one of Sally's routines, Mrs. V said, "No, Sally. Your cartwheels were fine, but the splits and bounces need more. Do you understand?"

"Yes! I mean … Yes, ma'am!" Sally did it again with more bounce, which almost made her boobs fly out. She stole a jealous look at Brenda and wondered how her gigantic display would behave.

Next the three girls demonstrated a cheer: "We're the Tigers and could not be prouder, and if you can't hear us, we'll yell a little louder." They repeated the cheer at the top of their lungs.

After about an hour, the three final candidates had finished everything Mrs. V required. It was time for the judges to decide, so they conferred with a lot of hushed talk. Finally Mrs. V introduced the judges and said, "The selection process has concluded and we've made a decision. Pam Walls and Judy Neel have been chosen as alternates. Sally Anderson, you've been selected as our new cheer team member. Congratulations, everyone! Let's give them a hand!"

The judges and cheerleaders clapped loudly and hugged each other, and a general chatter ensued. Then Mrs. V said, "You can pick up your new uniforms on Monday. You're a lucky bunch, because you're getting the new shorter outfits just like UCLA and Cal Poly. When I was a cheerleader at Bakersfield High School—I won't say when—we had dresses down to our ankles."

When Brenda hugged Sally and said, "You're the best," Sally's feelings of hate and envy grew more confused.

Mrs. V let them all go, and Sally changed back into her dumpy clothes and started for home. One of the many things she had to consider was how to increase her bust to compete with Brenda. After careful thought, she wondered if that was even possible. After all, Brenda's were the biggest she'd ever seen.

Sally had taken note that all the girls had well-developed figures. She recalled the magazine she'd taken from the beauty parlor, which advertised bust-enlarging cream and suggestions for exercises. She decided on both cream and exercise, recalling a rhyme she'd heard in the gym: *We must, we must, we must improve our bust.* That might work, but where to get the cream? She'd have to work on that and how to get past Grandma.

She decided that the best plan when she got home was to make a big deal of her success. She hesitated at the front door, then rushed in yelling, "I made it! I'm on the cheer squad. Yippee! Oh, Grandma, I made it!"

Grandma stood there in surprise, but Sally grabbed Gail and Zoe and danced around the living room. Before any questions could be asked, she handed the permission papers to Grandma and rushed to her room. No use having to explain the nice things and makeup in her gym bag.

She took out the magazine she'd taken from the beauty parlor and found the page with the breast-enhancement ad. She could only order it by mail, which was going to be a problem getting it by Grandma and her sisters. A *big* problem!

CHAPTER 11

Brenda

Sally spent half her time figuring out ways to fool, trick, and get around Grandma and her sisters. She had to leave home every day looking dumpy but arrive at school looking stylish, which became a kind of dance involving hair at the bus stop, makeup on the bus, and clothes in the locker room. Many other girls were also doing this, so they all—even those who didn't get along—worked out a chaotic underground system of cooperation, barter, and exchange. It turned the bus ride into a makeup parlor on wheels, and the stolen few minutes in locker rooms and bathrooms became bedlam. The social combat of school life included pushing, shoving, and arguing before first period even began, and the objective was to outdo the other girls and attract boys.

Classes and grades were not totally forgotten, but that venue was controlled by teachers. This struggle took place in the jungle, with no holds barred or prisoners taken. The leading girls controlled this social order any way they could. Cliques were common, and underground bullying ensured that no nonconforming girl upset the balance. Boys were almost oblivious to this subterranean current of social climbing. The boys were a kind of social Omaha Beach for the girls, and their weapons were hair, makeup, and a good figure. A big bust was as valuable as heavy artillery, and lunch break, after-school activity, and parties were the battlegrounds.

Of course, most girls and boys didn't compete at this level, and they were just a forgotten blob of "them" to students who strove for high levels of social prominence.

Sally wove in and out of the social scene while learning cheerleading routines. Her school day consisted of classes until three o'clock, followed by cheer team practice.

Brenda was high priestess of the social order, which made her no friends among the other girls. Only two other people, Coach Charles and Mrs. V, garnered anywhere near as much attention as Brenda. They were unofficial powers, with Mrs. V running the cheer team and Coach running the football and boxing teams.

Sally often saw Brenda between classes, in the locker room, and at cheer practice. Her envy knew no bounds, and she fantasized about having a figure like Brenda's—or even better. One day in the cafeteria, Sally dropped her pencil on the floor. When she bent to pick it up, a pair of legs appeared next to her. She looked up to see Brenda, who bent over in an exaggerated pretense of helping her. The bottom of Brenda's loose blouse ballooned out, revealing all her assets for Sally to envy. Brenda then strutted away, looking back at Sally with a shy smile.

When the stunning new cheer team uniforms were issued, the girls were thrilled and spent the whole afternoon adjusting their fit. They'd be wearing them at Friday's football game against Paso Robles High School. The short skirts were the biggest hit, and the girls all jumped around, showing off and guessing at the comments to come. They knew that some older fans would consider the new uniforms too risqué, but that was exactly why the girls liked them. They would be the first cheer squad in the county to have uniforms like the college girls.

On Friday afternoon, the football team, marching band, and cheerleaders bused up to Paso Robles, thirty miles north on Highway 101. Night games drew the biggest crowds, and it would be the new girls' first opportunity to perform. As the only freshman, Sally would be closely watched. She knew if she didn't do well, an alternate would replace her, which would be a humiliating demotion.

Sally noticed that Coach paced the sidelines with a degree of authority that no one could miss. He exuded power and grace, and even Mrs. V seemed demure in his presence.

All through the first half, the cheerleaders did really well, and they could feel the increased attention the new uniforms drew. It was exciting to feel mature and sexy. Sally did perfect cartwheels, and then Brenda did a whole series in front of the grandstand. The crowd drew in a breath of surprise as she cavorted around.

The game wasn't even close, and the Tigers went into the locker rooms at halftime with a twenty-point lead. Then it was time for the band and majorettes to perform, so Mrs. V told them which routines to do. Foremost was the exchange of cheer squads with Paso Robles High, and she wanted to make an especially lasting impression with the new uniforms. "Make sure your makeup, hair, and outfits are perfect. Is that understood?"

As the girls touched up their hair and adjusted their uniforms, Mrs. V went around helping and even adjusting some clothing. When she got to Sally, she said, "You've a nice figure Sally, so try to show it off a little more. Follow Brenda's lead." Turning back to the rest of the squad, she asked, "Are you all ready?"

In unison, they answered, "Yes, ma'am!"

Their routine, first in front of their fans and then the Paso fans, drew heavy applause—and envious looks at their new outfits from the Paso cheer team. Mrs. V watched with obvious pride. Sally was nervous as she watched Brenda make her bouncing cartwheel run, to gasps of surprise from the spectators, and then she did her own run. She drew lesser gasps, but she still felt good about her performance. Her hatred of Brenda was fading, though her envy remained.

After their halftime performance, the girls ate, talked, and flirted with boys before preparing for their next routine. Sally looked into the bleachers and was shocked to see Todd standing in the third row. She waved and yelled, "Oh my, it's Todd! Hi, Todd!"

Then it was time for the second half kickoff, with the crowd yelling and all eyes drawn to the field. Todd apparently didn't recognize Sally amid the standing, screaming fans. She was surprised to see him wearing a Junior ROTC uniform, which made him look even cuter than before. She wondered why he hadn't seen her. Could her new hair, makeup, and uniform have changed her that much?

Sally was thinking of running over to the stands to get Todd's attention, when suddenly Mrs. V grabbed her shoulder and spun her around violently. "None of that now. Didn't you hear me instruct you to get out there with the others? One more missed cue like that, young lady, and there'll be punishment. Or maybe you'd rather be an alternate? Is that clear?"

"Y-yes," Sally stammered.

"What was that?"

"Yes, ma'am!" Sally was scared now. She knew what *alternate* meant, but what about *punishment*? Could Mrs. V have meant corporal punishment? It was the first time she'd seen Mrs. V's hard side. The other girls smiled at her mischievously, as if to say, "We told you so."

As Sally prepared for the next cheer, she scanned the bleachers, but Todd was nowhere in sight. All eight girls kicked in the air and yelled, "Re, re, hit 'em in the knee. Rass, rass, hit 'em in the other knee." Then they jumped in the air waving their pom-poms, came down, and did the splits.

They continued cheering for the rest of the game, which the Tigers won thirty to ten. After the game, there were friends to meet, parties to go to, and dates to begin. Sally searched for Todd in the milling crowd but couldn't find him. Her searching was so obvious that a couple of girls asked who she was looking for, but Sally said, "Oh, just an old friend."

"Oh yeah? What's his name?" Marylyn asked. The others gave low, knowing laughs.

The team, band, and cheerleaders all went back to San Luis Obispo on the same bus along with Coach and Mrs. V. On the way home, several girls and football players sneaked off behind the pile of equipment in the back. At the school, when everyone piled out, the kids behind the equipment came out straightening their clothes. Brenda was the last one out, hurriedly tucking in her blouse.

In the parking lot, the cheer team gathered around Mrs. V, who congratulated them. But then she jerked Brenda aside and said, "You were back there without permission, weren't you?"

Brenda's normal haughty look vanished, and she said, "We weren't doing anything. We were just—"

"Don't you lie to me, Miss Barbano!" said Mrs. V. "I know exactly what you were doing and with whom. Don't lie to me now."

Kenny, a senior football player with a car, looked pretty nervous. He said, "Yeah, what of it? We were studying ... for next week. That's okay, isn't it? It was Brenda's idea anyway."

"It wasn't my idea. It was him!" Brenda insisted, without much conviction.

Mrs. V said, "It doesn't really matter whose idea it was. You're on my cheer team, aren't you, Brenda?"

Now totally lacking confidence and looking quite crestfallen, Brenda said, "Yes, I guess."

"What was that, young lady?" asked Mrs. V.

"I'm sorry. Yes, ma'am!" said Brenda.

"That's better. Report to my office after classes on Monday. We'll see about this." Mrs. V said this in a caustic tone that made all the cheerleaders blanch.

Sally was confused. Why would Brenda—or any of them—need permission to make out with a boy? Wasn't that always against the rules? Who'd give permission to do that? But she knew better than to ask Mrs. V. Sally was beginning to get an idea of just how strict Mrs. V was. She had two thoughts while heading home: *What punishment is Brenda in for? And how can I find Todd?*

~

Keeping her secret from Grandma, Zoe, and Gail was getting to be beyond Sally's ability. She was getting her stories mixed up, and too many questions were being asked. On Saturday morning, Sally found that her sisters had been poking around in her room while she was outside. They hadn't found anything, but that was the trouble. When Sally came in, Gail said, "Where's your new stuff? Did you hide it or take it to school? Grandma said you're not supposed to wear that trashy stuff. That's the rule! I'm gonna tell on you."

"Me, too! I'm tattling on you, Miss Prissy Face!" Zoe chimed in.

Sally said, "What are you talking about? I didn't do anything."

Pointing at the empty drawers, Gail said, "Yes, you did. You took all your stuff so you could wear it at school. It's not here, so where is it?"

"You snoopers shouldn't be in here. It's none of your beeswax." Sally was trapped, and she tried to think of something to prevent them from telling Grandma. "If you tell, I won't babysit you, and then Mrs. Tate will have to do it. How about that?"

Looking scared, Zoe said, "No fair! Grandma would make you babysit us."

"I'd just say I had cheer practice, and she'd let me go," said Sally.

Zoe and Gail looked at each other. Sally knew they hated Mrs. Tate, who was really strict and wouldn't let them snack or watch TV. They had to play old parlor games with her, too. Sally said, "If you don't tell, I'll let you play dress-up in some of my things when Grandma's out, okay? And I mean all the time, too—not just today. Well?" Sally knew she was on the right track. Just the thought of Mrs. Tate was enough. "Well?" she asked, more forcefully.

Finally Gail said, "Okay, but when can we do dress-up?"

"While Grandma's at the social," Sally said, "I'll bring some stuff home. But you've got to be careful, okay?"

"After church?" asked Gail. "How about then? Grandma's gone, and we can help you lie to her."

Sally hesitated. Gail was getting too big for her britches. "It's not a lie," Sally explained. "It's …"

It was Gail's turn to look triumphant. She was learning the art of girl combat.

Sally narrowed her eyes and looked at both of them. "Okay, I'll bring things home, but don't get that self-satisfied look on your faces quite yet. If you slip up on this, I'll put Mrs. Tate back in the picture lickety-split. Understand?"

Agreeable nods from both sisters sealed the deal, and they left the room.

Sally wondered what had changed. She never would have contradicted, disobeyed, or argued with Grandma even a few weeks earlier. Now she was plotting to disobey everything Grandma demanded. Thoughts of cheering and Todd washed her doubts away. Now if she could just figure a way to get ahold of some of that bust-enhancement cream.

~

Church the next day was boring as usual, and Sally was getting closer scrutiny than ever from Deacon Jennings, even in her dumpy little-girl clothes. As everyone gathered on the front patio of the church to gossip, Sally heard Mrs. Sondheim's voice behind her.

"Sally, is that you? My word, what's happened to all those cute clothes? And your hair and makeup? I'm stunned. Don't you like them?"

Sally turned to greet her sheepishly. "Hi, Mrs. Sondheim."

Grandma heard them and moved to where they were conversing. "She looks like a well-dressed Christian young lady, if I do say so myself. I hope you think so too, Mrs. Sondheim."

Mrs. Sondheim rebuffed Grandma. "Not at all. We spent days picking out new, conservative attire for Sally, and now she's wearing *this*? Sally's a young lady now, and she should dress appropriately." She pointed at Sally in an almost insulting way and added, "Oh my, don't you agree? Sally would be much better attired in the new things we bought."

Grandma was obviously intimidated by Mrs. Sondheim. "Well, for school and such, but church? I'm not sure if—"

"Come now, Mrs. Anderson," interrupted Mrs. Sondheim. "I'm trying to help, just as you've asked me to do. Church is a place where a girl should look her best, especially one as attractive as Sally."

Sally could hardly believe her good fortune, but she knew better than to intercede in the confrontation. She decided that just looking sorrowful was her best tactic, so she hunched her shoulders and put on a sad face. Her sisters shot her a "Think you're pretty smart?" look.

Grandma couldn't go back on her request for help with Sally. After all, Mrs. Sondheim had actually paid for some of it, so Grandma said, "On issues of fashion, I guess you'd be much more aware than me. And of course, we're very appreciative of your help."

This drew a satisfied smile from Mrs. Sondheim. "I hope I can look forward to seeing this beautiful young girl in more ladylike attire next week. Maybe a little more makeup too?"

Sally smiled and said, "Oh, Grandma, I promise to make you proud of me. I really do."

Before Grandma went to her social, she dropped Sally off at school to get her stuff and take it home. Zoe and Gail got to play dress-up, which Sally knew would keep them busy. She'd still have to tone down her hair and makeup until she was on the bus in the morning.

When Grandma got home later, she went in Sally's room for a talk. "Sally, I appreciate the help Mrs. Sondheim has given us, but I want to make it perfectly clear that these new clothes are to be worn in a demure way. Mrs. Sondheim's idea and mine are different. Tops will be buttoned up, skirts long, very little makeup, and no stacked-up hair. Is that clear?"

"Yes, Grandma," Sally replied in her most obedient voice.

Grandma opened the dresser drawer, reached in, and pulled out Sally's new items of lingerie. She held them in front of Sally's face and said, "These go out, understood? And to make absolutely sure, I'll dispose of them myself! Shocking, just shocking!"

Sally's newfound confidence drained away. Outside her door stood her sisters with self-satisfied looks on their faces. They both stuck their tongues out at Sally, who stuck hers right back at them.

~

On Monday, classes went as usual, but Sally felt more eyes following her in the hall. After second period, she applied more makeup and teased her hair. By lunchtime, she'd hiked up her skirt and opened a button on her blouse. Between classes, she saw that Brenda was making the most of her stacked figure. In particular, Brenda's cleavage drew Sally's attention. Then she looked down at her own chest and thought about the bust cream.

When classes ended, Sally went downstairs to the dim corridor and walked past the nurse's office to the meeting room. As she opened the door, she saw the other girls huddled together around a table, obviously not engaged in their usual joking and gossiping. They were stealing furtive glances at Mrs. V's open office door.

Sally said, "Hi! What's—"

"Shh!" interrupted Marylyn. "Mrs. V is getting ready to punish Brenda." They could hear Mrs. V talking forcefully to Brenda in the other room.

Brenda said very softly, "I didn't mean to break the rules and ..."

"And what?" Mrs. V barked.

"Yes, ma'am! I did break the rules, and I deserve to be punished for it," said Brenda.

Mrs. V said, "That's better. Now you girls pay attention. I'm going to punish Brenda. Also, no boyfriends until I release her from her punishment period. Is that clear? The rules are important, and I will enforce them strictly. Understood? Sally, this is your first lesson in obedience!"

In boisterous unison, all the girls said, "Yes, ma'am!"

Mrs. V closed her door slowly. Then the girls could see only murky shapes that hinted at what was happening. Muted sound of slaps were heard, over and over again.

The girls exchanged looks, and someone said, "Well, it's better than being off the team, isn't it?"

The other girls nodded in agreement, and Sally asked, "Have any of you, uh …"

Marylyn broke in and said, "Look out for her wide belt."

~

By the middle of the week, the cheer squad's balance was restored, though Brenda's behavior was, if anything, even bolder. Because Sally had classes near Brenda's, she was privy to all of it.

On Thursday, as Sally was standing near the co-op, she heard a familiar voice. Turning to see who it was, she was thrilled to see Todd standing in a small group across the hall, and he was even more cool looking than she remembered. She pushed her way through the crowd, tapped him on the shoulder, and said, "Hi, Todd!"

He turned around and said, "Sally? Wow, it's you. I can't believe it!"

She batted her eyes and put on a coy face. "Yeah, remember me?"

Then those soft, gray-green eyes looked down at her, and he nodded so that the lock of hair fell down over his forehead. "Oh, I remember you," he said. "Of course I do!"

Sally's heart pounded, and hardly believing how forward she'd become, she stepped up and pressed herself against him. At that instant, Brenda appeared just behind Todd—gypsy eyes flashing, blouse open, and red lips pouting. The two girls fixed their competitive eyes on each other.

Todd put his arm around Sally, who felt like a princess. But the moment was fleeting, because Brenda said, "Let's go, girls. Time for practice. You know how Mrs. V feels about us being late." Then she leaned her head—and chest—in close and looking squarely at Todd, said, "Sally, it's time for practice, so we'd better go."

Todd said to Sally, "You're a cheerleader? I didn't know freshmen girls could be cheerleaders. You look great!" His eyes looked at her in a way that made her feel special—and self-conscious.

Preening for him, Sally said, "You've changed, too, Todd. You're at school here now?"

Todd explained, "I started late because my permission paperwork wasn't ready."

Brenda said again, "Come on, Sally! No time for lollygagging around now."

As Sally let go of Todd, Brenda pushed up against him and said, "I'm a cheerleader too, and—"

"He knows, Brenda!" interrupted Sally. "He doesn't need you to tell him. We're friends from last summer."

Todd had a slightly confused look on his face as the two attractive girls argued around him.

Just then Mrs. V walked up and said, "It's that time, girls. Get inside now!" Her eyes fell on Todd, and as she walked toward him, the girls took a step back.

Todd reached out his hand and said, "Hello, I'm Todd Wyrum. You're the cheer coach, right?"

Mrs. V was not used to this kind of casual advance with friendly words and extended hand. "Yes, I'm Mrs. V. I see you're getting acquainted with my girls."

The girls noticed that Todd seemed neither impressed nor intimidated. Maintaining his relaxed smile, he replied, "Yes, nice group! I'm on the boxing team with Coach. I've seen you around—at the games, I mean."

"Yes, of course," said Mrs. V. "If you need help with your classes, I could have one of my very resourceful girls help. They're good students, I assure you. Right, girls?"

Sally and Brenda could hardly believe their ears. Everyone deferred to Mrs. V, but not Todd. They were shocked to realize that Mrs. V was almost flirting with him.

"Yes, ma'am! We'd be happy to help anytime, day or night," all the cheer girls said in unison.

The inclusion of the word *night* wasn't lost on Mrs. V. "Todd, it's nice to meet you. Girls, as I said, it's time for practice. Come on now!"

Sally said, with a hint of urgency, "We've gotta go, Todd. I'll see you later, okay?"

Brenda chimed in, "Me, too."

Todd said, "Have a good time. Work hard."

As they went in the gym, Sally shouted back at Todd, "Can I see you after practice? At four, maybe?"

Still looking somewhat confused, Todd said, "Yeah, I guess. Where?"

Brenda shouted, "I'll meet you anywhere you want. I've got more than Sally."

"No, you don't!" was Sally's sharp retort.

As Mrs. V held the door open, the girls filed into the gym. Then Brenda turned toward Todd and gave him a full view of herself. A button popped off her blouse as their eyes met.

The gym door slammed shut behind Sally and the other girls. The image of Todd—his big hands, his firm six-pack stomach, and the lump in his jeans—excited Sally. A moment later, she returned to the confused chatter of the gossiping cheer squad and Mrs. V's commands: "Get in your places. Boys aren't your concern today. Remember the rules—especially you, Sally, as a new girl."

Sally and Brenda hung back before going into the exercise room, arguing as they went. When they entered the room, Mrs. V patted her belt and said, "Well, I guess you two wayward souls have decided to join us. Just in time, too. You all know what that means, don't you?"

They all answered, "Yes, ma'am!" Another intense practice session had begun.

~

Sally didn't see Todd after school that day as she'd hoped, at the Friday game, or over the weekend. She was worried sick that something— Brenda—had butted in. The following Tuesday, she was surprised to see him at lunch in his JROTC uniform. JROTC was considered to be for nobodies, so none of the popular kids would be caught dead in it, but Sally didn't care. Todd still looked as cute as ever.

Todd was talking with two other guys, also in uniform. Making sure Brenda wasn't nearby, Sally hiked up her skirt, adjusted her blouse a bit, then went up to them and said, in her most coquettish voice, "Hi, Todd. I missed you the other day after school."

All three boys turned to her, and Todd said, "Hi, Sally. Sorry about that, but I had JROTC duties. This is Hector Raza, and this hulk is Helman Smjorberg. They're both on the boxing team."

Sally surveyed Todd's friends. Hector was a dark, wiry guy with jet-black hair and a lean, intense face. Helman was about five nine, blond, stocky, and dangerous looking.

Hector said, "Nice to meet you, Miss Sally," and Helman just nodded at her without smiling. They all talked for a while, and then Hector said, "We'd better get to the meeting."

Looking at Sally, Todd said, "Go ahead, guys. I'll be along in a minute."

As they walked off, Hector said, "Hope we see you again, Miss Sally."

Without taking her eyes off Todd, Sally said, "Yes, nice to meet you, too."

"They're nice guys," Todd said. "I didn't know if I'd be welcomed here, but they've been great. And I'll tell you this—Coach is a *serious* guy. After just a few days of practice, he's already got us sparring for real."

Sally looked closely at Todd while he talked about the boxing team and his new friends. There was something different, she thought—the look in his eyes, the way he carried himself. He had the presence of an older boy, and she felt warm all over when he was near. She said, "They look tough."

"You're right about that, too," Todd agreed. "If we had to mix it up, you'd want them on your side."

"Mix it up?"

"You know, a fight. That happens now and then. Not that I go looking for trouble, you understand, but sometimes it just finds you. Nice to meet your cheer team friend Brenda, too."

Sally said, "She's maybe ... not your type."

"What do you mean by that?" he said.

"Well, she's kinda ... Oh, never mind. Do you have to go in?" Sally asked.

"Yeah, I do, but it's only a short check-in and schedule meeting."

Sally said, "Will you walk me home after school? It's not far."

"Oh yeah, sure! I'll meet you over by the parking lot.

Pushing her bust out, Sally said, "See you soon."

Todd gave her a wave.

Sally actually wanted Todd to give her a kiss to show off in front of Brenda, but that was really too much to wish for.

~

After school Todd came walking toward her in his school clothes, smiling and waving. She waved back, so excited that she could hardly think.

Then she noticed Mrs. V come out of the gym and walk toward the staff parking lot. A few strides along, Mrs. V saw Sally, stopped, and shaded her eyes against the late afternoon sun.

As Todd drew nearer, Sally panicked. If Mrs. V saw her walk off with Todd, she would draw the wrong conclusion—actually the right conclusion—and punishment might be in store for her. Visions of Brenda and the *smack, smack* sound filled her mind.

Sally quickly stepped behind a hedge that shielded the parking area, so that Mrs. V wouldn't see her. Looking between the scrubs, she could see Mrs. V stop.

As Todd came around the far end of the hedge near Mrs. V, he saw her and said, "Hello again."

"And hello again to you, too, Mr. Wyrum." Mrs. V got a big smile on her face and reached out to shake his hand.

Todd took her hand and said, "Great cheerleaders you've got, Mrs. V."

"Why, yes," said Mrs. V. "Oh my, what big hands you have. Helps with the boxing, I'll bet."

"Summers on the ranch, my hands take a beating—roping, barbed wire, and such," Todd said.

"Well, I've got to run. You can call me anytime," said Mrs. V, running her hand down his arm seductively.

"Bye, Mrs. V!" Todd said as she walked to her car.

Sally came out of her hiding place and asked, "What was that? She touched you, didn't she?"

Todd said, "Yeah, something wrong with that?"

"She did, she did! And I'm here because I forgot a book," she lied, showing him a book she was carrying.

Todd looked skeptically at Sally's book and said, "Okay ..."

"Hi again," Sally said, taking a quick step forward and pressing against him. She expected him to be surprised when she pressed her breasts against him, but he wasn't. As he took her hand, she realized her blatant attempt to entice him had worked.

The sun was setting as Todd drew Sally into the dim recesses of the hedge. His eyes were calm as he bent his head and kissed her. She closed her eyes, heart pounding. The kiss was very gentle, and then he pulled back a little and looked at her. She ran her hands up and around his neck, parted her lips, and another kiss began, more passionately this time. For Sally, this was different from the grabby junior high boys and Brian next door. Todd was patient and didn't force the kiss, which made her even more excited, and she pressed her lips to his harder.

Sally wanted Todd's hands to explore her, but they didn't. She loosened his shirt and ran her own hands up his hard, sinewy back. She had always let boys do whatever they wanted and then pushed them away to entice them further, but this didn't work with Todd, who just continued the soft kiss. Sally wanted more as the warm spot in her settled lower. When his mouth parted from hers and moved down her neck, she whimpered and pressed her hips to him.

Todd didn't reach behind Sally and undo her bra, though she wanted him to. Finally she couldn't wait any longer, so she undid the snaps herself and pulled his hand under her blouse. Her bust cried out to be fondled, and finally his hand found her softness, moving round and round but not yet touching her nipples. Now his lips matched hers in passion, and feeling his erection, she rolled her hips tight up against it. With a slow rhythm, they kissed and pressed their bodies together. Finally the tips of his fingers flicked across her upturned cherries, and her body leapt as the tension of her long anticipation was released. The warm spot dropped lower and grew wet, and she thought she might even erupt.

This went on until Todd pulled back a little and said, "Sally, I've wanted this from that first moment."

She breathlessly replied, "Oh, Todd, me too!" Gradually, softly, his face descended to her breasts and she felt the wonder of his mouth sucking first one, then the other of her crowns. The sucking sound was almost music. She'd long imagined her own erotic seduction, and it was now being fulfilled by Todd. Her visions went further and she imagined him exploding in place of Brian. She wondered what that would feel like inside.

It was almost dark now, and just as their passions peaked, cars started to pull noisily into the parking lot. As headlights flashed past the hedge and highlighted them for just an instant, Todd said breathlessly, "I think it's about time to go, don't you?"

"Oh God, I guess so, but ..." Sally panted this out while buttoning her blouse.

"We'd better vamoose unless we want to be the entertainment for these folks," Todd said.

"Oh, Todd, I've dreamed of seeing you again—and now these people show up. Darn!"

Todd said, "Don't worry, Sally. We'll meet again."

"Yes, I'm sure!" She thought again about Mrs. V's hand running down Todd's arm. She knew not to trust Brenda's, but did she have to watch out for Mrs. V, too?

During the long walk home, Sally and Todd held hands but said little. She kept thinking, *I want more, much more of this. How am I going to get Todd alone in the house so we can't be disturbed?* He was her new project, with homework that she looked forward to.

When they got to Mitchell Drive, Sally said, "I'd better go from here by myself. I'm late, and Grandma will be fuming. My busybody sisters will be teasing me and looking for stuff, too." She waited for Todd to ask about their next meeting, but to Sally's consternation, he didn't. He sure wasn't like other boys she'd known. "Will I see you at school tomorrow?" she asked. "I'm free after cheer practice."

"Yeah, maybe," said Todd. "Let's play it by ear. I've got a long walk to downtown. Bye, Sally!"

In a disappointed voice, she said, "Well, I'll be around after practice. Bye, Todd!"

He gave her a last wave, then turned and walked back down the dark street.

Chapter 12

Put-Down

At home, Sally lied to Grandma about the library, barely caring if she was believed. Over the next few days, she rarely connected with Todd, and even when she did, Brenda was standing with him. Now Sally's jealousy knew no bounds. Brenda cavorted around, using the power of her figure to maximum effect. Mrs. V knew it, too, and played this sideshow. They'd all been chosen for their figures. In some quarters, the cheer squad was known as the Bouncing Babes.

One day, Sally saw Brenda and Todd walking together, and after they rounded a corner, she threw a tantrum. "That bitch! Hell, I know what she wants. That ... that tramp!"

Against her every instinct, Sally decided to ignore Todd—no following him, talking to him, or even just thinking about him. Weeks passed, classes continued, games were played, the Bouncing Babes did their thing, and Sally forgot Todd. Wrong! Of course, she couldn't stop thinking about him. In fact, she became even more obsessed in the absence of any clues about a hookup between Brenda and Todd.

For all Mrs. V's threats of punishment, cheer squad girls broke the rules. Behind the gym, in the park, in cars—the girls found ways. Sally figured that if she broke the rules and Todd found out, he'd be jealous. She knew for sure she could get Brian, next door, to do some heavy petting. A few days later, the opportunity came up at his house, but Brian's grabby hands and hard mouth were boring. It was an ordeal, compared with being with Todd. And Todd did find out through the school grapevine, but he showed no jealousy at all. In fact, the whole ignoring him and making him jealous thing was a flop.

One thing did happen as a result of Sally and Brenda working closely on routines and bust exercises. In spite of Sally's jealousy, Brenda helped her develop. It seemed her bust was increasing even without the cream. Among the cheer squad, she and Brenda were now the most developed.

After practice one day, Sally and Brenda stayed late to improve on a dance step, and then they went downstairs to the girls' dressing room to shower and change. Sally took a shower, dried off, and then came out of her stall and sat with a towel wrapped around her. Sitting on a bench, she lowered her head into another towel and worked her tresses to dry them. Hearing a noise, she looked up to find Brenda standing over her, also wrapped in a towel.

Brenda wasn't wearing makeup, and her hair was a giant mess. She looked down at Sally and said, "Sally, do you want to see them?"

Surprised, Sally said, "Oh, hi, Brenda. I didn't know you were here. Uh, see what?"

Brenda said, "You know, what you want. I know you want to see them."

As Brenda bent over and her face came closer, Sally said, "I don't know what you mean. See—"

"I see you stealing looks at them all the time," Brenda said softly, with a smile. "They're big and beautiful, aren't they? Come on, Sally, don't be shy. I know you want to, and I don't mind."

Sally knew what Brenda meant, but she didn't want to let on that she'd stared at the girl's bust. "I don't know ... really," she stammered.

Brenda stood up, pushed her shoulders back, and said, "We'll see about that!" As Sally stared up at her, mouth agape, Brenda reached down and gently stroked Sally's lower lip gently. Then she unwrapped her towel, holding it loosely in her hand. For a few seconds, she just stood there proudly, then slowly let the towel slip lower and lower. "I know you want to see them, Sally," she said. "I've seen you looking at me for weeks now. Well?"

With her eyes riveted on Brenda's chest, Sally whispered, "Well, maybe I did look, but I ... I didn't want to! I'd like to if I could just maybe once ..."

With victory in sight, Brenda took a deep breath and gently jiggled in front of Sally's amazed eyes. Brenda's silky skin was milk white and topped off with her huge, almost black, gypsy eyes. "Well, Little Rosebud, pull it off," Brenda said.

Sally said, "I—I don't know if ... I want to see, but—"

"What? I finally give you a chance to see them, and you shy away? What should I think? You're hurting my feelings, Sally. Are you rejecting me? Do you think I'm too much, or what?"

"Oh no, I want to be like you, Brenda. You're so beautiful, but—"

"Are you afraid? That's it, isn't it? Should I call you silly Sally from now on?" asked Brenda.

"Brenda, I didn't mean to hurt your feelings. I want to see! Please?"

"Maybe later, if you behave. We'll see," Brenda said.

"Yes, Brenda, I'll behave. Can I seem them, if I behave?" Then Sally heard the sound of high heels coming down the hall. It could be only one person—Mrs. V.

Brenda ducked back into a shower stall. Sally grabbed her towel and sat transfixed, waiting for the wrath of Mrs. V. Meanwhile Brenda's image played on a loop in her mind, over and over again.

Mrs. V came around the corner and asked, "What are you still doing here, Sally?"

Sally said, "Oh, hello, Mrs. V. I'm just finishing up and about to get dressed. I'm a little late because of ... Well, Brenda and I have been practicing the new routines."

Mrs. V interrupted Sally and asked, "What's this? Who's in that stall? Come out now."

Brenda came out looking relaxed, wrapped in her towel and smiling innocently.

Mrs. V, clearly suspicious, asked, "What new routines?"

Sally said, "You know, the ones we saw the Paso girls do."

Mrs. V replied, "Yes, that is a good idea. Do you need a ride, Brenda?"

"Uh ... Yes, Mrs. V, I do, if it's not too much trouble."

Mrs. V eyed Brenda, her suspicions not completely dissipated. "No trouble. Just hurry!" As she walked out, she said to Sally, "I've noticed you're developing, but your underwear is atrocious. It's got to go. Brenda, take Sally to Flo's to get some new things." Then she left the locker room.

Wide-eyed, Sally said, "Whew, that was close! What would she do if she knew?"

"Oh, poo, it wouldn't be so bad. You should see the other stuff that goes on. Mrs. V's no saint. You'll find that out soon enough. Why do you think she wants to take me home?"

"You mean, like what happened to you in the ..."

Brenda said, "Yeah, but that's not as bad as getting kicked off the team. Other things are worse, too."

"Uh, like what?" Sally asked.

"We'll go to Flo's next week. I'll let you know. She's right, Sally. Your stuff is yuck, for sure."

Sally said, "I want to see, tomorrow. Can I?"

"Well, maybe, if you're good," said Brenda. "Are you gonna behave?"

"I will! I'll behave, I promise," Sally said, wondering exactly what *behave* meant. Brenda ran off to the parking lot, and Sally dressed with images of Brenda fresh in her mind.

CHAPTER 13

Pinhead Ford

Todd's birthday, October 28, was only a few days away. The truck was finished—engine restored, painted, and new upholstery. Miss Lady's anticipation was so powerful that it made her shiver.

The weeks since Todd had departed had been like purgatory. Memories of him, especially the rodeo week, were everywhere. She heard an old song on the radio, and one particular phrase jarred her: "We play the game, I stay away, but the costs are more than I can pay. Without you, dear, I can't find my way. I surrender, dear." Miss Lady's heart had surrendered completely. She did odd things. At the bunkhouse, she opened his locker and took out his clothes, tack, and chaps to fondle and fold. She even changed the sheets on his bunk and curled up on it.

She went to the high pasture among the boulders under the big live oak tree, but it was unbearable. She wept openly, calling his name. Even when she'd regained her composure, she knew the longing would intrude again. It wore her out, her appetite dropped off, and she lost weight. Nothing was fun. She turned her roundup chores over to Cruz and Zeke, and she just let the house go. When the Boss complained, she said, "Do it yourself if you don't like it."

But now the restored 1940 pinhead Ford pickup was ready, and she could take it to Todd. The old pile of junk had been transformed with tuck-and-roll upholstery, new paint, and a radio.

Todd was boarding at the Houson House, but he didn't have a phone, and the messages she'd left there hadn't been returned. She fantasized about horny high school girls and what Todd now knew. She pictured them standing at a pool table, ogling Todd and giving him boob shots in their low-cut blouses. Lambs to the slaughter—but willingly, she thought. She pushed the mental picture away with difficulty.

It was Tuesday, and she wanted to see him on Friday, so she decided to call Houson House again. She dialed the number with shaking hands and asked, "Can I speak to Todd Wyrum, please."

A boy's voice on the other end of the line asked, "You got the room number?"

"I don't know his room number, but I know he's there someplace," said Miss Lady.

The boy said, "Lemme go find him. I'm pretty sure he's here. He came by with a girl a while ago." Miss Lady heard him yell something, and then he asked, "Who do I say is calling?"

"Mrs. Wyrum."

The boy yelled, "Todd, phone! It's your mom!"

Miss Lady gritted her teeth and waited. About five minutes later, a girl's voice came on. "Hi! Are you waiting for Todd? Are you his mom? He's really cute. He's coming—hold on!"

Miss Lady didn't even get a chance to respond, so she just kept holding. Another five minutes went by, and then she finally heard the phone being picked up.

"Hi, Mom. If this is about the money, it's okay. I'm getting it regular, so don't worry."

Almost sobbing, Miss Lady said, "No, Todd. It's me, Miss Lady. I've got your truck."

Todd exclaimed, "The truck! It's great to hear your voice, Miss Lady. Sorry about that Mom thing. These guys are a bunch of jerks."

Miss Lady had hoped for more focus on her, not the truck, but Todd *was* a guy. "Yes, it looks like—"

He broke in, "Wow, oh wow! Are you gonna bring it to SLO, or do you want me to come and get it? Miss Lady, it's great to hear your voice. I think about you lots, and I hope you think of me some, too."

Miss Lady said, "More than you could ever know, Todd. Always, oh my, always. I miss you so."

After a long pause, Todd said, "When can you bring it?"

"I'll come in Friday, so we'll have—"

"No, I've got a match Friday, in Arroyo Grande at the high school, and

I have to go. Could you come? No, that wouldn't work, either. How about Saturday, late morning?"

"Okay, Saturday," agreed Miss Lady. "But picking you up there wouldn't be good. What's a good place?"

"Uh, let's see. The mission is right down at the end of Monterey Street, which dead-ends there. It's a short walk for me, and there are places to park. How about that?"

"Yes, Todd, and I want us to go off someplace together," said Miss Lady.

"Me, too, Miss Lady."

"Do you know Avila Beach, where the old Surf Motel is? It's nice and secluded, and we could even swim. There's a bar called Barbara's by the Sea, too. I went there years ago. It's the kind of place no one would bother checking, you know?"

"Doesn't matter anyway," said Todd. "During boxing season, we're on a strict diet and drink regimen. You know, for our weight. The football blowhards drink, but not us. We're in much better shape."

There was commotion behind Todd, and an irritated girl's voice called out. He drew the phone away from his mouth and said, "Yeah, all right. Keep your shirt on. I'll be off in a second."

Miss Lady asked, "Is that a girl's voice I hear? I thought the Houson House was a boys' residence only." The "keep your shirt on" comment had prompted an unpleasant picture in her mind.

Todd hesitated and then said, "It is, but girls from Cal Poly come over and hang out, you know?"

"Yes, I do know, Todd," said Miss Lady. "I know very well. Do any of them come over to see *you*?"

"They're college girls, and I'm just in high school. So I'm kinda, well, beneath them."

With an edge in her voice, Miss Lady replied, "You mean they're older, so they wouldn't be interested in a mere high school kid? Is that what you mean, Todd?"

The lights went on, and Todd said, "No, not like that. I meant like ... Oh shit! Pardon the language, Miss Lady. Age doesn't mean anything to me. I'm just—"

"You're stepping in it, Todd. Let's just move on. I might be just a tiny bit oversensitive on that score, considering. She does have her shirt on, doesn't she?"

Todd exclaimed, "Sure she does! I just want you to know that ... You're right, Miss Lady, let's move on."

She laughed self-consciously and said, "Oh my, Todd, we're getting on like an old married couple. How about Saturday at ten at the old mission. Will that work for you?"

He laughed. "You're right, but I'm still sorry for any implications of ... You know?"

They laughed together, and then Todd said, "I'm gonna kick that girl, Fran or something like that, out. Her nickname is Hinge-Heels, which gives you some idea of her interests."

More laughter, and Miss Lady said, "If she's at the mission when I get there, I'll hog-tie her. I will!"

"I'll tell her. See you Saturday, Miss Lady. I can hardly wait."

"You don't know the half of it, Todd. Happy birthday, my darling! See you Saturday."

~

But Miss Lady altered her plans and went to see Todd box on Friday night. She had a quick dinner in Pismo Beach and then drove over to the school, which was crowded. So that Todd wouldn't recognize her, she did her hair differently and wore clothes he wouldn't recognize. She sat in the back, away from his team's corner.

She watched several matches before Todd's and disliked what she saw—a lot of blood. By the time Todd entered the ring, Miss Lady's heart was pounding with concern for his safety. Her heart leapt when she saw him in his Tigers uniform, looking lean, rangy, and determined. That lock of hair still fell over his forehead, which made him look even sexier.

The other boy entered the ring to the sound of lots of cheers. He was shorter, but much heavier built with bulging arms and an air of confidence. Miss Lady's heart rate increased.

When the first-round bell sounded, Todd crossed the ring and immediately started jabbing. That backed the other boy up, but he threw a haymaker in the process. Todd kept jabbing, and the other boy landed a few wild punches. As the round went on, it was obvious that Todd was winning, and at the end of the first round, the other boy had a bloody nose.

Between rounds, several girls gathered around an older woman at ringside. They were wearing matching school colors outfits, and when the woman spoke to them, they stood and gave a cheer. Miss Lady noticed they were sure a curvaceous group. One girl in particular stood out, with her huge bust in a low-cut blouse. She bounded around, obviously enjoying the rapt attention of the crowd. For a fleeting moment, Miss Lady thought the girl looked familiar, but she couldn't place her.

During the next few rounds, Todd kept up his left jabs, but he followed up with rights. By the middle of the third round, the other boy was spent. However, when Todd backed him up against the ropes, the boy came back off with a long, looping right hook that sent Todd to the mat. As the referee began to count over him, Coach yelled, "Get up, Todd. Damn it, get up!"

When Todd went down, Miss Lady screamed in fear, not realizing how loud she was. Several fans looked at her with curiosity, and a woman in front of her said in an irritated voice, "That your boy, ma'am? He's going to take a lickin' from Bob, you know?"

With some effort, Todd got up, and after staggering a bit, he went back to his jab and right cross combinations. Just before the round ended, he knocked the other boy down. He was still down when the final bell rang, ending the match. The crowd growled its displeasure.

Miss Lady, who had moved down by the ring, yelled at the woman, "See, Todd's better!"

After a few minutes, the referee called both boys to the center of the ring and raised Todd's gloved hand as the winner. The boys shook hands, and Todd went to his corner, where Coach took off his gloves. As Todd stood there, two girls—including she of the big bust—came to the ring apron, leaned in, and spoke to Todd in an intimate way that Miss Lady didn't like.

As Todd came down the ring steps, with a towel around his wiry shoulders and a little trickle of blood running from his nose, Miss Lady gave his sweaty arm a squeeze. She said awkwardly, "That was wonderful, Todd. A superior display of fisticuffs, I'd say. I congratulate you."

In shock, Todd stared at Miss Lady and stammered, "Why, why … Thanks, uh, ma'am!"

Coach barked, "Todd, go on in. I got Hector up next." Then he turned to Miss Lady and said, "Todd's really sharp, ma'am, and we appreciate your support. You related?"

Miss Lady replied to Coach, while looking at the two girls, "Yes, I'm his aunt."

"Well, you can be proud of him. We sure are!" Coach said. Turning to Sally and Brenda, he said, "You two playthings hurry along now!"

Miss Lady said to Coach, "Oh my, yes, we are very proud."

"Pay no mind to them, ma'am," Coach said. "Sally and Brenda hang on my boxers like a couple of trollops."

Just then Mrs. V appeared and barked at Sally and Brenda, "Get back with the other cheerleaders."

As the two girls reluctantly walked away, they waved at Todd. He acknowledged them with a nod and headed off toward the dressing rooms, and Mrs. V and the cheer team began preparing for their next routine.

Walking back up the aisle, Miss Lady turned and studied the cheerleaders and their scowling leader from a distance. There was something familiar about Mrs. V, but what was it? One thing was for certain—Miss Lady now knew that this band of promiscuous girls and their leader was trouble.

~

Miss Lady stayed at the Surf Motel in Avila Beach that night and prepared for the next day. Lingerie, perfume, and champagne topped her list. The town would be empty this time of year.

The next morning, Miss Lady parked at Monterey and Chorro Streets, near the park, in front of the mission. It was a cloudy autumn morning with a storm forecast for later. She sat and admired the Spanish mission, founded by Father Serra, with mixed memories. She'd been married there a lifetime ago.

~

Todd walked happily down Monterey Street to the park. Not only was he about to see Miss Lady, but he'd won his match the previous night—big time with a TKO! Then he saw Miss Lady from the corner, and she looked even more beautiful than he remembered.

When she saw him, a broad smile spread across her pretty face, and she waved. He waved back, and they ran toward each other, meeting in a crushing embrace. He lifted her and swung her around as they kissed passionately on the almost empty street.

As Todd embraced her, Miss Lady noticed a mouse under his right eye and kissed it. "Oh, Todd, I missed you so. Oh my, hold your Miss Lady forever and ever, my Todd!"

"Miss Lady, so much has happened, but now there is only you and me, together."

"Todd, you *are* happy to see me, aren't you?"

"Happy? Oh, Miss Lady, far beyond that. See, I've got you with me all the time." He held up his wrist, showing her the bracelet she'd given him.

"You're with me too." She held up her pinkie so he could see the ring he'd given her.

Todd threw back his head and gave a big laugh, and that lock of hair fell down over his forehead. "You inspire me in so many ways, as you know full well. Hey, where's the truck?"

Boys will always be boys, she thought. "I thought you'd never ask! It's right over there in front of the old adobe, see?" She pointed at it.

Todd leapt up, grabbed Miss Lady's hand, and ran toward the truck. "Man, oh man, you did a great job. It's just beautiful."

"And the upholstery?" asked Miss Lady.

Taking Miss Lady's hand, Todd led her to the passenger door, bowed, and asked, "Will you ride shotgun for me, my princess?" Then he went around and got in behind the wheel. "Wow, it's a clean, flathead V-8 with new shocks and flicker hubcaps. Jeez, is it mine?"

His boyish joy thrilled her, and she answered, "Yes, it's all yours, Todd. All yours!"

Todd checked out everything and then said, now more soberly, "Cost a lot, I bet. I don't know what to say. I knew I'd get the truck, but this? Did the Boss pay for it all—paint, engine, tires, everything?"

"Yes, he did," said Miss Lady. "I guess a bit of the old Myron came through. Think of it as a reward of sorts, certainly more than that pittance of an allowance you got. I guess he finally appreciates your hard work.

They reminisced for a few minutes, then drove to Scrubby and Lloyd's off lower Higuera Street for a burger and milkshake. Todd then drove to Avila Beach and the Surf Motel.

~

They took the See Canyon cutoff from Highway 101, laughing and talking all the way. Todd said, "I've got lots of love for you saved up, Miss Lady. Oh yeah!"

Miss Lady said, "Well, you better have. I'm not leaving a thing, even a tiny morsel, for those horny girls I saw at the boxing match. Especially that obnoxious cow who pranced around like—well, you know. And her perky little sidekick, too. Understand?"

"Oh, the cheerleaders?" asked Todd. "Yeah, they're known as the Bouncing Babes. Funny, huh?"

"No, not funny! Who'd let a group of high school girls behave like that, anyway?"

"Mrs. V, that's who. She's the cheer team coach, and she's a piece of work. *Strict* doesn't begin to tell the story. They gotta have permission just to go out with their boyfriends."

"And you, of course, get on very well with the cheer girls, right?" asked Miss Lady.

"Miss Lady, no foolin' around. I swear, I've never!"

"Oh, shut up, Todd. I know girls and women, and you don't?"

"Wow, Miss Lady, we can pull over right here, and I'll prove—"

"No, no! Let's get to the motel so we can really relax."

~

The whole town looked like it was 1920. The Surf Motel was an old run-down group of bungalows nestled against the hillside across from the beach. Gray paint was peeling off walls, doors, and window frames that showed evidence of salt damage. The front of their room was overgrown with a creeping vine that almost hid the door. A long wooden fishing pier jutted out from a breakwater, dimly lit by a row of lights all the way out, a hundred and fifty yards or so. Farther along was the Union Oil Company tanker pier, where a large ship was being loaded. The only thing lit up in town was a blinking neon light way down the block.

Their room was clean, but every piece of furniture was damaged and/or stained. Tilted venetian blinds hung at the windows, and a frayed rug lay crooked on the linoleum floor, with a basic kitchen to one side. The bedroom was just barely that—and nothing more.

Outside it was raining heavily, the surf rose in the bay, and wind whipped the foliage against the windows. Todd and Miss Lady had their clothes off in minutes. During the drive, they'd controlled their desires. But now, alone at last, their desires flowed like vintage wine, and they got lost in each other. Their ardor was satiated only after several hours of intense sex, and then they slept.

Two hours later, they were awoken by driving rain and wind that shook the little cottage. Todd said, "You know, I'd like to walk out on the pier. We don't get much weather like this in town, and even less on the ranch. How about it? Or did I wear you out?"

Miss Lady said, "Let's grab some coffee and doughnuts at the general store, okay? But first I've got to clean up."

Todd dozed. He wasn't the cleaner-up type anyway. As Miss Lady well knew, cowboys were notorious for being messy and immune to cleaning, other than their wrangling gear. If asked, he'd probably do it, but things would inevitably end up a bigger mess. Anyway, it was her life. She worked happily, quietly humming "You Are My Sunshine."

~

By the time they left for the pier, it was dusk. Though they were bundled up and careful, the wind and rain almost blew them over. The surf was way up and crashing so hard on the sand that it shook the beach. But Todd and Miss Lady took their coffee and walked to the pier as if it was a spring day. Each circuit of the pier took about twenty minutes, and they talked, cuddled, and laughed all the way. The waves were so high that they slapped up under the decking and sent up geysers three or four feet high between the boards the whole length of the pier. It sounded like someone shooting a BB gun. The roar of the wind and rain drew them together in their bundled cocoon. Never had they been closer, as they dodged the leaping waters.

~

Front Street, the main drag, ran just above the beach. Arm in arm, Todd and Miss Lady strode along until a blinking neon sign invited them into Barbara's by the Sea. It was a scene right out of a 1940s B movie, with a bartender to match. At a broken-down table at the back sat what looked like a local fishermen, and another slumped on the far end of the bar. A line of chrome and plastic bar stools stood along a mahogany bar, which sported the requisite mirror lined with bottles. The only decor was neon beer signs and a pool table that had seen better days.

Todd and Miss Lady sat at a booth, and the owner, Barbara herself, came to serve them. "What'll it be, folks?"

Miss Lady laughed and said, "I'll have a Rheingold if you've got it. Todd?"

With a self-conscious smile, Todd said, "Just a Coke. Nice place! Yours?"

Barbara replied without pride or embarrassment, "That it is. What are you two lovebirds doing out on a nightmarish evening like this?" A bartender with over twenty years' experience couldn't be fooled. In any case, it was the kind of place where it simply didn't matter, as long as you covered the tab and didn't make trouble.

With obvious pride at not having to lie, Miss Lady said, "We're out for a night on the town—and having the time of our lives, too. Aren't we, Todd?"

"You bet, Miss Lady. For sure," agreed Todd.

Barbara focused a sly smile on Todd and said, "In that case, are you sure you want a Coke? How about backing up this beautiful lady with your own Rheingold—which I do have, by the way."

Todd glanced at Miss Lady and said, "Uh, okay. Rheingold it is!"

"I'll be right back with two beers in iced glasses," Barbara said.

Todd and Miss Lady had a couple more beers and listened to vintage music on the jukebox: "Moon Glow," "If I Didn't Care," "San Antonio Rose," and so on. They danced and sang along with "You Are My Sunshine." Laughter, reminiscences, and jokes filled the evening in this place that time had almost left behind. Even on a stormy night, the cold beer was good, so they had two more. They were in their own world.

An hour later, Miss Lady left ten on the bar, and they walked back to the motel. On the way, Miss Lady noticed that Todd was sloshed.

They got undressed, and she went in the bathroom to get into her sexy evening attire. When she came out ten minutes later, Todd was asleep on the disheveled bed, mouth open and snoring. She was a little surprised, but it didn't matter. She turned off the lights and sat for a few minutes in the dark, sipping flat champagne. She was bushed too, so she got into bed next to him and fell fast asleep.

Dawn filtered through the soiled curtains and across the room. Todd and Miss Lady lay entwined on the crooked mattress half covered in mismatched bedding. They made soft, romantic love among the clutter, then dozed.

Todd awoke with a yawn and said, "Breakfast! I could eat a cow."

"You can eat something else if you want, Todd," offered Miss Lady. "Oh, Todd?"

"Okay, I'm up for that," Todd exclaimed, "though *down* for that is perhaps a better description."

"Oh no, Todd, I was just kidding. Really, I'm all sexed out, and it's okay. Later is fine, just fine. What a man—my man! Breakfast sounds good."

They showered together, then dressed and drove to Pismo Beach and the same clam joint where Miss Lady had eaten dinner on Friday. It overlooked the ocean and boardwalk. Todd wolfed down fruit, chicken-fried steak, eggs, bacon, hash brown potatoes, and coffee. She had coffee and a doughnut. When they were just about finished, Miss Lady said, "Well, unless you still want to eat that cow you mentioned earlier, I think we can plan our day now, okay?"

Todd replied, "Sure, I don't have to be at our roundup until four. Yeah, it's important because of the guys who lost or got injured, like Billy. You didn't see that match, Miss Lady. Wow, he got his bell rung, so a new guy from the second string will move up. Anyway, I've got to be there at four o'clock. I hope you weren't planning anything late today. I'll be gone until six or seven, okay?"

It was not okay, and she was obviously disappointed. "Todd, I thought this was our day together."

He could see she was upset. "Oh, I should have told you yesterday. I have to be there, because Coach is really strict about attendance. I'm really, really sorry, Miss Lady, but it's a big deal for the team."

Trying to hide a sad smile, she said, "Oh, it's okay. Perhaps I should have asked, but this isn't so bad. We've got until three o'clock!"

"Yeah! How about that drive up the coast we talked about?" asked Todd. "I haven't been up that way, you know? You could show me around. I'll bet there are lots of beautiful sights."

"It is most beautiful," she replied, holding back the "tomorrow without him" feeling.

Todd said, "Sounds like a plan!"

The drive out to Morro Bay and up the coast was beautiful, as expected, and even more special in the truck. There were sea lions on the beaches, and the storm had tossed up lots of driftwood. They explored several places and sat romantically among the flotsam, talking and cuddling each other.

Four o'clock quickly closed in as they drove closer to San Luis Obispo, and the lump in Miss Lady's throat grew. The small talk wasn't working, and she was on the edge of panic.

About halfway back, when Todd again mentioned wrestling practice, she asked, "Do the cheerleaders, the Bouncing Babes, ever go to these practices?"

"Well, not officially," said Todd, "but they always seem to be around. Don't know why."

"Yeah, for no reason, right? Right! Men are so dense," she said. "And that Mrs.— What's her name? What about her?"

"She's just their coach, though she teaches health too. I've got her for that class, which is really easy. I'll get an A for sure. Her class isn't even in the same league with math and bio. By the way, I got the periodic table completely done. Know it all, backward and forward. You were a big help to me this summer."

Miss Lady's effort to choke back her anger was failing. In a begrudging tone, she said, "That's good, Todd. Congratulations. Those girls? Do you date one or both of them?"

Todd said, "No, no. Uh, well, I ... Sally is kinda ... Well, but Brenda ... I'm—"

"Are you fucking them? The one with the huge tits sure does want it!" exclaimed Miss Lady.

"What? She wants ... I'm not, uh—"

"Oh, you're not?" said Miss Lady. "Ha! Brenda would go down on a doorknob if it had a man attached to it. And that Sally? If you tripped and fell, she'd be on the floor, legs open, before you were."

"Oh jeez!" Todd exclaimed. "I'm just trying to ... I mean, I do date some. But that's normal, isn't it?"

She had completely lost it now. "Dating them, holy shit, in the back of cars? Like that, Todd? They want cock, and you give it to them, right, Todd? Blow jobs too?"

Suddenly Todd's frustration and confusion boiled over. "Well, what about you and the Boss, huh? You're with him, aren't you? Well, aren't you? And he fu—"

Just as she swung to slap his face, he looked out the window at a passing car. He mistook her intended slap, which just grazed his shoulder, for an effort to get his attention. Turning back to her, he said, "Miss Lady, I'm ... I'm out of line. I'm sorry, so sorry."

Realizing her mistake, she sobbed, "Oh Todd, I had no business, none! I knew you'd date in high school, and ... Oh my, this isn't us. It's not us, Todd!"

He pulled to the roadside and put his arms around Miss Lady as she wept. "Oh, Miss Lady, what have we done? I love you so much!" By now, he had tears running down his face too.

"Me too, Todd. Me too," she cried.

After a few minutes, the tears banked their anger. They hugged and kissed, apologizing to each other over and over again. Then Todd drove on, and as they approached the bus station, he said, "Holy cow, I forgot! How will you get back to the ranch? What a dunce I've been."

Miss Lady lied. "I'll be fine. It's all arranged. Just drop me at the Greyhound depot next to the Freemont Theater. I'll catch the bus to Atascadero, and Zeke will pick me up there. It's no trouble, Todd."

"Are you completely sure that's okay? Because if it isn't, I can—"

"No, Todd, darling, it's fine. Not to worry. I'm a big girl, and I can get around on my own, even if I'd rather be with you." She gave his leg a squeeze, but it wasn't fine at all in her heart.

Todd kept giving her guilty looks for the rest of the drive. As they pulled up in front of the bus depot, he asked again, "Are you sure this is okay? I feel like I'm—"

"Todd, stop it. I've taken buses my whole life."

He pulled up in front of the station and said, "Hold on. I'll drive around and find a parking place and then come in with you."

"No, Todd," insisted Miss Lady. "There's the bus now. See it loading in the garage? I'll just grab my bag and be off." By now, she was shaking with fear and barely in control of herself.

"Miss Lady, this has been the most wonderful time for me—for us, I mean!"

"Shush, Todd. Remember only that I love you. I'm always, forever yours. Now I'm off." She gave him a quick kiss, got out, and grabbed her bag from the truck bed. With a wave at Todd, she walked to the waiting bus and climbed on board. The sadness of unrequited love crept up in her throat.

As the bus pulled out, Todd was still double-parked behind a delivery truck. She took a last look at him behind the wheel as they passed. As she turned away and the bus gathered speed up Monetary Street, the floodgates opened and she sobbed openly. Every wrenching sob said, *My love is gone from me.*

Hers was a look back at the joy of her yesterdays.

Todd drove off to his late practice and his tomorrows.

Chapter 14

The Locker Room

"Why haven't you bought that new lingerie I told you to get? My word, I can't have my girls attired like that, Sally. It's unseemly, not done!"

"But Mrs. V, I didn't because of the money."

"What was that, Sally Anderson?"

Sally answered, "Yes, ma'am!"

"That's better. Now what was the reason?"

Seated on a dressing room bench, Sally felt like she was in a police interrogation room. Luckily there was no one left in the dressing room to see or hear what was going on. On the verge of tears, she said, "I couldn't ask Grandma for the money, and she threw out the nice things Mrs. Sondheim bought me. I wanted to wear the new things, but ..."

"We'll just see about that!" interrupted Mrs. V, arms akimbo. "Brenda, are you there? If you're still here, I mean it."

A voice from a few stalls away called out, "Yes, ma'am, I'm here. I'm coming!"

"Get over here, *now!*" said Mrs. V.

That instant Brenda walked out of her stall clad in a towel, without makeup, hair a mess and dripping on the linoleum floor. She stood in front of Mrs. V and Sally and declared, "I'm here!"

"Well, Brenda, my sweet," said Mrs. V, "I was depending on your nefarious, scheming ways to see that this child got into the proper lingerie. Now I see you've failed me, but why?"

Brenda said, "What could I do? I didn't have the money either, and I couldn't just go buy it, could I?"

Sally surprised herself by exclaiming, "Yeah, it wasn't Brenda's fault. It wasn't mine, either."

Surprised at Sally's words, Brenda saw her with sympathetic eyes for the first time.

Sally's raised eyebrows said "Thank you" to the object of her jealousy.

Mrs. V pointed at Sally's things and said, "We're going to have to do something about those things."

Sally said, "I can't just ask Grandma for money. She'll ask what it's for and want to see it later. Do you see, Mrs. V? I'd be grounded for a year—for life, really."

With a knowing look, Mrs. V said, "Brenda?"

Brenda was now her old self. "We could go together. Flo would like Sally, you know?"

Mrs. V replied, with an evil smile, "Oh yes, Flo would indeed like young Sally."

With a mischievous smile, Brenda said, "Oh yes, Mrs. V."

"Then I'll leave it up to you," said Mrs. V. "And another thing, Sally: you're to leave the new lingerie in your locker. You can change here before and after school. That way Grandma won't find out. Agreed?"

Sally and Brenda said, "Yes, ma'am!"

"One more thing!" said Mrs. V. "Sally, follow Brenda's instructions. I don't want to dish out any more punishment." Walking out of the locker room, she let her hand brush against Sally's bust. "Oh yes, Flo will like you for sure!"

As Sally collapsed on the bench, Brenda said, "You know what we're gonna do?"

Confused, Sally shook her head and said, "I've got no money!"

"On Wednesday, we're gonna sneak off to Flo's and get your new sexy stuff. Oh, such fun!"

"But it's really expensive, and I can't pay for it," Sally said. "I get two dollars a week for allowance."

Brenda said, "Oh poo, I know what Flo likes. And anyway, you'll need that sexy stuff for the adventures that I'm sure Mrs. V has in mind for you—for both of us." She snickered and blew Sally a kiss.

Not knowing what Brenda meant, Sally replied, "Okay then! I love the silky stuff. It feels really nice on my skin, and I feel different in it too, you know? But what about the money?"

"Oh yes, I do too. And as far as the money goes, you'll need the new stuff to make money. Now for our plan. Hey, I look a mess. Will you help me with my hair and makeup?" Without waiting for Sally's answer, Brenda pulled her into the washroom.

Watching Brenda do herself up was amazing. Within ten minutes, Brenda was a sexy gypsy princess again, her hair a sensual pile of cascading ringlets fastened with red barrettes. She vamped her eyes and said, "You wanted to see them, didn't you? Yes, I see it in your eyes. You've behaved, haven't you? Do you want to look now?"

Sally's heart pounded. "I'm not sure what you mean by behaving—and the money? How can that be? But I think I've—"

"Mrs. V will explain about the money, your stipend, the booster club, and 'adventures' soon enough, so don't worry. Now do you want to see them or don't you?" asked Brenda.

Sally replied hesitantly, "I don't know what you—"

"You haven't been able to keep your eyes off me for weeks, Sally! You know very well what I mean. Yes or no, or I'll leave." Brenda reached across and loosened her towel.

Sally's eyes were riveted on what she hoped was to come.

Brenda took a deep breath and loosened the towel further. With a predatory look in her eyes, she said, "What a silly little girl you are. Touch them!"

Sally reached out, and as she did so, Brenda took her hand and moved it to the towel's edge.

"I don't know, Brenda. I—"

"Remember what Mrs. V said about obeying me?" asked Brenda. "Pull it!"

As Sally's fingers grasped the towel's edge, Brenda took a half step back. The towel fell away and revealed everything—huge, perfectly formed, pink tipped, and proud.

"Oh, Brenda, they're beautiful. Oh my!" Sally stared for a long moment, then reached out hesitantly.

Brenda said very softly, "Touch them, Sally."

Sally's hand moved to obey, but still she hesitated. "They're so—so perfect."

"Are they too big?" Brenda asked.

"Oh no, they're wonderful, really wonderful."

"Yes, and they're yours to touch if you want to. Do you want to, Sally?"

"Oh yes, Brenda." Sally's eyes were pleading, but she still hesitated.

"Oh my, you're being little girlish today. I guess I'll have to help you, won't I?" Brenda took both of Sally's shaking hands and placed them on her mounds. Then she began to slowly stroke her globes with Sally's fingers, like a soft paintbrush.

"Aahh!" Sally drew in an excited breath at the sensation of touching this perfection that she so envied and wanted for herself.

Brenda continued with the stroking motion until Sally's fingertips got to the most sensitive tips of her pride. A tiny purple vein stand out on her forehead as the sensation stimulated her. She looked down at a worshipping Sally and asked, "Do you like them, little Sally? Do you? Tell Brenda."

"Oh yes, Brenda. Oh my, yes. They're so beautiful."

"So you're not afraid anymore?"

Sally said, "No, I'm not."

"Okay then, you can go ahead. I want you to."

Sally was so excited by the look and feel of these wonders that she shook.

As they both got more excited, Brenda drew closer to Sally. In a few minutes, they both were breathing heavily and whimpering. Brenda put her fingers under Sally's chin, lifted it, and kissed her softly on the lips. Then she pulled back just a little and said, "Kiss me back, little Sally."

Captured by the heat of the moment, Sally didn't need any more coaxing. She did as she was told, and her own desire drew her along. The kiss increased their passion, and Brenda ran her hands across Sally's smaller but growing bust. Within a minute, Sally was uncontrollably excited. There was now nothing between them. Every inhibition had fallen away.

It was a feast of flesh, but Brenda was still in control. She asked, "Do you love them?"

Sally said, "Oh yes, Brenda, I do. Oh my, yes."

"Open your rosebud mouth." Brenda raised herself up while pressing Sally's face down to her crowns. With her other hand, she lifted a nipple into the wet of Sally's waiting mouth.

"Oh, they're so beautiful. I want mine to be like this," Sally said.

"Kiss them, Sally."

Sally gave a little whimper and began to kiss them—first one, then the other, over and over as Brenda moved her head back and forth. After a few minutes of this, she turned Sally's face up to hers and said, "Now lick them."

Sally didn't hesitate. Her tongue worked over the pink, cherry-tipped hills with wonder and joy. All the while, she fantasized about being so stacked and the attention it would bring.

A few minutes more of this had Brenda swooning with pleasure, too. Sally immersed herself in the taste and feel of Brenda's cherries on their soft beds of puffy pinkness. Meanwhile her smaller mounds were being seduced by the expert fingers of Brenda's teasing touch.

After another passionate kiss, Sally could wait no longer. Without encouragement from Brenda, she opened her mouth wide and sucked, in and out, over and around. Brenda stroked Sally's hair with one hand and her bust with the other.

Finally Brenda lay back on the bench and pulled Sally on top of her. Their legs entwined and their wet clefts pressed against each other as their hips rotated. The intensity grew and grew with moans and cries amid desperate kisses and fondling. Their carnal exertions reached a crescendo together, and they came once, then again, spilling over each other in release and joy.

Moments later they tumbled onto the pile of towels on the floor spent and happy, but then hearing a door slam down the hall, they quickly sat up. Exclamations in Spanish drifted their way, and Brenda said, "It's the janitor."

Breathing hard, they pulled towels around themselves and went into their dressing stalls. From her stall, Brenda said to Sally, "That was close, but—oh my!—wasn't it fun?"

"Oh yes," exclaimed Sally, "they're so wonderful. I love them. When can I—"

"Be patient, little Sally. If you behave, then maybe ... and even further, understand?"

"Yeah, I do. But Brenda, what's a stipend?"

~

When she was younger, it would never have occurred to Sally to deceive Grandma. Now she did it every day, sneaking next door to make out with Brian, and now going to buy lingerie with Brenda. Today was the day, and Sally was a little scared. How was Brenda going to finagle a way to pay for Sally's lingerie? Mrs. V had called her "scheming" Brenda, and Sally wondered what that really meant.

But most of all, Sally swirled in passion about those soft, mountainous breasts. In her dreams, they enticed her eyes, stimulated her fingers, and filled her mouth. She would do anything to get some for herself and reap the envy of other girls and the desire of the boys.

A week went by before it was finally arranged for Sally and Brenda to go shopping for the lingerie. Sally waited anxiously outside the gym. Finally Brenda came out and immediately started teasing her, saying, "I guess you're wanting to get those new things, aren't you? Come on, that's what you want Brenda to help you with?"

Sally replied, "Yes, but I thought we were going to do it last week like Mrs. V said."

"Well, I had to get some things done. And I do remember that Mrs. V said that you've got to do everything I say." Brenda looked around to see if anyone was about, then reached up and undid two more buttons on her blouse. She pulled back the fabric, revealing the curvature of her cleavage and the pink-and-blue lace of her bra, which just barely held in place the bounty Sally wanted to possess herself.

Sally's envy grew, but she said, "Yes, Brenda!"

"That's right, that's the way to address me!"

"Can we get something like this at Flo's?" Sally reached out and ran her hands across the silken fabric, letting her fingers linger in the milk-white valley.

As the door behind them opened, Sally quickly withdrew her hand and Brenda turned away. It was Kenny and Terrell, two football players. Kenny said, "Hi, Brenda, what's up? Is this the new girl?"

"Yeah, Kenny, this is Sally," said Brenda. "Sally, this is Kenny, and he's a back. This other lug is Terrell. They're on the football team, but I guess you can tell that." Both boys were huge. Kenny was blond and heavyset, with really bad skin. Terrell was swarthy, handsome, and tall.

Kenny said, "Need a ride, Brenda? We're at your disposal. Car's right over in the parking lot. Your friend there can come along, too. How about it?"

Even with her limited experience, Sally could tell what the boys wanted to do in the car. And both she and Brenda were willing, but not today! Every fiber of Sally's being wanted to get the new things at Flo's.

With a knowing glance at Sally, Brenda replied, "No thanks, guys. We've got an important errand to run, don't we, Sally?"

With great relief, Sally said, "We sure do, and we'd better get going."

Kenny said, "Suit yourselves. It's no trouble, really. We'll take our time. Go to the movie later, if you want? Catch the early one. Be out early. You won't get home late." Both boys smiled confidently.

"No thanks, Kenny. We've got stuff to do downtown," Sally said.

"How're you gonna get there?" Kenny asked. "We can drop you off, and it's no trouble at all. Really, Brenda, we could. No obligation from you or Sally, right?"

Sally and Brenda exchanged glances, and finally Brenda said, "Well, if it's okay with Sally."

Sally knew full well what the boys wanted, and she was sure it would delay or even cancel their plan to go to Flo's. "Come on, Brenda, let's just go. We can do that stuff with them later."

Brenda picked up her gym bag and took a couple of steps away from the boys, pulling Sally with her. She opened the bag, took out a small jar, and held it up for Sally to see. "If we go with them, it will only take a few minutes. I know what they want, and it will be fun. You'll see! And if we do, I'll give you this cream that I know you've been wanting. See?"

There in Brenda's hand was a jar of the breast-enhancement cream. "Oh my God, where'd you get it?" asked Sally. "You know that I've looked and looked for that."

Brenda said, "You have to do what I say anyway, like Mrs. V said, remember?"

The girls turned back to Kenny and Terrell, and Sally said, with barely concealed glee, "We'll go, but we've got to be down on Morro Street pretty soon, okay?" Sally and Brenda headed for the parking lot, giggling and skipping as they went. The two football players followed close behind, anticipating the fun to come.

When they got to the car, Kenny opened the door and folded forward the front seat. Terrell got in the back seat and said to Brenda, "Come on in, sweet thing!" coaxing her in with a flourish. Then Kenny got in the back seat on the other side of Brenda, who gave Sally a little finger wave, smiled mischievously, and said, "You're in front, kid!"

Sally felt like a child being told she couldn't go out and play. She knew what was in store for Brenda, and she wasn't sure what she wanted. She climbed in the front seat, pulled the door shut, and turned to see what was going on. Immediately the boys had Brenda's arms up over the back seat, and her blouse and bra off.

Brenda said, "Gently now, boys!" But all the while, her eyes were on Sally.

Sally watched Brenda's gigantic bosom trundled out while those big black gypsy eyes teased her. She recalled the locker room and wanted to tell them to leave Brenda alone. Only she, Sally, could touch ... Confusing jealousy boiled up and overpowered her, even as she was mesmerized by it all. She continued to watch, and Brenda's eyes continued to tease.

Terrell pulled back from his feast and started to unbutton his Levi's, and then Kenny did the same. Brenda said, "No, not today! Sally and I have to go. No jacking you off today, guys." But the boys already had their pants pulled down.

Brenda's voice wavered as she said, "Come on, guys. Sally and I have important things to attend to."

Terrell said, "What do you mean, no? You get us all hot and bothered, then turn off? That's not fair. You're not going to turn into a PT, are you? Like those hoity-toity girls?"

Sally asked, "What's a PT?"

"Come on, Terrell, you know I'm not like that," said Brenda. "Some other time, okay?"

Terrell touched himself and said, "Look at me, Brenda. You can't leave it like this."

Brenda said, "This is dumb, guys. You know I always put out. It's just that today we've got stuff to do."

Kenny said, "We're not leaving until you do what you're supposed to do."

With a smile, Brenda said, "Yeah, okay, if Sally will help me. What do you say, Sally?"

"Yeah, I guess." Before Sally finished saying this, Kenny already had her hand on him. It was over almost before it started, and then she watched Brenda finish off Terrell. It turned out not to be exciting at all, and Sally's feelings were all mixed up.

Brenda said, "Boys, are you all better now that Brenda's taken care of you? Oh, and my new little helper, too. You should thank her, too, you know? Well?"

Kenny said, "Yeah, thanks, Sally! I would have exploded without you. You're pretty stacked too."

After a few minutes, the boys drove them downtown. As the girls got out of the car on Morro Street, Kenny leaned over and said, "Hey, Sally, say hi to that twit Todd for me. I'll let him know we met. Mrs. V, too!"

Quick as a flash, Brenda said angrily, "If you do, we'll tell Coach about your curfew and booze stuff. He'd like to hear about that, don't you think?"

Kenny's face lost its arrogant look. "Hold on now, that's not—"

"We'll tell, and it'll be no more football for you," said Brenda. Then she thrust out her chest and said, "No more of this, either."

Kenny shut the door and drove off.

Brenda pulled Sally to the sidewalk, and they walked to Flo's dress shop. Along the way, Brenda cozied up to Sally and asked, "Wasn't that fun? They won't say anything. The football and boxing teams don't get along, to say the least."

"How do you know so much about the teams anyway?" asked Sally.

"I just know, because we take care of them. Most of us sneak around with them. But if Mrs. V catches you, look out. On the cheer team, we take care of their needs, but only when Mrs. V says to. If she finds out about our little HJ party, she'll come down hard on us and more! So don't talk about it with *anyone*, especially the other cheer girls. We're the stars now. They're jealous and will tattle on us."

Sally asked, "Take care of them? What's *HJ* mean?"

"Hand job. There's lots more ahead for you. Mrs. V will have you involved, for sure, and soon. From the way she looked at you during practice, I'd bet on it."

Sally pulled up short and looked at Brenda. "Sex? That's what Mrs. V tells us to do?"

"Yes, of course! That's how Mrs. V and Coach control, reward, and punish the players. If they play good, then they get it. But if they play bad? Well, they get nothing. Understand now? It's really fun. We get to have sex with all the big-shot players and put one over on all those hoity-toity, stuck-up girls from Aquila Alta they go with. See? It makes them really jealous, and they can't do a thing about it. I've had lots of boys on the first string. You see, with my figure *I'm* the first string on the cheer team—not Marylyn."

"You mean Mrs. V will tell us—you and me—to do stuff with certain boys to reward them for playing good?"

"Yes, exactly! She tells me, and now you too, which players to do. Today was just heavy petting for starters. Mrs. V will have more for us later. You like it, don't you? I mean, sex and screwing? I forgot, you're still a virgin. Sally, sweetie, you're wet now, aren't you?"

Both embarrassed and excited, Sally said, "Yeah, a little. But I didn't like how they ..."

Brenda smiled slyly. "You wanted to stop them so you could do the touching, like in the locker room, right? I know. Me too! Your touch is better. What about Todd? He's really cute."

Sally turned her eyes away and nodded. She didn't like how Brenda mentioned Todd. It was all very confusing.

Flo's, on Higuera Street, was small but elegant, tucked in between bigger stores. When Brenda and Sally walked in, the place was empty of customers. After a few minutes, a tall, austere women of about forty-five, well dressed, came out from behind a display case. "Why, it's you, Brenda. I haven't seen you since last spring. My, how you've grown. How quickly all you young girls do develop these days! And who's this cute friend of yours? I'm Flo, and this is my cozy little shop."

"Flo, this is Sally, my new friend. She's a cheerleader too, and she needs new lingerie. You know, just like Mrs. V said to get for me last year, remember?"

At the mention of Mrs. V, Flo's eyes narrowed. "Well, we'll see what we can do." She locked the front door and led them to the back of the shop.

After showing Sally the things from which she could choose, Flo raised an eyebrow at Brenda and the two of them disappeared. Ten minutes later they returned, with Brenda looking triumphant and Flo mildly embarrassed.

Brenda said, "I think it's time to go. Can Sally have this stuff?"

Flo replied, "Whatever she wants. Go ahead!"

Sally and Brenda headed for the front door, and as they walked out, Flo asked, "When will you be back? I'll get more things, I promise!"

Brenda said, "I'm not sure, but we'll let you know." Then she took Sally's hand, and the two girls walked quickly down toward Morro Street.

Sally said, "I'm wearing the red ensemble. Can I come over to your house later?"

"We'll see!" Brenda replied.

CHAPTER 15

Sisters

Weeks went by, and Sally's new modus operandi, with Brenda's help, worked to perfection. Grandma and her sisters never suspected, and the bust cream was working too. Sally felt more eyes on her in school, and Mrs. V commented on her appearance.

The looks from boys and envious stares from girls thrilled Sally. She and Brenda became close friends, though still competitors. Without realizing it, she began to emulate Brenda. Short skirts, cleavage, makeup, and bigger hair were all part of Sally's daily routine. The attention she craved was an aphrodisiac. The more she received, the more she wanted—and it was such fun.

Sally invented phony stories to fool Grandma, who still told her what to do and wear. She was not permitted to go out in the evenings, even on weekends. Except for things to do with the cheer team, she had no freedom to be her new self or spend time with Brenda.

She left most of her new things at the gym and hid the bust cream, which she applied twice a day, in her bedroom. She hated going to and from school each day looking dumpy, but she gritted her teeth and did it. Of course, all her acquaintances noticed the change in her appearance at school, but none of them knew Grandma. In fact, all her old friends just fell away as Sally focused her attention on cheer team and, most especially, Brenda.

In her frustration, Sally became bolder in finding outlets for her new womanliness. She snuck off during lunch period and even cut classes to make out in cars, behind the gym, or in the equipment room—often with Brenda, but not always.

She still had strong feelings for Todd, but even though her new look dazzled most boys, it didn't seem to register with him. They talked a few times, but always about things Sally didn't care about, such as boxing, science, and the ranch. She tried to show interest in Todd, but still he didn't ask her out, and she continued to obsess about him with other girls. He was often at Cal Poly for boxing, so was he spending time with college girls?

Finally, Sally decided that the only reliable source of knowledge about all this was Brenda, who would know for sure. But before Sally could ask her, something came up that seemed like it could help her find the answer she was looking for.

One Monday, after a football game, Mrs. V summoned Sally to her office. Sally walked down the long corridor of the gym basement to the cheer team office. Being summoned to Mrs. V's office was always serious. She knocked nervously and heard a sharp, "Come in, Sally. You're expected."

Mrs. V sat behind her big, polished oak desk, impeccable as usual. Brenda stood just to her left with a pleased look on her face. Using only her eyes, Mrs. V indicated for Sally to stand in front of her. She then said, "You know, Sally, I was helpful to the football players as a cheerleader when I was in school. You can be, too. It's fun. Do you think she's ready, Brenda?"

"Oh yes, Mrs. V." Turning to Sally, Brenda said, "Rosebud, do you want to show Mrs. V? You have them on, don't you?"

After weeks of practices, events, and parades, Sally had somehow acquired the nickname of Rosebud. Cecilia, whose flat chest hadn't responded to her own application of bust cream, was called Fried Eggs. These names came up in that catty way that girls have with each other.

Without Brenda having to saying anything more, Sally smiled proudly at Mrs. V and lifted the hem of her skirt to reveal the edge of her new lingerie.

Mrs. V said, "Well, I see you're developing too. Challenging Brenda, are you?"

"Aah … well … yes, ma'am!" Sally replied, with her heart pounding.

"Very good, Sally. Do you want to help Brenda reward our successful football players?"

Feeling the glow of beauty and acceptance, Sally nodded. "Oh yes! I mean, yes, ma'am!"

This elicited a quick response from Brenda. "Oh goody—we're going to have such fun."

Mrs. V said, "Yes, you two will be a great success. And Brenda, don't forget to be careful. We don't need any trips to Pismo Beach, do we? Do you have what you need?"

Brenda responded by patting her big cheerleader bag, while Sally didn't understand or care. In the glow of her new status, Mrs. V's question just faded away.

Brenda and Sally used the school corridors like fashion runways, but each day got more complicated for Sally. Deceiving Grandma and fooling her nosy sisters was not difficult. But almost every other girl on the cheer team had some issue to keep confidential, so no one was broadcasting what went on.

The hardest thing was avoiding Todd except when Sally was dressed down a little. Brenda kept telling her to be at her sexy best around him, but Sally wasn't quite ready for him to see that side of her yet—or maybe ever. The image question—whether to be nice or sexy—was confusing, though she generally pushed it aside because the attention she got overwhelmed everything else. She loved it, even though looking sensual was a lot of work, and she took Brenda's cue on almost everything.

One Thursday, as Sally and Brenda stood near the student snack bar, Kenny and Terrell came by. Brenda said, "After practice tomorrow, will you give us a ride home?"

Terrell put his arm around Brenda and said, "We'd be happy to help. Parking lot at five, okay?"

Sally bent over and gave the boys a good look at her developing figure.

After the boys walked away, Brenda said, "We're on with Kenny and Terrell after practice. Remember Joyce, that hoity-toity senior with the car? Terrell's her boyfriend. You go with Kenny. I'll do Terrell, because he's not so nice. See you after. Wear the pink stuff, okay?"

As Brenda skipped off, Sally called out, "What did Mrs. V mean about being careful?"

Brenda turned back to her and said, "I'll bring everything and explain later. Don't worry, it's gonna be fun!"

The next day they met Kenny and Terrell out by the parking lot. Terrell said, "You look great! It's Sally, isn't it?"

Brenda said, "She's a cheerleader too, in case you hadn't noticed."

"Yeah, hi!" Sally said flirtatiously.

Terrell said, "Oh yeah, everyone notices. You cheerleaders are great. Right this way, girls." He pointed at the car across the parking lot.

They walked over to a blue late-model Buick, a four-door sedan that must have belonged to Terrell's dad. Sally and Brenda had noticed it around with the Aquila Alta clique—the rich kids. Kenny ushered Sally into the front seat, and Brenda got in the back with Terrell.

Brenda said, "That was a good game you guys played. What's with the blood, Terrell? Did you get that cut on your hand in the game?"

"Yeah, but it's nothing," said Terrell. "It'll stop bleeding in a while."

Brenda said, "We want to make sure you know you're appreciated. That's how Sally feels, too."

Sally looked at Brenda for reassurance and said, "Mrs. V wants us to show you our appreciation."

~

It took only a few minutes to show the boys how appreciated they were. Sally didn't really want to be with Kenny. Instead, she kept thinking about Brenda or maybe Todd. Her feelings were in a confused stew—the touching with Brenda, her feelings for Todd. She gave Kenny only a hand job like before, but Brenda and Terrell didn't notice amid their own noisy sex.

Kenny asked, "Where you girls want to go, get let out?"

Brenda waved at them and took Sally's arm as they walked off. "Bye, boys. See you!" Then she turned to Sally and asked, "Well, did you like it? Did it hurt? You got blood on you."

Now Sally had to do some major faking to cover up what she hadn't done. "Uh, just a little, but in a really good way."

Brenda pulled up Sally's skirt and looked. "Your panties are spotted! Boys are grabby, not like girls. Not like me and you. It's the way they are. Men are better than boys, you'll see. The hurt part is because—well, he busted your cherry, but that won't happen again."

"My what?" asked Sally.

"Your hymen, silly. Didn't Grandma have the talk with you? You know, about sex and babies? Being safe, using protection?"

Sally said, "No. Did your mom with you?"

"No, I found out in eighth grade, with a friend of my stepbrother who was in the army up at Camp Roberts. I had these, almost, in sixth grade." She stuck out her chest.

"Sixth grade? Holy cow!" Sally blurted out.

"You're gonna be stacked, too," said Brenda. "That little rosebud mouth isn't the only thing you'll have. Keep using the cream. You still haven't told me anything about how you *really* felt."

More faking it! Sally said, "It just felt really good! I don't even remember exactly."

At the corner of Woodbridge Street, Brenda needed to turn to go to her house, so they stopped. She said, "Mrs. V will have more for us to do. Remember not to do it with anyone else, especially Todd. If Mrs. V finds out you did it without her permission, you'll get it."

"Todd? Why?" Sally asked.

"Did you see the way she looked at him outside the gym that day? I can tell. She's got a special project in mind for him, so be careful."

"What do you mean by *special project*?" Sally asked.

"I don't really know," said Brenda. "It's just the way she looked at him. I've got intuition for that kind of thing, believe me. I got it from my mom, who knows everything. She does *it* a lot."

"But Todd's my boyfriend! Can't I go with—"

"Does he think you're his girlfriend?" asked Brenda.

Sally said, "Well, we've been together—"

"How many times have you been with him? Once or twice?" Brenda asked condescendingly.

After an awkward silence, Sally said, "Oh my, what time is it? Late, I think! I'd better get home. I'll see you tomorrow at practice, okay?"

Brenda said, "Okay, party girl. We're gonna have us some fun. See you tomorrow."

~

"Where have you been, young lady? Do you know the time? You're late and supper's past. What's the world coming to, when a young girl is out without permission after dark?"

As Sally stood in the front hall, Grandma pointed toward her room. Sally said, "I was at practice, and then Bren—"

"What, that hussy? I told you to stay away from her. Didn't I make myself clear on that?" asked Grandma.

As Sally took a few tentative steps toward her room, her nosy sisters butted in. Gail said, "She was with a boy. I seen her, I did, the other day."

Grandma asked, "Is that true? I do hope it's that Jennings boy, right?"

In a flash, Sally saw a way out. "Yes, and he's from a good family too."

"He looked older," Zoe practically shouted. "He did, he did, Grandma!"

"Well, of course he's older now, stupid," said Sally. "We were talking about church and—and the barn dance. You know, next week? Remember?"

This explanation seemed to placate Grandma, but Sally's sisters wouldn't let it go. "She's not allowed—and anyway, it's not for church. She can't go, can she, Grandma?" Gail asked.

"I know Deacon Jennings's boys are going, so I guess it's okay. You will behave, Sally? No close dancing. That print dress with the puffed sleeves would look nice, don't you think?"

Sally almost choked when the puffed sleeves were mentioned. Barely restraining a scream, she replied, "Yes, that will look really nice." Then she quickly took the opportunity to go to her room. From down the hall, she heard Grandma call out, "I'll have the leftovers ready in a few minutes. Come to the kitchen then."

When Sally got to her room, she remembered that she'd have to hide the lingerie with the blood on it, but where? As she contemplated her dilemma, Zoe came in the room without knocking, and Sally said, "Zoe, you're supposed to knock."

With a smirk, Zoe said, "The leftovers are ready, Miss Smarty Pants."

"Just a minute!" Sally stuffed the panties and other things under her pillow, then went to the kitchen for supper. After eating she did a few chores, made notes in her diary, and went to bed, all curled up around her mixed feelings—Brenda or Todd?

~

The next morning, Sally got up late and went to the bathroom. When she came out, she heard the clothes washer going. "Oh no, it's wash day," she exclaimed. "My room, my sheets, *the lingerie!*"

Back in her room, she saw that Gail had stripped her bed. Sally ran to the washer on the back porch. No sheets there, or on the clothesline either. Her heart sank. Gail had found her lingerie. She sat on the porch, dreading what she'd find in the kitchen. Finally she got up and went down the hall to the kitchen. Sure enough, hanging over the back of a chair was her new bra—but not the bloodstained panties.

Grandma glared at her, picked up the bra as if it were a piece of trash, and asked, "Where, young lady, did you get this garish thing? And how on earth did you pay for it? Was it that Barbano girl—or worse, her mother? Oh my, that woman! I can't believe you'd ... Oh Sally, this is awful."

Sally's mind raced in search of an idea, and found one. "Mrs. Sondheim helped me, Grandma. I thought if it was okay with her, it would be all right with you. It's cute, don't you think?"

Gail and Zoe stood back looking smug, smiling ruefully at Sally's discomfort. As Grandma dropped the bra in the trash, Gail stuck her tongue out at Sally, and then Zoe did the same.

Grandma said, "That'll be all. You're grounded for a month, Sally, including cheerleading. No barn dance next week either. You will come directly home from school every day, understood?"

"But Grandma, it's so nice and cute. Why? I'm a good girl!"

"You won't be if you go on this way," snapped Grandma, "with these things and that girl. We're going to have a talk with the deacon after church. This can't go on."

Sally took one last chance. "Mrs. Sondheim won't be happy if we reject the things she bought me."

Grandma said, "We'll see about that. You're grounded, Sally. What would your poor, sainted mother think?"

This last sentence struck home with Sally. Indeed, what would her mother have thought? That question argued against the exciting adventures that Brenda had introduced her to. In bed, Sally considered the question about her "sainted mother"—and ways to pay back her sisters.

~

That question! Sally saw her "sainted mother" at the dressing table amid makeup, combs, and lingerie. Getting ready for a man? Which man? Her father was a long-haul truck driver, gone, mostly. Sally had only a blurry memory of a Peterbilt truck cab, way up high. It might be him, but maybe there were others? At any rate, "sainted mother" sure didn't fit.

Cool and detached from Sally, for sure. Warm, but no more than warm with the men who paraded through. Was Sally like ... No, she was nothing like her mother, though she looked just like her. Blond, short, petite except—and with the cream ... *But why use it if I'm going to be shaped like her?* Short skirts, cleavage, big hair, legs crossed. These images swam by alongside martinis, cigarette butts, and a waft of perfume. Still, no, not me. I'm a cheerleader! Brenda will know. I'll ask her.

At Sunday church, the deacon's eyes fell on Sally, as usual. He asked her, "Afterward, please?" As the crowd dispersed, Grandma told her to go with him while she waited in the reception room.

The deacon ushered her into his office, and she sat and slowly crossed her legs. His eyes followed her, and he reached over and patted her knee. "There, there, just relax! Grandma is concerned, and frankly so am I, but I'll not scold you. How's everything at school? You can tell me anything, okay?"

Sally's nervous squirming in her seat had made her skirt ride up, and she watched his eyes take this in. She leaned her shoulders back as she'd often seen Brenda do. Another button popped on her blouse, and the deacon's eyes grew a little wider.

"Well, I'm on cheer team, so I need to dress better. Mrs. V, the cheer team coach, says so. I've got to do it, but Grandma thinks it's not ladylike or Christian, so I don't know what to do. I'm a good girl, as you know." She could see that she was having the desired effect on the deacon.

He moved closer, slid his hand further up her leg, and gave it a squeeze with his eyes on her cleavage. "Sally, everything is going to be okay, I promise. Just do as I say."

Sally's inner voice said, *Brenda was right.* Feeling her power, she slid forward in the seat and pressed her boobs together. "You're not going to tell Grandma that I'm bad, are you? You're so good to me. Can we talk more often? I'm not a bad girl for wanting nice things, am I?"

The deacon's face grew animated, and his hand moved to the inside of Sally's leg. He said firmly, "No, of course not. Not at all, Sally. You're a good girl, and I'll tell Grandma so. Now about our talks, it might be preferable to meet at some other place—"

Suddenly there was a knock on the door and a woman's voice said, "Deacon, can I come in?"

He jumped about a foot, pulled his hand off Sally's leg, and stood up. In a not-quite-controlled voice, he said, "I'm almost done now, Bernice. I'll be out momentarily."

Sally asked, "Shall I go? I don't want to keep you. You'll tell Grandma that it's okay for me to dress nicely? I'd be ever so grateful when we meet again. Please?" She batted her eyes, then looked away so he could look down her cleavage. Her inner voice said, *Brenda, you're so, so right.*

"Yes, you can go. We'll meet again soon. And not to worry! I'll speak to Grandma."

Playing her role to the fullest, Sally stood, gave an almost curtsy, and went to the door. "You're so understanding! I don't know how to thank you, but if you think of something I can do …"

In the foyer, Grandma and the deacon were talking, a good sign. She wanted so badly to tell Brenda how she'd enlisted Deacon Jennings's help, remembering his hand on her leg.

At home, Grandma said stiffly, "I hope your talk with the deacon was fruitful. Against my better judgment and upon his advice, I'm going to let you stay on cheer team. You're still grounded, however, and must come directly home afterward. He will also want to meet with you again later."

Sally pleaded, "Can I go to the dance, please? The deacon trusts me, so you can too."

"We'll see!" Grandma promised.

~

By midweek, before the barn dance, Mrs. V had more rewards to hand out, and Brenda and Sally were slated to do Kenny and Terrell again. Sally now fully realized the power of her figure, just like Brenda. Knowing they could have any of the hoity-toity girls' boyfriends was thrilling. Because of her confusion about Brenda and Todd, however, she made up an excuse about Grandma's grounding her, so that Mrs. V would let her off. This was fine with Mrs. V, and Brenda too, who didn't mind a bit.

When Sally told Brenda about her meeting with the deacon and putting one over on Grandma, they both giggled and schemed to do more. Her plan to get back at her nosy sisters fell away amid the fun of enticing the boys.

Sally had to put on an act when she saw Todd, because she didn't want him to know about the other stuff. Nevertheless, the duplicity of her actions bothered her. Somehow Todd was different, and she was confused about whether she should try to entice him.

What really convinced her that Todd was on another level was that Brenda couldn't decide about him either. When Brenda fawned more blatantly in front of him, he just brushed her off. He even ignored her a couple of times, which made her visibly upset. She pretended she didn't care, but of course she did. Brenda wanted every boy and man to want her and every girl to be jealous of her. So she began disparaging Todd, claiming he wasn't her type and that Sally could have him.

After boxing practice one day, Coach and Todd passed through the cheer team practice room. This, of course, roused the interest of every girl. Mrs. V called them over and asked Coach to explain how important the cheerleaders' performance was to all the teams.

He began, "This is Todd Wyrum, a member of the boxing team. A few of you may know Todd."

There was a general murmur, and Sally said, "I know Todd pretty well. We're friends."

With a nod at Sally, Todd said confidently to the group, "You're the best. Every performance inspires us. I might also mention that we really like your new outfits. They're cool—really becoming."

"Thanks, Todd. I'm sure you inspire them, too. Am I right, girls?" Coach asked.

The girls heaped praise on the boxing team in a general frenzy of giggling adulation.

"Now girls, calm down a little. I'm sure Coach and Todd have things to do." Mrs. V reached out and grasped Todd's biceps, letting her hand linger. The girls took careful notice.

Without moving his arm, Todd looked directly at Mrs. V and said calmly, "We're happy to show you all how appreciative we are."

Coach said, "Thanks for the support, girls!"

Just as Todd and Coach headed for the door, Kenny and Terrell walked in and respectfully greeted Coach. Todd hung back and waved at Sally, but Kenny told him, "Nice try, but no sale. She's easy, but only for football players. Boxers are off limits, especially you."

"What was that, fatso? Watch your mouth," Todd said, turning to confront Kenny.

From just outside the door, Coach yelled, "Todd, forget it! Come on, we've got practice. Now!" Todd backed away, and he and Coach left the building.

Brenda said, "Sally, did you see how Todd stood up to Mrs. V? I could hardly believe it."

"And how she touched his arm. Did you see that?" asked Sally.

"Yes, but did you see Coach? You could see his—his thing, too. He's the best-looking teacher in the school. I wish Mrs. V would ask us to reward *him*. Did you notice how big his hands are? Oh my, I'm all a-flutter thinking about that."

Sally said, "His hands? What do they have to do with anything?"

"Silly! Big hands mean a big you-know-what," Brenda explained. "My mom told me, and she knows everything, believe me. She's been with every guy in town."

"Your mom?" Sally asked.

Brenda said, "Yeah, my mom. You'll understand when you meet her. She's even better developed than me. You should see all the free stuff she gets! I'll arrange for you to meet her later. I've watched her do all kinds of stuff. It'll be fun, but I've got to wait for the right time. I'll let you know ... But poo on all that. What about the barn dance? Is Grandma going to allow you to go?"

~

Sally's good behavior, helping out at home, and being nice to her sisters hadn't changed Grandma's opposition to the dance. It was sponsored by the Future Farmers of America, but even that wasn't enough for her. Desperate, Sally lied and said Mrs. Sondheim would chaperone, but that didn't change Grandma's mind.

Then, completely out of the blue, Todd asked her for a date. Sally knew this might be enough to turn the tables with Grandma, because Todd made a favorable impression on almost everyone. When she brought up the invitation, Grandma said, "Oh my! What a nice, polite boy."

Sally put on her most innocent, pleading face and waited with bated breath. After a long pause, Grandma relented. "All right, Sally, you can go. But you must promise to dress demurely and be home no later than eleven. Promise?"

"Oh yes, Grandma, I promise. Thank you, thank you, thank you!" Sally excitedly jumped up and down, shooting a triumphant sideways glance at her disappointed sisters.

"I'm surprised the dance is being held at that run-down Edna Farm Center. So what time is Todd going to pick you up?" asked Grandma. "Will he be bringing you a corsage?"

Sally said, "It's a barn dance, Grandma, so it's very informal. He'll be here at six thirty."

~

Because of the chaotic parking lot scramble, Todd pulled the truck around behind the old building. He and Sally walked arm in arm through the mess of cars to the front of the hall. They greeted many friends among the diverse, happy crowd. Many of the boys were wearing their letter jackets, and most girls wore full skirts and blouses. The band had just started to play. As usual, most of the dancers were girl couples looking to coax the boys onto the floor, which wasn't working just yet.

Spotting Brenda across the floor with their fellow cheerleaders, Sally pulled Todd toward them and said, "Hi, Brenda! You all know Todd, don't you?"

Sally immediately realized her mistake, as Brenda stepped forward and said, "Remember me?"

Without enthusiasm, Todd lied and said, "Yeah, sorta, but I don't recall you being a cheerleader."

This obvious put-down got all the girls snickering and eyes snapping back and forth. Obviously surprised at Todd's answer, Brenda said, "Well, I am!"

Mrs. V appeared and interrupted them. "Girls, girls, girls, come on! Get out there with these boys and dance. Look at them all, just standing around. Get going!"

Sally pulled Todd away from Brenda and onto the dance floor. Lots of other girls followed suit, and the floor filled with awkward couples bumping clumsily into each other.

Todd was not an especially good fast dancer, but when a slow song finally played, Sally was thrilled that he was much better. He held her in his arms most romantically. His hand at her back drew her to him, but not hard against her bust as other boys usually did—though now she wanted him to. His cheek was close against her neck, which sent a little shiver through her body.

Then a hand abruptly pulled her back, and Mrs. V's voice intruded on her happiness. "Sally? Todd? Not too close now. You must be a hand's width apart at all times. Is that clear?"

Todd spoke up and asked, "Since when? I haven't seen you separating any other couples."

Mrs. V said, "Todd, you know full well that Sally is a cheer girl, so I'm being extra careful of her reputation. Go on and dance, but make sure you're separated by the appropriate space."

By this time a small group of dancers had formed around them. Because of Mrs. V's reputation, some of them were openly shocked at Todd's near defiance of her.

Her knowledge of Mrs. V's general conduct caused Sally to suspect something, especially considering what she and Brenda had been doing at their coach's instruction for weeks.

Sally and Todd danced away, and he drew her close again. A minute later, however, Mrs. V was right back in front of them, saying, "This isn't your first time to break the rules, Todd. We'll see about that. Be in my office after practice on Monday. Is that clear?"

Todd smiled and said, "Sure!" Then he danced Sally away, just barely keeping distance between them.

The dance gradually became more and more fun—and a bit rowdy, because lot of kids from other high schools showed up. With the exception of Mrs. V, the chaperones weren't too strict, and the spiked punch gave several of them a buzz. Most of the time Todd and Sally danced together, but they had other partners, too. Sally kept a close eye on Todd, especially when he slow danced with Brenda.

About nine o'clock, the band played "Smoke Gets in Your Eyes," and Todd and Sally got really close. Kenny walked up and said to Todd, "I'm cutting in." It was clear he'd had more than his share of the punch.

Todd stepped back, but Sally said, "No, Kenny. You're drunk. Let's go, Todd."

As Sally turned away, Kenny grabbed her shoulder and spun her back around. "Oh no, not with him," he said. "We can go out back for some personal fun, you know? The kind of fun you like, Sally."

Todd stepped between them and said, "She said she wasn't interested, Kenny, so shove off. Have another drink—or whatever. Sally's with me."

Kenny shoved Todd out of the way and pulled at Sally's arm, but she pushed him away.

Todd said more forcefully, "Go home, Kenny! This isn't your night. Come on, Sally."

But Kenny wouldn't go. He shoved Todd and said, "I know her—and what she likes—better than you."

"Butt out, fats. Sally's with me!" Todd shouted.

With a pleased look on his face, Kenny said, "Tell him, Sally. Tell Todd about the four of us—you, me, Brenda, and Terrell. Go ahead, Sally."

Sally looked from Todd to Brenda, then back at Kenny, and said, "Uh, I don't know what you're talking about."

Kenny exploded, "BS! You and Bad Brenda were in my car. You remember, because you're easy!"

"What did you say, Kenny?" Todd asked forcefully.

A crowd had formed around the confrontation, with lots of yelling. A group of football players stepped up, ready to help Kenny, but Hector and Helman were also there. The football players outnumbered the boxers, but nobody really wanted to fight a boxer—and especially not the heavyweight Helman.

Kenny landed a punch squarely on Todd's nose, immediately shooting blood all over Todd's face and Sally's dress. He yelled, "Screw you, Todd!"

This was nothing new to Todd, who quickly recovered and put two jabs in Kenny's face followed by a hard right. Kenny threw a big roundhouse swing that missed, plus several wild punches, some of which landed. But when Todd hit him in the stomach, Kenny went down with a great *whoosh*. He tried to get up, but obviously the fight was over.

Mrs. V and a male chaperone stepped into the circle that had formed. The guy grabbed Todd, pulled him back, and said, "That's all, kid. It's over!"

Sally gave Todd a big smile. But when Brenda took his other arm and said, "My hero!" Sally blurted out, "He's not your hero, Brenda. He's mine. Butt out!"

On Mrs. V's face was a vengeful expression that Sally and Brenda had seen before, so they knew Todd was in trouble. Mrs. V said to Todd, very pointedly, "My office. Monday. Don't be late."

Not appearing the least bit intimidated, Todd replied, "See you Monday."

Sally quickly pulled Todd toward the restrooms out back. Luckily Brenda didn't follow. Sally said in a gentle way, "Come on, Todd. I'll get you cleaned up. You're my hero, you know?" For Sally, it was a complete thrill to have a guy—her guy—fight for her. The rush of adrenaline made what she wanted next even more highly anticipated.

On a bench out back, she took a towel and cleaned up Todd's face. His aura grew in her eyes, and they sat close, his arm around her. His face and soft green-gray eyes enthralled her, and she moved closer until their faces were only inches apart. His arm was firm and his mouth was close, but he didn't grab her or push his mouth against hers—so different from other boys. She wanted him, but he didn't move. When he leaned back, his lips brushed her neck and her warm spot grew. She put her lips near his, but he didn't respond.

Then, in a serious tone, Todd asked, "What was that about you and Brenda being *easy?*"

Sally replied, "Let's go now, before Kenny comes out."

But Todd pulled her behind a car and said, "Kenny's not going to bother us. What about that *easy* stuff?"

"Oh, Todd, it's—uh—just talk. I don't even know what *easy* means."

"Well, I sure do. It means only one thing, as far as I know. I'm pretty sure it applies to Brenda, and you hang out with her. So ...?"

Sally mostly pulled Todd through the randomly parked cars. Occasionally headlight beams reflected off the cars and partly lit their way. The crowd noise faded as they drew farther from the barn. Finally they found his truck and got in.

Todd looked directly into her eyes and asked, "Well?"

Sally replied, "Oh Todd, it's just that ... Well, it's so—"

"No, it isn't!" Todd said, interrupting her. "Just tell me why he said *easy.*"

She took a deep breath and looked away so he couldn't see the lie in her eyes. "Kenny asked me out, and I said no. But he persisted and said he'd get even because he's captain and, you know, important ... And his dad is a doctor and ... Well, stuff like that."

"Go on," said Todd.

"Go on *what?*" asked Sally. "Don't you trust me?"

Todd asked, "And you didn't do anything with him, or go out, or ... Oh shit, I know he'd be pissed if you wouldn't date him. He's an arrogant guy. I do trust you, Sally. Maybe it's all wrapped up in how Brenda behaves—or, more accurately, misbehaves. She's tried to kiss up to me, too. You may not believe this, but she's pretty sly."

At hearing this, Sally nearly jumped. That was more than believable—it was almost certain. She found it hard not to scream, but seeing a possible diversion helped her maintain control. Her emotions were flooded with a mix of jealousy and betrayal, with her feelings for Todd pitted against her desire for Brenda. She wanted Todd for love and Brenda for lust, and the fight roiled within her.

After sitting quietly for several minutes, finally Todd said, "Lean against me, Sally."

She did much more than that. She took his face in her hands and pressed her lips to his. Her wish was fulfilled, for the softness of his mouth spoke of love. Todd kissed her back, and slowly their bodies became entwined. His response was not to press harder, but to draw back slightly and let her passion catch up. Their mouths pressed, their hands explored, and it was almost like their clothes undressed themselves.

Soon Sally was completely naked, and she felt the lump of him ready as she swung her legs over his hips and sat down. He was there, and when she relaxed, he slid into her without effort, wet, hot, penetrating, and—oh, yes—huge. Her gushing inside closed around him. The tree of life was growing, pulsing, flared and deep, deep in her vagina, then a small, quick, joyful pain. They fucked each other in crazy, gyrating, self-fulfilling thrusts. Sally clawed Todd's back while he sucked and bit her nipples. Their yells and screams filled the truck, and the windows fogged up. The crescendo of his ejaculation into her, like a wet lance, seemed to reach almost to her throat. Then again, unhinged, overwhelmed in joy, their bodies soaking wet. Sally's insides filled to overflowing with his seed, then running down her legs and all over him. Finally they collapsed, gasping for breath and clinging to each other.

~

Time stood still for a long time, and then Todd said, "You're so fine, Sally. I love your twins, too."

"My twins?"

"Ha!" he exclaimed. "I've seen you bouncing along in the halls."

As Sally blushed, her inner voice said, *Take that, Brenda.* "Todd, am I nicer than Brenda?"

Todd said, "I don't know Brenda, remember? Forget her. You're the best!"

"Oh Todd, I'm so glad! You're my dream."

They snuggled for a while, then drove north on Broad Street. Parking the truck in front of the house, they talked for a while. Todd said, "You got some blood on your things. Are you okay? I didn't hurt you, did I?"

"No, Todd, it was ... Oh my, you—we!—were wonderful!"

"I'm feeling pretty good myself," said Todd.

Sally laughed and said, "Yes, we seem to be doing okay. But if I tell Grandma about the fight, she won't let me date you. What should I do?"

"I could go in and say you got a nosebleed," suggested Todd. "That might work. What do you say? After all, I've got blood on me too. See? You just danced too hard."

By the time Todd left Sally's house, all was well. She went to bed glowing with happiness, but very sore. That full feeling that Brenda had told her about was more than great. It stayed with her all night and the next day. Sally was no longer a virgin. She couldn't believe how loving Todd had been, even saying sensual things to her in French. In short, he was sexy *and*—even more important—romantic, and she could hardly wait to do it again.

Excited to tell Brenda about it, Sally suddenly fell victim to her competing feelings. Todd and Brenda swam in and out of her thoughts in their confusing love-versus-lust competition.

CHAPTER 16

Mrs. V

Sally's anticipation of telling Brenda about her night with Todd kept her on pins and needles. Before practice, she caught up with Brenda and could see from her expression that she was just as eager to hear about it. They ducked into a storeroom, and Brenda blurted out, "Oh my God, tell me everything! Did you have one? I hope you did. Tell me!"

"Twice," said Sally. "At least, I think so. It was beyond wonderful. I can't even begin to tell it all."

"Did you touch yourself while he—"

"No, silly. I mean, yes. Well, he did—not me. I don't know, maybe even more. It was beyond ... Brenda, he's huge! That full feeling you told me about? Wow, and his rolls around inside too! You were so right. I'm sore in other places too. I almost couldn't put on my new lacy bra. Oh my, it was just so wonderful!"

"How big? Bigger than Kenny?" Brenda gasped, and suddenly Sally realized that Brenda's enthusiasm for knowing such things about Todd wasn't good. Brenda grabbed her wrist and wrapped her fingers around it. "How big, really? Like this?"

Sally said, "Well, I'm not exactly sure, but ... No, Brenda, that's between Todd and me."

Looking a bit sheepish now, Brenda said, "We're friends, Sally. You can tell me, can't you?"

"No, Brenda, some of this is just between Todd and me," insisted Sally.

"You felt him come in you? Inside, right?"

Hesitatingly, Sally replied, "Well, yeah, of course I did."

Brenda said, "So he didn't wear protection? No rubber, Sally? Nothing?"

"Oh jeez, I was so excited that I forgot that thing you gave me," said Sally.

Now Brenda got in a huff. "I'll bet Todd isn't that big anyway, and maybe you'll get pregnant and visit the house in Pismo Beach. If I told Mrs. V, you'd get it worse than me."

Sally stood, mouth agape, as Brenda walked off. "Brenda, I'll tell you more, really!"

Fear crept in as Sally began thinking, *Pregnant? The house in Pismo Beach? Could it happen? I only did it once—but inside me! Would Todd want a baby? Would he still like me?*

~

At school on Monday, Sally was even more incensed about the teasing about her clothes and nickname. When they saw her on the bus, several of the nastiest girls called her Little Bo Peep. It was no wonder, given that she was wearing a long print dresses with short puffy sleeves, oxfords, pigtails, and no makeup. Even after she'd changed at school, they kept it up, but she was determined to show them. Brenda, for sure, would help her do that.

One morning Sally found a note taped to her locker: "See Mrs. V before class. Now!" Without changing clothes, she went straight to Mrs. V's office and knocked on the door.

A voice on the other side of the door called out, "Come in, Little Bo Peep. We've been expecting you."

Sally knew this meant trouble, but she walked into the office and said, "I'm here, Mrs. V."

Mrs. V pointed to a chair and said, "Sit!" Next to her sat Brenda, legs crossed and looking quite self-satisfied.

"Yes, Mrs. V," said Sally, promptly sitting in the straight-back chair.

Mrs. V said, "Brenda tattled on you, just as she should have. You were with that Todd boy without my permission. Little Bo Peep broke the rules, which is cause for punishment. I guess you want to do what the big girls do, right? Well, yes or no, Sally?"

The words rang in Sally's ears. In a meek voice, on the edge of crying, she blurted out, "I couldn't help it. After the fight, I wanted to comfort him. To hug him, you know? And it felt so good. Mrs. V, I know the rules, but Todd's my boyfriend. Isn't it allowed when—"

"Stop this incessant babbling, Sally!" Mrs. V barked.

Brenda broke in, "She broke the rules, so punish her like you did me. I was just making out on the bus, but she let him go all the way!"

"Oh shush, Brenda. She'll be punished," said Mrs. V. "Sally, if you're truthful, I could be forgiving."

Sally said, "Oh, Mrs. V, I do promise. Brenda wanted to know everything, but I wouldn't tell her."

When Mrs. V turned away for a moment, Brenda stuck her tongue out at Sally. Then Mrs. V asked, "How big?"

"No, Mrs. V!" exclaimed Sally. "I don't know. I just ... I think I love him!"

In a sarcastic tone, Mrs. V replied, "Love *it* is more like it, don't you think, Brenda?"

Brenda replied, "I saw it in his jeans. Pretty big!"

Then Mrs. V said, "Sally, not a word—not one—to Todd about this. You're not to see Todd again without my express permission. Is that clear? Because if it isn't, you're off the squad. And Brenda, that goes for you too. You can acquaint Sally with the next big girl step in her journey, which will be both fun and rewarding for us all. I've got more rewards for you girls to pass out to the players—and also, if you're really good, to the booster club. I'm a sharing person. You cooperate and you'll stay on the team, but if not, bye-bye! And you need the money, don't you, Sally?

"Uh, yes. But Mrs. V, I don't know—"

"Listen carefully, Sally. You entertain the football players to help the team, right? It's just a normal part of your cheerleader responsibilities. Well, we need money to support other activities too. So we do favors for them, mainly the booster club, and they give me—us—financial support. I collect a small amount on the team's behalf, and you get a stipend for your own use for helping out, understand? You've noticed Brenda receiving an envelope from a booster now and then, haven't you? Anyway, if you still have questions, Brenda will explain things further, I'm sure."

Brenda said, "Oh Sally, it's so much fun. And the money is just a reward that Mrs. V is generous enough to give us, see?"

"Well, yes ... I guess," replied Sally.

Mrs. V said, "Now the both of you get outta here!"

~

Todd wasn't worried about his visit to Mrs. V's office and any discipline she might have in mind. Coach wouldn't buy into anything like that after a fight at a barn dance. He might lay into Todd for *not* fighting, but this thing with Kenny was a big nothing. In fact, Todd was so unconcerned that he skipped Mrs. V's instruction to be there on Monday.

After health class with her on Tuesday afternoon, Todd knocked on Mrs. V's office door and prepared himself for a lecture on the school policy about nonviolence.

"Come in, Todd. I've been waiting for you!" Mrs. V leaned against her big oak desk. She wore a short skirt, heels, and a low-cut blouse, with her hair pulled back in a bun and perfect makeup. She pointed at a straight-back chair to her right and said, "Have a seat."

Todd casually stepped into her office and said, "I'll stand, Mrs. V, okay?"

She slowly picked up a folder from her desk, opened it, and said, "Todd, I think I'm going to have to report you to the dean of boys for cheating. The fight at the dance, which some say you aggressively started, will also be considered. Kenny's parents are asking for your suspension, and I saw the fight and may support their accusations. Another thing, which is definitely under my jurisdiction, is how you took advantage of a young girl on the cheer team later that evening. Disgraceful, just disgraceful, Todd! She'll be reporting on that too, I expect. You may not be going to this school much longer unless you fully cooperate."

Todd gulped and sat down. "What are you saying? First, I didn't start the fight—Kenny did. You saw him hit me in the face! Second, I've never cheated, because I don't have to. I get straight As, as you know. And third, I mean, I didn't do anything like that. How can you say that, Mrs. V? Sally Anderson said I did ... something?" Todd could sense Mrs. V's effort to take control.

She leaned toward him, letting her skirt hike up a little more, and said, "Well, she hasn't said anything yet, but I can tell she's upset—and as cheer coach, I am her mentor. I'm sure that her friend Brenda will back up all of this if I choose to press on with it. You're acquainted with Brenda?"

Then Mrs. V leaned over Todd and looked down at her disconcerted prey with a triumphant smirk. "Now, Todd, none of this has to happen. I may be able to persuade the dean and Kenny's folks to be merciful, and I'm certain that Sally would forgive you and forgo bringing charges. But you have to help me do this by cooperating fully with my wishes. Do you understand, Todd? Will you do as I say—to help you?"

Mrs. V bent over, showing him more cleavage, but Todd didn't take the bait. Looking her directly in the eyes, he said, "I don't know what you mean, Mrs. V. I did nothing wrong."

Mrs. V looked back into Todd's steady eyes, then abruptly stood up and put her fists on her hips. "Well, if you aren't willing to meet me halfway, then you'll be dismissed, I'm sure."

He replied calmly, "Maybe so. We'll see. Do what you've gotta do, Mrs. V."

Todd's confidence put Mrs. V completely off her game. He towered six inches over her. Nobody—teacher, administrator, or student—had ever so blatantly defied her. Her eyes blazed, but she took a step back and said, "Well, I guess that's all for today."

Todd smiled. "Then I'm off. Let me know what you decide. Bye!"

~

After practice on Thursday, Todd was called to Coach's office and handed a note. "What's with this, Todd? It's from the dean of boys. Are you in any trouble? You're usually the last student to get nicked. I heard about the fight, but no big deal. Kenny's always looking to mix it up, but his folks? The doctor, you know, he's got lots of pull in this county. Stay out of his way, Todd. Mrs. V seems to have gotten her shorts in a wringer, too. What's going on?"

No one intimidated Todd, but he needed to play it straight with Coach. The man was strict, dedicated, respected, and fair. If he was in your corner, everything was good, but if not? Todd thought carefully and said, "Coach, I did mix it up with Kenny, but it was no big deal. Scraps like that happen at dances all the time. You're right about him—if trouble doesn't find him, he goes looking for it. And everyone knows there's bad blood between boxers and ball players, so—"

Coach broke in and said, "Come on, Todd, get to it. I know all that."

Todd gulped and continued, "The fight was over my girl, whom he wants to think is his girl. Sally is a new member of the cheer team, and she was my date for the dance. Kenny tried to butt in, and he said some nasty stuff to her, and ... Well, everything went downhill after that. I won, like you'd expect, but I sure didn't expect him to blab to his folks."

"And then? There's gotta be more than that," insisted Coach.

Now uncomfortable, Todd said, "We did go to my truck and ... Well, we made out some."

"*Made out* how much, Todd? That can't be everything, can it?"

After another deep breath, Todd said, "Yeah, you're right. It got pretty heavy, but I got her home on time, and she was happy when I dropped her off. Mrs. V's just making up stuff to get me in trouble for some reason, but I don't know why. I swear, Coach! Mrs. V also said I cheated on my health class test. Really, no shit! That class is so easy. Who needs to cheat? Get real. I'm getting straight As."

Coach nodded, knowing not to ask what *heavy* really meant. He walked to the window for a minute, then asked, "What's Brenda Barbano got to do with all this?"

Todd said, "You mean, uh, the girl with the big—"

"Yeah, that one."

"She saw the fight, Coach. That's all I can think of, plus she and Sally hang out together."

Coach gave a hearty laugh and said sarcastically, "Hang out together? That's not the half of it. They've got a lot more going on than ... Well, enough of that. It seems she's a witness to you starting the fight. That's not in the note, but I heard it around. If Kenny's folks press the issue, Brenda corroborates their version, and Mrs. V says you cheated, then you've got *real* trouble. I can fix the fight thing, but I have little influence with the cheating accusation."

"Sally won't say I did anything wrong. I'm pretty darn sure of that."

"She just turned fifteen, Todd, and Mrs. V could make a lot of that. When that woman gets a bee in her bonnet, look out. She treats the cheerleaders like her private girls army. But why would she go after you? You're just about the best-behaved athlete at the school. It doesn't make sense."

Todd said, "When I didn't go along with her version of things and 'fess up to cheating, she seemed upset. Even invited me to her house for a talk. No kidding! Try figuring that out."

Coach said, "I think I understand that one, Todd, but let's leave it there for now. I'll see what I can find out, and maybe we can defuse this situation, okay?"

"Okay, Coach. I'll just hang in there until I have to go before the dean."

~

Todd's appointment with Dean Walsh was the following Thursday after the final class period. Officially it was a disciplinary hearing, but unofficially it was known as a "kick out" meeting.

Todd arrived a few minutes early, not knowing what to expect. He was dressed in his freshly pressed Junior ROTC uniform. Coach had agreed to vouch for his character, attendance, and future prospects. Dr. and Mrs. McKay came in, along with Kenny, and sat down. Kenny nodded at Todd but said nothing. Last to arrive were Mrs. V and Brenda.

Mr. Walsh came out of his office and asked the McKays and Coach to come in. He and Dr. McKay exchanged a few words and a bit of laughter before the door was shut. Todd was left waiting outside with the others and hearing muted conversation coming from the dean's office. When a buzzer went off at the secretary's desk, she indicated for Todd, Mrs. V, and Brenda to go inside. As Mrs. V passed Todd, she whispered, "We probably could have avoided this if you'd agreed to meet and talk it all out."

Todd didn't react. They entered the dean's office and were told where to sit.

Mr. Walsh said, "Todd Wyrum, it looks like you're in some trouble. New at our school, and already you're here in my office awaiting a ruling that I regret having to make." He opened a folder and continued, "I have here a list of infractions. Anything to say, Mr. Wyrum?"

Todd straightened up and confidently said, "Yes, I do. First, I did *not* start the fight at the barn dance in Edna. Kenny hit me first. Second, I did *not* cheat on my health class test. I'm a straight-A student, and my record will show that. And third, Sally Anderson was my date for the dance, and I got her home on time without any complaint from her regarding my conduct."

The dean said, "We'll see about that. First we'll hear from Kenny McKay."

Kenny spoke nervously. "Me and some other players were having a good time. The boxing team was there too. I asked to cut in on Sally and Todd, but he stopped me and used foul language. Cutting in is normal. He said 'Scram,' and pushed me. Sally wanted to dance with me, I could tell, but Todd stopped her. I tried again, and he hit me when I wasn't looking. Then we went at it. I was down, and he kicked me. Then the chaperones stopped it. Mrs. V can tell you."

Mrs. McKay broke in with a harsh voice. "He came home all bloody. I had to take him to French Hospital, where Tom was working that night. It was just awful, Ted—I mean, Mr. Walsh—just awful. These new kids in town are out of control. These boxers are vicious!"

"Tom—I mean, Dr. McKay—what were Kenny's injuries when he arrived at French Hospital?"

Dr. McKay said, "Well, let me start by saying that these boxing team members are nothing but trouble."

"Can you move on to the actual injuries Kenny sustained?" suggested the dean.

"He had a nosebleed, split lip, abrasions, black eye, and bruises," said the doctor. "My son had taken a beating."

Mr. Walsh then said, "Mrs. V, you witnessed the fight? Can you tell us what you saw? Briefly, please."

"I didn't see Kenny try to cut in on Todd and Sally, but I did see Todd hit Kenny," said Mrs. V. "The blow knocked him down, and there was a scuffle. Brenda saw it too, didn't you, dear?"

Brenda said, "Yeah, I saw it all. Todd pushed Kenny, then hit him and kicked him, too. He thinks he's so smart, but he's not. And he took Sally out in his truck and—"

"Okay, okay," interrupted the dean. "We're here about the fight and the cheating. If there is another matter, involving Sally Anderson, that inquiry will be handled by the dean of girls. Is that clear?"

Todd spoke up and insisted, "I didn't start anything, and Sally will confirm that."

"That's all, Todd," said Mr. Walsh. "Now we'll hear from Coach, who handles both teams. Coach?"

Todd watched as Coach, surely his best defender, began. "I did not see the scuffle at the dance, but I know that these dustups aren't unusual. I was told after the fact, by someone who would know, that the punch was spiked, and that's not unusual either. That factor alone may have significantly influenced these events. As for Todd's involvement, I can't say, because I didn't see it."

Mr. Walsh said, "Coach, we're more interested in—"

"Hold on!" interrupted Coach. "Dean Walsh, you and I have seen each other before on this matter. I'm not suggesting that Kenny started the fight, but the crowd, music, spiked punch, and pretty girls in the balance may have had an unintended influence. Isn't that just possible, Kenny?"

Kenny, looking very put upon, glanced back and forth between Coach and his folks. "Well, I just wanted to dance with Sally. That's all, and Todd wouldn't let me!"

At this point, Mrs. McKay's motherly instinct bubbled over. "Kenny had every right! He's a good boy and co-captain—and did nothing wrong."

"Can I continue?" Coach asked.

After a nod from Mr. Walsh, he said, "I'm not blaming anyone, Mrs. McKay. I'm trying to see things through the perspective of a barn dance, spiked punch, competition for the attention of some very pretty girls, and a situation that, for whatever reason, got out of hand. Mrs. V here had one of her very attractive charges involved. Sally Anderson was the focus of all this. Would it be possible to get her perspective?"

"I'm sorry to say she wasn't available to attend this meeting," lied Mrs. V, somewhat nervously. "But yes, I think she may be able to shed some light on this situation."

"It's Todd's fault," Brenda blurted out. "Why can't you take *my* word for it?"

Mr. Walsh held up his hands and said, "Calm down, Miss Barbano.

Your opinion is not being dismissed. Coach is just trying to put everything in perspective. Anything else, Coach?"

"Yes, there is! Todd is one of the best students I've had the privilege of coaching. Kenny, I don't doubt your version of what happened—or Miss Barbano's, either. But isn't it possible that this mix of young people and spiked punch just got out of hand, and it's really nobody's fault?"

Todd started to speak. But before he could get a word out, Mrs. V jumped to her feet, pointed at him, and yelled, "You've heard the evidence. It's him!"

Then it was the doctor's turn to say something, but first his wife jumped up and yelled, "Mrs. V's right! He did it—he hit Kenny for no reason! He should be expelled."

Mr. Walsh again raised his hands. "Please, let's all just relax. The fact is, Mrs. McKay, that I don't have the authority to do that. This is just a hearing. After this, I'll make a recommendation to Principal Jennings, who will decide Todd's fate."

Dr. McKay stood, and the room went silent. "Mr. Walsh, you now have the facts. We expect you to act on them as an accurate rendering of the truth. This Todd Wyrum struck Kenny without provocation, and he deserves to be disciplined. Nothing less will do. Is that clear?"

Mrs. V looked on in triumph, and Todd slumped in his seat. Dr. McKay was the voice of power and influence, and everyone, especially Mr. Walsh, knew it.

"I will act promptly on what's been presented here today," said the dean. "After that, it will be in Mr. Jennings's court. He's a fair and decisive leader, and I'm sure he'll take all the facts and opinions presented here into consideration. His decision will be final, and I'll support it. Now, does anybody else have any evidence to present?"

No one spoke up. As everyone else moved to the door, Todd stepped over to Mr. Walsh, extended his hand, and said, "Thank you for your consideration."

Mr. Walsh said, "Todd, I'll do my best in this matter. I hope you trust my judgment."

Todd gave a last nod at the dean and walked out. The main hall stretched out before him with all the display cases of the school's many trophies and banners. He'd hoped to add some trophies himself, but now he wondered if these would be his last days at San Luis Obispo High School.

Everyone was standing at the end of the sun-drenched hall, with Kenny to one side. As Todd passed by, Kenny shifted over to him and said, "Sally and I are hot for each other. I've had her in my car more than once." Before Todd could react in surprise, Kenny walked away.

After the McKays and Coach left, Mrs. V said to Todd, "All this could still be avoided if you'd help me find a compromise that will satisfy everyone. Brenda here could probably be persuaded to amend her version of events to more closely align with yours. We could meet—privately, of course—to arrange this. After all, there was much confusion amid the dancers."

Todd replied, in a sarcastic voice, "Privately, of course! Would that be in line with a compromise that would suit you? And, of course, I'm sure your trusty little helper Brenda would contribute to the fullest extent of her abilities. Wouldn't you, Brenda?"

Brenda's eyes widened, and her hands came up under her boobs. "Oh yeah, Todd … I'd help you for sure in any way I could. Right now if Mrs. V said to."

"Enough, Brenda, please," said Mrs. V. "My word, calm down, girl. We all know full well your willingness to help with your unique talents. I'm only suggesting possibilities."

Todd said, "I didn't start any of this. I just want to stay in school, and I don't need Brenda's help for that."

"No, I don't expect you do," agreed Mrs. V. "Brenda, let Todd and I set up a meeting to resolve this."

Brenda said, "But Mrs. V, I could help lots. You might need—"

"That's enough, girl. Now go!" insisted Mrs. V.

Todd got a parting comment from Brenda as she walked out. "Don't forget me now! I can be *very* helpful, you know?"

For a moment, Todd and Mrs. V stood eyeing each other. Then Todd turned and walked away, saying over his shoulder, "Let me know where and when, Mrs. V. I'll be ready."

In her best conspiratorial voice, Mrs. V said, "Oh yes, Todd. Oh yes, I will."

~

Todd knew the McKays wouldn't be easily assuaged, even if Mrs. V argued in his defense—assuming she would agree to come to his aid. He knew what a *private meeting* meant.

The next day, Brenda caught up with Todd outside the gym. She was dressed provocatively and tried to press her most prominent feature against him. She handed him a note, saying, "This is from Mrs. V, but I can help you too, if you'll let me. Mrs. V's just being mean to you, Todd. I'll tell the truth like it really happened if you'll give me a ride home. Will you, please? I want to help you. I can comfort you if you're feeling bad or ... Well, you know."

Todd said, "Yes, I know, and I'll think about it. Tell Mrs. V I'll get back to her."

Todd was facing two unpleasantries. First, was Kenny's statement about Sally true? And second, if he was to be expelled, he'd have to tell Miss Lady. Deciding to face the second thing first, he waited until just before dinner at Houson House to make the call. As he expected, the phone at the ranch rang a long time. But finally Mrs. Cruz answered "Rocking W. Who am I speaking with, please?"

Her voice was a happy sound to Todd's ear. "It's Todd, and a big hello to you, Mrs. Cruz!"

"Oh, Mr. Todd, I get Miss Lady!" After a few words in Spanish, off she ran.

Todd heard Mrs. Cruz and Miss Lady excitedly talking as they ran to the phone. Then Miss Lady's unmistakable voice came over the line. "Oh Todd, I'm so happy to hear your voice! How's school and the truck? Oh, I'll bet you're the toast of the school, with girls trying to meet you. Oops, forget I said that! Tell me all about your classes and boxing. You're not hurt, are you? Oh my!"

When Todd interrupted her questions, the intoxicating sound of his voice lifted her spirits. "Hold it, Miss Lady!" he exclaimed. "I'm fine! The boxing team is winning, and me too!"

A cascade of questions and answers ensued, concerning everything except what he had called about. Miss Lady described the ranch activities in detail. She was exercising Splash regularly, but not giving him any sugar cubes. They both laughed about that, because Todd was the only person who gave sugar cubes to Splash.

Finally Todd said, "So I'm okay, and I'm glad that you and the ranch are okay. But I'm calling with some not so good news." He explained the fight with Kenny and how it had started, leaving out his session with Sally in the truck.

Miss Lady asked, "If you were only defending yourself, then what's the matter?"

"Mrs. V and a cheerleader said I started it," Todd explained. "They're going to try to have me expelled."

Miss Lady's voice rose. "What? They can't do that! And who's this Mrs. V woman and this—this cheerleader girl?"

"There's more, Miss Lady. Mrs. V is my health class teacher too, and she says I cheated on a test. So that's another part of this ugly ball of wax. It's a lie, but she's got backup from Brenda!"

"Expel you? And who's this Brenda slut anyway?" Miss Lady was outraged.

Todd said, "Coach defended me, but he didn't see the scuffle, so he couldn't help me on that score. Also Kenny's folks are big wheels in town, and his dad is a doctor at French Hospital."

"Todd, why would she and—"

"It's complicated!" Todd exclaimed. "You actually may have seen both of them that night at my match. Mrs. V is the cheer coach, and Brenda, because she's got these huge—"

"Oh my, I *do* recall them. The dominatrix and the cow, and there was another girl."

Todd said, "The other girl is Sally, my date for the dance. She could've backed up my story, but they didn't ask her to attend the meeting with the dean. Why she wasn't invited, I don't know."

"They're trying to railroad you, Todd, but why? What did you do to warrant this treatment? Did the dean give you a way to redeem yourself and stay in school? Anything?" asked Miss Lady.

This was deep water that Todd didn't want to wade into. "No, but there's something else. After the fight, Sally and I—"

"Stop, Todd!" exclaimed Miss Lady. "I don't want to hear anything—nothing—about you and Sally. Is that clear? I was in high school once, you know? So we'll just completely drop that subject pronto, agreed?"

"Yeah, okay. But you know, Miss Lady, I just want you to ..."

Miss Lady said, "Stop, Todd. My darling, it's okay. I know that things, girls, will come along, and it's all right."

The phone in Todd's hand felt inadequate, and his voice broke as he said, "Miss Lady, I can't even ... Maybe I should deal with this on my own, and there is a way out. Perhaps it would be better."

"What way out? You didn't say there was a way out of this. What way?" Miss Lady asked.

Todd explained, "Mrs. V said we could work this out if I'd meet at her home one evening—"

"Holy hell, Todd! I know *exactly* what she wants to work out," said Miss Lady.

"But Miss Lady, I didn't mean for you to go and—"

"Oh yeah? I'll barrel rope that sleaze ball into a corral she'll never get out of," said Miss Lady. "We'll see about this, Todd. Oh yes, we will. When is this so-called expulsion meeting going to happen?"

Somewhat shocked, Todd said, "It's next Wednesday at four thirty in the principal's office."

In a very businesslike voice, Miss Lady asked, "And who's going to be there?"

"Well, I guess everyone who was at the last meeting."

"Is it possible to get this Sally girl to attend, Todd?"

"I'll give it a try, Miss Lady. I'm absolutely sure that she wants to help."

"Okay, Todd, I'll be at the meeting with backup. You just tell your side of the story, and I'll handle the rest. Oh, will I ever. That cunt isn't getting away with this. Oh, and one other thing. How did she get wind of what happened in the truck? I'm pretty sure you didn't tell her, so how did she know?"

This was yet another hurdle that Todd didn't especially want to leap over. "Well, Sally shared it with Brenda, as girls will do, and I guess Brenda told Mrs. V."

Miss Lady said, "And so Mrs. V heard all about you. Oh well, never mind. You're going to continue at that school, Todd, and no lowlife cheer coach is going to stop you. I was a cheerleader once upon a time, so I know what goes on. We'll show this gang of brats and their floozy leader, won't we?"

"Yes, Miss Lady!" Todd had never seen this side of Miss Lady before. His classy lover could be a tough rancher when the need arose, indeed, and this was such a time. It humbled him.

"You go to the meeting at four thirty. I'll arrive separately. And Todd, I want you to wear your JROTC uniform for the meeting. Questions?"

"No, Miss Lady, none. I'll be ready, and I sure do look forward to seeing you again."

Miss Lady was mad as a hornet and prepping for battle, but she and Todd both calmed down after a few minutes of small talk and ended the call.

Todd knew that regardless of the outcome, he and Miss Lady were going to put up a good fight.

~

The days before Todd's meeting with Principal Jennings were frustrating. Brenda and Sally were prancing through the halls, but he couldn't get Sally alone to talk with her. In fact, he began to think they were avoiding him. Part of him was mad at Sally for doing Kenny, but another part of him didn't believe Kenny's story. Todd had to know the truth—and also maybe, just maybe, persuade Brenda to change her story.

He decided to ambush Brenda after cheer practice. When the cheerleaders came out, Sally wasn't with them. They all filed past him with coy greetings, until Brenda stopped in front of him and said, "Hi, Todd! I hope you're not mad at me. I had to say those things, because Sally told me to. She doesn't like you anymore because ... well, because of what happened after the dance, you know? You hurt her, Todd. She's a little girl, and so she—"

"I didn't hurt her," insisted Todd. "Not at all. She was happy! Jeez, what a mess. I can't believe she'd—"

"She asked me to tell you that so you wouldn't try to see her," said Brenda. "Maybe I can help you, because I'm a big girl and put out. Then maybe I could change what I said at the meeting. You know how good I am at helping, don't you? Give me a ride home and I'll show you, okay?"

Todd said, "I can hardly believe she's so mad and that I hurt her. She seemed so happy."

Brenda said, "Oh, Todd, don't worry about that. I do what big girls do. Take me home and I'll show you, or let's get in your truck. Mrs. V and Sally don't have to know."

Todd said, very calmly, "Brenda, I'm in enough trouble already. Going all the way with you now could make it worse. I'll just go home now. Tell Sally that I'm really sorry I hurt her."

"What? I'm willing to let you fuck me, but you want to go home?

Every guy in school, in the whole town, wants me, and you won't ... I can't believe it. Look at me. Touch me! See for yourself." Brenda raised her bust, undoing two buttons in the process.

Todd said, "I do see. I know you're hot, Brenda, and that I could score. But right now I'm in a real jam, so I'm leaving, okay?" Todd turned and walked away.

Brenda stared after him, pleading softly, "I'm better than Sally. Really, I am!"

~

Todd and Sally spent the day before his hearing at Avila Beach. It was warm and romantic, but not so physical. The next day's hearing hung over them. He read her a couple of French poems, and she gave him a massage.

As the sun set, Todd figured it was time to bring up Kenny's remark. He couldn't figure a way to be subtle about it, so he just said, "After the first hearing, Kenny told me that he made love to you. Is that true?"

There was a moment of shock when the things Sally had done with Brenda weighed on her. She reached for an answer that would bypass that issue. "Oh no, I didn't. How could you believe him, especially after our time in your truck? Oh Todd, I couldn't—I wouldn't. He's lying. I didn't, I swear. How could you believe—"

"I didn't believe him," Todd said, "but I had to ask, in case you'd rather be with him than me, understand? I had to find out for sure, especially in light of what's going to come up tomorrow."

"No, Todd. I love you!" Sally exclaimed, and they threw their arms around each other.

~

Wednesday at four twenty, Todd appeared in uniform outside Principal Jennings's office. He was the first one there. It was a typical school waiting room with vinyl floor, plaster walls, acoustic ceiling, and plastic-covered chairs and couches. The late-afternoon sun slanted in through the windows, and photos of past school events hung on the off-white walls. Everything was clean and impersonal. Todd introduced himself to the receptionist, and then sat and waited.

The McKay family, including Kenny, arrived next. They sat and glared at Todd. Minutes later, Coach came in and sat next to Todd in silence.

Mrs. V, without Brenda, came in next and gave Todd a dirty look. Finally the receptionist ushered them all into the office, where Mr. Walsh and Principal Jennings awaited them. Todd was concerned because Miss Lady wasn't there yet.

They sat in a semicircle, backs to the door, in front of Principal Jennings's desk, where he greeted them. "Welcome! I hope these proceedings can promptly be concluded to everyone's satisfaction. First let's all introduce ourselves."

Coach started to speak, but then the receptionist came in and interrupted him. "Mr. Jennings, two more participants have arrived. You may want to talk with them before the meeting."

"Excuse me for just a moment," said Principal Jennings. He rose and went into the reception area. Five minutes later he reentered the office and said, "Excuse me, everyone, but we have two more participants. Todd's guardian and her attorney are here on his behalf. In spite of her absence from the prior meeting with Dean Walsh, she does have every right to be here."

Turning to the newcomers, Principal Jennings said, "Come in, Mrs. Wyrum. You too, Mr. Pearson." Miss Lady was in a knockout red dress, stockings, and heels, with her hair piled up and perfect makeup. Mr. Pearson looked every inch a lawyer. Mr. Jennings introduced everyone, and when he got to Mrs. V, she stood and nodded.

At that instant, Miss Lady shot out her arm, pointed at Mrs. V, and said, "It's you! I might have known a lowlife like you would start this inquisition of Todd. Get out now or I'll—"

Mrs. V broke in and exclaimed, "Barbara? Is that you, from Bakersfield High?"

Miss Lady stepped in front of Mrs. V, but Mr. Pearson quickly wedged himself between them and said, "Now ladies, take it easy. Remember, we're here to resolve an issue with Todd."

Miss Lady said, "Folks, this here is Valery Valverte, a real snake in the grass if ever there was one. She should leave—now!"

Having regained her composure, Mrs. V shot back, "This rodeo tramp shouldn't be here. She's probably more than Todd's guardian. I'm not leaving. Where's her authority? She probably made this whole guardian stuff up. She might even be helping Todd corrupt one of my girls."

"One of your girls?" said Miss Lady. "That's a laugh! They're a bunch of—"

Principal Jennings shouted, "Ladies, please, for Todd's sake, control yourselves!"

Everyone was stunned into silence. Mr. Pearson coaxed Miss Lady to a chair, and Mrs. V sat back in hers.

Principal Jennings took a deep breath and continued, "Mr. Walsh has recommended that Todd Wyrum be expelled, but now that Mrs. Wyrum and her counsel are involved, I think we should hear from them too. Mrs. Wyrum, please, what is your input?"

Before Miss Lady could speak, Mr. Pearson quickly stood and said, "Mrs. Wyrum has given me instructions on how to proceed. With your permission, may I, Mr. Jennings?"

"Go ahead, Mr. Pearson," said the principal. "The floor is yours."

Mr. Pearson said, "I've been in negotiations with, and on behalf of, this and other school districts around the state for many years. So we will deal with the district and school issues first." He opened a manila folder and looked over a few papers, then handed a few to Principal Jennings. "I have here copies of everything we'll be dealing with today. You need not peruse them now. I'm going to review them as we go along. Any questions before I start?"

The shock of the confrontation between the two women had dissipated somewhat, so Principal Jennings said, "Please proceed."

"I will try to put all this in the proper context," said Mr. Pearson, "so please bear with me. Number one: The dance in question was in the FFA's hall at Edna Farm Center and its grounds, including the parking lot. It was sponsored, organized, and paid for by the FFA.

"Number two: In spite of the attendees being from local schools, the school district has no jurisdiction there. The volunteer chaperones were not there in any official capacity. They had no authority to do anything other than observe, counsel, and/or participate in the activities.

"Number three: Had any discipline been needed, it was the FFA official on-site—and yes, there was one—who had the authority to, for example, call the police or fire department. He did not call for help, nor was any note made by the FFA of a 'scuffle' during the dance.

"Number four: Mention has been made of 'spiked punch' that may have played a part in all this, which may or may not be true. There is no hard evidence to prove that the liquid refreshment contained anything other than actual punch.

"Number five: This concerns the alleged injury to Kenny McKay. I checked with French Hospital and other regional health care facilities, but there is no record of a Kenny McKay being treated that night.

"Number six: The allegation that Kenny McKay was injured by a blow that Todd threw first is unrecorded and is therefore only hearsay.

"Number seven: Regarding the allegation that Todd cheated on his test—"

Mrs. McKay broke in and shouted, "Kenny was hurt and bloody, just as my husband said, so that's true! Tell this attorney person from somewhere out in the wilderness. Tell him!"

Miss Lady stood up and pointed her finger, first at Mrs. McKay and then at Mrs. V. "You're all lying and trying to railroad Todd for something that didn't happen!"

By this time, everyone was on their feet. Principal Jennings said forcefully, "Ladies, let's let Mr. Pearson finish. We'll get to all your comments after that, but for now, please sit down! Go ahead, Mr. Pearson."

Mr. Pearson continued, "Number seven: As far as the alleged cheating in health class by Todd, I ask now for Mrs. Valverte or Principal Jennings to produce any records, tests, or other documentation that supports the allegations. Mr. Jennings? Mrs. Valverte? Do you have anything?"

Principal Jennings looked at Mrs. V and asked, "Do you have anything to support your allegation?"

After a long pause, Mrs. V replied, "I saw him do it repeatedly. I didn't write it down at the time, but I did see him do it."

Mr. Jennings asked, "What about your grade book? Was he marked down for cheating? Better yet, did you bring your grade book so we can confirm your accusations?"

Miss Lady said harshly, "Oh yeah, teach. You got it, or don't you?"

Mrs. V, now looking rather uncomfortable, said, "No, I don't. I had no intention of getting Todd in trouble, but it just kept happening. You'll just have to take my word for it. I'm a teacher of long standing, and my word should count for something. Indeed, it should be quite enough."

Mr. Pearson nodded and continued, "I think we can now make our closing statement in Todd's defense. If it's all right with you, Principal Jennings, I'll do so. The school district had no authority to discipline Todd for something he is alleged to have done outside their jurisdiction. The chaperones have no authority to bring this up as a school matter, as they were there as volunteers. Neither the FFA official on-site nor law enforcement were called, notified, or otherwise involved, so no official record of any of this is on file for any reason, anywhere. No proof of spiked punch is offered anywhere. Kenny McKay's alleged injuries were neither recorded nor photographed. Therefore, it is a matter of hearsay at this point. Who threw the first punch can't be clearly determined. Dr. McKay, I don't doubt your word as far as treating Kenny's injuries, but how he got them is open to question. Am I clear, Doctor?"

Doctor McKay nodded his agreement. Miss Lady looked pleased. Mrs. V looked angry.

Mr. Pearson said, "No records, test papers, grade books, or other evidence have been produced to support Mrs. Valverte's allegation of Todd cheating. As his counsel, I maintain that—based on what's been presented—none of the allegations leveled against Todd Wyrum have been proved or otherwise substantiated in any way. We therefore move that all allegations of misconduct by Todd be dismissed. Thank you for the opportunity to represent Todd Wyrum here today. That's all we have. Again, thank you. Any questions?"

Mr. Pearson sat down, and a hush filled in the room.

After a moment, Principal Jennings said, "My goodness, I may need some counsel with my brother, Deacon Jennings, after today's proceedings."

Todd said, "I want to thank Mr. Jennings for his patience and fairness. I don't know what you'll decide, but I do feel that I've received fair treatment, so thank you."

"You're more than welcome, Todd," said Principal Jennings. "More than welcome, for sure."

As the McKay family slumped in their chairs, Principal Jennings said, "I'm pretty sure, based on what Mr. Pearson communicated to us today, that we should drop this whole thing and chalk it all up to a big mix-up. And I don't, by a long shot, cast aspersions on anyone for their stand on the issues. For darn sure, it has been a big mix-up."

Mrs. McKay had an angry look on her face, but the final word came down to the most influential person in the room, Dr. McKay, who echoed the principal: "A big mix-up. For sure, a really big mix-up."

Principal Jennings came out from behind his desk, and they shook hands all around. That is, everyone except Miss Lady and Mrs. V, who came face-to-face at the door.

Todd thought an actual physical fight might break out, so he gently stepped between them and said, "Ladies, it's over. Everyone can go home a winner."

Miss Lady whispered in Mrs. V's direction, "No, my darling Todd. We've won!"

But Mrs. V wasn't through. She replied, under her breath, "He's still in my school, in my class, and with my girls. Try that on, rodeo slut."

Before things could get any worse, Todd took Miss Lady's arm and guided her out of the room and down the hall. When they were alone, she said to Todd, "If she touches a single hair on your head, I'll kill her!" Todd was shocked, and his understanding of the predatory nature of women was definitely changing.

At the other end of the hall, the McKay family was filing past Brenda. When she blew the doctor a little puckered kiss and finger wave, he gave a slight start and quickly exited the building.

The confrontation, tension, uncertainty, anger, and relief of the day weighed heavily on Todd and Miss Lady as they drove away from the school. They had dinner at a fancy inn just off Highway 101. Afterward they lingered for a long time at their secluded table to talk about both fun and serious things.

Todd asked, "I don't want to pry, but what's with you and Mrs. V? Did you know her before?"

"It's okay, Todd. You're not prying. After what just happened, you have a right to know. I sorta expected to tell you this long-ago stuff someday, though I've dreaded it in a way." Miss Lady stopped there, looked away toward something lost, and took a deep breath. "Val—Mrs. V, that is—and I go way back to before the war. She was a cunning bitch even then. We were both cheerleaders. She was a year ahead of me. I was quite innocent at the time, and she … Well, she …"

Todd stopped her and said, "Miss Lady, you don't have to explain. Your word is good enough for me."

She turned to Todd, patted him on the leg, and gave him a peck on the cheek. "I love you, my Todd, and I always will. I also know what's ahead of you in high school. Those girls—oh yes, girls—will be part of your life, but that conniving, lying hag cannot be part of anything. If she messes with you, we'll get her. You've still got the note, don't you? Keep it in a safe place."

"I do," said Todd, "and I'll keep it!"

Miss Lady put two fingers to Todd's lips and said, "Hush, Todd, and let me fill in a few gaps for you. When I attended Bakersfield High School, it was a bigger deal than it is now. We did cheering at all the big events, enjoying lots of success and fun. But midseason during my junior year, Val—as she was known then—got hurt, and I replaced her as head cheerleader. She deeply resented that, and when she came back, she took revenge on me. She was a switch-hitter, meaning that she liked both boys and girls. The cheer coach was like that, too. They made me do things with boys ... and men ... for—oh God—for money. Our coach pimped us out, and now Mrs. V is doing the same with her cheer team. That's when I quit cheering and took up rodeo. Oh Todd, I was young and didn't—"

"You mean that Mrs. V—Val—was on both the girls' baseball team and the cheer squad? How'd she do both? I mean, she couldn't just ... just ... could she? Do you mean that she'd cheer, then bat? I've never heard of that!"

"Oh my God, Todd, it's just too complicated. She was bad news, really bad news. Let's just leave it at that, my young, darling, adorable Todd."

A look of bewilderment shaded Todd's face, and he said quietly, "I don't understand."

"Sex, Todd. Not baseball. She went both ways. She liked boys and girls, men and women, sometimes all at once. I was so young, Todd, and they made me do it. Mrs. L and Val ... How can I tell you this? I got pregnant, Todd. Then they kicked me out of school, and I had to go live in a special home. Todd, I had a miscarriage. Then later, after I recovered, I graduated from a different high school, got into rodeo, and met the Boss. Now can you see why we're bitter enemies? Oh Todd, it's a long story, and I hope you can understand—"

"It's okay, Miss Lady," Todd said gently. "I understand, and it's okay."

They finally left the restaurant and went to the truck, where they sat while he held her for a long time. She sobbed while Todd rocked her back and forth, humming French tunes to her. This went on for half an hour, and finally Todd said, "I understand, and I accept it all. You're my Miss Lady, and you always will be."

Exhaustion set in, but also understanding. At midevening, Miss Lady dropped Todd off at Houson House and drove back to the ranch.

CHAPTER 17

Fifty Cents

Ping, ping, ping was a sound Sally had heard before, but Grandma hadn't. She called out to Sally, who was on the patio with Todd, "What the dickens is that pinging sound?"

Sally came into the kitchen and replied, "That's Todd making a fifty-cent piece into something, but he won't tell me what. Do you want me to ask him to stop, Grandma?"

"Make a what into a what?" said Grandma. "It sounds strange to me. And yes, I do want it stopped. I'll bet you can hear it all over Mitchell Drive, and it's Sunday."

Sally went back to the porch where Todd was still beating on the edge of the coin with a tablespoon. She'd seen this odd behavior before, but just chalked it up to a guy thing. Her sisters also took an interest in this unusual activity, and Zoe chirped, "What're you doin' with that spoon thing, Todd?"

That was when Sally noticed that he was using one of Grandma's cherished silver soup spoons. "Oh Todd, you can't use that. Grandma will go through the roof. Please stop!"

Todd said, "I didn't know this was special or I wouldn't have used it. Put it back. I'll work on this later." He handed it to Sally and put the now partly modified disk in his pocket.

Sally put both her hands on her hips and asked, "What is it? What's it for?"

"You'll see! It's something I learned from a wrangler who'd been in the navy. Fun, too! Well, anyway, you'll be surprised when I'm done." Todd said this in a teasing way.

Sally said, "It looks pretty funny to me, Todd. Does it have anything to do with, you know, us?"

After Sally had returned the spoon, Grandma came out on the porch. Looking at Todd approvingly, she whispered in Sally's ear, "Remember what you said? 'I will marry that boy.'"

Sally and Todd had been going out for months, and their sex had become more intense and mature as time went by. They kept it secret from everyone, and the only person who knew was Brenda. Sally knew Brenda would keep her secret, because of the wild times they were having at Mrs. V's direction. She and Brenda and Mrs. V now had so many secrets that it was hard to keep track of them.

The biggest hush-hush thing was Mrs. V's policy—if you could call it that—of letting her girls have boyfriends if they "entertained" as she directed. The stipends she gave out helped too.

Sally felt guilty about this, but it was the only way she knew to stay on cheer team and have Todd too. Brenda kept this all to herself, but she really wouldn't care who found out.

The "entertaining" Mrs. V was directing them to do had gradually changed. By spring, sessions with the players had declined, and evenings with booster club members had increased. This mature clientele was more fun, and definitely more rewarding.

One morning after entertaining two members of the booster club, Sally and Brenda were called to Mrs. V's office. "Girls, you are much appreciated, so your stipends are being increased. Isn't that nice of me?" She handed each of them an envelope and said, "Open them, my sweet, beautiful, obedient girls."

In each envelope were two ten-dollar bills. Brenda said, "Oh, wow! This is really cool. We can use this, can't we, Sally? I guess they like us, right?"

Mrs. V said, "Oh yes, they do. Use it any way you want. Make sure your fans, as it were, stay satisfied, and there will be more. And girls, don't forget, this is completely secret, right?"

"Oh yes, Mrs. V, we will, for sure," Sally said enthusiastically. "It's really fun too, and a bigger stipend? Wow, I never expected this. Did you, Brenda?"

"No, I didn't. We can get new stuff at Flo's. Holy-moly, twenty dollars! That's lots more than we ever got before. Thanks, Mrs. V, thanks."

There was only one fly in the ointment. Based on the way Brenda looked and talked around Todd, Sally was certain that she wanted him for herself. It just wasn't in Brenda to stop flirting.

There was an old line shack out Highway 58, about halfway to the Carrizo, that had once been used as a temporary overnight stop for cowboys working the range. It was at the end of a narrow gravel track that wound into a small clearing. The shack was really old, tumbled down, and messy. But it had a window, the roof didn't leak, and the door worked. The nicest thing was the seclusion and the creek that ran year-round from a spring up the hill and ended near Santa Margarita. The water gurgled over big rocks into a small pool a few yards from the shack and was shaded by big live oak trees. It was just deep enough to get into and cool off. Todd had stashed a couple of old, army-surplus sleeping bags, water, a cooler, and a Coleman lantern there too. He intended the shack as their getaway place, because he had something special to share with Sally.

One Saturday, Todd asked Sally to go away with him for the day, without divulging where they were going. Sally assumed it was to Avila, because the bluff up behind the Union Oil storage tanks was one of their favorite spots. But when Todd turned north on Highway 101, she asked, "Where are we going? I thought we'd go to Avila, but I guess not. I know that you're familiar with this area."

Sally had on her cheer team jacket, but she took it off just after they passed through Santa Margarita. She was wearing one of Todd's old white cowboy shirts over a new blue-trimmed bra that was almost too small for her now-D breasts. She snuggled up to him and coyly said, "Want to make friends with my twins? They've been waiting all week. Boo-hoo for them, waiting and waiting for attention. They thought you liked them. Do you, wrangler guy? Tell them so!"

Todd said, "Sally, at least wait until I get to our surprise spot."

Sally got up on her knees facing him and said, "No, Todd, we come first. The twins won't wait!"

As he pulled the truck over to the side of the road, Todd's mind momentarily cast back to the cutie he'd met on Mitchell Drive only months earlier. She had sure grown up, for darn sure.

Just as their roadside romance was heating up, an elementary school bus chugged up the hill, pulled over, and parked near them. Out piled kids looking closely at the goings-on in the truck. Sally quickly put her bra and blouse back on while Todd laughed and said, "Guess we'd better vamoose if we don't want to be a learning experience for these kids. Oops, there's the camp director."

"Busybodies! Look at that old bat staring at us. I'll bet she wishes she was me, in here with you!" Sally said in an irritated voice as she tucked and primped in the mirror.

Todd had lipstick on his face, but he didn't care. He pulled the truck back onto the road, passing close to the kids and counselor, who gave them a dirty look. Sally stuck out her tongue at her.

Todd laughed uproariously and said, "Sally, my hot little nymph, calm down. We'll be there in five minutes. In any case, they wouldn't know us from Adam anyway."

Still irritated, Sally said, "I am *not* hot—I'm just really romantic. Oh phooey! How long until we get where we're going anyway?"

"Patience, my little nymph, patience!"

"What's a nymph?" Sally asked.

Todd explained, "Well, it's kind of like a fairy, an elf, a sprite, a pixie—cute like you!"

Sally gave him a satisfied smile. "I'm kind of like a pixie except for my twins, right?"

Todd laughed and gave her a squeeze. "Yep, except for the twins!"

Minutes later, he turned onto the gravel track, then stopped at the shack. "Ta-da! Our castle, Sally."

"Oh my, what's this?" asked Sally.

"It's for you, Sally! You'll see." Todd jumped out of the cab, came around to her side, opened the door, and helped her out. Kneeling in front of her, he took a little pouch out of his shirt pocket and tipped its contents into his hand. The reformed fifty-cent piece and a fine chain fell out. As Sally stared at him in wonder, he placed the coin—now a ring—in his left hand.

Then he looked up into Sally's bewildered eyes and said, "Sally, I love ... Will you go steady with me?" Threading the chain through the ring, he reached up and fastened it around her neck.

Sally's lower lip began to quiver, and she threw herself into his arms and said, "Oh Todd, yes. Oh yes, forever and always!"

He led her to the shack, picked her up, kicked the door open, and carried her inside. They pulled the clothes off each other and made love on the sleeping bags.

Awhile later, they took a couple of Cokes and went down to hang their feet in the pool. Todd said, "I guess you've made lots of new friend besides Bren—"

"What? Poo on her!" exclaimed Sally. "I've got Todd, and he's all mine. Oh yes, he is! Brenda doesn't get him, because he's mine. My boobs are better than hers—nanny nanny, boo boo!"

Todd said, "What's this BS about Brenda's boobs anyway? I'm not going to have—"

"No, no, no, you're sure not going to have anything to do with bad Brenda. Mine, mine, mine, all mine! I got the ring. Nothing for her, nothing. Just me, Sally!"

As Todd took in this theatrical performance of female possessiveness in all its power, he thought again, *What a transformation from last summer!* Little did he know.

They took a dip in the ice cold creek, and Todd explained about the coin, pinging, and how it transformed the fifty-cent piece into a ring. Then a hole was drilled in it of the proper size. It was an old navy trick by sailors who couldn't afford real rings.

When they drove off and stopped at the highway junction, Todd looked east and saw a different silhouette there on the far Carrizo horizon, under a tree amid some big boulders.

The shack became their refuge from prying eyes from then on.

Todd and Sally's new steady relationship went forward, but their old routines continued. For Todd, it was school, boxing, Sally, and that not-so-distant silhouette. For Sally, life was much more complicated thanks to Mrs. V, Brenda, and their secret adventures.

Sally's competitive friendship with Brenda was a winding road of secrets, lust, and temptation all swirled together. Their carnal pleasure adventures became almost an addiction. Along with the stipends, it drove them—clothing, makeup, hair, and cheer squad. They strutted the halls, overshadowing the other girls. But as Sally worked to integrate her steady relationship with Todd into this swirling mix, truth became the victim. It was a lie of omission, but still Sally anguished. She loved Todd, but it wasn't enough. Her obligations to Mrs. V and her love for Todd waged war inside her.

The power of her newfound beauty and voluptuous figure seduced others, but also herself. And then there was Brenda, whose super-aggressive sexual drive overpowered Sally's hesitation, pulling her deeper into lustful interests. And there was one more thing, for Sally loved that full feeling she had when copulating. When it took hold of her, she was helpless to stop, even if she wanted it, too. In some ways, it was more wonderful than her orgasms.

CHAPTER 18

Going Steady

Sally wore Todd's ring proudly every day at school, but she took it off to go home. While Grandma did like Todd, she didn't approve of going steady, so that was just another secret for Sally to hide. Brenda teased her, but Sally knew it was because Brenda was jealous. She wanted Todd, and she mentioned Todd's big hands often.

Sally and Todd went to their secret getaway spot whenever they could. Sally even decorated the shack with curtains and an old rug, plus pillows for the sleeping bags. They stocked it with soft drinks and canned goods, and Todd brought up a table and small camp stove. The day they put up the curtains, put down the rug, and cooked their first meal of hot dogs and potato salad was thrilling. For Todd, the shack meant rest and relaxation from his intense studies, JROTC, and boxing. For Sally, the goal was to forget the overlapping, competing parts of her life. At the shack, life was simply about Todd.

In spite of all that might have interfered, Todd took over Sally's heart. No one could love her like he did, and now she knew the difference. Sometimes just petting was enough, but at other times Todd introduced her to things she'd only heard of—and other things she'd never even imagined. When he filled her, there was only that feeling for which her entire world stopped.

Other aspects of Sally's life were also changing. She learned a lot from adventurous Brenda, who was in control when they did Mrs. V's bidding. Sally and Brenda were both in control at school, where they used their seductive beauty to rule the corridors and force boys, girls, and even teachers to look at them. At school, the two girls felt omnipotent in a sensual way.

As Grandma's suspicions grew, Sally was able to cover with lies and Brenda's help, though Brenda demanded payment in return.

Only Mrs. V's ironclad control and threats of wrathful punishment interfered with their world. Sally and Brenda disobeyed only when they thought they could get away with it. Mrs. V's punishment usually involved taking something important away from them. For instance, Brenda had to miss two cheer games for breaking Mrs. V's rules with an unauthorized boy.

Sally's turn came a few days later. Mrs. V ushered her into the office, shut the door, and said, "Now, Miss Sassy Mouth, you've been bad, haven't you? You were doing it someplace with that Todd boy, weren't you?"

"Why does it matter?" Sally asked. "I was with Todd, my boyfriend, and you said we could do that. Don't you remember?"

Mrs. V said, "Sassy, sassy mouth. That's you lately, Sally. Tell me right now!"

Sally's mind raced to find any kind of answer, but finally the strain of inventing a story, excuse, or outright lie wore her down. "I was with Todd—that's all!"

"Drivel! That's a lie," replied Mrs. V. "Tell me, or else."

"Honest, Mrs. V. Really!"

Mrs. V had worked herself into a complete rage, and spittle flew from her mouth as she yelled at Sally. "Do you think me a fool? Do you think I set you up with all these opportunities and stipends for the fun of it?"

Sally said, "Oh, Mrs. V, I'm really—"

"Get out! You're off first team for two weeks," said Mrs. V.

Sally quickly walked out, realizing that Brenda must've tattled because she wanted Todd for herself. A few minutes later, she found Brenda in the cafeteria and said, "You told Mrs. V about Todd and me, didn't you?"

Brenda's look turned defensive. "What could I tell her? I didn't know anything about your so-called secret place."

"Yes, you did, tattletale! I know you want Todd. You're bad, Brenda, just like people say, and we're not friends anymore. Your big, floppy tits and fat ass aren't everything. That's why people point at you. I'm better, and I've got more feelings too. Todd said so—so there!"

"No, they aren't," insisted Brenda. "Bigger is better, and mine are the biggest. Ask anybody!"

Sally realized she'd hit a sore spot. "What about your mom, huh? You said hers are bigger than yours."

Brenda's gypsy eyes grew dark and avenging. "You lie! She's a tramp, and I'm ... Well, I can have Todd anytime I want. I just let you have him because I'm nice. I'll bet he's not big like you said either, and I know about your feelings because of what we did together! You want them and me, don't you? Like in the locker room? Yeah, like that!"

Sally sucked in a gasp, because she'd tried hard not to dwell on, dream about, or crave that feeling. And in truth, it was a feeling that Brenda had given her. Todd versus Brenda was the real war within Sally, which she struggled to keep submerged. Now Brenda was making her face it—and yes, Sally craved them both.

The two girls glared at each other, but deep down they knew that they couldn't feud for long. They had too much in common. Minutes passed, and finally Brenda asked, "You want to come over when my mom's at work tomorrow?" After a long poignant silence, Sally lowered her eyes and nodded.

~

The successful boxing team was popular with fans and the booster club. A smaller pep band went with the cheer team to those matches. All the girls, including Brenda, were always preening for Todd. One day Sally would be with Todd, and the next day she and Brenda would sneak away for an intimate interlude. The Todd versus Brenda situation whipsawed Sally back and forth between feelings of jealousy and desire. These compulsions frustrated her, but she couldn't stop. Todd came first in her heart, but she couldn't put him first in the confusion and cravings of her life.

Sally and Brenda still had duties to perform for Mrs. V. Since football and basketball seasons were over, the focus was on the booster club. More secrets to keep!

In spite of their differences, Sally and Brenda became closer. Brenda led Sally into more sensual behavior. At first Sally went reluctantly, but as their success and fun grew, she became hooked on adulation and carnal pleasures. The stipends from Mrs. V grew too, which was nice, but the money was secondary.

Keeping all these secrets was a huge job. Sally lied every day to Grandma, Todd, Brenda, and her teachers. When she couldn't explain away something, she just made up another story. When school let out for the summer, their "appointments," as Mrs. V called them, went on. Sally had more spare time, but Todd was in summer school, so she spent even more time with Brenda.

Todd was an A student taking extra classes at Cal Poly, studying subjects that Sally and Brenda found boring. He planned to be a doctor, which was, for them, as far afield as Mars.

Sally and Brenda became ever closer, though they were still quite competitive. When other girls were catty toward them, they were even snottier back.

One day at Brenda's house, her mom's figure was mentioned for the umpteenth time. Sally finally challenged Brenda's story, saying, "I think you're exaggerating. They can't be that big!"

"Okay, smarty-pants, you'll see," replied Brenda. "The market delivers on Thursdays, so she'll be entertaining. We can sneak behind the house and watch through the window, okay? You'll believe me then."

Sally said, "Okay, but she'll be really mad if she catches us, you know?"

"Oh pooh, she won't care. She's caught me sneaking a peek a couple of times, and she just says that she's a real woman and I'm just a child. She's catty to me now 'cause I've developed."

On Thursday afternoon, the two spies went to Brenda's, hid behind the stone wall under the window, and knelt on some pillows. Brenda's mom was home, and the coast was clear. They crouched and waited. Minutes later, they heard men's voices, truck doors slam, and the doorbell ring. They scooted together, held hands, and exchanged mischievous glances.

Through a crack in the curtains, Sally could see a big room with out-of-date, overstuffed furniture and tan walls and ceiling. In the room was a fireplace, old floor rugs, and knickknacks on shelves and tables.

When Brenda's mom came out from the kitchen, Sally saw, for the first time, a woman in her midthirties of medium height with stacked dyed black hair and heavy makeup. She wore a short pink dressing gown, heels to match, and nothing underneath. Her gigantic bust ballooned out. She was an older, bigger Brenda with the same gypsy eyes, but aged skin and not as pretty.

Sally drew in a breath and whispered, "You're right, but she's a cow!" Wide-eyed, she and Brenda snuggled closer and giggled softly.

"Hi, Dick," said Brenda's mom. "I've been waiting for you and your helper. Come on in."

A big, heavily muscled man walked in, followed by a younger man with unruly blond hair. Both men had their arms full of groceries. Dick, the older guy, said, "We've got lots of stuff for you, Gwyn. Want them in the kitchen?"

Sally turned and whispered to Brenda, "Gwyn?"

"Yeah, Gwyn. Dumb name, huh? Stands for Gwendolyn," Brenda replied.

The groceries were put in the kitchen than Gwyn led the big men by the hand into the bedroom and shut the door. She called back over her shoulder. "Don't worry, blondie. You'll get yours later. There's more than enough of me to go around."

"You've seen this before?" Sally asked.

"Oh yeah," said Brenda, "but not when I had someone cute to share it with." She gave Sally a little rosebud kiss, and they snuggled even closer.

The scene that now transpired was riveting to Brenda but almost beyond belief to Sally.

Gwyn did them both in half an hour—under, on top, from behind, and then orally. Finally the men lay exhausted, but Gwyn looked very pleased. She got them cold beers from the kitchen. When she returned, the blond guy said, "You're the real deal, Gwyn. A real woman!"

She handed each man a beer and said, "Damn right!"

They relaxed for a while, and then Dick said, "Well, I guess it's time to hit the road."

"*Come* back anytime," said Gwyn, and they got in their truck and drove away.

Under the window, Brenda gave Sally a shy smile and said, "See what she does?"

Sally replied, "Holy cow!" Both girls were breathing hard.

"Yeah, there's more," said Brenda. "I mean now, if we want ..." She smiled and kissed Sally again.

Sally replied, "Well, I don't know. Maybe it's too, uh ..." Then Sally slid down and lay back on the pillows. When Brenda leaned over to kiss her, she opened her mouth. Brenda's lips were so soft, but then she pulled back and asked, "More?"

Sally nodded and raised her open mouth. Brenda's big brown eyes slowly came closer as her mouth opened wider. The kiss was firmer this time, and her tongue slid across Sally's parted lips slowly, then pulled back again. "More?"

Sally opened her mouth wide, reached up behind Brenda's pile of raven black hair, and pulled Brenda's open lips to hers. "Yes, more!"

The kiss was deep, Brenda's tongue seeking the recesses of Sally's throat, wet and waiting. Arms entwined, they writhed to find every wanting part of each other's desire. They swooned and were drawn deeper and deeper into passion, undressing each other as they went. Hands unsnapped bras, panties were pulled away, fingers probed, and wet kisses smeared lipstick as both girls gasped for breath between ever more impassioned caresses.

Sally's mouth found the heaping mound of Brenda's crowns and the firm cherries waiting to be kissed, sucked, and gently bitten. She swooned even more as Brenda did the same to her.

The further they went, the more Sally's contradicting desires of love and obsession bubbled out. "Oh Brenda, I didn't know. If I'd ... Oh my, do I want more?"

"Oh yes, my dear, you do," insisted Brenda. "Take my hand." Sally took her hand, her own fingers trembling. She knew!

Brenda's mouth moved to Sally's earlobe, and she whispered, "Put me there, in your soft place."

Sally guided Brenda's red-tipped fingers down, caressing her tummy, then farther until she touched it softly. Her body spasmed as Brenda's fingers probed gently against her clit. As each touch drew Sally closer to an eruption, Brenda said, "Help me, Sally, please!"

Sally found it, and Brenda forced Sally's fingers up and deep inside. Then with a yell, she arched up and back, twisting in joy as she was convulsed by her orgasm. Without the slightest bit of control, Sally's body responded as she convulsed in rhythm with Brenda. Twisting and gyrating, their legs parted and they rubbed their wetness against each other. Together at last, again they convulsed, bathing each other in a flow of passion.

Sally lay back, spent in the most wonderful way, as Brenda got up on her knees. "Oh Brenda, I didn't know what ... If I ... Oh jeez, we ... Oh, Brenda!"

Brenda stood up and said, "I knew, and now we both know. You're so soft and sweet, Sally. We—yes, we!" They straightened themselves and walked around to the front yard—close, holding hands, and whispering excitedly to each other.

As they rounded the porch, a voice exclaimed, "What naughty little girls you are!"

Sally jumped, and they clutched at each other. Standing on the porch, only a few steps away, was Brenda's mom. She'd changed into another outfit. Her legs were bare, and she wore pink-and-white open-toed low-heeled slippers with fake flowers on the front. Her dyed jet-black haystack of disheveled hair fell down over her smeared makeup, with a side helping of large hoop earrings. One upturned hand held a cigarette holder, and her arms were crossed underneath her drooping chest. She gave them a dismissive smirk.

Brenda said, "You, uh, scared us, Mom. We were, were …"

Gwyn would have none of it. "I know what you sneaky trollops were up to. Get enough? See what a real woman can do? What silly things you are. I saw what you did under the window, too. Naughty, naughty! By the way, say hi to Mrs. V for me. That conniving tramp is still up to her old tricks, pimping out you cheer girls just like in the good old days."

At this, Brenda and Sally looked at each other in shock.

Gwyn continued, "Yeah, yeah. I know, from way back, what Madam V's game is."

~

All summer, Sally and Todd didn't have much opportunity to get away. In August, Sally received an invitation to a cheer squad camp, so she invented another story so that she and Todd could sneak away.

"On Friday, Todd, how about we go to the Surf Motel at Avila Beach?" she asked.

Todd said, "Sounds like a plan—" Suddenly he remembered his last visit there with Miss Lady, and his face clouded over. The memory was vivid, with the room, rain, bar, and now the guilt.

Seeing him hesitate, Sally asked, "What is it? You don't want to—"

"We've already done that," Todd said abruptly. "How about a more romantic place? Maybe that place up the coast we heard about in Cambria?"

"Okay, but I thought you liked—"

"Then it's on!" Todd said, in a final sort of way.

Sally just shrugged.

~

Sally packed an overnight bag to support the web of lies that she now told so regularly to Grandma, and she even bribed Gail to confirm her story to Grandma. Then she packed a supper of sandwiches, potato salad, and dessert for Todd and her. They left on Friday afternoon, and the drive up the coast, which took about an hour, was filled with talk and happy laughter.

Todd pulled up at the Pines Motor Lodge, an old but well-kept-up place north of Cambria, on the coast right behind the beach. Two rows of rustic rooms stretched above the dunes about a hundred yards from the water, and the sound of the surf was constant. A stand of large pine trees screened it from the main road. It was nothing fancy, with parking in front of each room and a small office down at the south end.

While Todd checked them in, Sally waited in the truck. The reception office was small and spartan with a Formica countertop, a couple of plastic-covered chairs, a table with a stack of out-of-date magazines, and two vending machines. A middle-aged man greeted Todd and said, "I think I've seen you before, but I can't place it. Do you know me? How old are you, kid, and who've you got with you?"

His questions brought Todd up short, and he lied forcefully. "I'm nineteen. Why do you ask? My money's as good as anyone's, or I could go someplace else. Are we okay with that?"

The proprietor backed off and said, "Nope, no problem. Just curious. Like I said, you look familiar, that's all. You should have some great beachcombing. Have a nice stay!"

Todd left without replying, got in the truck, and drove down to park in front of room 6. The room itself was furnished in the same style as the office, with the addition of a big bed. A wide set of French doors opened onto a covered patio facing the beach, and the panorama of the ocean was beautiful.

Opening the doors wide, Todd hugged Sally and said, "Wonderful, don't you think? Our very own beachfront hotel!"

Sally hugged him back and said in her most romantic voice, "Oh yes, it's wonderful, my love!"

Todd shuddered slightly as her words launched a slideshow of memories, but he just hugged Sally tighter and said, "Let's eat. I'm starving! How about it? You and me out here on our very own patio?"

"I'll get the food," said Sally. "Oh, I didn't bring any cold drinks, but I saw a Coke machine outside the office. It's one of those old round ones where you pull the bottle out of the ice water. I'll run over and get a few while you set up the patio, okay?"

"I'll have it all set when you get back. Here, you'll need change." He handed Sally a dollar bill.

She hustled to the office, burst in the door, and went up to the counter. When the owner came out and saw Sally standing there, he said, "Can I help you, miss?"

Sally said cheerfully, "I need some change for the ... Mr. Hesselgren? Uh, I—"

"Why, Sally, it's you! What a pleasant surprise. Did Mrs. V send you?"

"No, Mrs. V didn't send me. No, Mr. Hesselgren, I'm here with my boyfriend, Todd."

"Let me venture a guess. You're with that boy from the truck, right? What's it been, a month since we had our booster club date? Wasn't that fun? You're so cute, Sally—the cutest, tightest stacked girl of the lot—and it was a real pleasure to be with you. If you ever need my help, just call. I'm a big booster club donor, and Mrs. V assured me that—"

"No, Mr. Hesselgren, I'm ... I'm with my boyfriend," Sally repeated, backing away from the counter.

"Oh yes, I'll just bet he's your boyfriend. One of many, I'm sure. You should've brought your buxom friend with you. We could've had a really big party."

Sally held out the dollar bill and said, "No, I just need change for the Coke machine, please. That's the only reason I'm here. I'm gonna leave now, Mr. Hesselgren."

"No? What do you mean, *no*? We could have a quickie right here and now. This Todd guy doesn't have to know a thing. It'll be over in a minute!"

"Oh please, Mr. Hesselgren, not now. I'm with Todd, and he loves me. I'll come back later, and I'll bring Brenda. I'll do anything—anything you want, but not now!"

Mr. Hesselgren laughed and said, "Sally, I'm just kidding. Really, just joking."

At that moment, Todd walked in and sensed trouble. "What's going on, Sally? I found some change."

Before Sally could say another word, Mr. Hesselgren took the dollar bill and slammed four quarters on the counter. "There you go, girl. Change aplenty. If you need more, I'll get it."

"Aren't you from the booster club?" Todd asked in a confused voice. His eyes moved back and forth between Sally, who looked scared, and the guy, who had an odd expression on his face.

"Hesselgren—Bob Hesselgren! I recognize you. You're a boxer. Nice girl you've got here. We met through Mrs. V's cheer team, didn't we, Miss Anderson? Or may I call you Sally?"

Sally grabbed Todd's hand and bolted for the door. Looking back over her shoulder, she said, "Thanks for the change. Bye!"

Having regained his composure, and with a sly smirk on his face, Mr. Hesselgren said, "Okay, Sally, see you again sometime. You too, Todd."

Standing at the Coke machine, Todd said, "What the hell was that all about? I got the impression he knows you. Does he? I mean, do you ... No, I don't know what I mean. But what's up with all that, Sally?"

In an obviously defensive tone, Sally said, "He was introduced to all the cheer team girls after a game, you know? Ask Brenda. She'll tell you."

"Brenda? No kidding, *that* Brenda? The girl you don't trust and told me to be careful around? Gigantic tits Brenda? There can't be another one. What's going on here, Sally? I don't need her to explain. What do you have to say?"

Sally said, "Can we please just get the Cokes and go back to our room, Todd? I'll explain later."

Todd didn't budge. "No, Sally. That was a confrontation in there. What's up?"

Trapped! Sally hesitated, trying to think of an acceptable lie, and she landed on a strategy she'd seen Brenda use time and again: attack your accuser. Todd wasn't actually accusing Sally of anything, but her behavior, longings, and guilt took her to a crossroad where no girl should be, and she lashed out. "Are you accusing me of something, Todd? Because if you are, I'm not your girl anymore, and you can have your stupid ring back."

She expected Todd to drop the subject, but he didn't move or object. He just asked, "What's Mr. Hesselgren to you, Sally?"

Sally knew immediately she'd made a mistake. Todd wasn't just any boy, and she should have known that. Practically in hysterics, she said, "He's my friend, stupid! I know him from cheer team—performing at booster club and stuff!"

"Booster club with Brenda? You do that with her? Yeah, I've heard rumors about that."

"Up yours, Todd! I'm a good girl. Here's your dumb ring! I don't need it or you, if that's what you think. Brenda's right. You're not so high and mighty." Sally tore the chain from around her neck and threw it down, then went back in the office.

She fully expected him to follow her inside and apologize, but the door didn't open. Dismayed and hardly believing what she'd done, she saw him walk by the window toward the room. She wanted desperately to go after him and explain, apologize, throw herself on his mercy—but her guilt and false pride wouldn't let her.

Sally was momentarily transfixed. Then from behind her came the voice of Mr. Hesselgren: "I heard that. If you need help, just ask. A place to stay? A ride? What can I do?"

Sally heard a vehicle, then saw Todd's truck pass on the way to the highway. She bolted through the door as the truck sprayed gravel along the driveway. She raised her hand toward his disappearing image, but it was too late. She looked down at the broken chain and ring at her feet, picked it up, and whimpered, "He's gone. Oh Todd, I didn't mean it."

From the doorway behind her, a voice said enticingly, "Come on in, Sally. He's just a kid. You and I can work something out. I've got a county supervisors' meeting tonight. You can ride into town with me, and I'll drop you at home on the way. How about it?"

"Well, I guess," Sally said, still looking off down the road forlornly.

CHAPTER 19

Obsession

Sally could barely remember her ride home with Mr. Hesselgren. Todd was gone, and her feelings for him were mixed up with Brenda, Mrs. V, cheer team, and the lies. And Mrs. V had more adventures for her too. She replayed the breakup in a loop of downward-spiraling remorse and crying.

When asked about Todd, she lied and said, "I don't know" or "He's nothing to me." She was emotionally wrung out. Brenda was her only outlet, and they delved deeper into each other. She gave up any last resistance to Mrs. V's will, and more adventures for her and Brenda followed.

Sally's will evaporated. Instead of picking and choosing which assignments to take, they took whatever Mrs. V gave them. Booster club invitations figured prominently. The stipends grew, and Sally's concerns about her reputation were forgotten. She and Brenda got ever more revealing lingerie at Flo's shop and wore it as seductively as they could get away with.

Brenda talked down Todd every chance she got. She and Sally criticized his truck, boxing, and all things connected with him, but it was all pretend. At night Sally dreamed of him. During the day she waited for him to appear around every corner, in every room, and on every street. She got snappy with cheer squad and her family, sharing only with Brenda. The two of them grew sneakier and wilder.

Days, weeks, and months came and went. Sally dove ever deeper into wild behavior, hoping to forget Todd, but she only obsessed over him more. She followed Brenda's lead, trying to replace love with lust, but love

---

persisted. She dated other boys, but they weren't even close to Todd. The search led to a dead-end street. She felt nothing—not even bad, just empty.

Avoiding Todd was easy in the labyrinth of the school, but still she looked for him. She'd make up excuses, even to herself, when he'd appear as if by accident, but she wasn't fooling herself or Brenda.

Sally and Brenda lured other girls' boyfriends into their web. The boys fell easily, but the other girls fought back. Insults, exclusion, and bullying were among their weapons, but there was more.

The cheer team had begun to do aerials, which were becoming popular in colleges. As the smallest girl on the team, Sally was the easiest to throw around. It also made her the focus of all the fans watching, so she made sure to make her bust bounce and her legs fly. During one game, Sally was hoisted by four girls. She stood on their grouped hands, then dropped into their arms. They were supposed to catch her, but they didn't—and she hit the turf!

Brenda rushed to her, whereas most of the other girls looked down at her with fake concern. The crowd roared in shock, and Mrs. V rushed over to attend to her. "Oh my, this is awful! Are you hurt, Sally dear? Don't move until we make sure you're okay." When Sally began to cry, Mrs. V exclaimed, "Oh, you careless girls. Get Dr. McKay—and hurry!"

Brenda pushed back the other girls and knelt next to Sally. As she held Sally, she scowled up at the three offending girls and said, "You sluts did this on purpose, and we know why, too. We got *you know what*—and you don't!"

The other cheerleaders faked concerned expressions, and one said, "You're the slut, Brenda. Oh Sally, we're so sorry we dropped you. It was an accident! You understand, don't you?"

Sally was still crying as Dr. McKay knelt at her side. He and Brenda exchanged intimate glances, and then he said softly, "Hello, Sally. I'm Dr. McKay. Is it okay if I examine you?"

Sally choked back her tears and said, "I remember you from booster club. It's my back!"

He checked Sally out and then put his instruments back in his bag. "Can you stand and walk?" he asked.

Dr. McKay, Mrs. V, and Brenda helped Sally up. The crowd gave her a hand, and she waved back at them. The doctor said, "Sally, you've twisted your back, but aside from that, you're okay. Come by the hospital to be checked in a few days. For now, bed rest is the best thing for you, okay?"

Sally nodded and limped off the field. Mrs. V drove her home, and Brenda rode along. Mrs. V said, "That was a nasty thing they did, but you know why, don't you? The school is a gossip mill, and it has caught up with you and their boyfriends."

Brenda replied sarcastically, "But you told us to, didn't you? Well, didn't you?"

"That's enough, young lady," said Mrs. V. "Now Sally, make sure you're nice—really nice—to Dr. McKay when he examines you, understand? And if you're too hurt, which I doubt, then get the boob queen here to help. Now go on inside and get some rest. I'll check in on you now and then, and Brenda will take care of your duties while you recover, okay?"

Brenda walked Sally to the door and said, "Don't worry, I'll take care of the *little* doctor." They both laughed, but Dr. McKay was a prominent member of the booster club.

Brenda asked, "What about Todd? Should he know? I could tell him, if you want."

Sally said, "No! I know what kind of help you want to give, Brenda. It's for Todd, not me." It was the perfect excuse, but Sally's stubborn pride won out and Brenda just shrugged.

Sally's back hurt for two weeks. She filled the time with boring games with her sisters, supermarket tabloids, and dreaming of Todd. These fantasies turned her tummy into hot Jell-O. Dr. McKay visited, but only his eyes trespassed. Brenda came by and dropped off Sally's homework.

Brian, from next door, tried to tempt Sally several times, but she just brushed him off. Then he showed up one day when Grandma and Sally's sisters were out, and Sally's steamy dreams overcame her hesitation. Wearing only a T-shirt and shorts, she pushed her bust out and said, "Hi, Brian! Come in. They've been waiting for you." She was lying, but not completely.

Anxiously Brian replied, "Uh, well, you look great, Sally. You're so beautiful."

Sally knew she could have asked him anything, but he'd only want one thing—her boobs. They went to her room, and he immediately began to feel her up with grabby hands. They fell on the bed, and within a few minutes Sally's top was off and they were making out madly.

Then the bedroom door swung open, and Grandma stood there shouting, "Oh God Almighty, what's this? Sally, Brian, what's this outrage?

Stop this instant!" With fists placed squarely on her hips, she put the evil eye on them.

Brian scrambled to his feet and said, "Mrs. Anderson, I'm so sorry!"

With a guilty expression, Sally just looked at Grandma. She'd been caught, but part of her didn't care. Then she got up and stood in the corner, arms across her bare breasts.

Without averting her eyes from Sally, Grandma said, "Take your things and leave, Brian. I'll be speaking to your mother about this later."

Brian brushed past Grandma in the doorway, then quickly glanced back at Sally as he started down the hall.

For a long minute, Grandma and Sally stood their ground. Then Grandma picked up Sally's bra from the bed, looked at the label, and said, "Lower your arms, Sally."

Sally didn't move.

Grandma's tone grew harsher. "You heard me!"

Sally turned and faced the wall, then lowered her arms.

"DD? Flo's? Aren't you ashamed, Sally? Turn around!" insisted Grandma.

Sally raised her chin a fraction but didn't turn around.

"Well, Sally?"

Finally Sally turned around, her eyes downcast.

"Oh, Sally, I'm so glad your mother isn't ... Was this the first time? Answer truthfully."

Sally shook her head, still not looking up.

Grandma exclaimed, "Jesus wept! It's that Brenda girl. It's her influence, isn't it?"

Sally replied sheepishly, "Brenda's my friend, Grandma."

"I knew it," said Grandma. "The minute I saw her with you, I knew it. She's just like her mother. Well, Sally Anderson, we'll see about this. And those cheer girls! I'll make an appointment with Deacon Jennings. You're growing up too fast. He'll help me put some moral backbone back in you."

Sally looked down to cover her tiny smile. She knew what Deacon Jennings wanted.

Grandma said, "I expect it was with Todd too, who I mistakenly thought was so nice. Was it?"

Sally just shook her head.

"From now on, Sally, no contact with that Brenda. Is that clear? As far as cheering goes, the deacon will have something to say about that.

Now get dressed and go sit in the dining room until I get back. I've got the unpleasant job of discussing this with Brian's mother. This is awkward. What must she think of you, of me, of us? God forbid!"

Sally reached for her bra, but Grandma grabbed it and said, "Oh no, you don't, young lady. This is going in the garbage. Do you have any other unseemly things?"

Sally shook her head. More lies!

"Okay, I'll be back from Brian's house shortly," Grandma said. "I can hardly believe that you would disgrace this house like this. I'm so ashamed, Sally Anderson. What would your poor sainted mother think? She'll be turning over in her grave."

When Grandma left to go next door, Sally sat down in the corner and cried. She wasn't afraid of Deacon Jennings, however, because she and Brenda knew how to fix that.

Returning from next door, Grandma found Sally sitting in the dining room with a blank look on her face. "All right, Sally, this wasn't your first time, was it?"

Sally sat up straight, cast her eyes down, and shook her head.

Grandma asked, "Have you been with other boys?"

After a long hesitation, Sally nodded.

"Oh my word, I just can't reason why ... Was it because that nice boy Todd and you are no longer friends? This is a good home—and a Christian one! How could you go so wrong?"

Refusing to look up, Sally just shrugged.

"You've been a very bad girl, Sally. Sex at your age—disgraceful! Sex is supposed to be reserved for the sanctity of marriage, and you know that. You've behaved like a tramp, and your reputation ... Well, you'll be punished, as you should be, and you must never do these things again."

"I'm not a tramp! I'm not! I'm a good girl!" Sally blurted out, and yet she was confused about the difference between a good girl and a nice girl. Which one was it?

"Oh my," said Grandma. "You do agree that you need to be punished, don't you?"

Sallie looked up pleadingly at Grandma, then nodded vigorously. Yet she knew full well that she'd go on with this behavior.

"Go to your room and read the appropriate passages. You know the ones. Meanwhile I'll contact Deacon Jennings. Now go!" Grandma reached over to the sideboard, picked up the family Bible, and handed it to Sally. Then she put her head in her hands.

Within a few days, after a talk with Deacon Jennings, Sally was allowed to continue with cheering. Fooling Grandma about Brenda was easy, and the two girls went on with their adventures almost as before. Sally also got new lingerie, but she hid it more carefully than before.

Brian's mother never spoke to Sally, but her eyes flashed hostility. Brian disappeared from Sally's life, and he and Sally were never again intimate—or even just friends.

~

In ways Sally could not have imagined, the incident with Brian and Grandma's scolding liberated her. Now Grandma knew. So what? Sally's anguished longing for Todd didn't stop, but it did change. No one could make her feel like Todd did, and the fact that she couldn't lure him in made him even more desirable. She and Brenda kept putting him down, but they also wanted him. And even though Sally knew that Brenda wanted him, their competitive friendship remained as strong as ever. Either girl would have slept with Todd without hesitation.

Without them even realizing it, Sally's life—and part of Brenda's, too—continued to revolve around Todd. Sally was practically obsessed with him. Even though they'd broken up, she still felt like she was his girl and he was her guy. Even in the midst of all her mixed-up, overlapping, contradictory feelings, that felt normal to her. How could that be *normal* between two friends as close as she and Brenda? And yet it was, and neither of them found their competitiveness unusual. Their lives gradually coalesced around a boy, a man, a giant in their eyes. His attractiveness was secondary only to his ability to resist them as no other boy could.

Brenda and Todd were in the same English class, and she made sure to sit near him when she could. She'd let the boys who helped her cheat on her classwork have a feel when the teacher's back was turned, but Todd never tried despite ample opportunity. He ignored Brenda and made friends with a dumpy girl who was a good student. Brenda shared this with Sally, and they avenged themselves on the girl by spreading rumors of her cheating, but nobody believed them.

Sally and Brenda joked about how trendy they were. Brenda had acquired a copy of *Playboy* magazine and noted that the centerfold was supposed to be the ideal girl next door. They perused the magazine, boastfully noting that both their busts were bigger than that month's centerfold model.

Sometimes they passed by the gym where the boxing team worked out, and one day they overheard Todd, Hector, and Helman joking around inside. The girls stopped, opened the awning window a tad, and peered in. Todd, Hector, and Helman were alone, and Sally and Brenda watched with rapt attention as Todd jumped with a *swish, swish* of the rope.

Helman grunted as he sent crashing blows into the big bag. He wore torn, discolored sweatpants, his heavy muscles bulged, and his bullet-shaped, prematurely balding head threw off beads of sweat at each blow. He just looked dangerous.

Hector worked the light bag with a staccato rhythm. His small, perfectly proportioned frame shifted, one foot to the other, as he switched hands on the bag. He had on a tank top, shorts, and black boxer's shoes, his body looked like coiled bronze wire, and he, too, glistened with sweat.

Sally and Brenda breathed excitedly and held hands. A look into the clandestine world of boys was priceless! They both felt that warm ball in their bellies.

Watching the boys grunt and flex their muscles was a turn-on. They swore, threw towels, and insulted one another in ways girls never did. The general camaraderie of the boys was also an education. At one point Todd pulled off his tank top, got a cup of water from the drinking fountain, poured it over his head, and let out a yell. He was wet, and the girls could see everything.

Brenda said, "Wow, I can see how big it is now. How could you break up with that, Sally? Do you not want him anymore? Why not me?"

"I don't care. I broke up with him because …" Her explanation trailed off because she wished she hadn't, and she didn't have an explanation. She hadn't told Brenda about Cambria.

"Oh God, I'll take him!" Brenda said.

Meanwhile the boys continued talking about girls, boobs, who was pretty or not, who was easy or not, and serious girlfriends. When they mentioned that Brenda put out, she gave Sally a pleased look. Brenda and Sally were also surprised to learn that a couple of girls whom they had thought of as prissy and goody-goody were not.

After a few more minutes of this boy talk, the side door opened and

Coach entered the gym. All three boys jumped to their feet and said, "Hi, Coach. We're ready!"

"Just a moment. I've got a couple of items to attend to, so relax," Coach said in a calm voice. He was wearing the team's tank top and shorts, rather than his usual slacks, jacket, and dress shoes. His legs were well shaped and muscled, his salt-and-pepper hair was wet, and he held a clipboard in his big, powerful hands. His muscles rippled as he moved, and he oozed sexuality in a way that even a handsome boy like Todd couldn't.

To Sally and Brenda, Coach was like a sword drawn from a scabbard—a personification of masculine, lethal power. They exchanged glances, and Brenda said, "Remember what Mrs. V said that time about Coach's big hands? Remember her sly smile? Do you think maybe ...?"

The boys and Coach worked out for a while longer. Then Sally and Brenda left their clandestine perch and went home, fantasizing about further opportunities and new prey.

~

Sally was continuously perused by Kenny, and she enjoyed stringing him along so she could ride around in his big convertible. She hoped Todd would see her and get jealous, and he did see her, but there was no reaction. Knowing about Todd's appetite for carnal pleasure, she wondered if there were other girls.

One day she had Kenny drive over by Houson House, again hoping Todd would notice her. She was surprised to see an older attractive woman driving Todd's treasured truck. At first she thought it must be his mother, but then she remembered that Todd's mom was in Germany. Sally's curiosity knew no bounds. A few days later, she saw Todd pick up this same woman near the school. The woman scooted over next to Todd, gave him a kiss on the cheek, and they drove off toward the highway.

The next day, Sally shared this information with super-curious Brenda, who said, "That's where he's getting it. Remember when you thought he was with girls from Cal Poly? Where do you think they'd go—I mean, what's up the highway?"

Instantly Sally knew where they'd go up the highway. As the green monster grabbed her in all its jealous rage, she yelled, "He wouldn't take her to our shack, would he?"

Sally had told Brenda that she and Todd had a secret spot, but here was

Brenda's chance to learn its location. She asked, "Well he might. Where is it?"

Sally answered with a long, anguished scream. She didn't connect Todd, Miss Lady, and the ranch, because his description of it didn't square with her own vision, which was more like something from a John Wayne movie. But seeing Todd drive off with this older woman transformed Sally's mental image of the ranch into something more like Moonlight Ranch. She was imagining a predatory, domineering, attractive witch taking advantage of *her* innocent boy, and she had to find out who this evil mystery woman was.

Sally persuaded Kenny to drive out Highway 58 toward the Carrizo, but as they got closer to the secret shack, Sally became nervous. What if Todd was there with the evil one? What would Kenny do? At the top of the hill, she got cold feet and—without explanation—told Kenny to turn around and go back. He was nonplussed by this turn of events, but he did as she asked.

At home that night, Sally anguished over the situation, but only one answer came up. *I can't stand life without Todd anymore. How do I get him back?*

~

In spite of her self-tortured jealousy, Sally's life went on much as before. She dated Kenny, but she obsessed about Todd and "that woman." She went to practice, the market, and everywhere else obsessing about "that woman." She and Brenda did Mrs. V's adventures, but she still obsessed about "that woman." They went to the beach in bikinis and flaunted themselves, drawing catty looks and comments from the other girls.

On an evening date, Sally and Kenny stopped at the A&W drive-in at Santa Rosa and Olive Streets. Todd's truck was parked a few spaces away, and he was in the driver's seat. Sally excused herself to go to the restroom, and walked right by the truck on the way. Just as she got to the ladies room, "that woman" came out, walked right by her, and got in the truck next to Todd.

Sally got her first good look at her competition, and she noticed every detail. The woman was of medium height and wore western boots, tight jeans, and a white sleeveless shirt. At her neck was a big, expensive-looking turquoise brooch, with earrings to match. She had a full figure with wide hips and long legs, golden hair spilled over her shoulders, and her makeup was perfect, including false eyelashes. She was definitely more mature than Sally might have expected, and she sat next to Todd in a "We're a couple" kind of way.

By the time Sally got back in Kenny's car, he'd evolved into an immature dope—and she felt inadequate. She asked him to take her home, though she got out at Meadow Park and walked the rest of the way so that Grandma wouldn't see her getting out of Kenny's car. For the umpteenth time, she desperately tried to figure a way to get Todd's attention, finally deciding that she'd just have to ask Brenda.

It was Brenda's opinion that Todd liked older girls, so now Sally needed a more mature look. Brenda's first idea sounded like something her mom might do, so that was out. Next she floated the idea that she would help Sally with Todd.

Sally said, "What? No, that's not what I want. I don't want to share Todd. He's mine."

"Well, he hasn't been for a long time now, has he? And there's us too, remember?" said Brenda.

"Yes, but ... Now you're being mean, Brenda. You know what I meant. I want him!"

So they put together a more mature look for Sally. Brenda's mom had everything they needed. They raided her makeup, and Brenda also got Flo to help out. A short skirt trimmed in red, wide belt, and scoop-neck, off-the-shoulder blouse also trimmed in red. Red open-toe shoes with ankle straps. Flo got her a strapless uplift bra that worked with the blouse—cute but revealing, and Sally already had sexy lingerie. Brenda did her makeup and hair, piling up Sally's blond tresses in a 1940s look, along with false eyelashes and perfume. Flo let them use the shop for all this.

Sally and Brenda learned that Todd had plans to meet Hector at the park in front of the old mission at the end of Monterey Street. Sally would ambush him there.

She saw Todd sitting on a bench close to the creek. Her first thought was that she was relieved that he was actually there. Her second thought was how handsome he was, sitting there browsing through a book, probably about the periodic table. With her heart racing, she took a deep breath, jaywalked across Chorro Street, and stood there a moment gathering herself. Todd's back was to her, so he didn't see her approach. The creek gurgled in the background as she walked the last few steps and stood behind and to his left. Just as she stopped, he heard her.

Sally said coyly, "Hi, Todd!"

Surprised, he put down his book and stood up. "Well, hello! What brings you here looking like that? I mean, you look pretty fine."

"Like what?" Sally asked. "I wanted to see you and—uh—talk, I guess. Find out how you're doing, you know?" Now that she was actually talking with him, she got tongue-tied and forgot all the things she and Brenda had decided she should say and do.

Todd said, "No, actually I don't know. I thought you, uh …"

Now at a total loss about what to say, Sally gave him a small curtsy and said, "Do you like it? My new look, I mean. It's more mature."

He looked her up and down. "Well, if you want to look like … that way. But that's not for me to say now, is it?"

Sally was surprised at his reaction to the new look on which she'd spent so much effort. She twirled around and said, "Brenda and I thought you'd like this. Do you?"

"Brenda? Yeah, I might have guessed," said Todd. "Your choice, Sally. Wow, Brenda helped you look like *that*? Her choice of perfume? Jeez!" He turned and shook his head.

Sally batted her overdone eyes and said, "A woman needs to look her best, don't you think?"

Todd just looked away, so she stepped more directly into his view and said, obviously irritated, "Yes, my friend Brenda. What's wrong with her?"

He still didn't look at her.

"Don't I look nice, Todd? I mean, like you want? Like more mature and stuff, you know?" Now she was mad. "Look at me! Brenda helped me look like what, Todd? Like *what*?"

Todd gave her a sideways glance and said, "Your eye things are coming off."

"You don't like how I look? But I'm beautiful and … and a woman. More than …" She reached up and touched her eye. Indeed, one of her false eyelashes was detached.

"Well, Sally?" Todd exclaimed.

Deflated, mad, and about to cry, Sally pressed on. "You're a mean person, Todd Wyrum, and stuck-up just like everyone says. I'm sorry I even came here!"

Todd still didn't look up, but just continued to shake his head slowly.

"I think that I look really cute, but you won't even look at how nice I am. Look at me, Todd!"

"Trampy. That's how she's helped you look, Sally. Like a tramp!" he replied coolly.

"What? You lie. I'm a nice girl, I am. I hate you, Todd. I hate you!" Sally could feel the tears begin, and her eyelashes drooped even farther.

Todd took a step toward her and held out his hands.

Sally jumped back and screamed, "Liar, liar, stupid liar! I don't ever want to see you again. Get away from me. You're stupid! You and that dumb periodic table stuff are ... stupid!"

Todd stepped back and held up his hands in surrender. "Whoa! You came here to see me, remember? If you want to look like that, then so be it. It's your life."

Sally erupted, "Damn you, Todd Wyrum! I'm cute, and much better than her. She's just an old hag. You'll be sorry."

Todd crossed the patio and said, "Go home, little girl. You're not even in Miss Lady's league. Your *friend*, Brenda? I can't believe it!" Then he turned and walked away, pausing at the street corner to look back and say, "Give my best to Brenda. Some friend she is. Wow, the joke's on you, Sally!"

Staring after him, Sally collapsed on the bench where he'd been sitting. He'd forgotten his book, still lying there. Feeling totally defeated, she pouted as she watched him walk away. In her mind, Todd's image gradually merged with Brenda's and all they'd done to prepare for this day. *Brenda!*

When Sally got back to Flo's, she broke into a full cry. Flo and Brenda were there, and Sally sat down in a pouty huff across from them and said, "Todd didn't like it. He thinks I'm trashy. He left me sitting there alone. All the other boys like me, and I don't want to see him ever again. Do you hear me? Look how cute and mature I am, aren't I?"

Brenda and Flo exchanged glances, and Flo said, "Oh no, I can't believe it. You look really cute, Sally. He just doesn't have good taste, does he, Brenda?"

Brenda answered, "Well, I guess not. I mean, we did our best, didn't we?" But the look on her face sent a different message, almost like she was pleased. "Sally, we'd better get on home, shouldn't we?"

Sally knew now that she'd been betrayed, but she couldn't really confront Flo. Seething with repressed anger, she said, with false humility, "Thanks, Flo!"

She and Brenda left the shop, walked down the block, and stopped at the corner to wait for the light to turn. Then Sally—her face a mask of tears, anger, and smeared makeup—turned to Brenda and said accusingly, "Lying slut, you knew. You did! You wanted him to see me just like you, a tramp. I was so humiliated. It was awful, just awful. Why'd you do it? Now I'll never get him back. In fact, I don't even want him back, and it's your fault. You and Flo. That bubby-loving bitch did all this so you could have Todd. You let her get her hands full so she'd help you, didn't you?"

Brenda said, with a hint of satisfaction on her face, "Well, you said you didn't want him anyway. And I'm not a slut—I'm sexy, and that's all! You wanted to look that way. It's your own fault, little rosebud mouth Sally. And it was your idea about the older look, after you saw that old lady with him. All I did was—"

Sally exploded, "Shush! You knew this would happen! You lied about the makeup, the older look, all of it. You gave it to Flo so she'd help, didn't you, Miss Droopy Tits?"

Pedestrians passing by began to stare at them.

"They're not droopy! They're the best—and bigger than yours. And yes, Flo helped, but ..." Brenda's explanation trailed off as Sally just stared at her.

The light changed, and they glared at each other as they crossed the street. As they walked past Mitchell Park, a car pulled up at the curb and Kenny yelled, "Hi, Sally, Brenda! Want a ride?" Both girls went into "boy attention mode" and got in the car. They shared a six-pack of beer with the boys, even though they didn't much like beer. Even to the one-track-mind boys, it was obvious that Brenda and Sally weren't in the mood. They made a few feeble efforts, but soon gave up and dropped them off at Meadow Park.

At Woodbridge Street, the girls stopped before going their separate ways. Brenda said, "Don't let Grandma see your face like that, or your top. Will you let me clean you up?"

Sally pulled at her blouse, then touched her smeared face. When she nodded, Brenda took out some tissue and worked for a couple of minutes, then lent her a lipstick. They touched hands for a moment, and their thoughts drifted back to shared interests and the usual competition between them.

Finally Brenda said, "Bye, Sally."

Sally said, "I don't like Todd. Why'd I try to get him back? I can forget him." But neither girl believed those words.

As Brenda walked off, she said, "There are lots of other boy, and men are better anyway." But they weren't.

Todd didn't call Sally, and Brenda's efforts to lure him flopped. Their "We'll show him" strategy had failed.

After that day, Sally and Brenda resumed their former habits. Mrs. V's adventures and the stipends continued, but it all became almost routine.

~

The next year, Todd was a senior, Brenda a junior, and Sally a sophomore. The girls became even more self-important and attention seeking. They were bored with the same old things, no matter what it was. Then opportunity came along in the form of a band and cheer competition.

The team was invited to a three-day competition at the Santa Monica Pier in Los Angeles. They traveled on buses, and it was a lot of fun from the start. But it was also real work, and competition was fierce. In the evening, almost everyone snuck out. The whole beach, boardwalk, and pier scene was wild, plus students were there from all over the state.

The crowds were quite enthusiastic. The cheer team didn't win, but the Bouncing Babes were popular nonetheless. Mrs. V accepted an honorable mention award, and the whole team drew a standing ovation at the pavilion.

Some of the spectators were in town to attend an airline convention, and they were especially appreciative of the cheer team and even spoke to them afterward with admiration. Brenda and Sally were very admiring of them in turn. The stewardesses were all attractive girls in powder-blue jackets, short skirts, and white blouses with trim to match. They wore cute little hats, dark-blue scarves, and low heels, and their hair and makeup were perfect. Even more impressive were the male pilots, many of whom reminded Sally and Brenda of Coach, in their tailed, dark-blue uniforms and visor hats. All the crew members, both stewardesses and pilots, carried themselves with casual confidence. They spoke to the cheer girls with the quiet assurance of professionals. The girls were impressed and talked about possible careers as stewardesses.

On Friday afternoon, after the awards ceremony, Brenda and Sally got to talk with crews from KLN, a foreign airline, who wanted to know about school, outfits, makeup, careers, and all thing cheer. Compliments and friendliness flowed easily, and Brenda and Sally's outfits seemed to be of special interest. It was the most fun they'd had in a long time.

When the competition concluded, the girls had some free time, so the KLN crew asked if they wanted to go to a party that night up the beach a few miles. There would be food and drinks, they said, and of course, only if it was okay with their leader, Mrs. V.

Conspiring privately, Sally and Brenda knew it definitely would *not* be okay. Sally said, "Mrs. V will never let us go. She most likely has some 'adventures' for us."

Brenda nodded and said, "So we've got to sneak away, and we'll come back really late when everyone's asleep, okay?"

"They'll be up all night, I'll bet," said Sally. "How many chances do we get to come to LA to perform and party? And we're not the only ones. Did you see those girls from Arroyo Grande yesterday? Wow, you know they'll be with those LA boys for sure. And I'll bet Mrs. V will be with some administrators, like that guy from San Diego. She won't be checking until morning roll call. Yeah, we'll be back late, but so what? Let's do it!"

They shared sneaky smiles, and Brenda said, "You're right. Let's just sneak off. I don't care if she catches us, anyway. Look what we do for her. We've got a few things in our cheer bags if we need to change."

When Sally and Brenda returned to the flight crews and accepted their invitation to the party, they were told to be at the pier at seven. Brenda asked about wardrobe and was assured that their cheer uniforms were perfect.

The two girls spent the intervening three hours in and out of the raunchy ladies' restroom on the pier, getting ready along with a gleeful, raucous crowd of other girls preparing for the same ruse. More mature makeup was applied, and the general atmosphere was "Boys, boys, boys! Chaperones be damned." What could possibly go wrong?

At seven o'clock, Sally and Brenda were waiting at the pier off Pacific Coast Highway. They stood close, holding hands in great anticipation of the adventure to come. Within minutes, a black limo pulled up at the curb, and two girls in tiny bikinis emerged through the open sunroof and waved at them. In accented English, laughing and gesturing, they yelled at Brenda and Sally to get in. They did so, opening the door only to be greeted by loud cheers from at least ten people cavorting inside the limo.

The scene inside was bedlam. Sally and Brenda were handed wineglasses, and arms went around them. Two girls were gyrating around a brass pole in the center of the huge car. Sally and Brenda were coaxed to stand up in the sunroof, and with the wind in their hair and drinks in their hands, they truly felt like part of the gang. Several crew members were making out in different stages of undress. A few girls were down to their bras, most everyone was tipsy, and all were happy. Foreign languages flowed freely. It was even more than Brenda and Sally had hoped for.

As they drove north, drinking and undressing continued. Without any encouragement, a big athletic girl kissed Brenda and peeled off her top. Everyone cheered loudly and pointed at Sally, whose blouse was off in a flash, to further cheers. Brenda gave a shake, and then Sally did the same, to even more cheers. They both put all the stewardesses to shame in the bust department, and it was lucky they were wearing their lingerie from Flo's. Both girls quickly became light-headed from the wine.

Next to Brenda, a girl was sitting on a man, kissing and pressing her little bust in his face, and nobody paid them any attention. Brenda and Sally stared as the girl rose up, lifted her small breasts, and said to Brenda, "You are big and nice, Brenda cutie. I want such but have only this." The man and girl leaned over and kissed each of Brenda's big nipples. Then the girl offered her bust, and Brenda kissed her little perky ones. The girl turned her face to Brenda and gave her a big wet kiss, saying in a clipped accent, "Thank you! You can have him next if you want, or your cute friend, or both. Wolfgang would like that. He's nice man. Your big boobies are *wunderbar.*" Everyone shouted "Yes," "*Oui, ja,*" or some such, followed by more clapping.

Sally and Brenda were proud of their figures, of course, but they'd never met a crowd so blatant in their admiration. For this group, sex was not a private, behind-the-scenes activity. Though the girls were a bit shocked, they realized they were indeed with the mature people they'd hoped to meet.

Brenda scooted next to Sally, gave her a little kiss on the cheek, and unsnapped her bra. Sally teasingly let it slip off her shoulders, and the group began to clap in rhythm. It was almost like being at a sports event. How different these Europeans were! They began to chant, "Brenda, Brenda, Brenda ... More Brenda!" Brenda gave Sally a coy look and nodded. Sally unsnapped Brenda's bra slowly, counting off as she went. The crowd did it with her: "Six, five, four, three, two, *one!*"

With her hands over the huge cups, Brenda slowly revealed her areolas. Then a cute brunette reached over and pulled off what was left covering her. The group gave a great sigh and gasped, in some foreign language, "*Sehr schön, sehr schön!*" Brenda gave Sally a follow-me look, and they did a short cheer team routine. More hooting, guffawing, and touching followed. One of the older pilots said, "*Ja, ja,* America great country!"

Several girls looked intimidated, but no one said a cross word. The tall girl, Katrina, touched Brenda, blew her a kiss, and then resumed her conversation with another girl. They both kept eyeing Brenda and Sally admiringly. The whole limo turned into kind of striptease display, which contributed to the party atmosphere.

Sally and Brenda both put their bras back on, and Sally asked Katrina, "What country are you from?"

"I'm from Netherlands, sometimes Germany and Spain on vacation. You been to Europe, Miss Sally? You study French, German, Spanish in school, yes? Where you from?" asked Katrina.

"We're from San Luis Obispo, up the coast. It's nice but boring. We haven't been anywhere." Sally felt she was among grown-ups for the first time.

A really tall pilot filled Sally's glass again, put his arm around her, and pulled her close. Then he kissed her and asked, "In gymnasium, *ja?* So pretty, so American, your outfits?"

Brenda gulped and said, "We're eighteen, just finishing high school. We're excused from gym class because we're cheerleaders, understand?"

He answered with a shrug, and Sally asked, "Are you going with any of these girls? The stewardesses, I mean?"

"No, it's not like that with us. We're free to be with others—and to change off, too, and love all. You understand, yes?" He turned away and left Sally and Brenda to watch the antics going on around them as they sipped their champagne from their wineglasses.

~

The party kept getting more raucous, until twenty minutes later they turned off the highway, went down a side street, and pulled up in front of the Palms Motor Lodge. A small group of double cabins was set back from the street amid a grove of palm trees. At the reception cabin out front, a blinking neon "Vacancy" sign hung in the window. The cabins were one-story, baby-poop-green, stucco affairs in the 1920s Spanish style. Each cabin had a covered porch in front and a red tile roof. The place looked run-down, with weeds growing all around. They parked alongside a second car in front of a cabin out back.

The moment the limo stopped, everyone piled out in a rush. One person ran off toward the reception building, yelling in a thick accent, "Home sweet home, yes! Our friendly little home away from home, yes? Do our new cheering friends like it, yes?" The half-dressed crowd shouted their agreement, and then helped unload the booze and sundries.

The cabin's interior matched its exterior. Two big four-poster beds with nightstands dominated the room, with a kitchenette to one side. The bathroom was small with a sink, toilet, and tub, and an open door led to the adjacent unit. In the darkened room, Brenda and Sally saw three people in a bed. Sally was surprised, but not Brenda. They sat in an overstuffed chair and hugged close. Now Sally knew what the party was *really* about.

Later a delivery girl came in the open front door and yelled, "Pizza! Your order is here. Where ya want it?"

Katrina said, "Yes, oh yes! The kitchen table, yes."

A hush fell over the crowd as attention was drawn to the beautiful, light-skinned black girl delivering the pizza. She was medium height with silken skin and short hair, and even in her work uniform, her big languid eyes and slim sculpted figure stood out. As she put the pizzas on the table, Katrina asked, "Will you join our party, pretty girl, yes? What's your lovely name? Sit down and have champagne, yes? These are California cheering girls." She pointed to Brenda and Sally, then asked, "And your name?"

"I'm Roxanne, or sometimes Roxy." The delivery girl gave a big smile and sat down. By now everyone was gathering around the pizza and Roxy, who accepted a glass of champagne. She raised her glass and took a sip, then said in a shy, girlish voice, "Thank you, but I can only stay a minute. More deliveries, you understand?"

Everyone was so enthralled with her that Brenda and Sally felt a little left out. Sally started a conversation with a pilot, and Brenda joined the crew with other girls. Someone put on music, and dancing began while more champagne flowed. Everyone was a little drunk now. Brenda got up to dance and coaxed Roxy up with her. Brenda's bust cavorted around and was the center of attention. Meanwhile Sally and the big pilot snuggled closer.

Then Sally got up and joined the crew in a strange half-dance, half-parade around Brenda and Roxy, who were going full tilt when Brenda's bra straps slid off her shoulders. Soon her full bust was exposed, which drew more cheers as the drinking, laughing, and making out grew more intense. In the other unit, the sounds of lovemaking were drowned out by the music.

It was now dark outside, with only a distant street lamp and the blinking "Vacancy" sign shining through the broken venetian blinds and adding a kaleidoscope effect in the room. Sally's figure was fast becoming a subject of cheering, along with Brenda's. And then Roxy's blouse came undone, and she became the object of much giggly attention.

Katrina, who seemed to be the crew leader, asked Brenda and Sally to demonstrate some cheers. They agreed, and thus began cheer demonstrations and teaching the crew. The crew's attempts to duplicate the cheers drew great peals of laughter and imitation from everyone.

This dancing, caressing, kissing, and general partying went on until well after midnight, when it finally devolved into a drinking, dancing, squirming, and fondling carnival of sexy fun. Sally and Brenda were kissed and fondled by both men and women, until it all became a blur.

Brenda blew Sally a kiss and a finger wave goodbye, then went into the other unit with a short pilot and Katrina. Roxy disappeared into the bathroom, from where the shower soon could be heard. At some point Sally got naked along with everyone else. Happily there wasn't the pinching and grabbing of young boys. Sally responded enthusiastically, even aggressively, and that was the last she would later recall of the evening.

~

The dawn light and the still blinking "Vacancy" sign woke Sally. Her head felt heavy, and she was tangled in among several arms and legs stretched across two beds. A woman's head rested on her tummy, and a man's hand cupped her left breast. Her legs were spread wide, and a man lay there between them. As Sally moved slightly and lifted her head, her whole body felt funny, a little sore, and her face was covered with a dry liquid that crackled when she yawned.

The dim room was still except for heavy breathing and the sound of the record player going round and round on a finished disc. She surveyed the prostrate bodies, empty bottles, pizza boxes, and discarded clothes. She ran her fingers over her face and hair, discovering that the area around her mouth was sore and her hair was a disheveled, matted mess. Her breasts had bruises on them, and the nipples were bright pink and very sensitive.

She heard a chirp next to the bed, and as she rose up on one elbow, she saw Brenda sitting on the floor next to her and snoring. Next to Brenda were a tipped-over nightstand, two empty bottles of champagne, and a torn curtain hanging off its rod. A giant mess of black curls fell over Brenda's shoulders, and her mouth was agape. Above her head, her hands were tied with her bra to a curtain rod. Her legs were stretched out in front of her, and a man lay partly over them. They were both naked.

Sally carefully unwound herself from the bodies and got to her knees. Then she reached over and touched Brenda on the shoulder. "Brenda, are you okay?"

Brenda's head jerked a bit, and a tiny moan escaped her lips. Then she looked up at Sally with squinty eyes, took a deep breath, and smiled. "Oh, Sally, are *you* okay?"

Sally nodded and asked, "What happened?"

Brenda wriggled her hands free from her bra. "I didn't know there was that much cum in the whole world. I see you got yours, too." Sally touched her stiff face, suddenly understanding.

Brenda got to her feet, and they viewed the room. Bodies lay everywhere, and some were in rather comic positions. A couple lay amid many beer bottles, including one standing upright between her legs, and an empty box sat squarely on his bare chest. Another had panties over his face as a mask, and a girl next to him was tied to a bedstead with her bra.

Sally saw something familiar on the box, which said "Rheingold Beer" and "My beer is Rheingold, the dry beer!" A little bell chimed in her head, and she heard Todd humming the phrase softly.

Two people were in the bathroom going at it—even now, so early. A swaying light gave the room a surreal look, and whimpers, moans, and splashing sounds could be heard.

All around them, people were waking and moving. A naked Katrina walked by them and started rummaging through piles of clothes. Finally she put on a big oversized jacket and began to drink out of a half-full wine bottle. She sat down next to Sally and Brenda, bent close, and said, "A good time, yes, cheer girls?"

Sally said, "Aah … yes! I'm hungry!"

Brenda replied. "Me, too."

Katrina said, "Yes … More you want? You had something to eat last night, yes? You had fun, yes? Your big boobies made for much fun, yes? I see you like to. That's good, yes?"

Katrina bent farther, lifted one of Sally's breasts, and softly kissed her nipple. "More fun, yes?"

Sally said, "No! I'd rather have something to eat."

"Nice little cheer girl." Katrina went to the couch and spread herself out seductively. "Oh yes, cheer girls! More fun, yes?"

"Uh, we meant breakfast," said Sally. But all they got was cold pizza, which they ate while sitting on the bed.

A man asked Brenda to continue the previous evening's activities. Brenda was game and they disappeared into the other room. Sally wasn't interested, so she finished the cold leftovers as the partying continued all around them.

By sunup, even the most ardent partiers had given up, and the room settled into a group clothing search expedition. After a few minutes, a cheer was raised to the "cheering girls." A vote was taken to decide which of them had been the best, and Sally and Brenda tied. They received stewardess flight jackets as a prize. When tried on, the jackets were more like complete outfits with very short skirts, which prompted another rousing cheer. Everyone showered, sometimes in groups, and then tried to sort out their clothes. This was only partly successful, resulting in a few odd outfits, but no one seemed to care.

Finally they were all ready to go, and everyone got into the limo. Roxy said goodbye and drove off in her little van still filled with undelivered pizza. It was just ten o'clock.

The drive back to Santa Monica was subdued, but still fun. They stopped at a tacky seaside café for brunch, since the tacky side of American life seemed to suit these Europeans. Brenda and Sally had never eaten so much. All in all, it was the most fun and by far the wildest time they'd ever had. They loved being so appreciated for their cheer routines, uniforms, and figures!

When Sally and Brenda were dropped at their hotel, everyone kissed them goodbye. Brenda and Sally told everyone, "See you later," but of course they never did.

~

When the two girls got to their room, there was huge commotion. Several girls yelled, "Where have you been? We thought you got kidnapped or something. We looked everywhere! Mrs. V is mad, mad, mad, and she's going to kick you off the cheer team!" Indeed, there was a note on their door instructing them to see Mrs. V immediately.

Just then the door burst open and Mrs. V stormed in, slamming it behind her with a bang. Scowling, she said, "You two girls have broken every rule, and you're in big trouble! Where in heavens have you been?"

Sally and Brenda jumped up, grabbed each other's hand, and cozied up together.

Mrs. V eyed them accusingly, but slowly an expression of curiosity came over her face. "Where did you get those cute blue jackets?" she asked. "They look like stewardess outfits. I'm waiting for answers, girls."

Sally was scared, but Brenda kept her composure and pirouetted to show off the new things. "We've been with our new friends, those airline people. You know, the ones who watched us perform. Do you like our new look?"

Mrs. V stepped up to Brenda and slapped her across the face, ripped the jacket open, and yelled, "Who have you two little trollops been entertaining—and where?"

Brenda put a hand to her red cheek, but she wasn't intimidated. She replied proudly, "Wouldn't you like to know? The limo, the food, the champagne, the new friendship. Oh my, they just loved us. It was really so much fun—and so fulfilling!"

Encouraged by Brenda's defiance, Sally stepped forward, spun around to show off her outfit, and said, "They saw us at the competition and liked us so much that they gave us these jackets as a reward, so there! And anyway, we know you were with that tall judge guy, Miss High-and-Mighty."

Brenda was now in full cry. "Yeah, him! And I'll bet you did that judge lady too—the one with the dyed red hair. Was it fun, Mrs. V? I'll bet you *ate it up*!

Their defiance shocked Mrs. V. "You can't ... You can't do—"

Sally broke in. "Yeah, you did it, you did it, you did it! So you can't make us do—"

Mrs. V replied by slapping Sally, who put her hands to her face and said, "You're mean and unfair, and you force us to do stuff. Isn't that right, Brenda? We do what you say, Mrs. V, and we can't even be with our boyfriends without permission. It isn't fair. Tell her, Brenda."

Brenda pulled her jacket open and yelled at Mrs. V, "I got so much that I can hardly walk, and Sally too. Look at my boobs. See how they've been loved? We loved it, and so did they!"

Sally nodded, but she was just barely holding back her tears. She leaned her head on Brenda's shoulder, and Brenda pulled her close as they looked up at a completely dumbfounded Mrs. V.

A long pause ensued as they stared at one another, and finally Mrs. V said, "You're both ... grounded. Is that understood? Grounded."

"No, we're not." Brenda had an edge in her voice.

"What?" Mrs. V asked scornfully. "Who do you think you are?"

Sally spoke up and said, "No, we're not grounded. Otherwise we'll stop entertaining. No more Mr. Hesselgren, no more Dr. McKay, no more booster club. And we don't care about the stipends, either!"

Brenda said quickly, "Well, maybe we can work *something* out. Sally? Mrs. V?"

Mrs. V replied, "I suppose we can, but—"

"No *buts* about it!" Sally broke in sharply.

Regaining her composure, Mrs. V stared at the two defiant girls, who stared right back. Without another word, she turned and walked out. The yelling had drawn a crowd of cheerleaders, who were huddled close in the hall. They looked intimidated, but said nothing. After a moment's hesitation, Mrs. V slammed the door behind her hard.

Brenda and Sally fell back onto the bed and hugged each other. Almost asleep, Sally said, "And I don't need that stupid Todd anymore, either."

Snuggled up close, they slowly fell into a well-deserved, exquisite, dream-filled sleep.

~

Before checking out of the hotel, Brenda and Sally paraded around in their cute stewardess jackets. Since they had belonged to much bigger women, with some adjustments they might be just right to wear as short-skirted outfits. An afternoon at Flo's would turn the jackets into perfect fits for Sally and Brenda.

The return bus ride to San Luis Obispo was the usual mix of fun and boredom. Since the team had been successful, everyone was in a good mood. Even Mrs. V seemed pleased.

Back at school, the outfits got lots of oohs and aahs from the girls and whistles from the boys. When Mrs. V saw this, she forbade Sally and Brenda from ever wearing them again, but they hardly cared. The new balance of power between them and Mrs. V had advantages for everyone.

During the new school year, the adventures and stipends continued. Brenda remembered that during their trip, Sally had said that she was totally finished with Todd. She also recalled other things that Sally had said, like bragging about how slow and manly Todd was. Sally knew that despite their recent fun, Brenda still had designs on Todd, and that in Brenda's worldview, stealing another girl's boyfriend—even Sally's ex—was part of the game. And as Sally was about to find out, sometimes things just happen.

On a particularly sunny day, Kenny drove Sally and Brenda to Avila Beach. He parked the convertible up the hill on San Antonia Street. As they walked down Front Street, Brenda remembered that she'd forgotten her beach bag and went back to the car to get it. At the corner of First Street, she saw a truck approach and recognized it as Todd's. *Bingo!*

No time for a plan—just a woman's reaction to opportunity. Pretending to stumble, Brenda fell to the ground. The truck stopped and a pair of jeans appeared next to her. She looked up to see Todd looking down at her with concern on his face. He knelt at her side and said, "Brenda, are you hurt? I saw you trip from up the hill. Can I help?"

"Oh, Todd, I think my ankle is twisted. If I could just stand ..."

"No, don't move. I'll help you. Here, take my arm. No, Brenda, don't lift—let me do that. We don't want to make it worse."

"Thanks, Todd. I do need some help. Can you look at it? I mean, to see if it's bruised or what?"

Todd bent and squeezed her leg gently. "Does that hurt? Is it sensitive to the touch?"

His touch sent a sensual surge through her. This was going better than she'd hoped. With a grimace, she said, "I'm not sure. It might be injured higher up. Can you check?"

"Let's see," said Todd, moving his hand up her calf, then her thigh, and squeezing gently again.

Brenda whimpered and said, "It does hurt! I'm not sure I can walk. What do you think?"

"I think you'd better not put too much weight on it," said Todd. "Let me help you up, and then we'll see."

While he had his arm around her, she pressed up against him. The next objective was to get into his truck. She stood, favoring her left foot, and said, "I don't think I can walk."

Todd said, "You're hurt, that's for sure. Let me help you into my truck.

I'll drive you to wherever you were headed. Is that okay, or was someone going to pick you up?"

What a gentleman he is, thought Brenda, *and what a chump Sally was to let him go.* She let Todd help her into his really cool truck, making sure he got a good look at her almost-open blouse.

Todd retrieved her bag and placed it on the seat next to her. "You all right, Brenda?"

Wearing her most helpless face, Brenda said, "Yes, Todd, and I'm so grateful. I simply don't know what I'd have done without you. I don't know how to thank you enough."

Todd started the truck. "No trouble. Where are your friends? I'll drop you off."

Now Brenda needed to stall. "Oh, them? I'm not sure. They were supposed to pick me up at the corner of First, right over there."

"Odd place to meet, isn't it?" asked Todd. "Are you sure it wasn't down at the beach?"

More lies and further stalling. Brenda pouted and said, "Well, maybe. I'm really upset and confused, or ... I don't know, maybe so. Maybe that's it."

Getting impatient, Todd asked, "Where else, and who the hell is it? Who would desert you?"

Not knowing what else to do, Brenda started crying and blurted out, "Maybe not every boy is as nice as you, Todd!"

Todd said, "This is getting way too complicated. Who are we talking about? It isn't—"

"No, it isn't silly Sally. It's Marylyn and Terrell." Brenda lied again. She really didn't care about any of this, except to get Todd alone someplace.

Todd just shrugged and said, "Those two? That figures."

Brenda faked it and said, "We were going to Cave Landing after the beach. I'll bet they went there."

"Okay, Cave Landing it is." Todd made a U-turn, then headed to Avila Beach Drive and off toward town. They turned up Cave Landing Road and parked near the oil tanks, but no one was there. "I guess they didn't make it here," he said. "Do you think they just left you? Would they do that?"

"I guess so," said Brenda, opening the door and sliding out.

He asked, "Where are you going?"

Brenda just walked off, knowing he'd follow, but she forgot to limp. He did follow her behind some rocks to a clearing that looked over the ocean and the town below.

"We might as well take advantage of the view, don't you think?" Brenda said in her best come-hither voice, and then she sat down on the only grass in the area.

Todd sat next to her and asked in a suspicious tone, "How's the ankle, leg, whatever?"

His tone told the story, and she knew her fib had been discovered. *Now or never.* She undid the rest of the buttons on her blouse and turned to face him. Her bust tumbled out and quivered seductively. "Todd, I want to thank you for helping. Can I do that, please?"

Taking in the view, he replied, "Uh, well …"

Brenda said, "No one will ever know, Todd. It'll be our little secret, okay?"

~

As they drove away, Todd said, "Brenda, I guess we found a place, if not your friends. Were there any friends, really? You forgot your limp, you know?"

"I wanted to get to know you better and …" Brenda paused and then said, "I'm sorry that I told a fib, but it was worth it, wasn't it? We did have fun, didn't we, Todd?"

He looked over at her blouse, which was still unbuttoned, and nodded.

When they got to the beach, Todd pulled over to the curb to let her out. At that instant, she noticed Sally across the street, staring at the unmistakable truck with her fists on her hips. Knowing she faced a confrontation, Brenda pulled Todd's face to her, kissed him, and then slid across and out the door. Looking at her, Todd was unaware of Sally's presence.

Then Brenda dug it in a little deeper. She waved at Todd and yelled, "See you at school, Todd. I had a wonderful time."

As Todd drove off, Brenda gave Sally a finger wave, took off her blouse, revealing her bikini top, and waited for the stairs to clear. Sally came up beside her, and they looked at each other but said nothing. Behind Sally came Marylyn and Terrell. Marylyn asked in a suspicious voice, "Brenda, where ya been? We waited and waited for you. Are you okay?"

Heading down the stairs, Brenda said in passing, "I fell and twisted my ankle, and Todd happened by and helped me. Nice of him, wasn't it?"

Marylyn said, "Todd helped you for an hour and a half? Sure he did! And where's the hurt now? I don't see anything. What did you do, huh?"

Sally gave Brenda a hateful look.

"Don't get pissy, little Rosebud," Brenda said. "He told me that you broke up with him."

"Brenda, you'd put out for any boy. But Todd's still mine, you tramp!"

A crowd formed as the confrontation grew heated. Brenda stepped right in front of Sally, so that only a few inches separated them. "Todd is not yours. He wants me. He said so!"

Kenny, who was standing right there, said to Sally, "I thought you liked me. My car's nicer than Todd's old truck. You said he was an arrogant jerk."

Sally replied, "Kenny, just butt out for a minute, will you, please?"

Brenda said, "Sally's jealous because Todd likes me better. I've got a better figure, see?" She posed for everyone to see.

The crowd liked this. Someone yelled, "Girl fight, over here! Show her, Brenda."

From up above them, a booming voice yelled, "What the hell's going on down there? Step back, everyone! Christ almighty, you kids got nothing better to do on a beautiful day? If I have to come down there, it will go bad for you all. Get outta here! You too, Brenda and Sally. Stop this crap. Anyway, Brenda, your mom's got you both beat. Get back to the beach, now!"

Everyone jumped back, and by the time the voice let up, they all had begun to go their own ways. This was because the voice yelling down at them was that of Big Earl, the San Luis Obispo County deputy sheriff. Earl was a huge, hulking, dangerous-looking guy standing six feet four with hunched shoulders. In his youth, he'd had an accident that made the left side of his face droop, kind of like a stroke victim, so his face was also scary, but Earl wasn't a bully. He chastised them occasionally, but he also helped them out sometimes. He was a fair, no-nonsense deputy, but everyone knew not to get on his wrong side.

When Big Earl and the kids left, Brenda and Sally walked into the water and waded out a ways. They stood hip deep in the small waves, giving each other dirty looks. Then they yelped as a bigger wave washed in and the cold water drenched them, so that they appeared almost naked. As they walked back to the beach, people stared, and one boy yelled, *"Hubba, hubba!"* This thawed their mutual hostility somewhat, because not even a fight could overpower their shared interest in being the center of attention.

Sally asked, "Your mom knows Big Earl?"

"Doesn't everyone?" asked Brenda.

They walked back to their friends at the seawall, and resumed their rightful place dominating the scene. The Todd thing of a moment earlier was somehow put aside, just like that.

Before Sally and Brenda left, they stopped at the refreshment stand. Big Earl sat at a picnic table eating a sandwich. They exchanged knowing looks and then walked up to him. He immediately gave them a dismissive look, but Brenda asked, "Is my mom really like that?"

Big Earl looked out at the water and said, "She lives a carnal life, just like you two."

Pondering his words, they walked away, and Brenda asked Sally, "What's *carnal* mean?"

CHAPTER 20

Breaking Away

The end of the year was also a time of new beginnings. The boxing team was having a winning season, and with one more win, they'd make it a record three in a row. If the boxers were winning, so was the cheer team. After commencement, the graduates would be moving on to jobs, college, military service, marriages, and new lives.

Todd, Hector, and Helman were among those leaving high school and headed into the great unknown world of adulthood. The girls were generally less confident about the future, but most of the boys were eager to bid "good riddance" to high school.

~

"Last year's championship tied the record," said Mrs. V. "If our boxing team wins this next match, they will have captured a record three championships in a row. Our cheer team is going with them to Santa Maria, along with the pep band. We can help them celebrate if, as Coach expects, they win. He is likely to get the Coach of the Year award also, so this could be a double win for us." Mrs. V scanned the girls, her eyes falling especially on Brenda and Sally.

All the girls jumped to their feet—hugging, clapping, and waving pom-poms.

Mrs. V said, "It will be as much fun as our own success in Santa Monica. Are you all going?"

"Yes!" shouted the girls. They exchanged giggles, glances, smirks, and guilty looks as they remembered how much fun Santa Monica was. Many of them would be graduating, so this really was a last hurrah. What would come next was still a mystery. Some would marry, some would go on to college, and others would get jobs. For many of the cheer squad girls, it was the end of a really fun four years.

For the boxers there was another obligation: military service and a smoldering event in the East.

Todd concentrated on his studies and boxing. His JROTC involvement had earned him an opportunity for a college scholarship. He dated older girls and continued to see Miss Lady now and then. He'd brought a college girl to the Senior Ball. Among the cheer girls, rumors swirled about him.

After their one encounter, Brenda had failed at luring Todd into an amorous relationship. Sally considered going steady with Kenny and his car, but decided against it. She still had Todd's *ping-ping* ring. With Sally's help, Brenda would probably be head cheerleader next year, if they continued to do Mrs. V's bidding. The stipends would continue, with Flo supplying the necessary items.

Grandma wasn't blind to Sally's activities and lame excuses. The big hair, makeup, tighter skirts and blouses, and frequent hanging out with Brenda didn't go unnoticed. Kenny's big convertible didn't impress her a bit, and she assumed that many of Sally's new things resulted from her dating Kenny, who came from a rich family. She'd tried several approaches to improving Sally's behavior, but nothing had worked, including the sessions with Deacon Jennings. This was especially disappointing, because Grandma had thought that he could influence an impressionable schoolgirl. She still lectured Sally from time to time, but nothing changed.

One day Grandma saw Todd downtown, and a new approach occurred to her. Would a reconnection with him bring Sally back into the fold? When Sally had been going out with Todd, things had been better, but how could Grandma make that reconnection happen? Gail needed help with a science project. Maybe asking Todd for help would get him to the house. It was worth a try.

Grandma took Gail's hand, stepped onto the sidewalk in front of Sinsheimer Bros. store, and called out, "Todd! Yoo-hoo, Todd!"

"Hi, Mrs. Anderson! It's been a while. Nice to see you too, Gail." He reached out to shake hands with Grandma.

Grandma said, "How fortuitous that we should run into you. Earlier today I was talking to Gail about your interest in science and that table you worked so hard on. You know what I mean, don't you?"

"Of course, the periodic table," said Todd. "It's important to understand the relationship between elements. Here's how it works. If you see the—"

"Oh, never mind explaining it to me, Todd. It's Gail who needs to know. Don't you, dear?" she asked, turning to Gail. "Your school science project, you know? That table thing you're doing?"

Confused at this turn of events, Gail replied, "Yeah, but I'm not getting very far without—"

"Well, never mind that," interrupted Grandma. "Perhaps we could impose on Todd for help. Wouldn't that be nice? Could we possible ask for your help, Todd? You're just so well versed in these science things."

"I guess so, if we can do it on an off day. See, I'm really busy with school and boxing. Sally probably told you. I mean, we're not going out or anything but—"

"Oh my, yes! I do very well understand. We'll keep you only as long as necessary. Could it be this Saturday? Does Saturday work for you, Gail?"

Pretty much bewildered at this point, Gail simply said, "Yes!"

"How about eleven o'clock, Todd? I'll make you a nice lunch, too." Before Gail could say anything else, Grandma jerked her off down the sidewalk.

~

On Saturday, Todd was at the house at eleven, and Grandma let him in. "It's so nice to see you here in our home again, Todd. Come in! Gail's at the dining table, all ready to get to work. Would you like some refreshments? I'm sure you would—how silly of me. I'll get them right now. Have a seat, Todd. Gail, say hello to Todd, and thank him in advance for going to all this trouble to help."

When he was finally able to get a word in edgewise, Todd said, "Glad to be here. Happy to do it."

Gail's project was ready, so they set to work. It was a big cardboard square with boxes for each element on it. Todd saw that this was going to be pretty easy, so he gave it to her to translate. They integrated and redrew the tables and graphs that went with them. Gail, now thirteen, was pleased that Sally's handsome ex-boyfriend was paying attention to her.

Grandma brought in sandwiches, lemonade, and fresh fruit. She was beaming as she set it all down on the table. "My, doesn't that look much more interesting, Gail? You're a big help, Todd." She seemed oddly preoccupied and kept checking the clock.

At noon, Kenny's car pulled up, and Sally started to get out. She was shocked to see Todd's truck in front of her house.

Kenny saw it too. "What the hell is that jerk-off doing here? I thought you were through with him, Sally. I told you that the next time, I'd kick his skinny ass, and I will."

"Kenny, please stop," said Sally, who then proceeded to lie to him. "Let me deal with this. I don't care for Todd even a tiny bit." She grabbed Kenny's hand to stop him from getting out of the car.

"Don't lie to me about this, Sally. What's he doing here?"

Sally got mad at the implicit accusation. "You're being rude and disrespectful, Kenny. I'm not lying, and how dare you accuse me? I have no idea why Todd's here."

Kenny said, "Well, I'm sorry, but you're my girl and—"

Sally interrupted him, "Just leave, Kenny, and let me get rid of Todd." She was of two minds—excited to see Todd, but wanting to keep the two boys apart. Kenny was six foot three and two hundred pounds, so he outweighed Todd by thirty pounds, but Sally knew that Todd wouldn't back down.

After a long pause, Kenny said, "Well, okay, if you promise to send him packing." Then he drove away.

With great anticipation, Sally skipped happily across the porch and went inside. She let the screen door softly shut behind her, took a deep breath, and walked deliberately into the dining room. Sitting with his back to her, Todd continued to talk to Gail.

"Oh my, what a surprise. It's Sally! Come in and see who's here, Sally. It's your old friend Todd." Grandma's faked astonishment seemed to work.

Todd turned in his chair and said, "Hi, Sally. I didn't know you'd be here. How're you doing?"

Disappointed, Gail said, "Well, I should've known. Sally, you're always butting in."

"Hush, Gail! Refreshments, anyone?" Grandma asked.

Todd stood up, and he and Sally looked at each other, but neither of them said a word.

"Well, let's all have some lemonade and cookies anyway. You too,

Gail." Grandma's happiness at this turn of events was obvious to Sally, who realized that she and Todd had been set up.

Seeing the handwriting on the wall, Gail picked up her project work and headed for the door. Before she left, however, she said to Sally, "You're always interfering, but we'll see about that. I know stuff!"

Sally knew that her sister's comment didn't bode well, but she was focused on Todd at the moment. Those soft, sexy eyes seemed to undress her, which made her even more self-conscious.

Grandma came back, placed the refreshments on the table, and discreetly left the room.

Todd said softly, "Nice dress."

Sally preened and replied, "I'm so glad you like it. Todd, I need to pick up my dress for the dance tonight. Can you drive me? Anytime you're ready would be fine. Bring the cookies, if you'd like."

"Yeah, sure!" exclaimed Todd, grabbing some cookies and motioning Sally toward the door.

She called out to Grandma, "We're going down to get my dress. Be back in a while."

Todd shouted, "Thanks for the cookies, Mrs. Anderson. I hope Gail does well on her project."

As they crossed the porch, Sally was so excited her knees shook. She got in the truck on the driver's side and didn't slide all the way over. When Todd got in next to her, there was a moment of high drama, but neither spoke. Then Sally slowly slid her hand across the seat and put it right next to Todd's leg. He reached down and squeezed her waiting hand.

"We'd better scram, or Grandma will see us and come out," Sally said.

Todd started the truck and pulled away from the curb, weaving up Mitchell Drive. Sitting so close to him made Sally's head spin, and she couldn't take her eyes off him. All that had happened since they first made love swam in her head. Although they'd been apart for a long time, somehow it seemed that they'd never been separated.

Todd said, "Oh Sally, I didn't know until you walked into the room how much I missed you. Oh God, it's been agony without you, just agony. Come here."

"Oh Todd, me too!" exclaimed Sally. They stopped at Broad Street and shared a long, passionate kiss.

A car pulled up behind them and honked. It was Cecilia and her mom.

Todd waved them around, but they frowned at Sally and Todd as they drove by. Sally stuck out her tongue at Cecilia as they passed.

Todd asked, "Where this dress place?"

"Forget the dress," said Sally. "I know a better place. Can you guess?"

"No need, fair maiden. We're off to the magic kingdom. Who said it's just a shack? Ha! But you'd better get off me, so that we don't become a statistic before we get there."

The path into the shack was even more overgrown than before, and Todd said, "I haven't been back here since before Cambria Pines and ..."

Sally nodded and looked away. She could feel his struggle, because it was her struggle too. When he hesitated, she picked up her purse and took out the little felt pouch. Taking his hand, she put the ring in it and squeezed. "Todd, I've carried it always. I said bad things to you, but I didn't mean them. I love you. Please put this ring on me, okay?"

He looked at it for a moment and then put the chain around her willowy neck. The ring dangled against the pearly white of her skin. He kissed her and the ring and said, "I love you, too. That never left me, either."

They went inside the shack, spread out the old sleeping bag, and made love for the rest of the afternoon. Before leaving, they sat on the rocks and dangled their feet in the cool water, cuddling in silence. Sally said, "Todd, I missed you so. But I also did some—"

Todd put two fingers against her lips to stop her from continuing. Then he whispered, "Hush, Sally, it's all right. I know you and Brenda did some stuff. I did some stuff, too. At the beach one day, a while back, Brenda and I met up and ... Well, she told me some stuff—besides cheering, I mean."

Sally hid her face and said, "Brenda blabbed to me, too. That's just how she is."

They both laughed, a bit restrained and guilty. Then Todd said, "You're better than her, Sally. Much better."

She prodded him in the ribs. "Oh, Todd! I know that, but it's nice to hear it from you."

Todd said, "You're better, you know? I mean, you've probably seen her around the gym, haven't you?"

Sally hesitated, in her mind imagining Brenda under the window, on the gym bench. In a an instant, her tummy was swimming again, just like in those earlier days, pulled back and forth between her love for Todd and her lust for Brenda. Would it ever let her rest? Her heart and her body argued as she sat there. Then a half-truth formed, and she looked away, "Well, maybe a little bit. She's pretty big—I know that!"

When it was time to go, she mentioned the dress. "I need to pick it up by five o'clock."

Todd nodded and said, "It's with Kenny, isn't it?"

She hugged him and said, "Todd, I feel so guilty, but I have to go because of cheer squad. We've got a dance presentation thing to do. It's to honor Coach, you know?"

"I understand, but damn Kenny!" Todd exclaimed.

Sally said, "Now I don't want to, but I have to. Please understand, okay?"

Again Todd put his fingers to her lips and stopped her. "Damn it, I do understand. And for Coach, it's cool. He's a great guy. But Kenny drives you straight home afterward, right? And don't have too much fun, okay? How about if I come by tomorrow and help your sis some more with her project?"

Sally nodded, then laughed. A few minutes later, they climbed in the truck and drove off.

Fortunately Todd had to double-park at Flo's. That way Sally didn't have to persuade him not to go inside with her, because she definitely didn't want him meeting Flo. She picked up the dress, but Flo didn't get her hoped-for reward this time. That was mostly Brenda's gig anyway.

~

The dress was beautiful—strapless, cream colored, lacy, and calf length. Flo had modified a strapless bra to go with it. There were shoes to match and white hose. She even had a tiara and elbow-length gloves. Grandma did Sally's nails and hair. Gail helped, too, after Sally told her about Todd coming back on Sunday to help with the project.

The only problem was that Todd's attention to Sally's bust left her supersensitive. She could still feel Todd's fullness down there, too.

Despite Flo's modifications to the bra, it still exposed a lot. Grandma said, "Oh my, Sally, that won't do. We're going to have to change or adjust that, for sure." But Sally liked the overexposure, which helped her be more competitive with Brenda.

Kenny picked up Sally in a clean car and tux, and he gave Sally a corsage. By the time they got to the Madonna Inn, she was ready to woo the crowd and outshine Brenda. She did wow her schoolmates and the assembled adult guests, but she did not outdo Brenda. When Brenda showed up with Terrell, her extremely low-cut dress drew gasps from everyone.

The dance was fun, and the cheer squad's short informal routine was a success. Coach got his award, to great cheers. Kenny was polite and didn't get too drunk with the other football players. All in all, it went as Sally expected—except for one thing.

As everyone was about to leave, Mrs. V took Brenda and Sally aside and said, "I want you to stay over. I've some special things for you to do. Tell your dates you have cheer team responsibilities and send them home alone. If they give you any guff, just refer them to me. After everyone has left, come to my room. It's number 212, and I'll explain more then. Is that clear?"

"What special stuff? And what if our dates won't leave?" Brenda asked.

"Hush! This isn't a request. It's part of your stipend, understood?"

Sally said, "But Mrs. V, Kenny is going to be ticked off."

"I know what Kenny expects tonight, but it's not happening," said Mrs. V. "Your special thing tonight is with Coach. And don't tell me you haven't considered that. I've seen you casing him for years.

Sally and Brenda exchanged knowing glances and said in unison, "Yes, Mrs. V!"

Kenny and Terrell weren't happy about the change in plans, but among the crowd at the door, they couldn't put up much of a fuss. Mrs. V stood right next to the girls as they told them, and the boys left in a slightly drunken huff.

When Brenda and Sally got to Mrs. V's room, she had them undress except for their lingerie and heels. Then she gave them big, fluffy, luxurious white bathrobes that engulfed them even with the sleeves rolled up. After touching up their makeup and hair, Mrs. V said, "Now we're going to walk down to Coach's room, and you're going to show him the time of his life. Remember, you're the very best. Are you both ready for this night of fun? And it *will* be fun, believe me. Those big hands aren't the only thing he's got. Here's a bottle of champagne each to take with you. I'll show you the room and usher you in. Are you ready?"

Brenda asked, "Uh, Mrs. V, how do you know—"

"Never mind how I know. Now, are you ready? I want you two

sex-obsessed trollops to prove your worth tonight. Your stipends will go up too. And Brenda, don't forget the envelope."

"Yes, ma'am!" said Brenda. As they approached Coach's room, Brenda was excited, but all Sally felt was fear.

At the door, Mrs. V knocked, and they heard Coach's deep voice say, "Come in." Mrs. V said to them softly, "Here you go." The door opened to a luxurious, dimly lit room with a huge bed. Wearing a big white robe, Coach stood there with a drink in his hand. He motioned them in.

Brenda went in, but Sally held back. Mrs. V said quietly, "Get in there, girl, right now!" All Sally could think about, however, was her afternoon at the shack with Todd—and his ring. She lied, "I can't, Mrs. V. I'm on my period. It just started this afternoon."

Mrs. V replied calmly, "No, you're not. I keep track of things like that. Do you think I set up all these adventures by some stupid accident? Now get in there."

Sally gave her a scared look but didn't move. "No, I won't," she insisted.

Brenda put her arm around Coach and said, "Come on, Sally. Coach is waiting."

"No, I'm not doing this. I've got my Todd back, and he loves me." Sally shook her head, though she couldn't help imagining Brenda in the throes of seduction with her and Coach. Once again, love and lust fought for control within her.

Mrs. V took Sally roughly by the shoulders and said, "Either go in or you're off cheer team. Do you want that? No more stipend, either. Do you understand me, Sally?"

Sally's lower lip trembled as she stood there.

Coach's voice rumbled, "Mrs. V, Brenda will do just fine."

Brenda had already loosened her robe and put Coach's arm around her. She simply said, "Bye, Sally. Sweet dreams with Todd. I've got Coach. See ya!"

As Sally stepped back from the doorway, Mrs. V pulled the door closed. Then she turned and slapped Sally, rocking her backward and throwing open her robe, which drew a muted scream from Sally. "You have so disappointed me," said Mrs. V with an ugly sneer on her face. "I thought you were the dependable one. Get back to the room, get dressed, and get out, ex-cheerleader. Right now!"

Sally ran back down the corridor to Mrs. V's room and grabbed her dress. Before she had time to get out of the room, Mrs. V walked in, shoved

Sally out onto the walkway, and said viciously, "You little tramp, don't come begging to me when you realize how stupid you've been. You're just lucky that Brenda was here to carry on for you. Now get out!"

Mrs. V slammed the door, and Sally turned and walked quickly down the corridor. Head down and not looking where she was going, she bumped up against someone. She looked up to see a large silhouette against the outdoor lights.

"Why, Sally, it's you," a man's voice said. "Where are you off to in such a rush? You look upset. Can I help?"

Sally replied simply, "Oh, hi, Mr. Hesselgren."

He said, "I was at the event for Coach. Didn't you see me? I saw you. Wow, you look marvelous! The other girls, too. Where's your buxom friend? Do you need a ride?"

"Oh, she's around somewhere, I guess," said Sally. "Thanks for the offer, but I've got a ride home."

"It's no trouble really," insisted Mr. Hesselgren.

Sally replied, "Like I said, I've got a ride, but thanks so much."

"Well, okay then. But I'm available if you need help, okay?"

"Okay, Mr. Hesselgren. Bye." Meanwhile the big question in Sally's mind was *How am I going to get home?* The answer, of course, was Todd. She went to the reception desk, gave the desk clerk her biggest smile, and asked to use the house phone. The clerk was obliging, confirming Brenda's frequently stated opinion that "Men are so easy."

Ten minutes later, Todd's truck pulled up in front of the inn. Sally ran as fast as her dress and heels would allow, and Todd jumped out of the truck and ran to meet her. Sally blurted out, "Oh, Todd, I am so happy to see you. I love you."

Todd took her by the hand and led her to the truck. They got in and hugged, and he said, "I thought *he* was going to take you home. What the hell happened?"

The first thing that occurred to Sally was to invent a good lie, but she realized that would put her right back where she was before. Her love versus lust, Todd versus Brenda conflict still loomed, however, so three quarters true was as close as she could get. "Kenny got drunk and left me alone. Then Brenda wanted me to go with her and some guy—together, like the three of us. But I wouldn't go, so ..."

Todd bought into the first part about Kenny, but he somehow seemed not to get the second part. He exploded, "Damn that jerk! I knew I shouldn't have let you go with him, Sally. This is partly my fault for letting it happen. Goddamn it!"

Sally immediately thought that she might have gone too far. With guys, this kind of anger often led to a fight, and if Todd confronted Kenny, the full truth might come out. That would be horrible, especially after today's reunion. She took Todd's hands and said, "Please just let it go, Todd. I'm so happy for us that I simply don't care, one way or the other, about Kenny. He's a jerk, and I promise that I'll never see him again if you'll just let it be. Please?"

Todd said, "I could beat the crap out of him if you want. He's big, but I'm tougher."

"I know that, but please just let it go," insisted Sally. "You and I are together, and that's all that matters. Kenny doesn't matter. I love you, Todd." Most of all, she wanted the other events of the evening to be forgotten.

On the way home, Sally snuggled and kept Todd from bringing up other things. He was a trusting, dependable guy. He saw her to the door and kissed her good night.

The day had been wonderful for both of them, though Sally had suffered a close call. She slept soundly that night, knowing that she'd broken free of the clutches of Mrs. V and her adventures. She'd miss the stipend, but so what? Brenda would still get hers. And even more important, Sally had regained Todd.

The only thing left was to make sure Brenda kept her mouth shut, and Sally knew that would cost her. Brenda would need placating to keep their other secret. Mrs. V was another matter.

CHAPTER 21

The Fight

The last three months could not have been more harmonious for Todd and Sally, who wore his ring around her neck. Mrs. V demoted Sally to alternate, instead of throwing her off the cheer team, but she was still the center of attention with her aerials. Sally spent less time with Brenda because of Todd, though they still paraded down the hall at school together. Keeping an eye out for competition from Brenda and other girls was a full-time job. Sally was surprised that Brenda kept her night with

Coach a secret, especially since it was obvious that she had a major crush on him.

Todd would graduate in June 1961, and Sally saw in him a younger version of the new president, John F. Kennedy—handsome, confident, and married to the perfect woman. When Sally imagined the future, she and Todd were married, successful, and in love. Any other pages in her book of life were simply blank.

Todd was polite to a fault—opening doors for her, helping her into the truck, pulling out chairs for her, giving her flowers. She loved it, and she noticed how the other girls envied her those attentions. The shack became their home away from home. Sally went to bed every night in complete bliss and dreamed about his marriage proposal, maybe even in romantic French, and their future together.

Their lovemaking was wonderful, and he introduced her to several new, stimulating things. She knew where he probably had learned these things, but she didn't ask. That full feeling she craved was even better with Todd. Sometimes it was gentle, at other times rough, but always careful.

When Sally missed her period one month, she didn't worry, because she was irregular anyway. Six weeks later, she awoke with a stomachache, but she didn't think much of it because of the beer they had consumed the previous evening. A few days later, however, it happened again.

At practice one day, when Sally got up from doing the splits, she felt a funny pain in her stomach that caused her to grimace. Mrs. V looked her over carefully and said, "You'd better see Nurse Jones after practice."

"I'm really not hurt, Mrs. V," Sally said. "I can go on."

Mrs. V replied, "No, Sally, you're not going on until Nurse Jones clears you. She's in her office now, so go let her check you out. Brenda, give her a hand, but come right back. We've got more to do."

"Yes, ma'am," said Brenda, and she helped Sally to the nurse's office. When they got to the door, Brenda said, "I'll bet she wants a full exam. Wanna bet?"

"No, I don't. I know you're right, but what can I do?" asked Sally.

"You got on your nice undies? You know the gossip. Be careful."

"It's okay," said Sally. "I'm wearing an old bra. Are you gonna wait for me? Well, here goes." She walked into Nurse Jones's office area and sat down.

In a minute, Nurse Jones came in and said, "Why, Sally, how nice to see you. I hope nothing's wrong. What can I do with—I mean, for—you today? Come in and sit there on the exam table. How cute you look today!"

As Sally sat on the exam table, the nurse patted her where the bruise showed. She pulled Sally's short cheer skirt up and began to feel the bruise. "Does that hurt?"

Sally winced and said, "Yeah, a little. I'll be okay if you'll just give me some pain pills, like you did for Brenda."

"Perhaps, but first we need to determine the extent of your injuries." Nurse Jones probed with her fingers all around Sally's thigh, pressing the area around a bruise that had formed. Finally she stopped and said, "This may be more serious than it appears. You'll need to disrobe so I can check further. Put on this smock, open in the back."

Sally looked at the smock and said, "I don't know about this. Maybe I should call—"

At that moment, Brenda entered and asked, "Isn't Sally's *doctor* supposed to do any full exams?"

"Normally that's true," replied Nurse Jones, "but in this case Mrs. V has authorized it, so it's okay."

Brenda said, "Well, okay, I guess." And Sally did, indeed, get a full exam, plus some tests she didn't understand.

The following Tuesday, Sally was back in the nurse's office while Brenda waited outside. Nurse Jones invited Sally into the exam room and said, "Sit down. I have interesting news." Her voice was pleasant, but her eyes were cold. "The rabbit died, Sally. You're pregnant."

Sally just sat there, speechless.

Nurse Jones continued, "Mrs. V will have suggestions about how to deal with your new condition. Being with child is serious, Sally. Do you know the boy? I'm sure he'll want to be informed—if you know who he is, that is. Your grandma too, and Principal Jennings, of course. I expect you'll be dismissed. Here's a booklet on pregnancy. Birth will be in about seven months. The scrapes and bruises I checked the other day are minor and will heal by themselves. Any questions?"

Sally sat in silence for a moment, until finally Nurse Jones said coldly, "Well, good day. Read that book, and keep in touch. Bye now!" Sally got up and left the office, not quite comprehending what had just transpired.

Seeing the bewildered look on her face, Brenda asked, "Is everything okay? Can you go on cheering?"

With a blank look in her eyes, Sally replied, "I don't know."

Brenda continued to question her on the walk home, but Sally remained mostly silent. She recalled seeing women with huge bellies waddling around town. *Oh my God!* Last year a girl from English class had gotten knocked up. She had been expelled from school, and nobody saw her again. Just an hour earlier, Sally's world had been filled with bliss. Now she sat in her back yard, convulsed by sobs that racked her mind and body. By the time she walked in the back door, Sally was an emotional wreck.

Grandma noticed her red eyes and asked, "Bad practice today, Sally? Go and freshen up, okay? Dinner in twenty minutes. You look upset. Is anything wrong?"

"No, Grandma, nothing's wrong," Sally said. Then she went straight to her room and quietly cried some more.

A few days later, Sally was approached after practice by Mrs. V, who pulled her aside and said, "Nurse Jones gave me the news. You've been working ever so hard toward this end, haven't you? I wonder who the lucky boy is. Do you know? Among all your many admirers, it will be hard to pick out the one to honor, but he'll be so happy. Have you told your loving grandma yet? I'm sure she'll be *just thrilled* to have a little one around. Your future, if you have one, will be decided on Thursday. Be at Principal Jennings's office at four. Don't be late!"

"But I can't tell Grandma," said Sally. "She'll make me go away, like that girl last year. What will I do? I'm confused, Mrs. V. People will treat me like ..." She sat down on the grass and began crying again.

With a self-satisfied look on her face, Mrs. V patted Sally on the head and said, "Well, yes, they will, but it's your own fault. You weren't careful, Sally. If you'd done as I told you, this wouldn't have happened—and you'd still have your stipend too. But, you know, Mrs. V can help if you'll let her, right?"

Sally just sat there and continued crying.

Finally Mrs. V said, "What a nuisance you cheer girls are, and you and Brenda are the worst of the lot. I don't know why I put up with all this. Be at Principal Jennings's office on time, okay?"

"Yes, I will, Mrs. V," said Sally.

~

Sally didn't sleep well that night, just like all the other nights since getting the news. She had always looked her best for school, but not that day. Her face was puffy, her hair was a mess, her clothes weren't coordinated, and she moped from class to class like a wrung-out dishrag.

After lunch, Mrs. V called Sally and Brenda over and said, "I've got a solution, in case you're interested."

Sally perked up and took Brenda's hand. "Yes, Mrs. V, I'm definitely interested, but what about the—"

"Never mind that," interrupted Mrs. V. "If you agree to my proposal, there won't be any need for a meeting. Have you told Grandma about your condition yet, Sally?"

Brenda quickly piped up and asked, "What condition is that?"

"Why Sally, you mean you haven't shared the joyous news with your frolicking pal? How very remiss of you!" said Mrs. V. "Well, Brenda, Sally's pregnant, assuming Nurse Jones is to be believed."

Brenda's eyes shot to Sally's midriff. "Holy shit, Sally!"

Sally immediately began to cry. "Todd and I, we ... Oh Brenda, I'm so scared!"

Mrs. V said, "Stop this simpering blabber, Sally. All's not lost. I have a solution, if you'll just listen."

Brenda snuggled up to Sally and said, "Yeah, Mrs. V's got a solution. It may be okay."

"Brenda, she isn't even sure it's Todd," said Mrs. V. "After all you girls have been doing, it's no wonder. Anyway, it doesn't matter much who the father is, if you take my solution."

Sally said, "Oh yes, it does matter, lots and lots. Todd and I are in love, and he'll want to marry me, and—"

Mrs. V exclaimed, "Stop this right now! He's not going to marry you, Sally, not by a long shot. Todd's off to college next year, probably on a scholarship. Do you think he wants to drag along a high school dropout with a whining brat? The answer is a big *no*!"

Now Sally began to *really* cry as Brenda hugged her closer. "Don't be mean, Mrs. V. She's got trouble enough already without you piling on."

"Okay, listen!" said Mrs. V. "I've got more adventures for you two, if you agree, and our stipend will go up. You'll be back on cheer team, too, Sally. Or you can ask Grandma for the three hundred dollars for an abortion. What's it gonna be?"

Sally exclaimed, "Abortion? No, not that! Grandma? Oh, no! Todd and I are going steady now, so I'm not sure I want an abortion. And anyway, maybe you're wrong and he'll want to get married! This is your fault too,

Mrs. V, because you had us do all that stuff! We're good girls—it's just that it was so much fun, and the stipend! We're good girls, aren't we, Brenda?"

Brenda said nothing, but she gave Mrs. V a leave-her-alone look.

Mrs. V said, "Don't make me laugh, Sally. You're not good girls. You strut the halls with your tits pushed out, cleavage, short skirts, and hair done up. That's not what good girls do. You like *it*—and lots of it, too. Everyone knows about you both. You're hot, and you want everyone to know it."

Continuing to gently rock Sally back and forth, Brenda gave her a couple of kisses on the cheek. "What about you, Mrs. V, and your own parade? We know what you did in LA."

"What was that, you busty tart? And how dare you speak to me like that?" asked Mrs. V.

Sally was still convulsing in sobs on Brenda's shoulder, but she managed to blurt out, "Brenda and I *are* good girls! We're popular because—well, just because!"

Brenda said, "Sally's right, Mrs. V. We're the most popular girls in school, that's all."

Mrs. V's eyes narrowed as she looked at her charges. She leaned over and put her face close to theirs, then poked a long, red-tipped finger into the front of first Brenda's blouse, then Sally's. She said softly, "These will get you what you want, because you both love to fuck—and for money, too. You know what that makes you, don't you?"

A bit intimidated, Brenda replied, "We're not ... What?"

Mrs. V said softly, "Try *escorts*, *call girls*, *prostitutes*, or maybe go whole hog—*whores*, that's what you are! You've known it all along, haven't you? I can see it on your pretty faces. Yes, you know what you are."

Shocked, they both stared at Mrs. V's perfectly made-up, vengeful face. Then Sally broke into another full bout of crying.

Brenda yelled, "We're not like that! Mr. Hesselgren said we were nice!"

Mrs. V straightened up, eyes still cold as ice, and dug her dagger in a little deeper. "Oh yeah, Mr. Hesselgren, is it? My, my! What I heard, Miss Boob Queen, was that you'd suck the chrome off a trailer hitch. And you, Sally, go bananas for that full feeling. It doesn't take much imagination to figure out what your favorite pastime is. No, you won't walk away from all that sex and money. You'll do my bidding or else."

Brenda started to protest, but decided instead to continue consoling the still-whimpering Sally.

Mrs. V said, "Now, can we calmly look to the future and a solution? You won't show for weeks, Sally, so it won't interfere with the entertainment I've scheduled. On Saturday, you'll go up to Paso and meet the doctor and a friend. Wear your things from Flo's. I'll drive you up and then bring you back on Sunday. Make an excuse to Grandma about cheer activities. I'll call and make sure she knows it's for real. Your mom, Brenda, is no problem. Does she still hang out at the Mission Bar?"

They both nodded. Sally's sobs had died down to a whimper.

"I won't be notifying Principal Jennings about your pregnancy, Sally," Mrs. V continued. "And as long as you're obedient, your secret is safe, but no more of that backing out like you pulled with Coach. Brenda took care of that—and most successfully, I might add. But Sally, you're on notice that if it ever happens again? Well, you know what will happen, right?"

The girls again nodded.

"Now for the good news. Sally, after school's out for the summer, we'll have you down to the house in Pismo Beach and end your condition once and for all. I will cover the three-hundred-dollar cost. Isn't that nice of me? Why yes, it is! But again I warn you, Sally, that any hesitation to obey will result in expulsion, plus you can take care of your condition on your own. Is that crystal clear?" Mrs. V gazed at the dejected girls with a look of complete triumph on her face.

More nods from Brenda and Sally.

"Good! Then it's settled. I'll pick you up at six o'clock. Be in your cheer outfits."

The girls stood up. Brenda lifted Sally's chin and said softly, "Come on now, it's not so bad. We'll have the same fun as we've always had. We'll just make sure Todd doesn't find out, okay?"

Sally said, "Oh my, Todd will be so ... I don't know if ... I know he loves me, and I don't want to deceive him. He'll be really mad and ... Oh my!"

Mrs. V said forcefully, "Don't be silly. He'll still want you. He's a guy, and that's what they want—sex. The rest is just words so that you'll put out. And you do, so he'll want you. He did it with Brenda, and you forgave him, right? Yes, you did, so what's the big deal? And don't forget your stipend. That's important, too, isn't it?"

Brenda had perked up. "She's right about that, Sally. We can work around Todd. He'll be busy with JROTC and boxing all summer. You'll see! It'll be fun and easy."

Sally gave Brenda a slightly dirty look and said, "I guess!"

~

Sally and Brenda did Dr. McKay and his friend, who turned out to be Deacon Jennings. By now, Brenda and the doctor were well acquainted, so they got their own room at a motel near Paso Robles. Sally and Deacon Jennings got the room next door. It was the quickest and most unrewarding "adventure" she'd ever done. A drunk Deacon Jennings fell asleep right after the event. They were dropped near Meadow Park the next morning. Grandma was none the wiser.

For the last two weeks before school let out, Mrs. V kept them busy, and the stipends rolled in. But for Sally, it became more of a chore than an adventure, stipends notwithstanding. The subterfuge and the lies she told to fool Todd began to wear on her. She loved him more every day, and Mrs. V's adventures were a growing ordeal.

Just a few days before school let out and Todd was to graduate, Sally didn't show up for an adventure that Mrs. V had set up. Mrs. V went to Sally's house and pretended to be concerned about her health. In front of Grandma, she questioned Sally in just the right tone of voice to scare her half to death.

When Sally walked Mrs. V out to her car, however, the threat was clear: "One more failure like that, and I'll let the whole story out. I'll tell Todd that the baby you're carrying isn't his, understand? What will he think of you when he hears that you fucked for money, huh? Do you think your grandma will front the three hundred bucks when she hears that? Your darling, loving Todd will leave you like a bad penny. Yes, Sally, that's what's in it for you if you don't behave. Obey and perform, or else. Is that clear?" Sally wet her pants right there on the porch, and the fear on her face was Mrs. V's answer.

Sally knew she was trapped in a web of her own making, and her only friend was in the same fix. The difference was that Brenda wasn't pregnant and didn't care. Sally began avoiding Todd as much as possible, because she thought the whole mess would show on her face—or she'd just break down and cry. She was caught in a downward spiral, and her appearance reflected it.

One Sunday morning, while trying to figure a way out of her predicament, Sally accidentally stumbled on an answer of sorts. She was at church with Todd when Deacon Jennings said during the sermon, "The truth will out. Good flows from truth, one way or the other. It's what Jesus said many times."

As they left the church, Sally looked at Todd, and his love for her shone out in all its simple goodness. She thought, *I'll tell Todd that I'm going to have our baby. He's good and honest, and he loves me, and he won't leave just for a college scholarship. No, he'll stay and marry me, and we'll live together blissfully!*

She decided that after the graduation dance, she'd tell him. After making this decision, Sally relaxed, was able to sleep again, and kept herself up better too. She reasoned that in a few days, everything would be done and she'd leave the adventures behind. It was actually a complete fantasy, but Sally convinced herself it was true. She didn't even consider the fact that Mrs. V wouldn't let her just leave without putting up a fight. Sally's clothes tightened, her bust grew, and her appetite increased, but even Brenda supported her fantasy. The house in Pismo Beach faded from the picture. Todd would be Sally's knight in shining armor and save her. As she prepared for the graduation formal with Todd, their false future looked rosy.

~

Sally and Brenda attended the mid-afternoon graduation ceremony, during which it was announced that several students were getting scholarships. Todd received a combined boxing and ROTC scholarship for Cal Poly, which was a big deal. There was a raucous gathering after the ceremony, and then everyone left to get ready for the evening graduation party.

Sally and Brenda, who was going to the graduation party with Terrell, prepared carefully. Flo was a great help in this, as long as Brenda continued to pay her a lot of attention, which she did.

Sally got an off-the-shoulder, floor-length white dress. The only trouble was that she'd grown since she had been fitted at Flo's, and the adjustment they made just barely did the job. She still wasn't sure the chaperones would pass on it. The addition of a white satin shawl was just the look she wanted, sensual and innocent at the same time. An acquaintance of Flo's did Sally's hair in a French braid, and she also had some dramatic makeup.

Brenda had picked out a slinky red satin dress that was so tight that she almost spilled out, along with red lingerie, ladder nylons, and red spiked heels. Her hair was piled with red satin ribbons woven in, and her makeup was dramatic with tiny, glittery flakes.

Sally also had other things to consider about attending the dance with Todd. For example, Kenny still followed her around and paid attention to her, even though she'd told him she was now going with Todd.

Grandma, Gail, and Zoe all three helped Sally get ready. It was the most fun they'd had together, and it took hours. When Sally stood ready in front of the mirror, she liked what she saw. When her sisters came into her room to see the finished product, they gave a collective gasp at Sally's beautiful, adult appearance.

Grandma followed Gail and Zoe into Sally's room, put a hand under her chin, and looked her up and down. "Oh my, I'm not sure that dress is quite enough. Your bust is a bit too exposed, don't you think? Perhaps we can pull the bodice up just a tiny bit. I'm sure you girls agree."

"No, Grandma, it's perfect. Yes, perfect! Sally looks just perfect," Zoe insisted.

Gail exclaimed, "I want to look like this for my prom someday!"

"Me, too!" chimed in Zoe.

Sally was pleasantly surprised to have the support of her catty sisters. Grandma did firmly pull up the bodice, which helped a little. But after Sally moved around a few minutes, the exposure grew even more. She was afraid she might just spill out completely, and she thought, *Brenda would sure like that!*

~

Just after seven o'clock, Todd pulled up in his nice clean truck. Sally, the girls, and Grandma were at the door in excited anticipation. As the four women watched, he got out and made the short wall to the porch. Wearing a tuxedo that fit him like a glove, he moved with the relaxed grace of an athlete, and his face radiated confidence. In one hand was a white box, and in his other was a bouquet of flowers. He arrived at the open door every inch the knight in shining armor they all wanted to see. "Hi, everyone. Holy moly, Sally, wow! Jesus, you look—wow! You're surely the most beautiful women in the world. I may need to sit down."

Sally's emotional roller coaster settled for a moment as she answered demurely, "Why, thank you, Todd. You look quite handsome yourself."

The girls watched this scene with rapt attention, getting a glimpse of the future that they hoped for. Grandma just beamed.

Todd handed the bouquet of flowers to Grandma and said, "Grandma, these are for you. Enjoy them in the spirit of our friendship."

Grandma said, "Oh my, Todd, you shouldn't have, but thank you! These are very nice. Excuse me while I go put them in water." She walked into the kitchen.

Todd looked at Gail and Zoe, who were paying close attention to all this. He handed each of them a white rose and said, "Here's something for you two cute girls."

Together they coyly said, "Thank you so much!" Giving Sally and Todd a quick look, they followed Grandma into the kitchen.

Sally said, "Oh, you charmer. You will forever be in their good graces now."

Todd said sheepishly, "It's nothing. They're nice—and kinda cute, too. They always welcome me warmly, and it's the least I could do on this important day. Sally, you look like a million bucks. I've got the most beautiful girls in the whole world."

Batting her eyelids flirtatiously, Sally replied, "I'm so glad. I did it just for you, Todd. What's that other thing you've got there. Could it be for little old me?"

Todd said, "Jeez, I almost forgot. Here's your corsage." Taking it from him, Sally accidentally dropped it to the floor. As she and Todd bent to pick it up at the same time, they bumped heads and laughed. Then he tried to pin it to her dress, but it didn't fit.

"Oh, thank you, but it has to go on my wrist." At this point, Sally noticed that her bending over had pushed her boobs almost completely out. She also felt the growing bump in her tummy, and all the recently banished fears came flooding back. Suddenly she felt less like Todd's princess, and more like the fat trollop Mrs. V had described.

With his eyes glued to her bust, Todd said, "How about we just forget the dance and go right up to the shack. Wow! That cute little girl I met two years ago playing hopscotch has been transformed. The year 1961 looks like a very good year. You're the sexiest woman alive."

These wonderful words thrilled Sally, but they also convinced her that

Todd would accept her pregnancy with grace and marry her. She batted her eyes and asked, "I haven't overdone anything, have I?"

"No, Sally, you haven't overdone anything. I'll remember you this way forever." Then Todd got a faraway look in his eyes as he recalled a past *forever* moment among some big rocks, under a spreading tree, with a tune on the wind from far off. Then, as quickly as it had come, the moment was gone.

Sally stepped up to Todd, looked to make sure the girls and Grandma were still occupied, and kissed him softly but passionately. She whispered, "I love you, Todd Wyrum. I really do!"

He gave her a soft smile, but the faraway look remained.

Sally wondered if those eyes said that this was the moment to give him the news. But just as this thought appeared, it vanished as her sisters and Grandma came back into the foyer.

Grandma looked up at the clock and exclaimed, "Oh, my dear! It's past seven. You two had better get going. Don't want to be late for this big night, do you?"

Todd helped Sally with her shawl. She took his arm, and he escorted her out the door. As they paused on the porch, Gail and Zoe both curtsied, batted their eyes, and said, "Oh, thank you, Todd. We want a boy just like you."

Sally thought, *Oh yes, they're learning. Oh yes, they are!*

The girls and Grandma waved goodbye as Sally and Todd drove off. Fifteen minutes later, they were at the Madonna Inn amid a huge array of guests. It was exciting to see the girls in formal dresses and the boys, who were usually in jeans and T-shirts, cleaned up and wearing tuxedos. The girls immediately got excited about all their outfits and makeup. Sally and Brenda's low-cut tops were not the only outfits drawing attention. A few girls had no back to their dresses and lots of cleavage too, and a couple of extremely short skirts drew gasps. Todd and Sally walked into the ballroom amid laughter, joking, camaraderie, and expectations of a bright future. Hope was in the air. What could go wrong?

~

The graduation dinner was the usual rubber chicken, and the punch got spiked, but the fun was all they'd hoped for. When Deacon Jennings gave the invocation before dinner, Brenda and Sally gave each other knowing looks. Dancing began right after dinner. The band was a local rock-n-roll group from Cal Poly, plus Little Willie Littlefield from the local El Morocco Club. He'd written the famous hit "Kansas City." The band included the Yasino brothers and the best guitar player around, Jim Pearson, doing solos.

Animosity between the boxers and football players had caused problems at past events, but tonight all seemed well. Coach had spoken to both groups, and his message was "Tone it down!"

A few odd things happened. For example, Brenda's mother, who was waiting tables, wore an Alpine dirndl-type dress that challenged even Brenda's display. Brenda and Sally tried to ignore her. Mrs. V was in a colorful dress, and she even danced with a couple of faculty members. It was also noted that the security officer posted outside was Big Earl, and Principal Jennings and Major LaBrie, Todd's JROTC commander, were chaperones.

When the lights went down after dinner, the mirrored ball spun, throwing its eerie beams across the floor, and a lot of secret drinking was going on behind the scene. A few of the school staff members danced. When several students asked their favorite teachers to dance, Brenda asked Coach.

Most of the music was rock-n-roll, which wasn't Sally and Todd's favorite. But even Hector and Helman, who seemed unlikely to dance much, joined in. Sally danced with both of them, and Todd danced with their dates and also Brenda.

Lots of the football players went out back to have a drink, then came back but didn't dance. Kenny asked to cut in on Sally, and Todd, not wanting to cause a ruckus, backed off and permitted it, much to Sally's consternation. When the piece ended, however, and Todd went back to dance with Sally, Kenny objected. "I've got the next one, too," he insisted, "if you don't mind."

Sally spoke up and said, "Yes, Kenny, I do mind. And anyway, you're drunk, so go back to your bottle and leave the fun to us. Come on, Todd, let's dance."

Todd said to an obviously drunk Kenny, "Butt out and leave us alone, okay, chump?"

This confrontation drew the attention of Kenny's teammates, plus Hector and Helman. If Todd hadn't used the word *chump*, all might have been forgiven, but that taunt set off the old antagonism. Coach and the chaperones weren't nearby to step in.

Kenny replied forcefully, "What's that you say, Skinny? Sally put out for me before, remember? She's a tramp."

Without hesitation, Todd hit him with a right hook that didn't land squarely but sent Kenny reeling. Unfortunately the miss threw Todd off balance. Kenny recovered and stepped into Todd with a straight punch to the face that put Todd on the floor—and Sally, skirt and tiara flying, with him. Kenny jumped on Todd, which violently forced Sally into the crowd forming around them. She screamed, but that got lost in the yells and curses issuing from the group.

Todd was hit several times before he finally stumbled back to his feet. Blood streamed from his nose and spattered over his tux. Now things were even. Kenny was much bigger, but Todd was quicker and a trained boxer. He hit Kenny with several jabs and a hook to the midsection that drew a gasp. Kenny charged Todd, setting off a brawl between the boxers, Hector and Helman, and the more numerous football players. Fists flew, blood ran, and girls scattered. Kenny's bloody face was livid with hate as he swung wildly, and Todd, too, was covered in blood. All around them fists were flying, girls were screaming, and boys were yelling.

It seemed like a long time, but actually only a minute or so passed before Coach and Big Earl rushed into the tangled, confusing brawl. They got almost everyone apart, as Big Earl hurled boys through the air. Todd and Kenny, however, continued to fight. Todd knocked Kenny to the floor, but then he wouldn't stop as anger and hate contorted his face. Todd kicked Kenny in the face and groin until Kenny screamed in pain. Even Helman and Hector tried to pull Todd away, but they couldn't calm him. Finally Coach came up behind Todd and lifted him clean off his feet. As Coach held him in an iron embrace, Todd screamed obscenities at Kenny.

Todd's temper, which no one had witnessed previously, gave his face the look of insanity. Even as Coach pushed him away, Todd tried to kick Kenny again. Finally Big Earl got hold of Todd and slapped his bloody face, which seemed to calm him down.

Fights were common, but this one was different. Kenny was really hurt and needed medical attention. Hector and Helman sat Todd down, and both Sally and Brenda went over to him. Sally said, "I'm so sorry I let Kenny dance with me. Oh my, Todd, you're hurt! Let me look at your face."

Brenda yelled, "Kenny's a jerk! He deserved it. He needed that, Todd. Good for you."

A moment later, Coach and Big Earl stood over Todd. One of the football players said, "Todd hit Kenny first. I saw it. Todd started it. All Kenny wanted was to dance with Sally. That's all!" Then another boy and two girls came up to Coach and Big Earl, and the boy said, "I saw it, too. Todd just hit Kenny for no reason. Kenny just wanted to dance with Sally." One of the girls said, "That's right, all Kenny wanted was a dance. Sally's easy—a tramp."

Finally Coach said, "Enough talk. Let's all calm down. Deputy, you'd better call an ambulance for Kenny. His jaw looks broken, and those eyes could be bad. Todd, what the dickens got into you?" More angry comments came from the crowd as Big Earl went to call an ambulance.

Brenda's mother tried to pull her away, but she wouldn't go. "You don't need to get mixed up in this," said her mother.

But Brenda insisted, "No, I want to stay and help Sally. Look at her dress. She's mostly spilled out."

Even as Brenda said it, Sally was tucking her boobs back in. Then she quietly put her arm around Todd, who sat in shock.

The band started up again, but only a few people went back to dance, and soon most people left the ballroom. Todd, Sally, Hector, and Helman sat quietly and cleaned up a little. Coach stood by and explained to a few people who hadn't witnessed the brawl what happened.

Mrs. V looked in and said, "Sally, I'm sure you were the instigator. You've been just wild lately, and that dress is so inappropriate. You're a disgrace to the team, the school, and all of us. I don't need any more reason. You're off the cheer team completely."

Todd looked up at Mrs. V and said, "It wasn't Sally's fault at all. Kenny called her a dirty word. I've got a right to defend Sally, don't I? Coach, don't I?"

With a look of resignation on his face, Coach patted Todd on the shoulder and said, "Well, yes, Todd, but not like that. You kicked Kenny when he was down—more than down! He was giving up, and you shouldn't have done that. You should've left him alone."

"But Coach, I didn't mean to—"

"I know, Todd, I know! Just sit tight. We'll deal with this later," said Coach.

Twenty minutes later, the ballroom had mostly cleared. Kenny, who was obviously hurt, was sitting with a couple of his friends and Coach, who had told Hector and Helman to leave.

A few minutes later, an ambulance crew came in with a gurney, followed closely by Dr. and Mrs. McKay. They made a big fuss over Kenny. As he was rolled out, he and Todd exchanged nods.

Dr. McKay came over to Todd and said, "His jaw looks broken, and he may have some broken ribs. But the worst is that left eye. You could have blinded him. You're a bad apple, kid, and we're going to get rid of you. Deputy, I want Todd arrested and taken to the courthouse jail. I'll call Judge Jackson and see if he can be arraigned on Monday."

Big Earl said, "Okay, doc, but are you really sure you want to do that? It was a hell of a brawl, but they're just kids, you know? And there may be other stuff to consider. Do you really want to file a complaint?" He looked at the doctor meaningfully.

Pointing at Sally and Brenda, Mrs. McKay said, "We sure do, Earl. Todd's a bad boy, and that girl? She's a tramp and everyone knows it. Look who she befriends! My word, look at that dress. She's just a tramp, really!"

Todd tried to speak, but Coach broke in. "Now, Mrs. McKay, let's not take this mess any further, okay? Big Earl and I will deal with Todd. Why don't you just go with Kenny? He needs you more than this situation does. Come on, let's be the adults. The law will deal with Todd. So how about it? Can we break this thing up now?"

Her dress a torn and bloody mess, Sally began to cry.

While this was going on, two more sheriffs came into the ballroom. One of them, the deputy chief, said to Big Earl, "What about it, Earl? Are we gonna take someone in?" He'd been looking over at Dr. and Mrs. McKay as he said this, knowing full well that they were prime movers in the county. The authoritative looks on their faces sent a clear message.

Big Earl, looking quite uncomfortable, replied, "Well, I sure don't want to, but I guess it's probably in the cards. You'd best tend to Todd's nose while you're at it. Stand up, Todd, so I can cuff you. Sorry about this, but it's policy. New procedure—not my idea, you understand?"

As Todd reluctantly stood up, Sally's crying increased. Big Earl said to everyone in general, "You know, not too long ago, a bunch of kids mixing it up would just be marked down as growing pains, and everyone would go home seeing it as a life lesson. Nowadays it's a big deal. It just don't figure, but it's the law, Todd."

When the cuffs were snapped on Todd, Sally jumped up, gave him a big hug, and said, "I love you, Todd. This'll be okay, you'll see."

As they started to lead Todd off, he looked back and said, "Sally, the keys to the truck are in my tux pocket. Take them, okay? I'll see you—well, when I see you."

Major LaBrie, standing nearby, said to Todd, "That was a bad move you made, Todd. If you're convicted, you'll probably lose your scholarship over this. It's a shame, a real shame."

Dr. and Mrs. McKay walked out with self-satisfied looks on their faces, though his smile vanished when he saw Brenda.

Big Earl and Coach walked Todd out with the deputies. Earl whispered to them both, "Like I said, this may not come out as they think. Too bad about that, too bad!"

Sally quickly morphed into Todd's girl and rushed out to the truck. She hardly knew how to drive, much less handle a stick shift. Grinding the gears, she pulled out behind the patrol car and honked the horn. She could barely see Todd turn in his seat to look at her, and a few moments later when she did it again, she could see him smile. She followed them all the way to the jail.

At the county building on Monterey Street, the officers got Todd out of the patrol car and took him inside. Sally parked a few spaces away, put on her cheer team jacket, and followed.

At the door, in the dark, Todd turned back to look at Sally, even as they pulled him through the door. He gave her that little nod, and the lock of hair fell down over his forehead. Sally waved and clutched her bosom as he vanished inside. She loved him more than ever, but she still hadn't had an opportunity to tell him about her condition, as she'd planned.

CHAPTER 22

Without Knowing

Sally was at the jail at 11:00 the next morning. She saw Todd through a small glass window, and they talked by phone, though they were limited to five minutes. His face was bruised and one eye was partly closed, but otherwise he seemed okay. She'd brought him a book to read.

Todd told her, "My arraignment is Monday at eleven. It's not a trial, so I won't be going anywhere, but I might need bail. Basically it's a hearing to level charges and put in process what's going to happen. That's when they'll decide what to do."

"But how will we know—"

"We won't know, Sally. Just be patient," Todd said. "You'll understand at the hearing, and there's other stuff to know. I expect Dr. and Mrs. McKay will be there, but probably not Kenny. The people who saw the fight will probably be witnesses. I asked Major LaBrie to be there, and Coach, of course. Big Earl said he'd be there too, which surprised me, but it could help. Who knows?"

Now that she'd heard it all, Sally got scared. "Todd, could they put you in ... in jail?"

Todd said, "Yes, they could, and I expect Dr. McKay will use his influence to try to do just that."

"But you were only trying to protect me! So I could tell them that and maybe ... Since I'm a girl, maybe they'll ... Oh Todd, what are we going to do?"

"Judge Jackson is a hard-ass, but he's fair, according to Big Earl. So at least I've got a good judge. It could be worse. I could get probation or military youth camp."

"Can I help? Anything?" asked Sally.

"No, I don't think so, unless the lawyer wants a character witness. I called Miss Lady out at the ranch and told her everything—about you and me, too. She'll have a lawyer for me at least. The same one who helped me before. He's pretty sharp."

Sally was suspicions. "Miss Lady? Your guardian from the Carrizo. Like that?"

"Yeah, like that," Todd said.

Down the hall, a shout rang out. "Time's up! Everyone out!"

What Todd had said about character witnesses sank in, and Sally knew who could help. She called Brenda, and they worked out a plan to assist Todd. The first question was how to dress to make the right impression. This was an area of expertise where they didn't need a lawyer's help.

~

Monday morning at eleven o'clock, Miss Lady and Mr. Pearson sat in the courtroom and waited as other people filed in—Dr. and Mrs. McKay; Principal Jennings and his brother, Deacon Jennings; Coach and Mr. Hesselgren from the booster club; and Major LaBrie, who came in alone and sat in the back. Big Earl was already there, seated next to the bailiff. Everyone spoke in hushed tones. When Mrs. V and Flo entered, the tension in the room rose. They walked around close in front of Miss Lady, and the two bitter enemies eyeballed each other with looks that could kill.

At that moment, Sally and Brenda sashayed in with enough presence to momentarily stop all conversation. They were dressed at the very edge of tasteful for grown women, with short skirts, cleavage, and makeup. The group that had formed around Dr. and Mrs. McKay gave a collective start at their presence, and Mr. Hesselgren shook his head. Big Earl indicated where they should sit, but they gave a little finger wave to Mrs. V and moved instead to seats near the McKays.

Brenda brushed the doctor's arm and in a lilting voice said, "Hello, Dr. McKay. And you must be Mrs. McKay. Nice to *finally* meet you. I'm Brenda, and this is Sally." There was actual fear on Dr. McKay's face as Brenda sat down and crossed her legs.

Sally stopped in front of Mr. Hesselgren, bent over, took his hand, and said coyly, "Oh, Mr. Hesselgren, I'm so happy to see you. It's been too long. Your visits to cheer team practices are so appreciated."

Mr. Hesselgren was no fool. He whispered quickly to Sally, "I get the message. Move away, and don't make a fuss. I'll fix this all up with you and Brenda later, okay?"

Sally sat down and pretended he'd given her a compliment. "Oh, thank you so much. You're so complimentary. We girls try so very hard to please you and all your attentive friends."

After that, things settled down a bit. The district attorney entered through a side door and sat at the right-hand table. A police officer escorted Todd in and directed him to a seat with Mr. Pearson. Minutes later the bailiff called out, "All rise."

Judge Jackson, who was blind, came in with his guide dog and sat at his bench. "Be seated, please. Are you ready, Mr. Neel?" he asked.

"Yes, your honor, the district attorney's office is ready."

Judge Jackson then said, "Hello, Mr. Pearson. Nice to have you in my court again. Are you and your client ready?"

"We are, your honor," replied Mr. Pearson, "and I'm happy to be representing this fine young man, Todd Wyrum."

"Yes, I'm sure, but more of that as we move along," said the judge. "Mr. Neel, you may proceed."

The DA stood and said, "Friday evening at the high school graduation party in Edna, Mr. Wyrum, who sits at the defendant's table, assaulted Kenny McKay. Kenny McKay is not here today, because of his injuries. He is still in French Hospital. Dr. McKay, his father, is here on his behalf. We intend to prove that the injuries Kenny McKay sustained were callously administered without provocation by the defendant during the dance. We are charging Mr. Wyrum with first-degree assault and ask the court to set a date for trial."

Judge Jackson asked, "Mr. Pearson, how does your client plead to this charge?"

Mr. Pearson and Todd stood up. "Not guilty, your honor," Todd said.

"Then we do have a case, don't we?" said the judge. "Can we have some quiet back there, please? This is a courtroom, not a social. Do I hear a bail proposal, Mr. Neel?"

The DA replied, "We ask for ten thousand dollars cash or bond, due to the severity of the assault."

Judge Jackson said, "Mr. Pearson, I expect you have something to say on this matter. Go ahead."

Mr. Pearson replied, "I do, your honor. Mr. Wyrum asserts his innocence and that he was only defending himself, although he deeply regrets the injuries sustained by Kenny McKay. Mr. Todd Wyrum is a local young man and just graduated on Friday from our high school. We further assert that he is not even remotely a flight risk and therefore should be released on his own recognizance. He can be released into the care of his legal guardian, Mrs. Wyrum, who is in the courtroom today. Thank you very much for your consideration, your honor."

At this point Dr. McKay approached the DA's table and, standing just behind Mr. Neel, spoke to him over his shoulder. Mr. Neel then turned to Mr. Pearson at the defense table and whispered something. Mr. Pearson nodded, and Mr. Neel said to the judge, "Your honor, another item has come to my attention that may or may not affect these proceedings. May we please have a twenty-minute recess to discuss the matter? With your approval, Mr. Pearson agrees to this."

The judge, showing signs of irritation, said, "What is it, Mr. Neel?"

Mr. Neel again said, "Items have just now come to the fore that may well influence this proceeding."

The judge glared at the two attorneys and said, "We'll recess until one o'clock."

After Judge Jackson departed, the room shifted to several small group discussions that seemed to be focused somewhat on Brenda, Sally, and Dr. McKay. Both attorneys went back and forth between Major LaBrie, Miss Lady, and Todd, and this continued throughout the entire lunch break. At one point, name calling and rude gestures erupted between Mrs. V and Miss Lady, who had to be separated. Finally the judge returned and asked everyone to be seated.

The DA rose and said, "After consultations with all parties, it is agreed that pending charges against Mr. Wyrum will be dropped if he agrees to go into the army as a private soldier. Major LaBrie will facilitate this, since Todd is already in JROTC. Todd will leave this afternoon for Fort Ord; otherwise he'll have to wait a month. If this is acceptable to the court, then we can conclude these proceedings." He handed the judge a sheet of paper.

Judge Jackson thought this over for a minute and then said, "Are there any objections? Hearing none, I rule that all charges against Todd Wyrum be dropped pending this agreement:

1. "Major LaBrie will facilitate Todd Wyrum's entrance into the army and basic training.
2. "Todd Wyrum will go through basic training at Fort Ord, up the coast.
3. "Upon successful completion of basic training, Mr. Wyrum will be admitted to the Medical Corps training program at Fort Sam Houston, Texas.
4. "Todd Wyrum's high school diploma, which has not yet been issued, will be forwarded to him at his next posting.
5. "If any further arrangements are required by the court, they will be handled by Mrs. Wyrum as Todd Wyrum's legal guardian.

Miss Lady stood, leveled a hateful stare at Mrs. V, and exclaimed, "The damn army! This is so unfair."

Todd, who was sitting next her, put a hand on her shoulder and gently pulled her back down. "It's okay, Miss Lady. Really, it is. Sit down and let's get on with this, please?"

Then Mrs. McKay said to her husband, "This is not fair. Kenny is badly hurt, and this vicious hoodlum goes free? You're his father and a doctor. How could you agree to this travesty?"

It was Dr. McKay's turn to pull Mrs. McKay back into her seat. "For the love of God, Judy, will you let it go? Kenny's jaw is not broken. Just sit, please!"

The judge asked, "Okay, do you all agree?"

Mr. Neel looked at Mr. Pearson, who nodded and said, "It's agreed." A general nodding of heads ensued, and then everyone stood and began leaving the courtroom.

Pointing at Sally and Brenda, Mrs. McKay said, "We should banish these tramps with him!"

Dr. McKay quickly pulled her down again and said sternly, "Judy, please!"

The two attorneys reached across the table and shook hands.

Big Earl slapped Todd on the back and pointed at Sally. "Don't worry, Todd. She'll wait for you!"

Major LaBrie took Sally, Todd, and Miss Lady to lunch at Scrubby and Lloyd's, where they sat around a table under a big tree and enjoyed burgers and milkshakes. There was obvious tension between Sally and Miss Lady, but confrontation was avoided. When they finished lunch, Major LaBrie excused himself to make a call.

Miss Lady said, "Todd, I'll pick up your stuff from Houson House and take it to the ranch. Maybe, uh, Sally can get your things from school?"

Todd nodded, then brought up a topic that he was afraid might cause a problem, "Sure, but I want Sally to have the truck if that's okay with you, Miss Lady. It's her only way around now, and I'm sure she'll take really good care of it. Is that okay? I mean, you did give it to me, and ..."

Miss Lady took another look at Sally. It really wasn't okay, but she felt she couldn't deny Todd anything, given the situation. "It's okay by me," she said, "if she takes good care of the old girl."

"I will, I promise. Now I have to excuse myself." Sally rose and went to the ladies' room.

Watching her go, Miss Lady said, "You can really pick 'em, Todd—and her buxom friend too."

"I'm really sorry about all this, Miss Lady. I let my temper get out of control, and Sally ... Well, it's just that ..." As Todd stumbled through an apology, his confusion was evident. His heart was divided between two vivacious women, and his future had just been deeply muddled by the past days' events. He turned away, not knowing what else to say.

Miss Lady lips quivered as she said, "I knew this would come, Todd. I'm not sad or angry, and I don't want to turn back time. We'll always be what we were that summer, but I know you'll be with other women and marry someday. I wish you happiness, Todd. May I hold you, just one more time? Come to Miss Lady, please. I'll always be yours. Oh Todd, your Miss Lady loves you so, if only for this last minute."

He turned back to her, and in one last desperate embrace, they both cried. Todd said, "We'll *always* have that summer at the rodeo—always, Miss Lady. And I'll wear this bracelet forever, no matter what. It will always remind me of you, of us. Oh God, this is tearing me apart."

Miss Lady extended her hand, so that Todd could see the silver and turquoise ring he'd given her. Through her tears, she said, "And this, my darling Todd, will always and forever connect us. I love you and only you, my Todd ... My Todd."

Todd, visibly shaken, said, "Oh yes, Miss Lady. Oh yes."

Knowing Sally would be back any minute, Miss Lady stood up. Barely under control, she wiped her tears away and said, "I can't bear to see you leave, so I'm going back to the ranch. I'll get your other stuff later. You're leaving with the major in a few minutes, and my heart is breaking, so you need to just let me go. Oh Todd, I wish this was until we meet again, but I know it's goodbye. So goodbye, my love."

Watching her walk away, Todd choked back a sob and whispered, "Miss Lady!"

~

When Sally returned, she didn't ask where Miss Lady had gone.

However, Major LaBrie said, "Where's your mom, Todd? I thought she'd want to see you off. You're leaving in less than an hour."

"She's not my mom!" Todd said harshly.

Sally knew what his answer meant. She was glad to see Miss Lady gone, because she needed to have a private talk with Todd. "Major LaBrie, can I have a few minutes alone with Todd, please?"

Major LaBrie said, "Okay, but we're already late. You can come along and say goodbye at the Greyhound station. Now let's vamoose!" They all stood and walked to Major LaBrie's car. During the ride to the bus station, Major LaBrie talked continuously, and Sally couldn't get a word in.

At the bus station, Sally and Todd stood among a throng of other recruits while Major LaBrie got it all organized. The depot smelled of sweat, stale cigarettes, and diesel fumes. A tired clerk, the crowd of recruits, and several dozing passengers were the only signs of life.

There was really no time for Sally to have a serious, private talk with Todd, but she tried anyway. "Todd, we need to talk about the future, about us and—well, important things. Also, I want to give you something. Please keep this close, so that we'll always be near each other." She put a lock of her hair in his hand and squeezed it shut.

Todd kissed her long and lovingly, then said, "Always, always!"

The major said, "There's the bus. Say your goodbyes and let's go, Todd."

Todd said, "Basic's done in a few weeks, Sally, and I'll be back on leave. Then we can go off together and get our tomorrows figured out. It's only a few weeks, okay?"

Sally's mind was busily figuring Todd's schedule in relation to nine months. "Well, okay, as long as you're sure that you'll be back on leave."

The major walked around and handed each recruit an official document, then a second envelope. He announced, "There's some kind of snafu, minor stuff, at Fort Ord. When we get there, hand this to the sergeant who registers you. He'll give you special instructions. I have no idea what your instructions will be, but like I said, it's probably a minor thing. Everyone understand?"

Everyone nodded, and the bus driver called out, "All aboard for Fort Ord." The new recruits began to file on to the big bus.

Major LaBrie said, "Todd, you'll have to put this off for a while. Say your goodbyes."

Sally and Todd shared a farewell kiss, and then Todd grabbed his small bag and started to get on the bus. He hesitated at the bottom step and said, "Oh hell, I almost forgot. Here's the keys and signed pink slip to the truck. Don't forget to get that driver's license, Sally. Take good care of it. Bye for a few weeks."

All Sally had time to say was, "Bye, Todd! I love you."

The big door closed with a hiss, and a minute later the bus pulled away. Sally and Major LaBrie watched it disappear, north toward the highway.

It was so quick, so final. Todd was gone without knowing. Sally clutched her belly.

CHAPTER 23

The Mason Jar

When the bus left the station enveloped in diesel fumes, Sally's world went with it. Todd had spoken of their separation in terms of weeks, but it could have been a century as far as her feelings went. Sally's womb had taken over.

Major LaBrie dropped Sally off at her home after the bus left. Todd's beloved truck sat in Sally's driveway, forgotten. Without him in it, it meant little. She forgot all about his locker things. At home she avoided Grandma and her nosy sisters, went straight to her room, and shut the door.

Trying to muffle her sobs, Sally finally fell asleep. When she awoke the next morning, dawn was just peeking through her window. The house was quiet, and she realized she'd slept more than thirteen hours but still felt exhausted. Her heart was empty, but her tummy was full.

Choking down her panic, Sally slowly started remembering—back, further back, gaining momentum as her mind raced. Finally she got up, still in the rumpled clothes she'd worn to the courthouse, and ran out on the front porch and down to the sidewalk. The street was quiet this early morning, and the glow of a not-yet-risen sun spilled across Mitchell Drive.

Sally looked down at the hopscotch squares, still barely discernible along the sidewalk. Jingling white, red, green, and blue tokens flashed by, and a whisper of words—"I will marry that boy"—jerked her back to the present. She ran back into the house and down the hall to her bedroom. Tearing open her lingerie drawer, she tossed out several things and finally found what her memory had latched onto—the mason jar. Sally clutched it to her bosom as if it were Todd himself and threw herself back on the bed, pressing the jar between her breasts, where he'd been so often. For a few minutes, the jar *was* him, but soon her crying began again. That night was the first of many when Sally would sleep curled around the mason jar, her substitute for Todd.

~

A hundred miles north, Todd sat half asleep on an old couch in a dimly lighted room, along with forty other tired and confused recruits. At the end of a hot bus ride, Todd and his comrades had been deposited in an old wooden barracks at Fort Ord, California. Two bare light bulbs illuminated a twenty-by-forty-foot room filled with assorted wood furniture. The envelopes they'd each been given at the bus depot stated in cold army language that an unknown virus had somehow come back to the States with soldiers returning from Vietnam. It was the first time most of the recruits had ever heard of the place.

An hour later, a master sergeant stood in front of them, clipboard in hand. He was a big bull of a man with a bulging gut, bald head, and ice-blue eyes that looked hungover. In a pronounced southern drawl, he said, "May I have your attention? I'm Sergeant Bradshaw, and I have important news. You're not in high school anymore, and soon you will be members of the United States Army, enlisted class of June 1961. Get used to a *big* change from civilian life. Moving on ... Right now you're at the old reception building off base, because a virus got loose on the base. Until they figure out what the hell it is, no new recruits are going to be inducted here, so you'll be transferred to other training facilities. We'll announce where you're headed later, so for now just sit tight. Someone will bring you some chow shortly. Any questions?"

The kid next to Todd said, "Yeah, can we call our folks and let them know?"

The sergeant glared at the kid and said, "So you want to call your mommy, do you? Yes, but not until you're told to do so, okay? And another thing—your induction will be done elsewhere."

Another kid asked, "Can we check out the base while we wait, Sergeant?"

"No, you can't leave this building! Even I can't go on base, since it's quarantined until they find out what this fucking thing is. So like I said, sit tight."

By ten o'clock, it was really getting hot in the claustrophobic old building. A few minutes later, a soldier showed up, plugged in a four-station phone bank, and left. Right behind him was a civilian who delivered bag lunches and soft drinks, and then he too left. Finally the sergeant returned and said, "You've now got your chow and a phone bank. Go to work on them, but make it quick. Your buses leave in an hour. I'll tell each of you where you're going a little later."

Almost everyone in the room called someone. Todd tried calling Sally twice, but he got no answer either time. By then the bag lunches and drinks were gone.

The sergeant said, "Sit down—and I mean right now!" Within a count of three, everyone was seated. "When I call your name, come forward and get your instructions. Then line up in alphabetical order at the door." He started down the list, handing each recruit a piece of paper indicating his destination. Toward the end, just before Todd's name, the sergeant called out, "Mr. Terry R. Wells?"

In the far corner, someone stood up and meekly came forward. It was a female recruit with short brown hair wearing jeans, a baggy high school letter jacket, western shirt, and boots. She said, "I'm Terry R. Wells, sir!"

"Don't call me *sir*, Mr. ... I mean, Miss ... Oh, I don't know what I mean." Someone snickered, and the sergeant yelled, "Cut that shit out!" Towering over Terry R. Wells like an avenging bird of prey, he said authoritatively, "Sit down, Terry R. Wells. Why are you here?"

"I'm supposed to go into the Army Nurse Corps. I just caught a bus ride here like everybody else."

"The Nurse Corps? You're gonna be ... Hold on, I'm gonna find out what's up. If this isn't a shit storm! Everyone just sit tight. I'll look into this." The sergeant looked closely at her and back at his clipboard, then left the room, muttering to himself.

Standing next to Terry, Todd said, "Don't panic, miss. It's the army. They'll figure it out. I'm going to be a medic myself, so we're in the same field."

Terry said confidently, "I just want to serve, you know?"

There were a few lewd comments tossed around, and then Sergeant Bradshaw reentered the room with an officer. In a much more controlled and authoritative voice, the sergeant said, *"Attention!"* The group of recruits abruptly jumped to their feet and stood in disorder.

At that, the officer, who was in dress uniform, took a step forward and pointed at Terry. "This is Miss Terry R. Wells. She is a candidate recruit for the Army Nurse Corps, of which you may someday—though I hope not—be in great need. She will serve, just as you will serve. Now Sergeant Bradshaw will inform you of your next posting. That is all. Sergeant?"

As the officer turned to leave, Sergeant Bradshaw said, "Yes, sir! Okay, outside are three buses, and each has a destination sign on it—Fort Dix, Fort Hood, or Fort Lewis. Get on the bus assigned to you, sit down, and shut up. Miss Terry R. Wells and Mr. Todd Wyrum, you're both going to Fort Dix. Now get a move on!"

As they filed out, Terry said to Todd, "We're the only ones going to Fort Dix, aren't we?"

"It looks that way," replied Todd.

The bus to Fort Dix was almost empty, so Todd and Terry talked to each other. The bus stopped in Salinas and San Jose, slowly filling with an assortment of draftees. It was a raucous trip with everyone excited to be headed to an unexpected location. Todd was still hoping to notify Sally, but no luck so far. He and Terry continued talking, off and on, for the rest of the trip.

At the Fort Dix terminal, the recruits were subjected to a series of interviews, tests, and exams. Oakland and the terminal, a dingy place without a hint of personal comfort, were disappointing. At the end of the day, each draftee was issued a food voucher and a room designation in a local hotel. The hotel was even dingier than the terminal, and the food was typical cafeteria fare. The recruits were all assigned to double rooms. After settling in, everyone congregated in a recreation room furnished with tables, chairs, a dartboard, and a pool table.

The pool table and Terry, as the only girl present, were the centers of attention. Most of the attention directed at Terry was good natured until someone got hold of some beer. Then some of the guys got bolder with Terry, and the pool games started drawing bets. Carlo, an older, swarthy guy, was winning. After a while Terry excused herself, at which point Carlo left the pool game and blocked the door. Terry's polite efforts to depart weren't successful, which drew catcalls and off-color remarks. After a few minutes, Terry looked at Todd, thinking that he was her only ally.

Watching the pool game, Todd hadn't paid much attention to Terry's dilemma. Now he looked over and in an offhand way said, "Give her a break, guys. It's late, and she's the only girl for miles around. Have another beer, and let her be on her way."

But Todd's comment didn't go down well with Carlo, who was hoping for the chance to fool around with Terry. "Butt out, Skinny! It's up to her to say, and she's still here. Right, Terry? She'll stay if we're nice, which we will be. Come on, Terry, sit down and have another beer. We're all in the same boat here."

Todd tried to ignore the "skinny" comment, but when Terry was again barred from the exit door, he spoke up again. "She wants to leave, guys, so let her."

While another guy stood between Terry and the door, Carlo came over to where Todd sat on a couch. "You'd best butt out—or maybe you want to do something about it, Skinny?"

Warily, Todd stood and confronted Carlo. "Shit, Carlo, she just wants to turn in. Take it easy. She doesn't want anything to do with you anyway. She's got more class than that."

This last comment drew a collective laugh from everyone except Carlo, who took a step toward Todd and shoved him back down on the couch with a thud. Todd quickly bounced back up under Carlo's off-balance upper body and shoved the bigger boy backward toward the pool table. Carlo pushed himself off the table and charged at Todd, but before he got there, two guys stopped him. A confrontation between several of the boys ensued, with a lot of shouting and cursing. Some took Terry's side, some Carlo's, and some just wanted to see a fight. The door was still barred to Terry.

"So you want to mix it up, schoolboy? I'm ready!" Carlo shouted. Todd motioned for him to bring it on, but Carlo was still being restrained.

A friend of Carlo's said, "Play a game of eight ball for it. Carlo wins, she stays. Todd wins, she gets to leave. How about it, guys?"

Carlo's smiled and replied, "Good idea. You up for it, Skinny?"

Todd turned his head in Terry's direction and gave her a heads-up. Still blocked at the door and getting angry, Terry said, "You'd better win, Todd. But no matter what, I'm leaving, so do as you want."

Watching Carlo play pool, Todd had recognized that he was a much better than average player. "Okay by me, and a ten spot on it, too," Todd said. "Rotation, one and fifteen, side pockets. Three games, unless you can't cover it, Carlo."

Carlo looked a little surprised but took up the challenge. "Sure, Skinny. Set it up."

Todd didn't have five dollars, much less ten. But he'd been in many pickup pool games, and showing confidence was half the battle.

One of the other boys set up the table. Todd found a halfway-decent cue, and both he and Carlo took some practice shots. They lagged for the break and Todd won, so he shot first. With a good break, he sank three balls and continued to run the table. Sinking the one ball in the side pocket, he won the game. He then promptly derided Carlo, "You're already a loser, and you haven't even shot yet. Get your ten ready. I'm all over this, Carlo."

In the next game, Todd got himself in a bad position off the break and Carlo won, though mostly by pure luck. Launching into his own bragging mode, Carlo said, "Old Skinny here done lost his touch, Miss Terry. So looks like it's maybe you and me from here on."

Todd won the third game easily, with Carlo showing signs of anger. Todd called over to Terry, still standing near the door, "You're outta here. This Carlo chump is a total loser."

"My hero," exclaimed Terry, planting a kiss on Todd's cheek. She then departed with a friendly wave.

Todd tried to call Sally from a pay phone, but the line was busy. When he tried again a few minutes later, it was still busy. Happy about the pool, but frustrated about not reaching Sally, he headed to his room.

Terry was standing in the hall, and she beckoned to him and then disappeared into a maid's room. As Todd walked by the room, the door was open and he heard Terry say, "Come in quickly, or someone will see. Hurry!"

Todd looked around at the tiny, cluttered space and said, "Maybe some other time."

"Oh, come on, Todd. Your girl's not here, and I am," said Terry.

Todd just shook his head and proceeded to his room.

~

The next day, the trip to Fort Dix continued, but Todd and Terry were on separate buses. Three days later, a tired bunch of recruits unloaded in front of matching dust-colored barracks.

At Fort Dix, Todd got one more chance to call Sally. After an eternity of ringing, the phone was picked up and a voice said, "Hello? Anderson residence. Zoe speaking."

"Hi, Zoe! It's Todd. Can I speak with Sally? Hurry, please, because I don't have much time." Greatly excited, Zoe bubbled with a barrage of questions, until Todd broke in and said, "Zoe, please? Please go get Sally."

"Okay, Todd, I'll do that right now. Bye!" she exclaimed.

Every three minutes, Todd put more coins in the phone slot. Finally he ran out of money, but still no Sally. Perplexed and disappointed, he had no way of knowing that in her excitement, Zoe forgot all about him being on the phone. Sally never knew that he'd called.

Sally's growing midriff and the mason jar were her only connections to Todd. Where was he, and why hadn't he called like he'd promised?

Flat broke, Todd did write Sally a letter.

BOOK III

Letters

CHAPTER 24

Letter #1

From: SPC-4 Todd Wyrum
c/o Bravo Co.
Training Unit B-22
Fort Dix, New Jersey

To: Sally Anderson
691 Mitchell Drive
San Luis Obispo, California

Dear Sally,

I made it, and now there's lots of explain. I'm in New Jersey at Fort Dix, not Fort Ord. There's some kind of virus at Ord, so they shipped us off to different places, Texas and Washington. I drew this dump. It's near the Pine Barrens, which is a hard place to train, we're told. We'll see. Today was just induction stuff. The real thing starts tomorrow.

The bus ride took us to Ord, several other stops, and finally Oakland Army Terminal, an even dingier place. We stayed the night, then took a boring, three-day bus trip here. During the trip, I got a big laugh. "I'm gonna sit right down and write myself a letter, and make believe ..." Remember that, from the day we met? Now I'm actually writing to you. Pretty cool, huh?

I called you several times, but no answer. Zoe answered the last time, but I guess she forgot. The bad news is that I won't be able to see you until my first leave, in ten weeks or more. I miss you, and I hope your summer isn't messed up because of me screwing up. The only upside to this is that I'll get into the Medical Corps, like I wanted.

I've got that picture of us, the one at the shack, pinned up next to my bunk.

I saw something really neat on the trip east—a cattle drive crossing in the mountains of Utah. It was the real thing with horses, cattle, cowboys, dust, and yelling. It made me miss the ranch. Thank goodness for Miss Lady. She sure stepped up, like she always does.

The guys are the usual mix of Americans. Most are draftees, but a few enlisted.

Sally, I miss you more than words can say. I'm so sorry for messing up. It was all my fault. I should have just left that dumb Kenny alone. I lost my temper, I guess, because I love you so much, and I won't let anyone insult you. I guess I just went too far this time. Sorry, darling!

But the good side is that you'll be a junior and rule the roost with the other cheer girls. Don't let Bad Brenda steer you wrong, okay? I trust you to be my girl. You're going to have a fun year, and in a few weeks, I'll be with you again and we'll have our usual fun. You know what that means?

So now I'm off to chow with these other rowdy guys. Then a good night's sleep in a real bed, not the bus seat of the past three days. I love and miss you more than I can say, Sally.

Love, Todd

P.S. I've got a poem in my head whenever I think of you, so here goes:

> I see a long trail winding,
> So along the path I go
> In quest of my Sally, time my ever foe.
> You're my destination, no matter how dark the way.
> You're always there at the end of every day.

~

The days without a word from Todd seemed never ending. Sally envisioned some other girl with him, in her many erotic nightmares. She touched herself at night, hoping it would fill the void, but it didn't. Had he forgotten her? She dressed in baggy clothes to hide her growing condition. When the phone rang, she rushed to answer—and was crushed when it wasn't Todd.

Sally poured out her confusion to Brenda, but all she got back was stuff about seeing other boys. Brenda teased her by recounting Todd's many attractive qualities, further stoking Sally's fears.

Grandma's curious looks made Sally resort to extreme measures to disguise her condition. Summers of dating, beach parties, and hanging with Brenda were now a distant memory.

One afternoon, Gail yelled, "Sally, there's a letter. I think it's from Todd. Come quick!" In an instant, Sally was lifted out of her lethargy and propelled down the hall, where she crashed into Gail. The letter flew from Gail's hand, and Sally pounced on it like a hungry cat. She took the envelope to her room, ignoring the sound of Gail yelling.

Sally sat on her bed, staring at the wrinkled, soiled envelope as though she'd struck gold. When she read the return address, her mind stuck on *Fort Dix, New Jersey*. She opened the envelope with shaking hands and read Todd's letter with tears in her eyes, especially when she got to the poem, and resolved to sleep with the letter that night.

Later that evening, Grandma knocked on her door and asked, "Sally, dear, are you all right? I'm so worried about you. Gail's not hurt—she was just trying to help, you know. She said you got a letter from Todd. Is that right? Sally, please open the door."

Sally opened the door and said, "Yes, Grandma, Todd's all right, but he's at a base in New Jersey."

"Oh, I'm so happy to hear that," Grandma exclaimed. "We women do pine so when our men are away. Let me hug you, poor girl. It's going to be okay, Sally. Now what's this about New Jersey? Can that be right?"

Sally said, "Yes, Todd's at Fort Dix in New Jersey. He explained in the letter about there being some sort of medical problem at Fort Ord. The bad thing is that I won't get to see him for weeks and weeks."

Grandma commiserated with her. "That's not so bad, Sally. My Jim, your sainted grandfather, was in the South Pacific for years. A few weeks isn't too bad."

In the kitchen, Sally grabbed Zoe by the hair, almost jerking her out of her chair, and yelled, "You're a liar, Zoe! Why didn't you tell me about Todd's call?"

"I did, Sally!" Zoe insisted. "Remember, in the yard? I did, didn't I, Grandma?"

"Girls, calm down, Grandma said. "My goodness, what a mess."

Zoe said, "Sally's mean, Grandma, and you need to punish her. You do!"

Grandma said, "In fact, I do recall that day, Zoe, and you didn't say anything about a phone call from Todd. You told us how cute he is, but you didn't say anything about a call. Why didn't you tell us?"

Gail chimed in, "Zoe's always fibbing, Grandma. This is just another one."

"Hush, Gail," said Grandma. "We don't need any more of that."

"But I did tell you, Grandma! At least, I think I did," Zoe pleaded.

Sally stood back and pointed at Zoe. "Why, you little—"

"Stop it, Sally. And Zoe, I'm sorry to say you didn't, but why not?" asked Grandma.

Zoe shrugged and tried to look innocent, then hung her head and replied in a whisper, "I guess I just kind of forgot. But I thought I did, Sally, and I'm really sorry."

Sally crossed her arms, shook her head, and walked back down the hall to her room, slamming the door behind her. She read Todd's letter over and over again, until she finally fell asleep. Sally's sleep had been troubled lately, and that night was no different. She had an erotic dream about Todd and awoke on the verge of an orgasm, wriggling and squirming around in frustration, willing her longing to pass. But the only thing that would relieve her frustration was Todd, and she yearned for him next to her.

The next best thing to talking to him was writing a letter.

~

Letter #2

From: Sally Anderson
691 Mitchell Drive
San Luis Obispo, California

To: SPC-4 Todd Wyrum
c/o Bravo Co.

Training Unit B-22
Fort Dix, New Jersey

My darling Todd,

Oh, my darling, I got your letter today, and I do remember the song. I've played it over and over again in my head. That memory is so wonderful. I am reborn and joyful, and I love you so. Please come back to me as soon as you can. I'm kissing you now all over. I love my Todd, and I want to go up to the shack right now and have our usual wonderful time.

I waited for you to call like you said. Now I know why you didn't, but you did, and stupid Zoe didn't tell me you were waiting on the line. Just blurted out how much she likes you and stuff. I got so mad at her. I pulled her hair and called her a liar, too.

I don't quite understand why they'd send you to New Jersey, so far away. Why?

Are the girls in New Jersey cute? I hope they're all ugly and flat. Stay away from them. I know how devious girls can be if they want a boy. They've got lots of tricks, so be careful. Only I'm allowed to love you like that, remember? Remember me and only me, your Sally.

I've read your letter twenty times. It's wonderful. I read the poem forty times. It's so loving and so much like you. You're so, so romantic.

I'm in my room now, curled up around your letter and the mason jar. Remember the lemonade? I got the mason jar you drank it from. It's been in the back of my lingerie drawer all this time. (The jar, I mean.) When you left, I started sleeping with it. That's a silly girl thing, isn't it? No matter. Your next-to-last paragraph gave me a feeling of our love. Me, too! Me, too! Me, too!

It's a boring summer here in Dullsville, and *slow*! I can't wait for us to leave.

I saw Hector and Helman downtown, and they said hi. They got boxing scholarships to Cal Poly. They're both really nice to me.

Grandma says hi and kisses. Gail and Zoe, too, even though I'm not talking to dumb Zoe anymore.

Cheer team gets together every week and does stuff, but mostly just gossip and boy talk. Girls are silly, aren't they? I've got you now, so I don't have to do that anymore. Well, maybe a little.

I've got lots of important stuff to tell you. Ten weeks, you said, right?

I wait every day at the mailbox. Please write often, because it brings you closer to me.

I wish I could write poetry like you.

Love, your Sally

P.S. I love, love, love you, my one and only Todd. Kisses, kisses, kisses, kisses.

~

Writing the letter helped Sally feel closer to Todd, but still ... She normally hated gardening, which Grandma loved to do. But today she needed something to distract her from her erotic longings, so she went outside to weed. It didn't work, however, so she went back to her room, took out the letter, and reread the paragraph about the truck. The warm, Jell-O feeling returned to her abdomen.

Sally thought the only thing that might help was a visit to Brenda's house. She told herself she was going for a distraction, but her subconscious knew that a visit with Brenda would have carnal overtones. Sally's heart and body were at war again, and she falsely convinced herself that she could maintain control. She arranged her balloon dress to hide her condition and walked the ten minutes to Brenda's.

Brenda answered the door dressed in Bermuda shorts and a halter top. "Hi, Sally! Come on in. Mom isn't home, so we're alone. You're getting kind of big. Come here and let me see." Brenda took Sally's hand, pulled her to the full-length mirror, and pushed out her own chest to compare it to Sally's. "You're almost as big as me. Are your nipples bigger, too? Let me see."

Sally pushed out her bust and said, "I don't know, but maybe."

Teasing her friend, Brenda said, "You always wanted bigger ones than me, didn't you?"

"Well, maybe," admitted Sally, "but now I've got big ones, too." Sally already felt better, and as the girls giggled like in old times, she momentarily forgot her condition.

Brenda said, "Undo my top. Let's compare!" Sally hesitated, but then reached around and untied Brenda's top. As the garment fell to the floor, Brenda exclaimed, "Oh yes, mine are still bigger, aren't they? Your turn, Sally!"

Sally looked at her very competitive friend, then back at the mirror. "I got a letter from Todd. He's in New Jersey, so I won't see him for ten weeks. He still loves me, but I'm gonna have a baby and he doesn't know. I planned on telling him before he left. What am I going to do?"

Brenda, still preening in the mirror, said, "You shoulda told him. If you had, maybe you'd even be married by now. But ten weeks isn't really much, Sally. And on the bright side, I think Mrs. V can help you with the baby thing if you help her with ... well, you know. We've had fun doing that, haven't we? Cheer up, Sally, and let's cuddle like we used to, okay?"

Putting her hands on her belly, Sally asked, "What about this?"

Brenda took Sally's hand and pulled her toward the bedroom. "It's okay, I still like you. And anyway, I've got something to show you. You're not going to believe this!"

"What is it?" Sally asked, reluctant but curious.

"Fun for us, that's for sure," said Brenda. "It's my mom's. You're going to be really surprised."

They sat on the bed, and Brenda took out a long box and placed it on the bed. It had a plug-in cord with it. With a conspiratorial smile, Brenda plugged it in and pressed a button. To Sally's amazement, it hummed. Brenda put it against Sally's inner thigh and said, "It's a vibrator. Feel it? It's for your little thing. This goes in, and this round knob ... Well, it makes you feel really good."

Sally picked it up and asked, "Can it really? Instead of touching, you know, like we do?"

"Yeah, Mom wouldn't have it if it didn't. She's gotta have it. Look at this, too." Brenda took out a blue velvet bag and laid it on the bed. "Look inside the bag, Sally."

Sally took out a long, floppy, wine-red object and examined it. "I wonder what . . ."

"It's big, and it's got two ends," said Brenda. "I forgot the name of it, but it's for both of us, see? Let's try it!"

~

Later when they were sitting around gossiping, Brenda said, "What are you gonna do? I mean, about—you know! Mrs. V's got more stuff for me, and you could help. You might need her help, too. Well, you know what I mean, right?"

"I don't know, Brenda. I intended to tell Todd when he had a pass up at Fort Ord, but now that he's back east and all ... You know what I want, don't you?"

Brenda said, "Yeah, you want Todd to marry you. Maybe I shouldn't bring this up, but are you sure it's his baby? After all, we've been doing lots of adven—"

"How could you ask that, Brenda? Yes, I'm sure! It was after my little visitor, and I thought it was okay."

"I'm on your side, Sally. I hope Todd does marry you, and I guess you can be an army wife for a while. At least until he gets out and goes to medical school, don't you think? Maybe like that?"

Only minutes earlier, Sally had been so satisfied, but now the doubts crept back in. A look of bewilderment came over her face, and she said, "Yeah, I guess. It would be our life. Fun, too, don't you think?"

Brenda asked, "But what about school in the fall? Mrs. V is going to want you to do stuff. It doesn't take a mind reader to figure that out. You know darn well she's in cahoots with Nurse Jones. How much does she want to, you know, fix it at Pismo Beach?"

That was a topic that Sally wanted to avoid. "I don't know, but let's not talk about it. Stop, please!"

Suddenly Brenda said, "Oops, hear that car door? Mom's home. Let's go out on the porch, and I'll put this stuff back. Fun, right? Come on, let's get going before she comes in."

Sally and Brenda were in the living room when Brenda's mom walked in the front door with Mike, her current boyfriend. "What are you two trollops up to anyway?" she asked. "Oh, this is my boyfriend, Mike Hawk. He's the manager at the Mission Bar on Higuera Street. Say hi and be nice to him."

"Hi, Mike, nice to meet you," Sally replied politely. Brenda didn't say anything.

Mike gave Brenda and Sally a bold look and said, "And nice to meet you, too, uh ..."

Brenda said, "It's Sally. Sally Anderson, my best friend. She lives nearby, and we're just leaving, so bye!" With a wary look in her eyes, she took Sally's hand and led her outside.

When they were outside, they stopped and Brenda said, "Mike's been trying to get in my pants ever since Mom brought him by. He asks me to sit on his lap when the TV's on and Mom's out. Guess what he wants.

Mom thinks he's a big wheel because he runs a bar. Can you imagine, the Mission Bar, of all places? It's a dump full of lushes. Be careful when he's around, Sally." Even after saying this, Brenda loosed her blouse.

Sally noticed this and said, "I'd better be getting back home now."

Brenda said, "Well, I like to tease guys, you know? Keep them guessing, know what I mean?"

Sally walked off with a wave. "Yeah, I do. See you Friday, okay? We gonna get together after you're done with cheer team, like always?"

"Yeah, and you can watch if you want," said Brenda. "Mrs. V can't do much about that."

~

Letter #3

From: SPC-4 Todd Wyrum
c/o Bravo Co.
Training Unit B-22
Fort Dix, New Jersey

To: Sally Anderson
691 Mitchell Drive
San Luis Obispo, California

Dear Sally,

I'm relieved that you got my letter and the explanation. Don't blame Zoe, because she's just a kid.

Well, training has started in earnest now, so I'm up every morning at five thirty doing calisthenics, followed by breakfast, classroom work, drilling, and stuff like that. The tests they give are dumb, and the questions are easy, like "What color's an orange?"

The army is made up of all kinds—guys from Puerto Rico, Guam, Maine, Canada. I've made new friends too. They'll never be Hector or Helman, but they're okay guys. One boxer has the crazy nickname of San Bruno.

We've had no training with rifles, pistols, or grenades yet, but everyone's looking forward to that. My JROTC training is a big help, and the other guys come to me for advice.

Fitness wise, no problem. Lots of recruits are out of shape, and the sergeant *really* gets on their case. Lots of yelling, which is normal! Some jokers in the outfit. Two guys are married.

Guys have pictures of their girls at their bunks. I've got yours up, and it gets *lots* of scrutiny.

The thing that keeps me from missing you too much is hard training, but still I think about you all the time. I go to sleep with your picture over my head and your love in my heart. I love you!

The mason jar? I do remember that day—the hopscotch squares, lemonade, Grandma, and your family!

Sergeant Rouna heads our platoon. He's a Swede from Minnesota, and he drives us hard.

It's night now, and I'm writing in the dark. So if this isn't too legible, that's why. Now I'm going to lean up and give your picture a kiss good night. Hold me close and remember me, okay?

Todd
Here goes again:

> "Empty Brook"
> I smiled as I heard the water's gurgling flow.
> I turned to see it pass.
> It was then I realized, I stood not next to the brook
> we love so well,
> But was alone, and what I heard was my life passing
> by without you.

~

Sally was at the mailbox every morning. She pined if the delivery person was late, and she was sad if she didn't get a letter from Todd. Today the mail was delivered on time *and* she got a letter, which she tore open. Getting a letter from Todd was like finding a treasure, and when she felt this way, a visit to Brenda's beckoned—though she resisted.

His mention of the creek and shack made her wonder if maybe she could tell him, "There's a baby there, Todd." Would he smile, kiss her bump, and whisper sweet nothings in her ear? "Happily ever after" meant a married couple, a home, and babies. Meanwhile Todd's letters filled one part of her life, and sessions with Brenda, when Sally's will faltered, filled the other.

Sally was now only observing the cheer practices, and her efforts to hide her secret was working. Mrs. V said a few things, but kept her secret. After a team meeting about new girls, Mrs. V dismissed everyone except Sally and Brenda. Then she said, "You're team leaders now, so act like it. Acquaint the new girls with the rules, and help me pick out the ones who might be interested in the other activities. Do you think you can do that?"

"Yes, Mrs. V!" the girls replied.

"Okay, Mr. Hesselgren's little seaside haunt in Cambria is going to be the site of a private party. You're the entertainment, as it were, next Friday and Saturday. Your stipend will be double—isn't that nice? Wear your cheer uniforms and hot lingerie, understood?"

Sally replied in a forlorn voice, "Mrs. V, I can't do that while I'm like this."

"Yes, you will, Sally, because I say so," insisted Mrs. V. "There are still things you can do. Isn't that right, Brenda?"

"Well, maybe she'd better not," replied Brenda.

"Hush! She'll go and help you, and that's decided. Sally, some men might even find your 'condition' a turn-on. In any case, you're going and that's final."

Shocked, Sally said, "Mrs. V, I'm doing fine, but not that fine. I don't want to."

Mrs. V said, "Stand up and show me your tummy." Sally stood up. "Yes, you're showing more," agreed Mrs. V, "but not enough for unknowing people to notice. In another month, Grandma will find out. After that, who knows?"

At the mention of Grandma, Sally broke into tears and said, "No, I can't!"

Mrs. V said, "Okay, you've got until mid-July, I'd guess. I'll set it up for July 19 at the house in Pismo Beach, agreed? It's three hundred dollars, which I'll cover as long as you agree to keep up the adventures."

Still crying, Sally nodded in agreement, not realizing the importance of her answer.

"Okay! Brenda, you'll help Sally and give her moral support. Oops, I mean *immoral* support. Funny play on words, right? Oh my, I'm so funny sometimes. Please forgive my ha-ha." Mrs. V's humor was completely lost on the girls.

Brenda said, "I'll help Sally all I can, but she'll be—"

Sally broke in, "I'm not sure! Todd will be back soon, and we might get mar—"

"Nonsense!" exclaimed Mrs. V. "He's probably not coming back. And even if he does, do you really think he'll want to be tied down to a brat and a fat high school dropout? No! He won't want a girl shaped like a bowling ball with tits down to her knees. Your friend here might become the object of his affection—as she was before, right? Oh yes, Brenda, I know about your tryst with lover boy down in Avila."

At this comment, Sally shot dagger looks at Brenda. Her self-esteem plummeted as a glance confirmed her worst fears. She gasped through her tears, "Todd loves me!"

Then Mrs. V closed in for the kill. "He'll be overseas with hungry girls all over him. He's gone! But Mrs. V knows how to take care of sluts in trouble, so let me help you. I've been doing this a long time. Get in line, Sally, and all will go well. Step out of line, and you'll be out on your cute little tush—abandoned, broke, and with a little brat to look after. You'll be a waitress in some greasy spoon and flirting with truck drivers! Yeah, Sally, it's my help or nothing."

Brenda protested, "You forced us to do these *adventures*, or else we'd be off the team!"

Mrs. V's temper flared, and spittle flew from her mouth as she yelled, "Silence, you two! That's a load of crap. You aren't the first high school whore to get in trouble, Sally, so don't lay this innocent baloney on me. I know what you do on these adventures. You're both hotter than firecrackers. You do whatever it takes and like it, too. Yeah, you've known all along that the money pays for escorts, call girls, prostitutes, or—let's go whole hog—whores. You knew. Oh yeah, you knew."

Sally yelled, "We're not whores! We did it for cheer team, like Brenda said. We did it for the players and booster club and ... and we help you, too! I'm not going to Cambria if—"

"Oh yeah, the money," said Mrs. V. "I forgot to mention that. Yes, you'll go, or I'll have you thrown out of school. Your loving grandma will be on the phone in ten minutes, so glad to hear that her adorable granddaughter's been fucking her way through high school."

Brenda spoke up. "It was a *stipend* you said, not money. For cheer team!

If you do that, we'll tell how you set this all up with the deacon and Mr. Hesselgren and all that."

"You lying little tramps. They won't believe you, and anyway Nurse Jones will back me up."

Feeling braver now, Brenda said, "You're ... you're a pimp. Yeah, a pimp! We'll tell the truth!"

Mrs. V stepped forward and slapped Brenda. With real fear on their faces, both girls backed against the wall to protect themselves. Now having instilled fear in them again, Mrs. V calmed down. "Girls, we've let this thing get out of hand. Let's calm down. Can we do that? Straighten yourselves up." A few moments passed while the girls hesitatingly pulled themselves together, and then Mrs. V said, "I'm leaving the room to let you decide: Cambria or expulsion?"

Brenda's jaw dropped, and she exclaimed, "Why me? I've done everything you asked, even that fumbling little jerk Dr. McKay."

"Yes, you did, Brenda, and I'm sure his little weenie is happy for that. But don't look so surprised. It will be you, too. Now talk it over and decide. I'll be right back." Mrs. V walked out.

The girls slumped to the floor, and Brenda said, "We don't want to be expelled, do we?"

Sally said, "I can't do that to Grandma. She's so good and proper. Oh God, what are we gonna do? What a total bitch Mrs. V is. But we've got to do something, don't we?"

Brenda replied, "Yeah, we do. Well, we could pull this whole thing off and earn double stipends if we just went up to Cambria. Mr. Hesselgren is pretty nice, and he did give us all that cute stuff. It probably would be kind of fun, like most of the things we've done with him."

"What about this—my baby? *Todd's* baby? Brenda, what if Mrs. V's right and he doesn't come back? All those girls in New Jersey will see in him what I see. He's so cute, and they'll put out for him for sure, don't you think?" Her lower lip trembling, Sally patted her baby.

Brenda nodded, reluctantly agreeing with Sally. "They'll for sure want to have him. What girl wouldn't? We've gotta go to Cambria. I don't see any other way, do you?"

Sally nodded and said, "You're right, but it makes me mad."

"Me too, but what other way is there?" asked Brenda.

When Mrs. V returned, Sally had stopped crying. Seeing the looks of resignation on the girls' faces, Mrs. V said, "So it's resolved that you're going to Cambria?"

Brenda took Sally's hand, glanced warily at Mrs. V, and answered for both of them, "We'll go, but we want larger stipends."

Surprise flashed across Mrs. V's face, but it quickly gave way to a sly, accusatory smile. She said, "You're learning, aren't you? Okay, I'll increase them, but you'd better hit some high notes—and in your best lingerie, too. I'd better hear glowing reports, agreed?"

"Yes, Mrs. V," they said in unison.

They did go to Cambria, and glowing reports did ensue, but it wasn't the same fun. New conquests, ego-boosting compliments, and a feeling of control were no longer the thrill that they had been previously. Not even the increased stipends helped. The happy, sexy cheer girl attitude faded, and it felt like a job. Sally and Brenda were no longer in awe of the prominent men they conquered.

When they got home on Sunday, there was no happy teasing and recounting of their success. Mrs. V's cruel words had hit hard, and unspoken between Sally and Brenda was the question: Could it ever be fun again? They also began considering an even bigger, more important question: How were they ever going to wriggle and squirm free from the grasp of that domineering, exploiting pimp?

~

Letter #4

From: Sally Anderson
691 Mitchell Drive
San Luis Obispo, California

To: SPC-4 Todd Wyrum
c/o Bravo Co.
Training Unit B-22
Fort Dix, New Jersey

Oh my darling,

Your letters make me so happy, but life without you is sad. See the tears on this page? Oh, so much for my silly girl ways of trying to explain. Todd, please hurry back to me. Can you take your leave sooner? You said it was about mid-July, right?

I'm doing cheer stuff, some with Brenda, but it's not as much fun as it used to be. She says hi. I went to Avila Saturday. I saw Big Earl there, and he says hi.

Grandma, Gail, Zoe, and I made two apple pies the other day, and it was fun. We got the apples from the tree at Brenda's house. Nice big ones, but I forget the name.

I've got one more year left, and I don't care. Brenda only has half a year left.

We learned new cheers last week. Got new cheer outfits, too. You'll like them, shorter. Do you think I've got nice legs? I know you like the other parts. Ha-ha! I cut my hair.

It got up to one hundred yesterday, which doesn't happen often. Gail, Zoe, and I lay under the sprinkler in the front yard, and it was nice and cool. We had fun until a bunch of boys came by in a car and yelled something at us. Don't know what it was. Something about my bathing suit.

Is training hard? Do you go into town? I guess you're not allowed until training's over, right?

I've got lots more to tell you, but it can wait until you're with me. Come back to me soon.

I love you,
Sally

~

After mailing her letter, Sally went into the backyard and stretched out on a blanket in the hot afternoon sun. Just as she started to doze off, she felt something like popcorn going off in her tummy. It took only a moment for her to jump up and realize that it was her baby moving. Shocked, she said out loud, "Oh my God, it can't be. It can't, but it is."

Gail yelled from the porch, "What're you doing? You're getting fat, Sally. Is Brenda coming?"

Sally quickly turned away and exclaimed, "No, I'm not getting fat. It's none of your beeswax anyway, so butt out. And no, Brenda's not coming. I thought you didn't like her."

"We don't like her. I do want big ones like her, though," said Gail, heading back into the house.

Sally was on notice. Other people could see. It was decision time—a decision that she really, really didn't want to make. *Please come home quick, Todd,* her tummy bump said.

~

Letter #5

From: SPC-4 Todd Wyrum
c/o Bravo Co.
Training Unit B-22
Fort Dix, New Jersey

To: Sally Anderson
691 Mitchell Drive
San Luis Obispo, California

Hi Sally,

Got your newsy letter. Training has been stepped up, so I don't have much time to write. It's just train, train, train, when I'd rather train with Sally. I'm really bushed, so this will be short.

I've got two new pals here. Both did some boxing, so we've got things in common. Rich is from Casper, Wyoming. He's a big guy, maybe 210, with a big head and quiet. A heavyweight and friendly. His family are ranchers way out of town. Sounds like the Rocking W. Frank—we call him "fearless"—is a wild man. Must have a hundred girlfriends all around Oregon. He's a middleweight. He works at golf courses and wants to be a pro. I haven't seen him play, of course, but I wouldn't know from whatever if he had talent. A wisecracking hellraiser ready to fight at the drop of a hat kind a guy. We're friends, so it ain't me.

Sergeant Rouna's focus right now is on how to build a fighting team.

He's drilling it into us, and I hope it works. We hear lots of stuff about Vietnam, way over in Southeast Asia, and it doesn't sound good. We also hear about new gear we'll be getting in 1962 that will help us in the jungle.

Our next training problem is in the Pine Barrens, which isn't actually part of Fort Dix, but we still train there. A guy told us that we'd best get ready. When I asked why, he just gave me a wry smile.

I've got to go now. I wish I could be where the mason jar is. Hold me close and put yourself in the shack with me, all cozy and warm and loved. I'll kiss you in all those places that make you quiver. So long, Sally. I love you. Only time for a short poem today.

Love, Todd

> "Our Shadows"
> Now our lives go on apart,
> So it's our shadows
> That must walk together
> Until we stroke together again
> And our love blooms anew.

~

Reading Todd's letter sent Sally into fits of desire, and she could barely keep her hands off herself. She squirmed in frustration, with thoughts of wild, all-consuming lust. When Brenda showed up at her house, Sally poured out her mixed feelings to her.

When Sally finished, Brenda had a story of her own to tell. Late that afternoon, she had bruised her thigh, so she'd gone to the gym, which was almost empty. There she had run into Coach in the downstairs corridor. As Brenda had walked by him, limping slightly, she'd said, "Hello, Coach! How are you?"

Coach stopped, looked her over, and said, "Brenda, you look your usual beautiful self, but I see you've got a limp. Have you been injured? Is it serious? Are you okay?"

"I fell and hurt my leg, see?" Brenda glanced around to make sure they were alone. Then she lifted her short skirt and indicated a faint discoloration on her upper thigh.

Bending down to take a look, Coach touched the bruise and asked, "Does that hurt?"

"Oh yes, Coach, it does. Can you make it all better for poor, helpless Brenda, please?"

Somewhere down the hall, a noise echoed. Sharp footsteps were approaching. Coach stood up abruptly and said, "I can recommend a treatment. Come this way, Brenda."

Brenda said, "No, Coach, I want you to—"

Coach showed her into the exercise room, which wasn't what Brenda wanted. She said, "But Coach, *you* fix it, like you know so well how to do. That will make it better, please?"

"Brenda, we've got a way to go to heal your injury. Follow me."

Brenda looked up at him with big, sad eyes and said, "But it isn't *you*. I want Coach to fix it."

He took her to a big new stainless steel tub and said, "Brenda, you'll really like this."

"Aw, Coach, I want *you* to do it!"

"That's not in the cards for today, Brenda, because I need to leave. You get in and have a nice, soothing swirl and healing time. This is a hot tub with jets that shoot at your sore spots." He turned on the water and checked the controls, saying, "I've got to take Mrs. Charles to dinner. That was probably her coming down the hall, understand?"

As Coach walked out, Brenda called after him, "Oh pooh, I'm better than her!"

At the door, Coach turned to her and said, "Nobody's arguing with that, Brenda. Now have a good time."

Brenda did like it. The jets were especially stimulating, but nothing could replace Coach.

Now she could hardly wait to tell Sally about the new experience that awaited them. "You won't believe how these jets make your thingy feel. It's really fun, and you'll feel closer to Todd."

When they got to the gym the next afternoon, they checked to make sure the place was empty. They'd brought bathing suits, but after getting into the tub, they decided that clothing was optional. It was indeed a thrill, and Todd and Coach were momentarily forgotten.

~

Letter #6

From: Sally Anderson
691 Mitchell Drive
San Luis Obispo, California

To: SPC-4 Todd Wyrum
c/o Bravo Co.
Training Unit B-22
Fort Dix, New Jersey

My darling Todd,

Your letters are the highlight of my life, but when will you be here with me? I want to know so that I can be with you and talk to you about important things, *really* important things. Do you have a plan? What will I do while you're in training, and then later when you're doing army stuff? I don't have any idea what army guys—I mean *medics*—do.

I like the poems, but you don't have to put them in if it interferes with something else important. Oh, Todd, I don't know what I mean, only that it's the letter that's most important.

Cheer team practice is starting next week, and Brenda and I are supposed to be leaders. I'm not sure that I'm up to that. I guess Brenda can, but I'm not sure I want to. Mrs. V is being kind of mean to us lately. Even with the new routines and outfits, it isn't as much fun as it used to be. Do you think I should quit? I'm not sure. I could do more babysitting if I quit. What do you think?

Grandma, Gail, and Zoe say hi. Deacon Jennings also asked about you. I didn't know exactly what to tell them, because I don't know anything about army training for a medic's job. I guess you fix hurt people, don't you? I mean, like if someone shoots them in a war? Do medics deliver babies, too? Are there girl medics, like nurses and all that? Do you see girls on the base? I guess there must be some, right? What do they do?

I'm all confused, Todd, about when you'll be with me—and what then? Can I quit school and go off with you in the army? I know wives do that, don't they?

I wish I could write you a poem. There's so much I can't do. You can do everything.

―――

313

I love you,
Sally

~

Sally felt the popcorn in her tummy pretty regularly now, so her life became focused on two things: Todd's letters and the baby. But she still didn't think of the baby as a real person who was coming. It was more of an abstraction that scared her.

July 19 was only ten days away, and Sally got more and more frightened thinking about the house in Pismo Beach. The only person she could talk to was Brenda, but she was absorbed in her own adventures. She didn't seem to take Sally's talk about the baby seriously.

During one conversation, Brenda said, "Lots of seventeen-year-old girls have babies. If you decide not to do the Pismo thing, can you still live with Grandma?"

That was one of many huge question that Sally couldn't answer. The only thing she knew for certain was that if Todd were there, everything would turn out okay. But he wasn't, so everything was a giant, confused, worrisome mess that she had to face all by herself. She worried day and night.

~

Letter #7

From: SPC-4 Todd Wyrum
c/o Bravo Co.
Training Unit B-22
Fort Dix, New Jersey

To: Sally Anderson
691 Mitchell Drive
San Luis Obispo, California

Dear Sally,

I read your letter over and over. You seem kind of confused, which worries me. Are you okay? There's nothing to worry about on my part, and there are no other girls, period. Relax on that score, Sally. Even if there were, I'm still your Todd and nobody else's.

It kind of alarms me that you're talking about leaving school and babysitting. Wow, what's up with that? You shouldn't quit school, Sally. Your education is really important. What's with that idea? I didn't even know you were babysitting, though I guess most girls do it sometimes.

Stick with cheering! Isn't that your focus? Academics are important too, you know? Just do what Mrs. V says. She may be a pain, but she's still the boss. It's like me and Coach. We don't always agree, but he's the boss—and he's usually right. Like I hear around Fort Dix, "Go along to get along." If she asks you to do something that's not right, just say so. What's she gonna do, kick you off the team? You and Brenda are the leaders now. She'd shaft herself.

To answer your question, medics attend to the wounded, but we do other stuff too. Delivering babies is part of the course at Fort Sam Houston, in Texas.

If I'm stationed someplace nice, then we can be together—I mean, after you're out of school. If it's war, which is looking likely with the Vietnam dustup, then I'll probably be gone overseas. In that case, you'd best stay in SLO at Grandma's. Maybe you could get a job as a secretary.

Well, this brings me to a topic that you won't like. The medic school at Fort Sam Houston is full up for classes in September, so if I want to get in, I need to take the August class. So I won't be coming back on leave in August like we planned. I'll be in Texas until the ten weeks.

I know you'll be disappointed, but it's better for me—for us—in the long run. This way I'll be home sooner, for sure. I know it's a long wait, but I hope you understand and can handle it. I need the medic training so that I can get out and go to premed someplace. The army will pay for it because of my JROTC stuff. It's best this way, don't you think? Me getting the experience and training to be a doctor is the best way to secure our future, understand?

I'm sorry we have to wait. I had a hard time making that decision, but knowing you were safe in San Luis with Grandma made it easier. I hope you agree, but in any case it's decided.

Don't quit cheer team or school. Just go on with your happy life, and I'll be back before you know it. Do stay away from Kenny though. I know he's got the hots for you, but he's a bad egg.

Hi to Brenda. Hector and Helman too. Kiss Grandma, Gail, and Zoe for me.

We start a field problem in the Pine Barrens tomorrow. Wish me luck. Our company will be taking part. We're the aggressor force, and Company D will be defending. I'll let you know who wins.

If you need cheering up, just grab the mason jar, read a poem, and think of me.

"That Honeyed Place"

Will you touch my arm, Sally?

Will you hold and stroke it as you've done so often to let me know you're mine?

Fold yourself around me in my morning slumber, as again I'm yours at dawn.

Kiss me awake, my love.

My ears will slowly wake to your whispered words, "I love you."

Feel my lips respond on your tender mounds.

Hold me against that honeyed place.

Let my ship of love fill you,

And feel a warm sea wash over those white shores of your inner life.

Let us share the rapture of eruption together.

And for a hundred—no, a thousand—yes, a million times, let us be only one.

I love and miss you,
Todd

~

On the second day of the field problem in the Pine Barrens, Todd injured his right hand while doing a rope climb. It wasn't serious, but it got worse when he didn't report it. Back at the base after two more days, his hand was swollen and inflamed. Among the things he couldn't do was write, so he went two weeks without sending a letter to Sally. He didn't give it much thought, but it was viewed differently on Mitchell Drive.

~

Letter #8

From: Mrs. Barbara (Miss Lady) Wyrum
Wyrum Ranch, Highway 58
San Luis Obispo County, California

To: SPC-4 Todd Wyrum
c/o Bravo Co.
Training Unit B-22
Fort Dix, New Jersey

My dear Todd,

Having not heard from you in some time, I decided to write. I know you're probably very busy, so I fully understand. Still, I miss you and hope we can keep up a regular correspondence.

You and I need to work out your future. You're a man now, Todd, not the boy I've known and loved these many years. I am happy, more than happy, to go forward with you in any way you want. Regarding her treatment of you, I must say that I find Major Wyrum, your mom, a cold fish. You're a wonderful young man, and a little stumble in high school is not a life-threatening event.

I've set up an American Express account for you. Your pay is meager, so I hope this little bit helps. It is one hundred dollars per month. Your mother's stingy seventy dollars wasn't enough, even while you were here. I think she's a selfish skinflint, but I better not continue in that vein.

Things continue as usual on the ranch. The Boss is also as usual—only more so, if you get my drift. All the hands send you a big howdy, and Mrs. Cruz wants to send you fresh tortillas. No kidding. I dissuaded her from that, but it was a nice thought. You're my darling Todd, and always will be.

Please, please do write to me more often. I can hardly stand it here without news of you.

I checked to see if your truck was still in one piece. It's sitting in the driveway at Sally's home, but I didn't see her anywhere about. I hope she's rightly sorry for the part she played in getting you in this fix. I'm not saying she's not a nice girl, Todd. I'm just saying that it was inconsiderate of her to put you in that situation.

I wish I could write to the army and tell them to be nice to you. Kind of funny that, don't you think? Well, it's a woman's perspective, so there. Be careful.

I have much to share with you, besides just missing you terribly. Yesterday I received this letter from Major Wyrum, who is still in Germany, it seems.

Love, Miss Lady

~

Letter #9

From: Major B. H. Wyrum
First Armored Division GHQ
Judge Advocate's Office
Building H-111
Warner Barracks
Bamberg, West Germany

Dear Mrs. Wyrum,

I received your letter and the note from my brother a few days ago. Thank him for me. I was in some shock at the turn of events, but if Todd is now safely in the army, I hope I can relax knowing his future is on track. Notice I did not say the *right* track. A private in the army is not a good start. I'm so disappointed. Please convey this to him in no uncertain terms. If any costs were involved regarding this unfortunate incident, please forward them to me.

Now that Todd is in the army, and not an officer as I'd hoped he'd be, I think it is no longer necessary for me to forward money to you to give him, especially in light of his lack of self-control and the trouble it got him into. Thank you so much for stepping in to assist him in avoiding a worse fate. Let's hope he makes the most of this reprieve and does something with his life besides making a fool of himself over a wayward girl.

Since Todd will likely be moving around a lot in the army and you still have power of attorney to act for him, I'll continue to communicate with him through you. Is that all right with you, Mrs. Wyrum?

As I said, please express to Todd my *extreme* disappointment in his behavior.

Again, thank you for all you've done over the years.

Very truly yours,
B. H. Wyrum, Major, United States Army

~

After mailing this letter to Todd, it still angered Miss Lady that the major would refer to her as Mrs. Wyrum. It was cold, as if Miss Lady was some servant or government official. "Cold bitch" was the right description of her, in Miss Lady's view. Todd's mother was a member of Mrs. V's league of bad women.

~

Letter #10

From: Sally Anderson
691 Mitchell Drive
San Luis Obispo, California

To: SPC-4 Todd Wyrum
c/o Bravo Co.
Training Unit B-22
Fort Dix, New Jersey

My darling Todd,

Oh no, Todd, this is really terrible! You're not coming back in August? I cried when I opened and read the letter. How could you make this decision without me? Don't you love me anymore? I'm so mad at you for putting the dumb army ahead of me. How could you? I've been counting on you being here. I've got lots of new things to talk to you about—new stuff we both need to do.

Todd, can you get them to let you go for a week or two? They've got lots of other guys to go marching and shooting and doing army things, but I've only got you. So just tell them you need time off for an important visit. They'll understand, won't they? I mean, if you promise to be back on time, of course. Or you could fake being sick with the flu. They might not even miss you because of all the other soldiers. A little fib to help me is worth it, isn't it?

Brenda agrees with me. You should keep your word to me first. The army comes second, doesn't it? If you come home, I'll continue to cheer, and I'll forget about babysitting. I promise!

I love the poem, and I sure do curl up around the mason jar, but it's not you. Please come back to me as soon as possible. I need you near me. You can help. I feel so alone without you.

Your very own Sally, who needs you *so very much!*

~

Sally spooled Todd's letters and fit them into the mason jar, kind of like a diary. It was what he *didn't* say that really bothered her. *Will you marry me? Let's get hitched, engaged, betrothed.* And why hadn't she told him of her condition? How dumb she felt. Part of her thought he wouldn't come back if he knew, and another part wondered if Mrs. V was right. Was it even Todd's baby?

The popcorn continued, so despite her fear, Sally decided to see Nurse Jones after practice. Nurse Jones was in her office, talking with Mrs. V. Sally took a deep breath and said, "Nurse Jones, I would like to talk with you in private, please."

Mrs. V spoke up in a loud, insulting voice and said, "I'll bet we know what this is about!"

"Oh, Mrs. V, don't be so hard on poor, innocent Sally," said Nurse Jones. "She just likes to screw and wasn't careful, that's all. All those nice boys had to be taken care of, didn't they? And she and Brenda are so good at that, aren't they? Oh yes, and I almost forgot about the money."

Mrs. V said, "Yes, you're so right. My adventure girls did an outstanding job at booster."

The nurse gave Sally's bump a poke. "It almost looks like Sally has three boobs, don't you think?" Both women laughed heartily at Sally's expense. Then four vengeful eyes fell on her as Nurse Jones asked, "Shall we have that exam now? Mrs. V can help. We'll check out everything very carefully, won't we, Mrs. V?"

"Oh yes, we will. Come along now, Sally. We'll be gentle with you, but still, of course, do a thorough job." They took Sally by the hand and led her toward the exam room. Sally tried to pull away and said, "I really only wanted your opinion about the popping." As they got closer to the exam room door, Sally finally pulled free. "No, Nurse, I don't want to! I'm Todd's girl now. I don't want to do *that* anymore. No!"

Mrs. V stopped pulling and said harshly, "Well, if we let you go now, will you continue the adventures without these silly protests? Will you obey me?"

Nurse Jones said, "We've got to examine her, Mrs. V. We've got—"

"It's better if she does what she's told," insisted Mrs. V. "Will you do as promised, Sally?"

"No, Mrs. V, I wouldn't like that. I'm different now, and Todd is coming—"

"Oh, you stupid little trollop!" exclaimed Mrs. V. "Todd's not coming back, and even if he does, he's not going to want to drag you and *that* around. Grow up, Sally. Do as we say, and everything will work out for the best. You'll see. Now I'm going to examine you."

Sally insisted, "I won't go with Nurse! I don't want to."

There was a long silence, with some tugging and pulling both ways. Finally Mrs. V said, "Then your appointment in Pismo Beach next week is still on, right? If so, a session with Nurse Jones isn't necessary. Is it still on, Sally? Yes or no?"

When Nurse Jones pushed the door open, Brenda was standing there. "Why Sally, I was wondering where you'd gone. I heard some loud talking, and I hoped everything was okay. Is it, dear?"

The two women were momentarily distracted, and Sally was able to pull away from their grasp and run to Brenda, who welcomed her with a hug. Sally said, "I'll go if Brenda can come with me, Mrs. V, but I won't go without her!"

Disappointment flashed across Nurse Jones's face. "Why, you little tramps, I'll get you!"

Mrs. V said, "Just settle down, Nurse Jones, and consider the other side of this. Working together, these two girls could be very profitable. We'll not find others so easily, and the booster club will be very happy."

"Okay, you're probably right," conceded Nurse Jones. "Go ahead."

Mrs. V said, "Okay, Sally, Brenda can go with you. But if you don't go, I'll have you thrown out of school by Monday afternoon. I'll be notifying Grandma, too, remember? Now, you girls get out of here before I change my mind and call Principal Jennings and Grandma this evening."

Nurse Jones was still scowling as they left.

~

Letter #11

From: SPC-4 Todd Wyrum
c/o Bravo Co.
Training Unit B-22
Fort Dix, New Jersey

To: Sally Anderson
691 Mitchell Drive
San Luis Obispo, California

My very dearest Sally,

Your letter floored me. I don't understand. I have to do this for medical school and our future. And getting leave to come see you? Pretty funny! The army doesn't give a hoot about you and me. There is war coming in Vietnam, and they'll need more medics in 1962. Medics are in short supply, so what I'm doing is really important. It's *very* important to me, and it should be to you, too. Would you rather I drove a truck for a living or went back to the ranch?

So there is zero chance that I'll be coming home until after my medic training, which will take about ten weeks. We've been together a long time, Sally. A few weeks more isn't really so bad, is it?

Your letter was kind of odd. Is something wrong? Are you healthy? If there is anything wrong, go to the school nurse or French or Serra Vista Hospital. What could it be? Find out and get help.

I've called a few times, but nobody answers. Twice I left messages with Zoe. What happened with that? Didn't she tell you? I can't call much because of the cost, so I hope these letters are okay.

Our training problem in the Pine Barrens was tough, and I injured my hand. That's why you didn't get a letter for a while. I kept it a secret from Sergeant Rouna so they wouldn't hold me back, which they might have done. Now my hand is okay, so I can train and write to you again.

Well, back to our training in the Pines. We marched about twelve miles every day, and then we had to assault an enemy position. Each assault was different. Pretty cool really, except we were all *really* bushed. The Pine Barrens are spooky at night, too. It's the darkest place I've ever been. We fired the new M-14 rifles, M-60 machine guns, and .45 pistols, and the shooting was cool. My JROTC training has given me an edge. I'm the top-rated recruit in our training class so far.

I've got a short crew cut now. I don't know if you'll like it.

Again, sorry I haven't written in the last couple of weeks. It was my hand. I think of you most when I'm in my bunk at night. Guess what I'm thinking about? Oh boy, do I miss your boobs.

I scratched this down for you while on the march in the Pine Barrens.

Love and kisses, your Todd

> If I call your name,
> Will you hear it from afar?
> Or will my voice fade into the shaded forest?
> No, your love will pull it from the shadows
> And wrap your woman's heart around me.
> Drinking your forever kiss.

~

When Todd received Miss Lady's letter, it pulled him back to the rodeo, the high pasture, and ... He sat in front of his barracks reading her letter over and over again. The next morning, he went to the American Express office on the base and inquired about his new account. It was there, just like Miss Lady had said.

Todd's mind and body dwelt on her, the rodeo, and that summer. He looked over at the disciplinary barracks and thought, *I'd be in a civilian version of that place right now, if not for Miss Lady's help. Her love, too.* Wishing he was back at the ranch eating Mrs. Cruz's breakfast and getting ready to wrangle, he hummed softly, "You are my sunshine."

Coming from behind Todd, a voice with a heavy Texas drawl broke into his thoughts. "You're singing pretty good for a California boy. We might make a Texan of you yet."

Todd looked up and saw Sergeant Johnson standing there. "I'm no Texan, sergeant, but I do know a thing or two about ranching and country music. My horse Splash and I'd ride fence for hours on end in the hot sun, singing to pass the time. Brings back a passel of memories."

Sergeant Johnson sat down beside Todd, and looking off in the distance, said, "I'll bet there's a girl at the end of that passel, too. Ain't I right? Always is, it seems."

"You're smarter than you look, Sergeant Johnson. How'd you know that?"

They both laughed, but then the sergeant got serious. "We got orders coming down in a short time. Might be a few weeks, but they're coming."

"Orders? Like how?" asked Todd.

"Vietnam most likely. They need medics bad, especially with the indigenous Vietnamese forces, you know? Working with them in the field as advisers."

"Advisers how? You mean along with them, instead of with our own army units?"

"You up for deployment? You're at the top of the class. My guess is that you'll be the first to go, and they can send you anywhere. But if you volunteer, you'll get another stripe and choice of station."

Todd said, "Volunteer? I thought that was a no-no with you career guys."

"Why, Private Wyrum, you're too smart. I guess I taught you too well—just too damn well. You think about it, you hear? Time for class, so get moving. It's field dressing again."

The sergeant and Todd walked off to class. Todd hadn't thought much about what would come after the training. Deployment, but where? The only place he didn't want to go was Germany and Major Wyrum. Mom. Yuck. He'd go anywhere, but not Germany.

Vietnam was where all the talk of war was coming from, so Todd figured he'd better get more details. How bad could a little pissant place like that be, especially for a member of the United States Army?

CHAPTER 25

The House in Pismo Beach

After another long sleepless night, Sally awoke to even more anguished longing for the mail and Todd. She'd not received a card or letter for more than a week! Even worse was when the mailman did stop but didn't have a letter for her. Sally's tortured mind knew no bounds as she imagined Todd in the arms of another girl. Her belly grew bigger, and her efforts to keep from showing grew more difficult, but Grandma and her sisters still hadn't guessed. They just teased her about getting fat.

Brenda was no help, either. She joked that Sally's boobs were now almost in her league, which was true. But Mrs. V was the worst, calling Sally at home and trying to coax her into taking on new adventures. She'd always mention the house in Pismo Beach and the fact that Sally's time was running out. Brenda hinted at that too, but Sally ignored their prodding. Her entire focus was on her condition and hoping for word from Todd about when he'd be home to marry her. Looming over all this was the question of how soon Grandma would find out and what she'd do.

The morning crawled by, and it seemed to Sally that eleven thirty, the usual time for mail delivery, would never arrive. She went to the front porch and peered up the block toward Broad Street every few minutes. Finally she saw the happy Filipino American mailman coming down the street at a snail's pace. She waited on the porch as he walked from house to house, stopping to talk with the neighbors. When he got to her box, Sally ran to meet him, yelling at the poor man, "Is it for me? Is it?"

"Ah, miss, it's ... Well, just a second. Let's see. Here's one for Sally Ander—"

Before he could finish his sentence, Sally grabbed the letter, tore it open, and walked back to the porch. Then she flopped down on the steps and began to read.

The mailman walked off, muttering to himself about the impatience of youth.

The first paragraphs were all it took for Sally to realize that she wasn't going to be rescued from disgrace, banishment, and ridicule. Todd wasn't coming home. She clutched the letter to her bulging bosom, slumped over on the brick porch, and broke into forlorn sobs. Should she tell him? If she did, he might never come back, like Mrs. V said.

Mrs. V's words had become Sally's new reality. Alone and abandoned didn't begin to describe it. She read the rest of the letter, dismayed that Todd could be so optimistic while she sat alone and hopeless an eternity away. As she sat there, the house in Pismo Beach loomed closer.

Sally read about the Pine Barrens march, and then read the romantic sections over and over again. The soft, romantic things she longed to read were included, but the reality that Todd wasn't coming home outweighed the romance. How silly of him to think that she wouldn't like his short hair. Sally leaned back on the cold bricks and sucked her thumb. She heard the phone ring, but it barely registered in her sorrowful brain.

Then Zoe threw open the screen door and said, "It's Brenda! Grandma said she's not supposed to call."

Sally said, "Okay, I'm coming in. Where's Grandma? I thought she was out. Oh, never mind." Picking up the phone, she said in a raspy voice, "Hello, Brenda. What do you want?"

"Well, it took you long enough," replied Brenda. "Where were you, in the shower? You sound upset. What's up?"

Trying not to start crying again, Sally said, "I got another letter."

"What did he say? When is he coming home?" Brenda asked, but there was no response on the other end of the line. Just a deep, labored breath. "What's wrong, Sally? What did Todd say? Come on, tell me. He still loves you, doesn't he?"

Finally Sally said, "He's going to a school for medics in Texas, and he'll be away for months. Oh God, no Todd—and I'm going to have our baby."

"Don't be so down on yourself, Sally, darling. You have options, you know? Anyway, I've got someone here who wants to help. Here's Mrs. V."

Brenda passed the phone to Mrs. V, and making an awful face, whispered, "Todd's not coming home. Sally's really upset. Talk some sense into her if you can. You know, the options?"

With no small degree of "I told you so" in her voice, Mrs. V said firmly, "This is Mrs. V, Sally. I know you were counting on Todd returning to marry you, and I'm so sad to hear that he isn't coming. I'm your friend, Sally, and I can help if you'll let me—with Brenda, of course. Will you let me?"

When there was no answer from Sally, Mrs. V shook her head and passed the receiver back to Brenda's anxiously waiting hand.

"Sally, please let us help," said Brenda. "It's a nice place, and Mrs. V has agreed to pay for it if we go on with our adventures. It's been fun, hasn't it? We can have more fun, and you'll be back on the cheer team. I know you want that. Dumb Todd seems not to care anyway."

Sally exclaimed, "Todd doesn't even know! And you, of all people, know how nice and thoughtful he is. Oh God, why didn't I tell him? I'm so stupid!"

Mrs. V took the receiver back from Brenda and said coldly, "Sally, everything will be okay if you let me help. Brenda agrees! It's a nice, secluded, clean, well-run place. Lots of girls have gone there and come away happier for it. Now that Todd has *deserted* you, I can't see another way. Telling your Grandma will probably be hard, but she'll forgive you, won't she?"

Those last few words from Mrs. V were the hardest blow. Sally sobbed, knowing that Grandma would probably be ashamed, condemn her, and then kick her out.

Mrs. V continued, "How about it? Shall I schedule a visit? It's only overnight, and then you'll be back at home, fit as a fiddle, in no time. We'll make up an excuse about cheer team having to overnight somewhere, okay?"

Brenda grabbed the phone from Mrs. V and said, in a confident tone, "I'll be with you, Sally. You'll see, everything will work out, and Mrs. V has more adventures and money for us. We can go tomorrow. It's Saturday! It'll all be over in a day, and then you'll be back to your old happy self. Cheer team starts regular practice in a couple of weeks too."

Mrs. V took back the receiver and said, rather forcefully, "Okay, Sally, I can set it up for tomorrow at two o'clock—or I can call Grandma and tell her about the other option, which is expulsion. Which is it?"

Defeated and exhausted, Sally said flatly, "I'll go to Pismo. Grandma's home now."

When Mrs. V heard the phone click, she turned to Brenda and said, "It's on for two o'clock tomorrow. Be here with her, and I'll pick you up. Have your cheer stuff all ready. She's so upset that she might forget the whole thing. We don't want Grandma to suspect anything's amiss."

Brenda said, "You don't care about either one of us. You know Sally doesn't want to do this, but you're pressuring her into it so that we'll do the stuff with the booster club, aren't you?"

Mrs. V said, "Just keep that to yourself, or you'll be off the team too. Is that clear? I've got new girls—pretty girls—coming along next year, and you can be replaced. Those two little twins from the junior high program look like good prospects. You've seen them throw themselves around at the gym. Do you think they might be up for some adventures? You bet they would! I'll lay money that with some stipend incentive and sexy lingerie, they'd be ripe for it. I can tell by the look on your face, Brenda, that you think so, too."

Resorting to her go-to move, Brenda said, "Those two *little* girls ain't got this, do they? I'm not worried. Ask our fans at booster club who's best, and you'll see."

After calling back and talking to Grandma, Mrs. V said to Brenda, "Be at Sally's house to get her ready. She'll need help—if I'm any judge, which I am. I'll be there at one o'clock."

~

The dreaded day had arrived. On Saturday morning, Brenda showed up to help Sally get ready. They were in luck, for Grandma and the sisters were out doing the week's shopping.

It was a good thing that Brenda was there to help, because Sally was in a complete daze. Brenda had to do everything—clothes, makeup, hair, and things to pack—and it didn't matter at that juncture that she kind of overdid it with everything. Sally's bra now overflowed, to Brenda's *oohs* and *aahs*. She persuaded Sally to stand next to her in front of the mirror for a comparison. Pretty close, they agreed, but Sally showed no enthusiasm.

Just as they finished packing, Mrs. V pulled up in her new Oldsmobile sedan and honked the horn. She was dressed demurely, with a head scarf and dark glasses. After a second honk, Brenda came out the front door dragging Sally behind her. They were wearing their cheerleading uniforms, but Sally's face was forlorn.

The girls got in the back seat, and Mrs. V drove up to Broad Street, then south toward Edna and west on Price Canyon Road to Pismo Beach. That was the less-traveled back way to Pismo Beach. There was little conversation at first, just a few questions about what they'd packed.

After several minutes of relative quiet, Mrs. V said, "Oh, Sally, don't look so depressed. This is a way for you to get back to your fun life. Think about cheer team. Tell her, Brenda!"

Brenda took Sally's hand and tried to coax her out of the deep funk. "Mrs. V is right. This is going to be easy, and it will be over in a few hours. Then we'll be able to go back to our fun life. Who needs Todd, anyway? There are lots of other boys."

Sally continued pouting and sighed a couple of times. "Well, I guess …"

As they got to the Cabrillo Highway and turned south, Mrs. V explained what was going to happen. "Sally, when we get there, Brenda and I will go in with you. But we'll have to leave once you get started with the procedure. Then when—"

"You're gonna *leave* me? I thought Brenda was gonna stay with me like you promised!"

Mrs. V said, "Don't be this way, Sally. I didn't promise you a thing. After all, I'm paying for this, aren't I? It's going to be simple, so don't worry, and Brenda can stay a few extra minutes if you want."

Clearly upset at the change in plans, Brenda said, "I thought I was going to stay with Sally, so why can't I?"

Mrs. V replied angrily, "No more back talk. You got in this mess on your own, Sally, and I'm paying to clean it up. You'll do as I say, and that's that—or I'll dump you both out right here. So shut up and calm down. We'll be there in a few minutes."

Brenda blurted out, "No fair. You *did* say—"

"I said shut up, and I meant it!" exclaimed Mrs. V.

"But you did say—" insisted Brenda.

Just past Pomeroy Avenue, Mrs. V pulled the car to the curb and parked. Then she reached around, grabbed Brenda, and gave her a good shaking. Pointing a dark-red fingernail at the two of them, she said, "Shut up and behave! I can find other tricks besides you. Don't think I can't."

The three of them sat in silence for a minute. Finally Mrs. V smiled and calmly said, "This has just gone too far. Let's settle down to the friendly way we've always—well, almost always—been, okay? Let's behave like grown-ups and get Sally taken care of."

Brenda and Sally exchanged glances, then nodded their grudging agreement.

Without further discussion, Mrs. V drove off down the highway. A few blocks later, they turned right onto Park Avenue. The housing along that street had seen better days. Faded paint, weed-filled yards, and abandoned cars was the order of the day. Both girls looked around with a feeling of foreboding. Toward the end of the street, Mrs. V pulled up in front of a gray house that was in slightly better shape than the rest of the neighborhood, but still nothing to brag about.

Mrs. V turned in her seat and put on her biggest smile for the two cowed girls. She pointedly said to Brenda, "Now please help Sally and me, okay? Sally is counting on you, and so am I."

The girls pondered what to do. With Mrs. V still leaning over the seat in a confrontational way, Brenda finally said, "We'd better get to it. It's what we came here for, right?"

On the verge of tears once again, Sally said, "Yes, I guess, but I don't want to!"

Mrs. V drove the knife in a bit deeper. "Todd's not coming back, so what else can you do? We can go back and talk to Grandma and Principal Jennings, if that's what you want. No more high school, cheer team, or money. Is that what you want, Sally?"

Sally said in a pained whisper, "No, Mrs. V, that's not what I want."

"Okay, then we're off!" Mrs. V got out and beckoned for the two scared girls to follow.

Brenda got out first with the little bag, and Sally reluctantly followed. They stood at the curb, peering over a peeling white picket fence at a weedy lawn that needed mowing. An old pickup truck with four flat tires stood in the driveway. There was no garage, and the faded gray house stood back from the street some thirty feet. All the windows were covered from the inside with blinds, some cracked and bent. A covered wooden porch sat at the top of five weathered steps. Part of the porch railing was broken, and pots of dead flowers stood at each side of the steps. The house looked almost abandoned.

Seeing the horrified expressions on the girls' faces, Mrs. V said, "The house is kept this way to avoid attracting attention. You understand, of course."

Sally tried to turn back, but Mrs. V blocked her way. Trembling, she took Brenda's hand.

Brenda pushed the creaking gate open and walked up the flagstone path, then up the steps and onto the porch. A big "Welcome" sign hung crookedly next to the door. Mrs. V's voice said softly but firmly, "Knock, Brenda. The bell doesn't work."

A moment later, a gruff face appeared in the door's small window, and an older woman answered the door. She wore heavy makeup, and a half-smoked cigarette dangled from her lips. Her hair was up, though just barely, and she had slippers on. She looked like she'd just gotten up from a nap—or was in need of one. When she smiled, she looked like a woman who'd once been attractive, but her eyes were hard and her warm welcome sounded phony. "Well, I've been expecting you, Mrs. V. These must be your young charges. Welcome, and come on in."

The room was filled with overstuffed chairs, couches, and stools of varying colors and fabrics. The walls were painted pale green with flowered wallpaper at the far end. The blinds were drawn, though sunlight slanted down across the room, and rugs covered the hardwood floors. Two table lamps lit an otherwise dim space, and several full ashtrays were scattered about. In the kitchen, off to one side, four chrome and plastic-covered chairs sat around a Formica-topped table and the sink overflowed with dirty dishes. The soft hum of a fan could be heard, and the place had the scent of cheap air freshener combined with cigarette smoke.

Standing behind the girls, Mrs. V said, "Hi, Bev! Sorry we're late. A little hesitation, it seems, but nothing serious. Just a bit of girlish jitters, as well you know."

"Oh yes, I surely do. Which one is it?" asked Bev. "No, don't tell me. I can tell at a glance that it's the blonde. Quite a bump you've got there, girly! And my, look at the tits on this one. Are you ever stacked, girl! Just like me once. What's your name, Bubbles?"

Mrs. V said, "Not now, Bev. It's Sally with the bump. You're ready, aren't you?"

Bev opened a door marked "Exam Room" and said, "Yep, all ready for you, Sally."

Brenda backed away.

Mrs. V said, "She's twelve weeks along. Any problem with that?"

Bev reached out, took Sally's hand, and led her to the door of the exam room. "No problem at all. Go ahead and disrobe, Sally dearest. Not to worry, I'm an expert. You'll be fit as a fiddle in no time."

With a sly smirk on her face and eyes as cold as Bev's, Mrs. V said, "Well, it's in your hands now, Bev. Brenda and I will leave Sally in your care. We'll be back within an hour of your call. Sally, you'll be brave, won't you?"

Dropping her coat on a chair, Sally said, "Brenda's supposed to stay with me."

Bev reached out and took the bag from Brenda, grabbing her hand as she did so. "No need for Brenda to leave. She can stay if she wants. Do you, dear?"

Again Mrs. V said, "Not now, Bev! We're all business today."

Bev eyed Brenda covetously, then led Sally through the door of the exam room.

The room shocked Sally. It was white with a powder-blue linoleum floor. Items she couldn't identify were strewn around, and it had that same air-freshener smell, only stronger. The room didn't exactly look dirty, but neither did it feel clean. A chair that appeared to lean back into a table sat in the middle of the room, with a set of stirrups attached, and the gurney sitting alongside was covered with instruments. The chair and array of shiny chrome items looked cold and institutional, and a bright florescent light hung overhead.

As Sally stood just inside the doorway and surveyed this scene, Nurse Jones stepped out from behind the door, gestured at the room's furnishings, and said invitingly, "Come in, Sally. I've been waiting for you. I'm Bev's assistant for the procedure. Everything is ready for just you, *darling Sally.*"

Mrs. V was leading Brenda toward the front door, but seeing Nurse Jones flipped a switch in Sally, who began yelling, "I can't! I won't! No, no!" Realizing this was the critical moment, and still holding Brenda's hand, Mrs. V turned around and shoved Sally farther into the exam room. "In you go, Sally. Don't be difficult! Mrs. V's here to help."

Despite Mrs. V pushing and Nurse Jones pulling, Sally managed to jerk away and call out, "Help me, Brenda! Please, I don't want to. Let me go. Let me go!"

"Don't hurt her! I'm here, Sally!" Brenda yelled. A little scrum ensued as Sally was pulled back and forth between Brenda in one direction and the two older women in the other.

Finally Sally dropped to the floor, which broke the grips of Mrs. V and

Nurse Jones, and crawled toward Brenda and the door. She kept screaming, "No, I won't do it! It's Todd's baby—*our* baby! I won't do it!"

Standing at the door, Sally and Brenda turned and glared at the two older women. Mrs. V yelled, "You're out, Sally! If you won't do what we agreed, you're through with school and cheer team, and I'm throwing you into Grandma's tender hands. Furthermore, if this is your final decision, you can find your own way back to town."

For a moment, the two girls and Mrs. V just angrily glared at one another. Then Mrs. V said, "One last chance to change your mind, Sally. One last chance. And you, Brenda, won't get off scot-free either, I promise you. Talk some sense into Sally. Oh my, this is a mess!"

Bev broke in, "I told you, Mrs. V, not to take on these high school sluts. The money wasn't worth the risk. Now look what's happened—a mess! A real ugly mess!"

Sally and Brenda stood with their backs to the front door as they resisted the imploring voices from across the room. The space that separated them from Mrs. V might as well have been a mile wide, and their fear had been replaced by determination. Sally said, "I won't do it! We're leaving. You can take your revenge, Mrs. V, but I'm not hurting my baby. We're leaving, aren't we, Brenda?"

Brenda nodded vigorously, and they slowly backed out the door and left the house. Holding hands, with hearts pounding, they descended the steps and walked down the path. At the gate, they looked back to see Mrs. V standing on the porch and glaring at them. She yelled, "You stupid girls. You'll be sorry, so sorry." Then she went inside and slammed the door.

After a moment, Sally said, "My bag and coat? What are we going to do now, Brenda?"

They looked back at the house, then at each other, and their eyes agreed. They walked toward the Cabrillo Highway. No need to even consider returning to the house in Pismo Beach.

~

What now? At a beachfront gift shop selling cheap trinkets, cards, T-shirts, and sunscreen, Sally and Brenda sat on a bench and tried to decide what to do. Among the possibilities were hitchhiking, walking, and calling Grandma or Kenny. In the end, they decided to call Mr. Hesselgren, of all people. He wanted what he wanted, but at least he was forthright about it.

Sally's tears and realistic portrayal of abandonment persuaded the man at the counter to let her use the phone, though Brenda's cleavage probably helped. So Sally called the Pines Motor Lodge, and Mr. Hesselgren came to their rescue. He picked them up an hour later in his big Cadillac and drove them to Sally's house. He didn't have any questions or demands— he just seemed genuinely happy to see them. Their lame excuse for being stranded in Pismo, though, wasn't terribly convincing. Their frightened faces, shrill voices, disheveled appearance, and lack of convincing reason for being there was a dead giveaway. When they got out of his car, they stood at the driver's side window and thanked him profusely.

Mr. Hesselgren gave them a crooked smile and said, "It was Mrs. V's doing, wasn't it?"

The girls looked at each other with guilt written all over their faces. They were caught, and all three of them knew it. A heavy silence hung in the air for a moment.

Looking at Sally's belly, Mr. Hesselgren said, "I've been around. You don't run a string of motels without knowing stuff, and I've got a pretty good idea of what's what in this part of Pismo. During the war, this was a really wild, wide-open town, though that was before your time, of course. You could get into trouble in any way imaginable—and out of trouble too, if you get my meaning. Booze, dope, whores, gambling, and floating craps games that went on for days, even weeks as I recall. I was—we were all—younger then, and wilder, for sure. I could go on and on." His eyes on Sally's bump could not be misunderstood. "You ever talk to your mom about those days, Brenda? Well, she'd tell you. Or how about Todd's buddy Big Earl?"

A look of surprise spread across the two girls' faces.

"Ha! You don't know! My, oh my, what stories I could tell. Oh yes, what stories—and Mrs. Sondheim too, by the way. She didn't get to be queen bee in these parts playing bingo and bridge at the Monday Club. She and your mom and Dotty—what a trio! They could shake a club to its foundation, though in different ways, of course. Oh yes, they sure could! Mrs. V ran with us back then, and I was there to see it, too. Great stories, and great fun."

Brenda exclaimed, "My mom and Mrs. Sondheim? Mrs. V, too? I can hardly believe it!"

"Oh yeah, Brenda!" said Mr. Hesselgren. "The Mission Bar, Barbara's by the Sea, Motel Inn, and a whole lot more. Jukeboxes going full bore, dancing, army guys fighting—Pismo was the wildest. Even the El Morocco Club out on Higuera Street. I owned the Surf Motel in Avila Beach in those days, and we were full every night. What a scene, and we all made a bundle!"

"Oh, Mr. Hesselgren, we are so thankful for ... for the ride," Sally said.

"You know, I bet Mrs. V's pulling down a grand a month, more or less, for your adventures. What's she give you—ten, twenty, thirty—for helping the cheer team?"

Both girls' mouths fell open.

Mr. Hesselgren smiled and said, "Yeah, I know about all that stuff. Like I said, I've been around."

"We didn't know that!" Brenda exclaimed. "We're so thankful for your help, Mr. Hesselgren."

"No need to thank me. We've had plenty of good times. You're both nice girls who fell prey to Mrs. V's scheming, greedy ways. She's been that way awhile. I hope your guy Todd comes back to you, Sally. I really, sincerely do, but if he doesn't, get in touch with me and I'll see what I can do." He reached through the car window and gave each girl a pat on the cheek.

Brenda said, "Sally can't, but I can show you how grateful we are, you know?"

"I'll be in touch," he said, and the car pulled away.

Sally's shock hung in the air as the car disappeared down Mitchell Drive. "Your mom, Mrs. Sondheim, and Big Earl? His motels? Holy cow, Brenda, could it be?"

Brenda's eyes narrowed. "Who would've guessed?"

Sally started down the driveway, but halfway to the front porch, she saw Grandma looking out through the screen door. Pulling up short, she glanced down at her bump, and said, "Oh God, I don't have my coat."

"She's sure to notice," said Brenda. "We should have gone to my house, and you could've borrowed my cheer jacket. Let's go over and get it."

Grandma waved at Sally and turned away. A long moment passed, and then she spun back around and came flying out the door. "Oh, Sally, what have you done? What, oh Lord, have you gone and done?"

Sally felt like she was nailed to the spot. She unconsciously pressed her hands to her tummy and lowered her eyes in shame. "Oh Grandma, I'm so sorry!"

Grandma collapsed in a rocking chair on the porch, almost like she'd been struck by a blow. Slumping over, she put her head in her hands and began to cry. Sally dropped to the lawn strip down the center of the driveway and began to cry. Brenda followed their example and cried right along with them, although she remained standing. Hearing the noise, Gail and Zoe came out on the porch and surveyed the scene in total incomprehension.

This went on for a couple of minutes, but then Grandma regained her composure and slowly stood up. After a long look at the girls, she pointed at Brenda and said, "You! I might have guessed you'd be a part of this shame. Get out of here right now. Scram!" Without saying a word, Brenda gently patted Sally on the head and walked away.

Grandma came down off the porch and slowly walked up to Sally, who was still slumped over and sobbing, her shoulders convulsing. She stood over Sally, hands on her hips, and said, "You're a disgrace to this family, pure and simple. I can hardly imagine what your mother might think of this—of you and me—from on high. Now get up, and stop feeling sorry for yourself. You've brought this on yourself with your bad behavior, makeup, risqué clothes, and befriending a tramp like that girl. And that cheer team crowd? I should've known. Poor Mrs. V too, after all the work she's put into molding you girls into an admired group."

These last words forced Sally bolt upright, and she replied defiantly, "Mrs. V? Why, you don't know. You *can't* know. It's all her fault—every bit of it!"

Gail got in her own little jab, saying, "You're in trouble, Miss Smarty Pants. You're in big trouble!"

~

Grandma coaxed Sally to her feet and led her into the house. When they got inside, Grandma sent Gail and Zoe off without explanation, and she and Sally sat at the kitchen table in silence. The kitchen, usually so warm and friendly, now felt like a prison cell to Sally, and the chrome and vinyl breakfast table and chairs felt about as welcoming as a police interrogation room. Grandma wasn't asking any questions yet, however. She just stood at the sink and puttered, with tears running down her face.

Finally Sally gathered her courage and said, "Grandma, I'm sorry! Todd and I just—"

"Hush. Just hush, young lady. I thought that boy was so nice, but we just never know, do we? Well, I know what to do." She went to the wall phone and dialed a number.

A minute or so passed, and then Grandma said, "Deacon Jennings, this is Mrs. Anderson. Sorry to bother you today, but I have a situation that needs your attention. Sally and I urgently need to talk with you. Are you free for a few minutes? We need God's counsel. Please, can you spare a minute?" She listened for a minute and said, "It's Sally, and it's terrible. I'd better wait to tell you." Pausing another minute, Grandma then looked over at Sally and said, "Yes, we can come in about twenty minutes. Oh, Deacon Jennings, thank you so much. See you in a few."

When Grandma faced Sally, she had the saddest, oldest face that Sally had ever seen. Sally's lower lip again began to quiver, but Grandma put a finger to her lips and pointed toward Sally's bedroom. As Sally got up and walked down the hall, Grandma called after her, "I never thought you'd become such a bad girl, even when you began to do makeup and dress that way. Oh Sally, you so disappoint me. Go and put on your best church clothes. You know where we're going."

Indeed she did. Could things get any worse? Well, yes, because Sally knew what the good deacon had been up to. She wished Brenda could come along, but she knew better than to raise that question. When she got to her room, Sally first went to the mason jar, took out Todd's last, heartbreaking letter, and read it over. Her thoughts drifted. He could still rescue her from this hell that was now descending on her, but Todd wasn't there. Oh, why hadn't she told him?

Chapter 26

Grandma

Sally despaired at her choice of clothes—drab, childish, out-of-fashion, colorless junk. She knew what the deacon would prefer to see her in. If only Brenda could come, too.

"Are you ready?" Grandma yelled. Her voice was harsh and sad at the same time.

Sally decided that rather than choosing what to wear, she'd just pull out the first thing she grabbed from her closet. When she brought it out, however, she realized that it was her prom dress. Bursting into tears, she threw herself on the bed.

Her loud sobs roused Grandma, whose unsympathetic figure soon stood at her door. "Get up and into something, young lady. We leave in fifteen minutes." When Sally didn't budge, Grandma went to the closet, took out a dress and shoes, and put them on the bed. "Get into these right now, Sally."

Sally roused herself, got dressed, and went to the bathroom to do her makeup, completely forgetting that Grandma had forbidden her from putting on anything except a bit of lipstick. When she emerged, one look was all it took for Grandma to grab her hand and forcefully jerk her back into the bathroom.

"No, that just will not do!" exclaimed Grandma. "Not by a long shot! I know how to take care of that. You'll not go to church and disgrace me even further by looking like a tramp." Grandma pulled her to the sink, filled it with water, and ordered Sally to sit on the toilet edge. Then she soaped up a washcloth, took a knee in front of Sally, and said, "Raise your face, young lady!"

"No, Grandma, please let me do it." Sally tried to shield her face, but it was too late. Grandma pushed Sally's hands aside and began vigorously scrubbing. When Sally tried to turn away, Grandma just scrubbed harder, which hurt, plus it was just humiliating. Sally felt like a child being punished. "No, Grandma, please don't. It hurts." In just a minute, the makeup was gone, and Sally's face was pale pink.

Grandma said, "You've been a bad girl, plain and simple. We'll see what Deacon Jennings sees as appropriate for a hussy. I can barely believe I'm going to see him over something like this. I'm so ashamed of you. You're a disgrace to yourself, our family, and your sainted mother. I'm almost glad she's not here to see this. Your body is a holy vessel to be given only to ... And that boy! Oh, the shame of it."

Now really scared, Sally blurted out, "You still love me, don't you, Grandma?"

Grandma coldly replied, "Get your wrap, and meet me at the car."

Sally finished dressing and stood before the mirror. What she saw was not a cute, proud cheerleader, but a drab shadow of her former self. She was nothing more than an unattractive child.

~

The ten-minute drive might as well have been an hour-long trip to prison. Sally's inner voice said, *Oh, Brenda, can you be here with me?* Of course she wouldn't be. The warden waited.

They were greeted at the church by Mrs. Jennings, who gave Sally a condescending look. She had noticed Sally's growing womanhood and the deacon's eyes on her.

When the deacon entered the reception room, he was smiling, but when his eyes fell on Sally, his jaw dropped. He stammered, "Well, uh ... Hello, Mrs. Anderson, and you too, Sally. What, uh ... What brings you here today?" His nervous expression revealed that he already knew the answer to that question, even before Grandma spoke.

With apprehensive eyes, Grandma glanced at Mrs. Jennings. Then she looked back at the deacon and asked, "Can we see you alone perhaps?"

"Why, of course, Mrs. Anderson. Right this way. My office will do just fine. Bernice, will you get us some refreshments, please?"

On her way out of the room, Mrs. Jennings walked close by Sally and whispered, with a dirty look in her eyes, "Serves you right." Millennia of women's indirect confrontations didn't have to be explained to Sally.

A death-row inmate couldn't possibly dread execution any more than Sally dreaded being in Deacon Jennings's office. When the door closed behind them, she sat down, already on the brink of tears. She looked at the deacon, and even to Sally's young eyes, the fear etched in his face was obvious.

Before the deacon could say a word, Grandma started in. "As you can see, Sally is in a family way—without having a family, as it were. That boy Todd, who I thought was so nice, got Sally into trouble. Now he's left for the army, and Sally is alone. I'm going about this all wrong, aren't I, Deacon? I'm so ashamed."

After a long hesitation, and with fear still on his face, Deacon Jennings said, "Well, now, it may not be as bad as it seems. Todd seemed like an honorable boy. Is it possible he'll come back and do as he should and—well, marry Sally?"

Both Grandma and the deacon looked questioningly at Sally, who looked down at her feet, afraid of the answer she was about to reveal.

The deacon said, "Come now, Sally, tell us everything. We're on your side. When you told Todd, what was his response? Is he coming back to wed you?"

Sally whispered, "Todd doesn't know. I didn't tell him. I was going to, but then I didn't, and he left. He's training at Fort Dix, back east."

Grandma just looked away and shook her head.

The deacon said, "Oh!" After another long silence, he asked, "Could you write and explain it to him? Do you think he'd respond honorably, as he should?"

A glimmer of hope crossed Grandma's face. "Yes, that would be best," she agreed. "Surely the army will let him leave for that reason—I mean, if he promises to go back. Won't they, Deacon?"

The deacon's face revealed no confidence that the army would, indeed, do just that. "Well, Mrs. Anderson, it sure would be a solution. But the army, in which I myself served as a chaplain, isn't likely to just let Todd leave, even for as good a reason as this. In their eyes, he's a soldier first. What do you think, Sally? Would Todd come back and make an honest woman of you, if you told him?"

Grandma burst out, "Good grief, Deacon, she's been wearing makeup, dressing in a risqué way, and behaving badly for some time now, besides befriending that awful Brenda girl. I mean, why would she not have told him? ... Oh my, oh my, Sally, are you sure that Todd is, well, that he's the—"

Suddenly looking even more scared, the deacon interrupted Grandma. "Let's all calm down now, Mrs. Anderson. We don't want to take things too far, so let's see now. Are you sure, Sally, that Todd is ... the one?"

The deacon's "honest woman" comment had jolted Sally into an even worse mood, and she just hung her head.

Realizing just where this might lead, the deacon tried to stop the inquiry. His voice rose, and his panic began to show. "Let's just stop with what might be ... Well!"

But Grandma wouldn't let the subject drop. "Oh my God, you weren't with other boys, were you? Is that why you didn't tell Todd?"

Sally's mind fixated on the fear on the deacon's face, and her inner voice said, *If only Brenda was here.* Grasping at that straw, she said, "Maybe if Brenda were here, she could help explain how ... well, you know, how I got into trouble!" He courage began to build as she continued, "You could have Mrs. Jennings call Brenda and ask her to come here and explain stuff— important stuff! Don't you think that might help, Deacon Jennings?"

Grandma said, "No, Sally, not her. How could a girl like that help?"

"Now Sally, let's not involve those who might, well, cloud the issue," said Deacon Jennings. "Don't you agree, Mrs. Anderson? Brenda might not be the appropriate person to clarify the situation."

The obvious discomfort on their faces gave Sally even more courage. She sat up straight, looked the deacon in the eyes, puffed out her chest, and said, "Yes, Brenda can help. I can call her myself, right now, and she can explain everything. Everything about *everyone*, Deacon Jennings. Everything!"

Sally's words pulled the deacon up short again. "No, that surely won't be necessary. In any case, it's a long walk, and our meeting is almost over."

"No trouble!" exclaimed Sally. "I'm sure her mom would drive her, and she may be helpful, too."

The deacon insisted, "No, that won't be at all necessary! Don't you agree, Mrs. Anderson?"

"Not necessary at all," agreed Grandma.

Sally considered going further with the Brenda thing, but she could tell by the look on his face that her intended effect had been achieved. Feeling that she had the upper hand, she felt better.

Mrs. Jennings entered the room with a tray of refreshments, shooting another disapproving look at Sally. "Here are some goodies. After all, there's nothing that God-fearing people can't resolve if the Lord helps. Oh yes! How entertaining you were, Sally, this past football season, with the other girls. I do hope you'll be involved again next year. You will, won't you, Sally?"

The deacon said, "Bernice, please close the door on your way out."

As Mrs. Jennings closed the door, she looked back at her less-than-composed husband and replied, "Well, of course, dear. We wouldn't want the goings-on here to get out and become common gossip, would we? Anyway, you have a wedding to plan."

The word *wedding* was aimed at Sally like a dagger, and her momentary good feeling deflated like a balloon losing all its air.

The door closed with a bang, and then the silence in the room was deafening. Sally didn't want to be pilloried any further, Grandma didn't want to hear that Sally had been intimate with other boys, and the deacon didn't want to have his adventures with Brenda revealed.

Grandma reached over and tried to fasten one more button on Sally's dumpy top. "You need to look like a nice young lady in Deacon Jennings's presence, Sally."

Sally had the deacon's full measure now. She fumbled the buttoning job just enough as to show even more cleavage. "Yes, Grandma."

The deacon had gotten the message too, especially regarding Brenda. Pulling himself together a bit, he said, "This is an unfortunate condition that Sally finds herself in. She's been victimized by a careless boy and left to fend for herself. While recognizing the seriousness of the situation, we must also extend as much support to poor Sally as our love for her allows. Don't you agree, Mrs. Anderson?"

Surprised at the deacon's apparent change in attitude, Grandma said, "Well, of course, I'll take your experienced advice on the matter. What punishment do you think we should mete out regarding Sally's lack of moral values? She's disregarded your teaching and scripture, and she's a disgrace."

Sally sat up straight and stared at the good deacon as if to say, "Brenda's waiting."

He got the message. "Mrs. Anderson, contrary to what you may have surmised, I believe that Sally has been victimized. This older, unscrupulous boy has perhaps coerced Sally into a behavior that she wouldn't have undertaken if he hadn't lied to her. He may have even physically threatened her in a subtle way. After all, he's an accomplished boxer, so that could be the case." Then he turned to Sally and said, "Sally, this behavior wasn't your idea, was it?"

With a sad face, Sally looked down at her ugly brown shoes and shook her head. Even though she knew the deacon's description of Todd was a complete lie, perhaps it would be her saving grace. A vision of herself and Todd making love at the shack coursed through her mind, and she thought about some of the adventures she and Brenda had so willingly undertaken.

Grandma said, "Well, I don't quite see it that way, but I place my full trust in you, Deacon."

The deacon reached over and patted her on the shoulder. "After all, Mrs. Anderson, you did come to me for advice and the Lord's help in this matter. Let's see if we can put Sally on the road to what the Lord might want and have some compassion for her frail situation. Can you help me—and Sally, of course—by doing that?"

Grandma replied, "Oh my, I guess so, if you say it's your—I mean the Lord's—way."

Sally and the deacon exchanged knowing looks, as if Brenda was right there with them.

"Here is what I propose," said the deacon. "I'll speak to my brother and see if there's a way for you to continue school. As you may know, the policy is for girls who get into this kind of, uh, *situation* to be expelled as an example to others. In spite of the circumstances that have befallen you, Sally, the Lord and his servant on this earth, being myself, wish you and your future child to remain in the church and live a wholesome life. This will not be easy. I hope you grasp this opportunity to return to a high moral path and devote yourself to prayer and virtue. As for the boy involved, I hope he returns and take full responsibility. If that's not the case, however, it will be up to you to put yourself on a moral path. Do you understand that, Sally? And you, Mrs. Anderson?"

The hypocrisy of the deacon's statement made Sally want to throw up. Their eyes met, and in that instant they both knew. *Brenda to the rescue*, thought Sally. She lowered her eyes and said, "Yes, Deacon Jennings, I understand."

With a touch of desperation in her voice, Grandma asked, "But what am I to do with her? I can't just put this aside. I've got to consider my position in the community and the church. What am I to do?"

More hypocrisy. "I hope you'll take this occasion to do some praying while you're here, and then consider the options," said Deacon Jennings. "We'll talk again next week. Mrs. Anderson and Sally, does that work for you?"

Grandma said, "The *options*?"

The deacon looked at them now without the slightest guilt on his face. Somehow he'd resolved within himself a way out. It felt to Sally like Brenda had left the room. "Now, ladies, I'm sorry but I need to bring this to a close. I hope you'll take this opportunity for some heartfelt prayer. I'm so glad you availed yourselves of the church's resources. Our prayers are with you. Now please excuse me. Bernice will show you out. Thank you!"

The deacon's cool dismissal was a further slap in the face. Grandma was surprised, but not Sally. On the way through the nave of the church, Grandma did stop to pray, while Sally waited out front. Even though the worst hadn't happened, the weight of it all sat heavily on Sally.

Sally and Grandma were quiet on the ride home. The clear path to resolution Grandma had expected to get from Deacon Jennings wasn't, in fact, clear at all. What should she do? What about Sally being expelled from school? Could Todd come back? And the biggest question of all, what about the baby?

~

At home, Sally went directly to her room, lay down, and fell fast sleep. She slept the rest of the day and through the night, finally waking up with what could only be described as a sleep hangover. She was still wearing the dumpy clothes of the previous day. She tried to remember all that had happened. Was it just yesterday? How could so much bad happen in only one day?

For the next few days, Sally and Grandma hardly spoke, which was okay with Sally. Sensing that something was amiss, Gail and Zoe didn't tease her. Sally napped a lot.

On the following Monday morning, Grandma could be heard talking on the phone with Deacon Jennings. She seemed pleased with whatever transpired. On Tuesday she sent Gail and Zoe off to a neighbor's house right after breakfast. Then she sat down with Sally for a talk, at the old kitchen table where they'd shared many talks in the past.

Appearing calm and composed, Grandma said, "Sally, after a lot of work, Deacon Jennings and I have come up with a plan for your future. I hope you'll agree to this, but if not ... Well, that would be another matter entirely. Pay attention now."

"Yes, Grandma, I'm listening," Sally said.

"We've arranged for you to go to a nice, clean, well-supervised home near Paso Robles. It's a home for girls who get in trouble—well, pregnant—where they can have their babies in a safe, out-of-the-way place, and it will—"

"What?" Sally interrupted her. "A home, a safe place out of the way? Grandma, *this* is my home."

"Hush now, girl, and listen, because I'm not going to do this again. After the birth, you can go wherever they want or put the child up for adoption. You'll be well cared for, and I can visit you occasionally. Deacon Jennings says the church will pay for most of it. If Todd returns, so much the better, but since I don't expect that, this is the best option. It's a nice place, I'm told, and we know of other girls who've gone there. We'll leave next Monday. It's a nice summer drive up there, and we'll have a chance to chat. Now, isn't this a good solution, and so nice of Deacon Jennings and the church to do?"

A shocked silence enveloped the room, until finally Sally composed herself enough to speak. "Grandma, I don't want to go to a home. *This* is my home. Why can't I stay here? I won't be a bother to you, I promise. Deacon Jennings said he'd speak to his brother about—you know, me staying in school. He's a nice man, and he'll help me."

"He is a nice man, but he has a school to run, and having girls with loose morals around doesn't help. Your example would be awful. You have to go, Sally. I have to look out for the reputation of this family too, and as long as you're here, the shame of what you've done is a family disgrace."

"But Grandma, I can't just ... This is my home!" Sally exclaimed.

Grandma got up to leave the kitchen. "No more back talk, Sally. We'll leave next Monday."

Alone without Todd, pregnant, penniless, and now about to be cast out of her own home. This was Sally's future as she saw it. *Abandoned* summed it up pretty well. She was too despondent to cry. Where could she turn? Was there a last straw to grasp? Was Todd her only hope, or was there something else?

~

Letter #12

From: Sally Anderson
691 Mitchell Drive
San Luis Obispo, California

To: SPC-4 Todd Wyrum
c/o Bravo Co.
Training Unit B-22
Fort Dix, New Jersey

My darling Todd,

Each day I awake from dreams of you and missing you more and more. I hope you're doing well in your training. I am with you in my heart all day and night.

I hope your hand is all better. Is it? What's so bad about the Pine Barrens? Could you ask not to go there if the training is too awful? Well, you could at least ask, couldn't you?

I need you home with me. I'm so unhappy. Dumb school starts soon, and I hardly want to go back. I can't believe I missed your calls and dumb, dumb Zoe forgot to tell me. I can't forgive her for that.

I'm so sad and confused. Please come home, or I could go and see you. It only takes five days on the train, you know? Flying is too expensive, I guess. Let's be together. I don't care where. School's dumb. I can drop out and come live with you at Fort Dix. The army will let us do that, won't they? Oh Todd, I don't know what to do. What do you want me to do? Grandma's mad at me because—just girl stuff, you know?

I haven't seen Helman or Hector, so I can't say where they are. Maybe they left for college. You want me to find out? I haven't been up to our spot. I won't go without you.

Gail and Zoe say hi, so hi. Grandma, too!

We've had some cheer practices, but I'm not doing any of the routines, just watching. Mrs. V is being mean to me about something. We do have some really cute new outfits again this year. We'll put the other schools to shame. The booster club chipped in for them, I'm pretty sure. New cheers, too, but I'm not doing aerials for now.

Remember how we said we'd always be truthful with each other up at the cabin? Well, I kinda should have told you some other stuff before you left, but I didn't. It was dumb. I should have, and I wish I had. I hope you're not going to be mad at me. You won't be, will you? I'm kind of confused. I don't know how to do this. Brenda says I should just do it, but I'm kind of scared, too.

I have some news to share with you that will be kind of a surprise, but good if we are together. It's not so good if we can't be together. Remember the last time we were up at our place? Remember how we thought that— well, at least I thought so. You wouldn't know about that stuff probably. I told you that!

Well, now! I love your letters. Sorry I missed your phone calls. Dumb Zoe forgot to tell me about one at least.

The doorbell is ringing! I think it's Brenda. I've gotta run. It's really, really important. I'll tell you later. Be careful in the Pine Barrens. I love you! I'll mail this quick.

~

Sally put the letter on the table and ran/waddled to the door. She opened it and said, "Hi, Brenda! Come on in. Grandma and my sisters are out, so it's okay."

"Yeah, sure," Brenda said.

Sally asked, "Where've you been? I'm so happy to see you. Why haven't you called or come over?"

"It's been a week, and you're bigger," said Brenda. "The new cheer outfits are here. Wanna see?"

"Yeah, come on in," said Sally.

"I kinda didn't want to, you know, Sally? With Grandma here and all. I can tell that she doesn't like me. She calls me those names, so I just stayed away. What's that on the table? Are you writing to Todd?"

Sally said, "Yeah, I don't know how to tell him about—well, you know. What if he's mad or doesn't want to come home to me? I cry about it all the time. I've written before but threw it out. How do I tell him so that he'll come home? It's so dumb that I forgot to tell him. And what if Mrs. V is right and Todd doesn't want a fat, high school dropout? That's me right now, you know?"

"Yeah, you should've told him—but you didn't," said Brenda, "and you can't go back and undo that. Maybe Mrs. V is right, but you can't change that either. But what if you *don't* tell him, and he comes back and finds you with a baby? And by the way, Mrs. V mentioned it at cheer practice."

"Mrs. V said that? Did she really? Oh, fudge!" exclaimed Sally.

"Well, the girls knew anyway, Sally, so it's not a big deal anymore."

Sally turned and walked into the kitchen. Brenda followed her, and they sat down at the old table. Sally quietly said, "Grandma's going to send me to a home for girls who get in trouble. It's up in Paso. I've never heard of it, but Grandma says it's a nice place. Deacon Jennings is going to pay for it. I don't want to go, Brenda. I don't want to be in a place like that. I'm not a bad girl."

"No, of course not," agreed Brenda.

"But Brenda, I've still got to tell Todd, don't I? And what will happen at this home anyway? It's full of girls who got in trouble, Grandma says, but I don't want to be stuck with a bunch of girls in trouble."

With no solution to offer, Brenda just shrugged.

Sally said, "I've got to go up there in a few days with Grandma. I don't want to go, but she says I can't stay here. I think I'm gonna cry some more now, Brenda." And she did.

Brenda put her arms around Sally, but the crying continued. After a couple of minutes, she said, "I've got an idea, Sally, and it just might work. Why don't you come and stay with me? Your grandma wouldn't object to that, would she?"

"Oh, Brenda, would you let me? I don't think Grandma would let me, but she might. What about your mom? Would she be okay with me there?"

Brenda just laughed. "Are you kidding? She's busy with her dorky waitress job and her new horny boyfriend, Mike. He's always looking at me that way, you know? Why don't you ask your grandma?"

Sally said, "Sure, it can't hurt to ask! The worst she can do is say no, but she might say yes. I'm not going to that place in Paso, Brenda. I'm going to mail this letter to Todd, and in my next letter, I'm going to tell him about my bump. Brenda, Grandma will be back soon. You'd better vamoose. I'll call you tomorrow."

~

Later that day, when Grandma seemed in a good mood, Sally broached the subject.

"No, Sally, you're absolutely not going to stay with that loose girl! How could you even imagine I'd let you? I'm going to tell Deacon Jennings about this. I'm sure he'll be shocked and agree with me. How could you even consider that? Your young mind is poisoned by such thoughts."

"But Grandma, the deacon did say there were options, didn't he?"

"I said no, and I mean no!" insisted Grandma.

Sally said, "But Grandma, you *said* we could consider other options."

"Sally, I may have said something like that, but I never considered you staying at that girl's home. My word! I'm sure the deacon will agree. We'll ask him after church on Sunday."

"Grandma, I don't want to!" exclaimed Sally.

"You just shush. No more of this foolishness. We'll see the deacon on Sunday. Saints preserve us, what did I do to deserve this? And your sainted mother, oh Lord!"

Sally was too discouraged to listen to any more of that "sainted mother" stuff. She'd tell Brenda later. She went to her room and perused the contents of the mason jar.

~

The next day, while Grandma and her sisters were at the store, Sally called Brenda with an update. They walked to Meadow Park and sat under a tree in the hot summer sun.

Sally said, "We'll see Deacon Jennings on Sunday after church. I think it's curtains then."

"The deacon is Principal Jennings's brother, right?" asked Brenda.

"Yes," said Sally.

"I never connected the fact that they're brothers. This might turn out okay, Sally. If you're going to see the deacon on Sunday, maybe *we* can talk to him together on Saturday. You know, I've had adventures with him too. I'll bet I can persuade him to let you stay at my house. If I give him the right incentives, he may see things differently. He's crazy for me, you know?"

"Who isn't?" said Sally, smiling.

"You too, little Miss Rosebud!" exclaimed Brenda. "Only you've got three bumps now, that's all."

"Brenda, you think you're so funny, don't you? This could've happened to you, you know? What if it was you and Terrell? Or you and Coach?"

At the mention of Terrell, Brenda grimaced. But when Coach's name popped up, Brenda rolled her eyes and hugged herself. After a moment, she regained her composure and said, "Well, it didn't, now, did it? Anyway, I always used protection. But you didn't, right?"

Sally said, "My little visitor had just left so I thought everything was okay ... too, too ..." They exchanged looks. Nothing more needed to be said on that subject.

"The deacon has a youth group meeting on Saturday afternoon," said Sally. "We could try to meet with him after that. That might work. A deacon in the church sure wouldn't want that to get out. By the way, his wife is bitchy to me, so I think she already knows."

Brenda said, "Well, maybe."

Sally laughed. "It's called the Moral Path. The youth group, I mean—not Deacon Jennings. If my grandma found out, she'd just freak out!"

Laughing, Brenda said, "I know just what to wear. Oh boy, this is going to play big with him. You want to help me? With your bump, you might not want to. But if you do, it's okay—and it might be fun, like before. Think about it, okay? What time on Saturday?"

"Three o'clock, at Meadow Park. We can walk. Brenda, do you really think this will work?"

~

Saturday at the park, as they walked toward each other, Sally shouted, "What are you wearing?" When they drew closer, Brenda checked to see if anyone else was looking, and then unzipped her jacket. She did a little pirouette, showing off her completely pink ensemble—pink athletic shoes, white bobby socks with pink frilly bands, a short pink skirt, and a darker pink leather belt with a huge round buckle. But that wasn't the whole story. She was wearing a pink bustier, bare at the waist, fastened with baby-blue cords at the front and sides. Her bust almost spilled out, for the bustier came up only high enough to just barely cover her. As they greeted each other, Brenda said, with a cute laugh, "Do you like it? I'll bet the deacon does."

"Holy moly, Brenda! You better zip up before anyone sees. Compared with you, I feel like a fat fashion blimp." Sally's outfit was cute but more subdued, with white athletic shoes and socks. Her skirt was short, but everything else was covered by her cheer jacket.

Brenda said, "You're okay, Sally. After all, you don't have to perform. I can hardly wait to see his face."

"Oh boy, me, too!" exclaimed Sally.

They walked the ten minutes to the church, chatting as if nothing of import hung in the balance. But both girls knew that what would happen in the next few minutes could make all the difference.

Mrs. Jennings greeted them in the rectory office with demeaning looks at their outfits, obviously guessing at what might be under the jackets. She said, "I'll tell the deacon you're here. What's this about? I'm going out, so he'll call you when he's ready. He's very busy, so be brief."

"Yes, we'll only be a few minutes. It's private," Brenda said to the notorious busybody.

"Hmm, why so? What's the matter? Perhaps I should stay," said Mrs. Jennings.

Keeping her eyes cast down, Sally said, "Like Brenda said, it's private. The kind of thing one would discuss only with one's deacon, you know?"

Just then, Deacon Jennings came out of his office. One look at Brenda, and his calm face transitioned to fear. "Oh, what a pleasant surprise to see you girls. What can I do for you?" he asked.

Before they could answer, Mrs. Jennings said, "Perhaps I should stay. I might be able to help."

The deacon was facing the girls, and Mrs. Jennings was behind them. Brenda looked down her front, batted her eyes, and slowly unzipped her jacket ... all the way down. Mrs. Jennings couldn't see what Brenda had revealed, but the deacon could. He quickly spoke up and said, "It's private, Bernice. Right, Sally?"

Sally said, "Oh yes, confidential. Please, Deacon?"

The deacon's eyes bulged just a little, and for just a moment he seemed to be at a loss for words. Then he sputtered, "Yes, she's right, Bernice! I'd better listen to this in private. Girls, will you come this way?"

Bernice raised her lapel pin watch and said pointedly, "Well, if that's the way it is, I'll go tend to my own *private* duties. Don't forget the Moral Path club meeting in thirty minutes." She left the room, slamming the door behind her.

Brenda took a couple of steps toward Deacon Jennings and fully opened her jacket. With his eyes fixed on her, she let the garment slide off her shoulders and to the floor. His stare followed the jacket down, then back up Brenda's voluptuous figure.

In the still of the room, Sally could hear his breathing grow ragged. Yeah, Brenda was in control.

Brenda took one of the deacon's hands and put it on her bare midriff. Then taking his other hand, she led him to his office. Before she went inside, however, she looked back, blew a kiss at Sally, and said, "See you later. We're going to discuss how the good deacon is going to help you. Right, Deacon Jennings?"

"Well, I don't know, but surely some arrangement can be …" His voice trailed off in a hesitant, embarrassed tone. He followed Brenda into his office and closed the door.

Even with the door closed, Sally could hear the lustful goings-on.

~

The room was small, but beautifully furnished with two overstuffed chairs and a matching couch, bookshelves, and a big desk. Windows looked out on the street, and Brenda said in a sexy voice, "Shall we pull the blinds?"

"Oh yes!" the deacon said, and he walked over and drew the blinds.

"I like you, Deacon Jennings, and we've had so much fun before. But I have obligations to consider also, and Mrs. V insists that I do right by you and the rest of the cheer team."

"Oh yes, Mrs. V often bandies your name around. I do want you around as much as you can manage, Brenda. I'll be as good to you as I possibly can, with all due consideration to my position, of course. Mrs. Jennings is, well, not very accommodating in her wifely duties, if you know what I mean. Not that I don't love her, and she's extremely helpful. No, it's not that. She's just so—well, I guess *cold* is the best word to use. And you're so—"

"Hot! Is that the word you're looking for, Deacon? I like being that way. I'm the most popular girl in school, too, and Sally's next. My figure's still the best, don't you think?"

"Oh yes, I'm sure! Your friend Sally is nice, but she's not you. You're just so, so—"

"Hot! You like to fuck me, don't you, Deacon?"

The deacon looked away in obvious embarrassment at Brenda's blunt truth, "Yes, I do! But it's getting late, and I've got Moral Path in a few minutes, so I think we'd better—"

"Sally is so nice, and she needs your help. She's pregnant and having Todd's baby, but she doesn't want to go to that yucky place in Paso. She wants to stay here instead, and we want her to stay at my house. You can persuade her grandma to let her do that, can't you? I know you can. Will you?"

"Well, I don't know, Brenda. It's not really acceptable for Sally to stay in town that way. People will talk, you know? And I'm not inclined to involve the church."

When he hesitated, Brenda continued, "Yes, you can, and we both know that. That's why Grandma brought Sally here in the first place. Sally's grandma always takes your advice."

The deacon hesitated again, then stammered, "But I—I can't do that. Really, Brenda!"

Then Brenda took the deacon's hands and put them to her breast. "If you won't help Sally, I won't let you screw me anymore."

"Whoa, Brenda! I do *want* to help Sally. It's not that at all, and I've got the group coming in a few minutes. Can we talk later, please?"

Listening to the conversation from the next room, Sally pushed the office door ajar and said, "Deacon, if you don't help me, we'll tell. Right, Brenda? We'll tell about all the stuff you've been doing with us."

"Yes, we will!" exclaimed Brenda. "For sure! And Principal Jennings and Mrs. Jennings might get upset."

Deacon Jennings said, "Hold on a minute! There's no need to go overboard. Let's just settle down—oh shit! Sorry about the profanity. I just let it out accidentally. I'm not myself today. Let me think a minute, okay?"

Just to remind him about the reward for helping Sally, Brenda slipped his other hand under her bustier. "We're just asking for a little help, Isn't that right, Sally? That's all, please?"

With his face flushed, the deacon nodded, put his head in his hand, and mumbled, "You know, this wouldn't have happened if only Mrs. Jennings ... What am I gonna do?"

Sally sat beside him in the big chair, and Brenda knelt in front of him, her bustier still undone. "If you can't help us, we'll have to tell," said Brenda. "But we want this to stay our little secret. Right, Sally?"

Sally said, "Yes, we sure do. But if you can't help, you know I'll have to tell—and other stuff, too!" Both girls snuggled up close to the deacon, looking first at his tormented face, then at each other. Brenda said, "We like you, and know you like us. So let's do this together, okay?"

"Oh, you two!" exclaimed Deacon Jennings. "How did I get into this fix? One look at your figure, Brenda, and I just go to pieces. And when you touch me—oh my!"

Brenda said, "Deacon, you're not in a fix. It's easy! Just help Sally, and I'll continue to make you happy. That's what you want, isn't it? And maybe you could even talk to your brother, Principal Jennings, about letting Sally stay in school? We won't even tell Mrs. V."

Hanging his head even lower, the man groaned and said, "Oh God. Okay, yes!"

The girls put their arms around his sagging shoulders, patting him comfortingly. Sally pleaded, "Please help me so we can all be happy, okay? Please, Deacon Jennings, will you?"

The deacon just nodded.

CHAPTER 27

The Pine Barrens

Letter #13

From: SPC-4 Todd Wyrum
c/o Bravo Co.
Training Unit B-22
Fort Dix, New Jersey

To: Sally Anderson
691 Mitchell Drive
San Luis Obispo, California

Hi Sally,

Wow, things are moving fast here! This dustup in Vietnam is looking more and more like the USA is going to have to step in and take out some bad guys who've infiltrated the south. There are local guerillas too, I'm told by some of the non-coms who've been here. They say it's a nasty, fouled-up place. We're going back into the Pine Barrens tomorrow. I'm getting lots of infantry training with rifles, sidearms, and grenades—and lots and lots of marching.

So here's what's happening. I leave for Fort Sam Houston in two weeks. I won't get time off except a couple of days in Texas. More disappointment for you, but as I said, I've got to do this to get a scholarship in premed school. There's just no other way, and you'll be with me.

And what's all this in your letters about being upset? I understand that you miss me. I miss you too, Sally, but you're going to be an upperclassman and a leader of the cheer team. So put on that winning smile of yours, have a good time, and study. You're beautiful, popular, and healthy, plus you have a good home and a grandma who loves you. You've got everything! And I haven't even mentioned your figure—wow! But be careful of Brenda, because she gets pretty wild. Don't let her lead you astray. I also hope Mrs. V recognizes your potential and gives you the opportunity to flower.

The Pine Barrens is a hard place to train. It doesn't look difficult, but the way the army pushes us, it is. It's filled with dense forest, gullies, and water courses, not to mention the mud. Some guys have a really hard time, but the NCOs training us won't let them drop out. It's the army way, which isn't like being on a team. Anybody who slacks off or complains really gets it, not to mention the yelling that the NCOs do. I just train and help out the guys who are having a hard time. My JROTC experience is a big help, although I caught a lot of flak for it in high school. The rich kids looked down on us because of the uniforms, marching, and all, you know?

I get a lot of ribbing from the other guys here because you're so good at writing to me. I tried the phone again, but still got no answer. Maybe it's the time difference. Oh well. I've got your picture up. It's the one of you in your cheer outfit, taken last fall. It gets lots of *oohs* and *aahs*.

We finish up next week after the Pine Barrens ordeal, then more weapons training, and finally a ceremony and parade. Those are usually attended by the families of the graduates and base army brass from the high command. I wish you could be here to attend.

I talked to our NCO about getting more time so I could go back home and see you, but he just laughed and gave me the usual "You're in the army now, kid" talk. Others who put in their own requests for more time got the same answer.

I'm looking forward to the medic training, but sorry for both of us that I can't come home. I know that I promised and it's not what you want, but it just hasn't worked out.

I need to stop here. Change of plans. I'll finish up this letter later. See ya!

~

It was even hotter than usual—a heavy heat that just sat on the place like a wet, scratchy blanket. The usual discomfort of a field problem in the Pines was greatly exacerbated by this extreme. They were led by Sergeant Wilkins, a huge black man who swore in almost every sentence he spoke. *Fuck* was his favorite word, and "Fuck you, soldier" was his favorite thing to say.

They marched, lugging sixty-pound packs, across shallow water courses that forced them to drag the gooey mud along. Of the forty-two men who had started, five had fallen out over the past two days. They had flopped down like filthy gunnysacks full of sour cornmeal, left for medical personnel to retrieve. The soldiers who went on were sympathetic but could be of no help, because it was going to continue for two more days.

Todd believed he could make it, but he questioned the extreme nature of the whole thing. Was it really necessary to actually *break* recruits in order to make good soldiers of them? Without thinking, he spoke up and asked, "Sergeant Wilkins, is it really necessary to—"

"Shut the fuck up, Wyrum! We'll break after the next gully. This is the new training regimen. There's a war coming, and they want to get you ready. Get moving, all of you, now!"

"Yes, Sergeant, but I still—"

"Shut the hell up, Wyrum! You girls can rest later. Move out! What a bunch-a pussies they're sending us these days. Shit, in Korea we humped through wet snow that was knee deep."

They continued to trudge along in a broken line of hunched-over zombies. Sergeant Wilkins came up to Todd, who was near the front of the single-file line, and said, "Listen, Mr. Wyrum, I know you're off to medic training in a few days and you've got some kind of background in this sort of stuff. I want you to keep your eye on the most done-in among these guys. At this point, you're the best qualified to spot any potential drop-dead cases. Some guys might need medical attention, and we're a long way from the field station, so just keep an eye out. Now, step aside to let the line pass by, and give each guy a good look. Let me know what you think. And another thing, stop questioning and complaining! You're a leader here, and these grunts will follow your example. So shut the fuck up and get to it. Move out!"

"Sarge, I really don't know shit. I just had some high school chem—"

"For holy motherfucking sakes, just do it! That's an order! And anyway, *you* know you don't know, and *I* know you don't know, but *they* don't know you don't know. Get it?"

Todd knew when to shut up. As the line of bone-tired soldiers moved by him, he looked closely at each guy. They all seemed ready to drop, but they still had two hours of marching and several water-filled gullies to cross. Would they make it?

Crossing two more muddy gullies, they came to a steep, meandering rock incline about nine feet high. To the left, it ran into a marsh, and to the right, it just kept going. The soldiers dropped where they were as the whole line met this impasse. It was about five thirty, when they usually were done for the day, but they were still an hour or more from the bivouac area. The extreme heat, water crossings, and now this cliff were all slowing them way down.

Sergeant Wilkins, who had been near the back, came up and looked over the latest obstacle. "Christ on a church! Who in the hell put this fucking thing up? I was this way before, and this motherfucker wasn't here. Fucker grew while I was on leave. No shit! That's what happened. Ain't that fucking right, Wyrum? The fucking Pine Barrens up and gave birth to a goddamn wall just to mess with me. A black man can't get a fucking break in this world, not even in a motherfucking shithole like the Pines. *Shit, shit, shit!*"

One of the guys spoke up and said, "I'm with you, Sarge! A brother can't catch a break even in this pine hell. I say we just let it slide and stop right now, okay?"

"Hell no!" exclaimed the sergeant. "Put a sock in it, Washington! Just shut your trap and keep moving."

A few guys snickered at this outburst, and an Italian kid from Chicago, whom they all knew was a wiseacre, popped off, "I'm with Wash! The thing wasn't issued to the Pines, so it can't actually be here because it's against regulations. Damn thing isn't actually in place. It's a figment of Lieutenant Wash's imagination, so it can't be real, right?"

Since everyone knew the lieutenant was an asshole, a full round of laughter erupted. This humor, and a reference to an officer whom no one liked, broke the ice. Even Sergeant Wilkins smiled as he said, "Well, yeah. It ain't here, so we'll act that way. But enough about the lieutenant, understood? This man's army ain't about being popular. Right now, we've got to get up this motherfucker."

A guy from Atlantic City piped up and asked, "How, Sarge? Do we just climb the sucker?"

Sergeant Wilkins replied, "No, we don't do that. Madrano, you and O'Donnell take your entrenching tools and start cutting some steps. By that overhanging tree over there looks about right. Then a couple of you can spell them. Now get to it."

The two soldiers selected for step-cutting duty looked unhappily at Sergeant Wilkins, but they did as instructed. Madrano said, "Rat fucked again!" Meanwhile the other guys slumped on the ground as comfortably as possible, happy for the rest.

Cutting steps into the wall was hard. Several of the guys took turns spelling Madrano and O'Donnell, but the work moved slowly. The rock, dirt, and mud kept breaking or sliding away. Working under the overhanging tree wasn't successful, so they shifted to another location, but it was still slow going.

Todd took his turn, and when he was exhausted, he handed the tool to another soldier. There were two guys going at it now, furiously swinging their tools. As one soldier backed off, the other guy swung his tool wildly, completely missed the wall, and hit the first guy in the chest, knocking him backward onto some rocks. He screamed in pain.

Sergeant Wilkins, who had gone looking for an easier route, quickly came back. He knelt over the injured man and exclaimed, "What the hell's going on here? Fuck me! This guy's hurt bad. He ain't breathing right. It looks like his neck's hurt, too."

The soldier who had swung the tool said, "Sorry, Sarge! It just got away from me as I was digging. Fuckin' wall is just a bitch, and I was—"

"Never mind how, shit for brains," said the sergeant. "We've got to help this man. Wyrum, you got any ideas about this breathing thing? If we can't get him breathing right, he'll croak."

Todd said, "First, let's get him laid out flat with his feet raised. Then we can at least see what's actually wrong with him. But you're right about the breathing, Sarge. We've got to fix that quick!"

As everyone gathered close, lots of crude advice and blame made the rounds. After they'd laid the man out, Sergeant Wilkins started massaging his chest, but it wasn't working. The man took a few gulps of air, but not much was getting into his lungs.

Sergeant Wilkins, an NCO who always seemed to be in charge, now looked confused and afraid. He barked, "Any ideas? Anyone seen anything like this before?"

Stooped over the writhing, prostrate man, Todd said, "Sarge, we got a few instructions from a medic when I was in JROTC camp one summer."

"No time to experiment," replied Sergeant Wilkins. "This guy's in a body bag if we don't do something fast."

"It's pretty fuckin' radical, Sarge," warned Todd. "His lung's collapsed. I mean, I *think* that's it."

"Radical, my ass! Him dying is what's radical. What do we do, Wyrum?" asked the sergeant.

"Well, we—uh—cut a hole in his throat, insert a breathing tube, and reinflate his lungs. It looks like both lungs are down. I don't know what happened. My best guess is the shovel and rocks hit him. Anyway, we really need to do that, I think. It's out of my league, but—"

Sergeant Wilkins said, "Cut a hole in his throat? Okay, if that's our best shot. His face is turning purple. How do we do it?"

"I need a knife or razor and a straw," said Todd. "Wash, I know you've got something we can use, right? And I think a straw from our field rations will work."

Lieutenant Washington produced his switchblade knife and said, "You could shave with this." Someone else pulled a straw from their rations pack and handed it to Todd.

Todd said, "Okay, we've gotta be clean about this. Anybody got any alcohol?"

Sergeant Wilkins handed him a pint of Old Grand-Dad and said, "This'll have to do."

"Well, here goes, Sarge!" Taking a clean handkerchief and the bourbon, Todd cleaned the knife, straw, and area at the man's throat. Hesitating just a moment, he then cleaned his own hands. Everyone could see that they were visibly shaking, but no one said a word. Sergeant put a hand on Todd's shoulder and gave him a look of trust.

Pausing a minute to steady his hands, Todd cut an incision in the man's throat and quickly inserted the straw. He then lowered his mouth to the straw and blew hard several times. Then he took his mouth away, and a moment later the man took a ragged breath, then another. His face began to lose its purple color, though the look of pain was still there. Todd removed the straw and put a bandage over the cut. A minute or two later, the man was breathing in gasps.

Someone in the crowd exclaimed, "Holy shit! You fucking did it. Doc Todd did it!"

Sergeant Wilkins's face relaxed. "Yeah, Todd, you did it. You're gonna make a hell of a medic—one *hell* of a medic."

Todd leaned back and deep a breath, nodded, and again looked at his hands. They were shaking again. He said, "I'm glad I took JROTC. Happy to help, and I'm fuckin' lucky!"

They made a litter for the injured soldier and managed to get up the cliff at a spot farther along. Two hours later, after sunset, there were back at the bivouac area. Exhaustion was universal.

The next day, they were back at it in the Pine Barrens, minus the injured man and one other. Two days later, they finally finished the field problem and returned to Fort Dix.

Four mornings later at the mess hall, an orderly approached Todd and asked, "Are you Private Todd Wyrum, Training Unit B-22?"

"Yes, I'm your man. What's up?"

The orderly handed Todd a note and said, "Dress uniform!" Then he walked briskly away.

Still pretty tired from the ordeal in the Pines, Todd sat down on the mess hall steps as all the other soldiers filed out. The note said simply, "Report to Major Adams, Regimental Headquarters, at 0900 Thursday." That was today, an hour and a half from now.

The "dress uniform" part surprised him because he hadn't been issued one yet. He knew he'd get one before graduation, but that was a week away.

After getting into his only clean recruit uniform, Todd reported to the major's office, where he faced a battery of high-ranking officers, the regimental sergeant major, and Sergeant Wilkins. Standing at attention, he saluted and said, "PFT Todd Wyrum reporting as ordered, sir. I don't yet have a dress uniform, sir."

The sergeant major said crisply, "Stand at ease, Private Wyrum. You're fine as you are."

Todd replied, "Yes, sir!"

Major Adams said, "This is Colonel Hasline, who has something to tell you."

"Private Wyrum, we've been informed by Sergeant Wilkins here of your exploits during the recent field problem in the Pine Barrens," said Colonel Hasline. "That was a heroic thing you did out there, and under the most difficult of circumstances. After serious consideration with the highest authority of the army, we've decided to honor you at the upcoming graduation ceremony. You will be awarded the Bronze Star in recognition of your act. You likely saved a man's life and have proven a fine addition to the army. I hope you will accept the army's and my own sincere appreciation for what you did out there. We are very proud of you, Private Wyrum. Congratulations."

Everyone in the room, including Sergeant Wilkins, shook his hand warmly. Then the major asked, "Private Wyrum, are you considering making the army a career?"

"Why, yes, I am, sir. I hope to be enrolled in the army's premed program at a university. I've worked toward that since entering JROTC in high school, sir."

Major Adams said, "After consulting your records, we hoped that might be the case. Why did you enlist as a private soldier instead of applying to the premed program directly when you graduated from high school? You were an outstanding student, as I see from your records."

With that question, Todd felt completely deflated and looked down at his feet. Then he took a deep breath and said, "Sir, I got into some trouble—a fight over a girl, *my* girl—just before graduation."

"Was it your fault?" asked the major.

After a long pause, Todd said, "Yes, sir, it was my fault. I lost my temper and hurt a boy pretty bad, sir."

Sergeant Wilkins stepped forward and said, "If I may interject, Major."

"By all means do," said Major Adams.

"Did you win the girl?" asked the sergeant.

Todd said, "Yes, sir ... I mean, yes, Sergeant, I did."

"Nice going!" exclaimed Sergeant Wilkins. "But if that was the case, why choose the army?"

Following another long pause, Todd said, "I was arrested, and when I went before Judge Jackson, he gave me two choices. The army, which I had intended to join anyway, seemed the best choice. The other choice was ... well, not so good, sir. Uh, I mean, Sergeant."

Major Adams said, "Well, be that as it may, you'll be awarded the Bronze Star at the graduation ceremony next week, and I know you'll do well at the medic school in Texas. Don't give up your ambition to be an army doctor, Private Wyrum. When your training in Texas is completed, or perhaps later, the army may be able to help you in that regard." He looked around at the others and asked, "Anything more for Private Wyrum?"

There were smiles all around, but no questions.

"That's all, Wyrum," concluded the major. "We'll see you next week at graduation. You're dismissed."

Todd graduated and was awarded the Bronze Star, capped off by congratulations from everyone. Then he spent two whirlwind days raising hell in Atlantic City, and set off to Texas by train.

~

Hi Sally,

I'm back. The Pine Barrens was a huge mess, but as a result of what happened, I got the Bronze Star. Pretty cool! I got it at graduation in front of the entire base personnel. I wish you could have been there. You'd have been proud of me.

We had two days off in Atlantic City. I got drunk with the guys, but nothing more, I promise. Now I'm on a train heading to Texas. We're just passing through the Blue Ridge Mountains. It's really beautiful with lots of little towns, like from a storybook, along the way.

I'll send you my new army PO box mailing address when we get to Texas. I have no idea what will be different. They don't tell us much except the usual "hurry up and wait" routine.

Please keep writing to this address. They'll forward the letters. I love you and miss you.

P. S. I'm glad you like the poems. Here's another one.

> "O Sky"
> O sky above, light the way
> At end of every day.
> By the stars I'll find you,
> Seeing at night the twinkle
> In your blue eyes
> And the hue of it all
> When the moon rises
> On my love for you.

~

———

Letter #14

From: Sally Anderson
691 Mitchell Drive
San Luis Obispo, California

To: SPC-4 Todd Wyrum
c/o Bravo Co.
Training Unit B-22
Fort Dix, New Jersey

Dear Todd,

Oh my God, Texas? I can't believe you went there rather than come home to me. Did you explain to them about me? They might have understood and given you leave to come home. I'm mad at you. Don't I come first? Aren't I more important than the dumb army? What did you do in Atlantic City? Are there girls there? Well, of course there are. Are they cute? Do they have big boobs, the way you like them? Bigger than mine? Did you meet any stacked girls who put out?

I feel so lost. What am I going to do? You said I have everything, but I don't have you.

I'm glad the guys like my picture. I'll bet they all have pictures of their girlfriends up too.

I'm glad you got a medal. I wish I could've been there when you got it. Send me a picture of you in your uniform with the medal. I'll bet you look handsome, like always.

Brenda says hi. She thinks you're being mean too. She's a good friend and wouldn't do anything bad. She's just, well, wild sometimes. You should know. I found out about you and her. Just because we broke up for a short time didn't mean you could do things with her. Well, you know what things I mean. That was wrong of you. It wasn't Brenda's fault. She told me. Yeah, she told me all about how you enticed and teased her. How she couldn't help it because she was lonely.

I've got to go now and be sad and alone some more.

Love,
Sally, but I can't wait forever. I like the poem.

~

-Two days later, Grandma and Sally met with Deacon Jennings.

"Mrs. Anderson, it's a tragedy that Sally is with child, but there are other things to consider. After further reflection, I think our first plan was flawed. Sending Sally away isn't going to help her deal with this or steer her toward the right moral path. After further inquiry, the place itself is not what it first seemed to be. We agreed to send Sally to a place with high standards, and this place just doesn't hold up. I'm sure you'll agree, once you've heard the whole story."

"Yes, Grandma, please let our wonderful, loving friend and deacon explain," Sally said.

The deacon said, "Yes, please. I met with Sally and Brenda yesterday, and we had a long, informative, even pleasant talk. This is really Todd Wyrum's fault, but now Sally is being forced to pay the price for his immoral behavior. Apparently he threatened her that if she didn't—well, you know, give in to his lustful desires ... The bottom line is that Sally's an innocent girl who was led astray, and unfortunately she's been made to face the result alone. Todd should, by all the moral standards that I've instilled in her, be here to marry her."

Turning to Sally, Deacon Jennings said, "You were victimized by this boy, weren't you, Sally? Isn't that what happened?"

With a face as sad and remorseful as she could muster, Sally said, "Yes, we went for a long ride in his truck one night. We did some kissing, and then he made me do bad things—things that your teaching said I shouldn't do, Deacon Jennings. And when I said no, many times, he said, 'Give it up or get out.' We were way up in the hills east of Santa Margarita. It was dark, and I was alone and scared. How could I have gotten home to my loving grandma and wonderful sisters?"

Reaching out to pat Sally on the leg, the deacon said in a comforting voice, "It's okay, Sally. We understand. You were alone after dark, far from home and in the company of an unscrupulous, selfish boy. We fully understand the awful choice you were forced—yes, *forced*—to make. You might even have put yourself in physical danger had you resisted further. That's how you felt, right?"

Sally nodded furiously and even gave a little pout. "I was so scared!"

Grandma blurted out, "Oh my word, that sounds more like—well, rape!"

Worried that things might be going a bit too far, Deacon Jennings said, "Well, I wouldn't go so far as to say that. Let's just calm down and look at this in the light of what to do now, rather than trying to dig into the past. Okay, Mrs. Anderson? Sally has enough to be concerned about. After all, you did come to me for counsel and advice."

"Yes, please, Grandma," said Sally. "I trust Deacon Jennings to be our moral guide."

The deacon continued, "After much consideration and prayer, I think it best if Sally lives with Brenda, at least until the child arrives. Can we agree to that, Mrs. Anderson?"

"My word, that immoral girl and her mother?" exclaimed Grandma. "How can I let Sally go there? No, Deacon, I can't do that. Oh my!"

Deacon Jennings moved over next to Grandma, took her hand, and looked her close in the face. "That's no longer strictly true, Mrs. Anderson. I've been pastoring Brenda over the last few weeks, and she's turned over a new leaf. She's toned down her appearance and started attending my Moral Path youth group. Why, just two days ago, she was there on her knees. Didn't you see her outside your house a couple of times, dressed very conservatively and without makeup? She's been helping Sally with moral guidance too. Isn't that proof of reformed, church-inspired ways? It surely is God's intent to forgive sinners if they come back to the fold. The moral, enlightened path to which Brenda and Sally have now returned is surely your own wish too, isn't it, Mrs. Anderson?"

As the deacon looked on, Grandma gave Sally the once-over and then nodded. "Yes, it is, and God does surely forgive those who stray but return to the fold. I know that, but Brenda's mother isn't returning to any fold, as far as I can tell. I see her now and then at her waitress job—the clothes, the makeup and hair! If she's reformed her ways, it sure doesn't show. You do know what past activities I mean, don't you, Deacon?"

From the expression on his face, Sally could see that the deacon was really going to have to reach for a good answer. She was learning to lie pretty well, so she spoke up before he could respond. "She's been to church, and our Moral Path club too, hasn't she, Deacon Jennings?"

Relief flooded the deacon's face as he said, "Yes, indeed she has, and with a degree of commitment I'd not have guessed even a few months ago. Yes, indeed!"

Grandma's shock was obvious. "I find that hard to believe, but if you say so, Deacon Jennings, then I guess Sally can go to Brenda's. I just can't have her living at my house, you understand?"

"Oh yes, I do understand, Mrs. Anderson," said Deacon Jennings. "Your standing in the church and community must be uppermost in your considerations. I fully agree with you."

Sally asked, "Well, can I, Grandma? Can I can stay at Brenda's for a while?"

Before Grandma could answer, the deacon spoke, not wanting to lose control of the final decision. He again took Grandma by the hand, looked her in the eyes, and said, "Yes, Sally, it's okay. I think your grandmother, in her love for you, agrees. Isn't that right, Mrs. Anderson?"

Grandma gave a slight nod. "Saints preserve us, I hope we're making the right decision."

As they left the church, in significantly different frames of mind, Sally and Grandma met Mrs. Sondheim going in. Grandma tried to steer Sally away, but it was too late.

"Hello there, Mrs. Anderson," said Mrs. Sondheim, "and Sally! Are you here for the Moral Path meeting? It begins in a few minutes, if you are."

Grandma replied, "No, Mrs. Sondheim, we were just leaving after a meeting with Deacon Jennings." As she maneuvered around Mrs. Sondheim on the narrow path, Grandma noticed her friend's eyes looking Sally over very carefully.

Mrs. Sondheim's gaze and what it revealed couldn't be avoided. Grandma stopped and said, "Sally's gotten in some trouble, Mrs. Sondheim, as I'm sure you've noticed. I—we—are so ashamed. That awful boy and Sally just—"

"Oh, Sally," interrupted Mrs. Sondheim, "I'm so sorry for your unfortunate accident. Yes, these things do happen, I'm sorry to say, and sometimes to nice churchgoing girls like yourself."

With her head hanging low, Sally said, "Thank you, Mrs. Sondheim. I didn't mean for this to happen. I thought that—"

"Hush, Sally! You have your grandmother here to look after you and spiritual guidance from Deacon Jennings, so you'll be okay. And I'm a friend, too. How can I be of help? I can, you know! Such an ordeal for such a young girl. How old are you?"

"I'm sixteen and still in high school, Mrs. Sondheim, and now I'm gonna have a baby."

Mrs. Sondheim put her arm around Sally and hugged her. "Poor girl, poor girl!"

Grandma cried softly too. "I've tried so hard, and now this. I'm just so, so ashamed!"

As Grandma pulled Sally down the path, Mrs. Sondheim said, "If I can help, please call on me! I might help pick out some appropriate cute new clothes for you, Sally. Think about it, okay?"

~

Two days later, Brenda, dressed demurely with only a little makeup, arrived at Sally's house.

She was greeted at the door by Grandma, who said, "Hello, Brenda. Please come in. I'm glad to see that you've turned over a new leaf—at least, I hope you have." She turned and called down the hallway, "Sally, Brenda's here!"

In a somber mood, the two girls finished packing Sally's things. Having to dress down had made Brenda almost as depressed as Sally, and she was afraid to look in a mirror.

When they had finished packing, they carried the suitcases out to the porch and Sally asked, "Grandma, can I leave Todd's truck here, since I can't really drive it in my ... my condition?"

"Yes, Sally, that's okay for now," Grandma answered sadly.

Carrying two suitcases each, the girls walked over to Brenda's house. Sally had packed her most precious possession, the mason jar overflowing with letters, in a cloth-lined box.

Before entering Brenda's house, Sally paused and said, "I haven't really asked about your mom. What does she think? Is she going to, you know, be angry or tease me?"

Brenda replied, "My mom? Don't worry, Sally. She's had plenty of extracurricular activity in her time. I wouldn't be surprised if she was knocked up, too, before my dad came along. Relax, it's going to be fine. My big bed will be cozy, and we can snuggle up like we used to do. Yummy fun!"

"Are you going to help me with that, too?" asked Sally.

"Of course, but we do need to be careful about Mike. He's got eyes for me, so he might have eyes for you too, even with your bump. I don't like him, but it's fun to tease him—only when Mom's not looking, of course. She blows a gasket when she sees me do it. She's such a bitch that I like getting back at her. Just watch out for Mike, and the rest will be a breeze."

A week went by, and Gwyn, Sally's mom, had very little to say to Sally. She'd just glance at the bump with a dismissive smirk. Mostly she wasn't home, so the two girls did as they pleased. The evening snuggling was nice again. They would lie there for long hours and talk of dreams, love, and past adventures. Sally even read parts of Todd's letters to her friend.

Brenda did get pretty excited when the bump kicked or moved around. A couple of times at night, it woke them to lots of laughter and jokes.

One evening, Mike showed up to take Gwyn to a movie. It was a hot August night, and Sally and Brenda were sitting in lounge chairs in the backyard wearing shorts, halter tops, and lots of lotion. After waiting a few minutes for Gwyn to get ready, Mike walked out on the back porch and noticed the two girls. They both had removed the straps to their tops, revealing more than the usual spread of bulging bosom. Engaged in their usual banter of gossip, they were sitting with their backs to the porch, and neither girl noticed Mike.

For several minutes, Mike enjoyed gazing down at the girls' display. Then he said, "Hi, girls! You've got a *Playboy* centerfold level of porn going on there. Wow, I could stand here for hours just drooling."

Brenda and Sally both leaped to their feet with yelps of surprise. In the process, Brenda's top fell completely off, and Sally's almost did the same. They both quickly covered up with both hands, and Brenda squealed, "That was sneaky, Mike. It's not polite to sneak up on innocent girls like that."

"Oh yeah, *innocent*," teased Mike. "Like you didn't know I was here. You can't fool old Mike. I've seen you on display plenty of times, Brenda. You're proud of what you've got, and you let everyone know it. Who's your friend? She's got a great set, too. You've got competition, Brenda, real competition."

Mike's forthright statement surprised Brenda momentarily. "This is my friend Sally. She's on the cheer team too, and she's staying here now. Be nice, Mike, and say hello."

Mike said, "Nice to meet you, Sally! Looks like you're in the family way, right? Should've used protection."

The girls said nothing.

Mike was a tall, raw-boned guy with long, dirty-blond hair, not well kept up. He had sneaky brown eyes, a wide sloppy mouth, and sallow skin. He was wearing a suit that had seen better days, no tie, and scuffed brown half cowboy boots. In general, the girls were of the opinion that Brenda's mom wasn't getting much of a bargain with Mike. Gwyn said he was well endowed, but at her age, she obviously wasn't choosy.

When Gwyn walked out on the porch and saw Mike staring at the two girls, who were still overly exposed, she exploded. "What the hell? You two little sluts are showing off like a couple of strippers. Cover up and stop advertising. Mike's a nice guy, and he's mine, understood?"

As Brenda and Sally scrambled to get their tops back on, Gwyn said to Mike under her breath, "Sally's knocked up, and she's been kicked out of school for next year. If you've got any friends who might want to hook up with her, I'd bet she'd be okay with that. Cost a couple of bucks maybe, maybe not. She's a regular punchboard, from what I've heard."

"I wouldn't be surprised," said Mike. "Wow, look at the size of those tits! How far along is she?"

Gwyn abruptly said, "I'm about ready, so we can go anytime. And keep your eyes off them!"

"No big deal!" agreed Mike. "I gotta hit the bathroom, and it'll take a few. We'll go when I get done."

Gwyn stepped down off the porch and walked over to the girls. She looked trashy in a low-cut blue top, short skirt to match, platform shoes, and heavy makeup. She had a big pile of dyed raven hair, just like Brenda, and it tumbled down off her head like a curly haystack. She scowled at Sally and said, "You show off like this one more time and you're out of here. Understood, tramp? Mike's a nice guy. If you want to do more screwing around, do it with your own guy."

In an instant, Sally's sense of Brenda's house as a happy sanctuary disappeared. She was no longer welcome there, but where else could she go? She determined to stay as far away from Brenda's mom as possible, because she just didn't see any other option.

~

Three days later, when Sally came out of the bathroom after taking a shower, Mike was standing in the hall. He'd come back to continue the remodeling. Sally was wrapped in a towel that barely covered her. Gwyn was at her waitressing job, and Brenda was around somewhere, though Sally didn't know exactly where.

Sally said, "Oh, it's you, Mike. What do you want? The bathroom's free now, so you can go in and finish up. I'm done."

Mike stood leaning against the doorjamb, so that Sally had trouble squeezing by him to get to the room she shared with Brenda. He reached around and pulled out his wallet. Taking out a twenty-dollar bill, he held it up and said, "I've got twenty for you if you go down on me. Right here, quick, and nobody's the wiser. I know you need the dough, Sally, so how about it? A quick buck and some fun, too. If you swallow, I'll throw in another ten. I've got a real load for you."

"No, I don't want to, Mike. I'm going to have Todd's baby, and—"

"Shit, he ain't gonna know. You think I'm gonna send him a letter or something? Come on now, Sally. We can be friends, and you can make a fast buck. With cans like that, you've gotta be hot. Your friend Brenda is cooperative! That girl's a real pistol, but you already know that, don't you? Even in your condition, there's stuff you can do. How about it?" He waved the twenty at her.

Just then, they heard Gwyn out on the front porch. The front door slammed, and Mike ducked into the bathroom. Sally quickly went to her room and twisted the doorknob to go in, but the door wouldn't open. She was still standing there in the hall when Gwyn walked in and saw her.

Noticing Mike pretending to work in the bathroom, Gwyn shouted, "Goddamn it, Sally! I told you to stay away from him and keep your clothes on. Now look at you displaying yourself. Did she proposition you, Mike? Did she open that towel to tempt you? Slut! Goddamn, I'll bet she did. Sally, you man-stealing tramp, you're outta here. Get your shit together and leave. You be gone by tomorrow or else, understood? Now where's that slutty daughter of mine? Did she have a hand in this, Mike?"

With a wry smile on his dirty face, Mike said, "Well, yeah, you guessed right. She came out of that shower, saw me, and opened that towel. She didn't say anything, but I got the message. Then she put two fingers in her mouth and sucked them. You guessed right, Gwyn. That girl is a package for sure. Damn, I don't know why you've been so nice to her, especially when she'd turn around and act like this. I think Brenda just kinda looked the other way, if you get my meaning."

Gwyn turned on a dime and started down the hall. "Brenda, get in here right now. I've got questions, you little tramp. Did you put this little pregnant bowling ball up to this? If you did, you'll be out of here, too. This is my house, and that's my man, goddamn it!"

A moment later Brenda unlocked the bedroom door and stepped out into the hall. She was just as mad as Gwyn. "Screw you, you flabby old bitch. Sally didn't do anything! She had just finished taking a shower when numb nuts here cornered her. You should be mad at *him*, not us. Mike's a liar. I would never do anything with him anyway, because he's just a lame, broke nobody who can only get an old tart like you, and that's the truth. Come on, Sally. Let's get dressed and get out of here. He's all yours, *Mom*. And Sally, you can stay here as long as you want. How's that for an answer, *Mom*?"

Mother and daughter stood glaring at each other, their faces just inches apart.

"Why don't we just leave these two alone, Gwyn," Mike said dismissively.

Brenda's mom turned and left, shaking her head, and Mike followed her, not quite so confidently now. Brenda and Sally heard them walk out on the back porch.

Brenda said to Sally, "You know what she used to be, don't you? Sally, I never did anything with Mike. Well, I did let him look at me once when I was coming out of the shower, but just to tease him. That doesn't count, does it?"

"No, Brenda, that doesn't count," Sally assured her.

Unfortunately the confrontation completely poisoned the atmosphere at Brenda's house. Both girls knew, without saying it, that Sally's days there were numbered.

Sally usually stopped by Grandma's house once a day to check the mail and pick up odds and ends she'd left there. She enjoyed seeing her sisters too, now that they'd stopped teasing her. Since Sally was no longer living there, they missed her and were nice to her. Grandma was polite, but still rather cold toward her.

On days when there was no mail, Sally got distraught. Images of Texas filled her worried mind. She imagined ranches, cowboys, oil wells, and cowgirls with big hats, tight jeans, and smiles for Todd.

A week after Sally's confrontation with Brenda's mom and Mike, a letter was waiting for her at Grandma's house. The moment she saw it, happiness flooded through her, but it quickly turned to disappointment. The letter was from Principal Jennings and addressed to Sally, in care of

Mrs. Anderson. Sally had been suspended from school, and she needed to report to the county health department for assistance with her condition.

Sally stopped reading, sat down on the porch swing, and cried softly. When she felt her baby move in her tummy, she gently put her hands on it and experienced, for the first time, that feeling that has existed for thousands of years—a woman nurturing her child. She sniffled and said softly to herself, through the tears, "My baby. My very own little baby."

Sally sat there a long time, feeling the tiny life pulling her deeper into the motherhood that was approaching. She was no longer in control. Her body, mind, and psyche were all now being driven by her baby, which was eternal and perfectly normal. She was going to be a mother.

Grandma called from inside the house, "Sally, I heard something. Were you crying?"

Without a word, Sally walked inside and handed the letter to Grandma, who read it and said, "Well, we knew this was coming."

Sally looked up with tears in her red, swollen eyes. "Yes, Grandma, we did. And I'm going to have to leave Brenda's, too."

Grandma wrapped her arms around Sally and said, "You poor girl. We'll go to church tomorrow and see if there is help from a forgiving God. Deacon Jennings may have some wise counsel, too. We shall see."

As Grandma spoke, there was understanding and compassion in her voice that Sally hadn't heard before. "Okay, Grandma," she said, hoping this was a sign of softening.

~

The next day, Grandma, Gail, and Zoe stopped by Brenda's house and picked up Sally. The car was unusually quiet as they drove to church, where the parishioners milled around in front before the service began. It was the usual crowd, and there were lots of covert glances at Sally. No one said anything, but the looks, especially from the women, told the story.

"Welcome, Sally Anderson! How nice to see you at church. You, too, Mrs. Anderson," said Mrs. Sondheim without the slightest tone of sarcasm in her voice.

Sally, Grandma, and the girls all turned to greet her. Her greeting was so warm that Sally answered with just a bit of cheer in her voice, "Oh, Mrs. Sondheim! Nice to see you, too."

Mrs. Sondheim said, "I guess school will be starting for you all in a week or so. Will you be one of the leaders of the cheer team again, Sally? I so enjoy all you beautiful girls doing your routines. I was once a cheerleader myself, as you know. It keeps a girl fit, too, doesn't it?"

Sally's smile vanished, and without saying a word, she just shook her head.

"Oh, that's too bad," said Mrs. Sondheim. "I'm so, so sorry. Why might you not —"

Grandma broke in and said simply, "Sally won't be enrolled this year, so cheering is out."

With a sympathetic look on her face, Mrs. Sondheim said, "I'm so sorry to hear this, Mrs. Anderson. I realize this is a private matter, but could we step over here out of the way for a moment?" At Mrs. Sondheim's urging, they moved away from the prying eyes of the crowd. "And how are things at home?" she then asked.

Before either Grandma or Sally could answer, Gail spoke up and said, "Sally's not home anymore. She's staying with Bad Brenda and her yucky mom."

Sally turned toward her sister, but Mrs. Sondheim broke in, looking very serious, and said, "Brenda's house, oh my! And the boy? Is he going to do the honorable thing?"

Moments passed in silence, and finally Mrs. Sondheim asked again, "Is he, Sally? Speak up now. This is serious, as you well know. Is he going to do the right thing?"

In a whisper, Sally said, "He doesn't know. I didn't tell him before he left."

"Why did he leave? And where did he go?" asked Mrs. Sondheim.

Grandma explained, in a hushed and embarrassed voice. "Todd got into trouble, and army enlistment was his only choice. Terrible! Judge Jackson, as you've probably heard, and that Todd Wyrum boy. It was in the newspaper, too."

"Oh yes, I did, but I had no idea," said Mrs. Sondheim. "My goodness, I'm usually so well informed about these things. So Sally, Todd's your boyfriend, and you're having his baby, but he doesn't even know? This is serious."

Looking terribly sad, Sally said, "And now I can't even stay at Brenda's. Her mom doesn't like me."

Mrs. Sondheim replied, "Well, her mom can just ... Well, my word, *she's* surely nobody to judge anyone else, is she? Can you inform Todd, and might he come home and join you? Is that possible?"

At this point, the parishioners began filing into the church. Deacon Jennings was standing at the steps. Mrs. Sondheim said, "This is an awful situation you're in, Sally, but perhaps I can help. I'll look into it, okay? Sweet child, don't worry. Something will turn up, but *do* write and tell him."

"Todd *does* love me, Mrs. Sondheim. He does!" exclaimed Sally.

As Sally walked past Deacon Jennings, she looked directly at him, but he didn't look back. Obviously he hadn't talked with his brother, Principal Jennings, about helping her. The helpless, begging look Sally gave him was ignored.

Inside the church, Mrs. Sondheim went to her usual seat, while Sally, Grandma, and the girls sat in the back. They all heard the usual sermon about good morals and not giving in to the devil's temptations. Sally recalled the last encounter that she and Brenda had had with him. Oh, the hypocrisy!

Outside after the service, as everyone stood around gossiping, Mrs. Sondheim said, "Sally, if you're not able to stay with Brenda, you'll be going back home, won't you?"

Grandma, looking uncomfortable, spoke up and said, "Well, no, she won't. I can't be seen as condoning Sally's behavior. My place in the congregation and community wouldn't stand for it, so she won't be coming home. We had originally planned to send Sally to the girls' home in Paso Robles, and I think that's still the best place for her."

Sally jumped back and exclaimed, "No, Grandma! I said I wouldn't go there, and I meant it. Please let me come home. You once said that this home is for bad girls, but I'm not a bad girl. I just—"

Mrs. Sondheim clutched Sally to her and said, "You poor girl! The boys always want what they want, but they don't care to be responsible for the result. Mrs. Anderson, I hope you'll permit me to see if there is some alternative to this ... this home in Paso. I've heard of it, and I think Sally's right to not want to go there. The place does some good work, it's true, but in Sally's case, I don't think it's the right place. May I help?"

Looking quite surprised, Grandma said, "Well, I guess, if it's no trouble."

Mrs. Sondheim said, "No trouble. None at all. I'll contact you. We'll find something for Sally."

~

Letter #15

From: SPC-4 Todd Wyrum
c/o Bravo Co.
Training Unit B-22
Fort Dix, New Jersey

To: Sally Anderson
691 Mitchell Drive
San Luis Obispo, California

My darling Sally,

I made it! We're at Fort Sam Houston now, and it's just about the most open, dusty place I've seen since leaving the Carrizo. It was a two-day trip, and like I said in my last letter, the Blue Ridge Mountains were really beautiful. The rest of the trip was interesting, too. We've sure got a big country here. At each place we stopped, I marveled at all the different regional accents. The slow southern drawl is real soft and polite, but this Texas drawl is different.

Lots of Mexican stuff around here, and I really like the food. I got a lot of the same kind of dishes back when I was on the ranch. Mrs. Cruz made fresh tortillas for us every day. Peppers too.

My army medic training started right off. A couple of the NCOs told me that it's the Vietnam thing that has accelerated the training. They expect to be engaged pretty soon to help the Vietnamese army. Just as advisers right now, but maybe as combat troops later. What that exactly means, I don't know. The army doesn't tell us much except "Do it." There are a lot of career guys here, and they seem to smell trouble over there. Some have been there already and didn't like it.

Word of my Bronze Star has gotten around. I'm already a leader in my training unit.

I haven't gotten my new mailing address yet, so keep writing to the Fort Dix one. They will forward mail to me. Oh, it's assembly! Gotta run! Your picture's still up in my footlocker.

I love you, Sally. Don't forget me.

~

Every morning began with assembly, and it was hot even then. One day an officer stood with the duty sergeant in front of Todd's unit, and the sergeant called out, "Spec 4 Wyrum, front and center."

Todd marched forward and stood in front. "Private Wyrum reporting, Sergeant!"

"At ease, Private. You're to report to Captain Covert in the office on the double."

Todd was six weeks into his training to be a medic, and although it hadn't been as physically hard as at Fort Dix, the demands of medical training was tougher. Some days he was even more tired than at the end of a long march through the Pine Barrens.

Todd kept hearing about Vietnam and the army's advisory role. Nobody he talked with had a single good thing to say about Vietnam except for one thing—the girls were beautiful. The hot, sticky weather and drenching monsoons were followed by even hotter, dusty, energy-sapping dry spells. Buddhist temples were interesting, but not necessarily safe. The list of bad stuff was lengthy: triple-canopy jungle, booby traps, punji sticks, snakes, spiders, and huge centipedes, to name just a few.

Entering the office at the headquarters building, Todd went up to the desk and said to the soldier receptionist, "Private Todd Wyrum, reporting as ordered."

A sly smile spread across the receptionist's almost pretty face, as she replied coyly, "Why, Private Wyrum, nice to see you again."

"Holy cow! Terry, is that you?"

"That it is! Just little ol' me, in person."

"How'd you get here?" asked Todd. "I mean, behind a desk? I thought you were going to be a nurse. I thought I might see you around, but not at a desk. What's up?"

Terry said, "Well, I'm a girl. That's what's up. The army's not looking for female medics, so I'm in the medical orderly training program. It ain't so bad. Well, here I am! What's up with you, Todd?"

"I'm here to see the captain. The training is pretty intense, as you might have gathered. I'm generally more tired here than at basic. Hey, at Ord, they let you in, Terry. How'd they get it wrong?"

"Same answer, Todd. I'm a girl, as I'm sure you've noticed."

Just then, the buzzer on Terry's desk went off, and a voice instructed her to show Todd in. As he walked past Terry to the door, she said, "Maybe we can get together, if you get a pass, and spend some time in San Antonio. It's really nice down on the River Walk. Might that be possible, soldier?"

"It's a plan," said Todd. "I'm in the B-unit. Call me, okay? I'd better go in now. See you!" Then he stepped into the office and said, "Private Wyrum, reporting as ordered, sir."

"Yes, sit down, Private. I've some good news for you. We're going to move you up to the more advanced training unit—that is, if you agree. Do you, Private Wyrum?"

"Yes, sir! I'm definitely willing to be advanced, but I'm a little confused about the reason, sir," admitted Todd.

"Good question, Private. One reason is that the army needs frontline medics, and the other reason is that you're way ahead of your classmates. That's especially true regarding courses relating to biology, chemistry, and so on. You're quite impressive! Have you considered our officer training program, Private Wyrum?"

"That was my intent all through high school, sir. I was in JROTC the whole way. As to why I didn't take that route ... Well, I think if you look my record over, you'll understand."

"I see, Private. Okay, this will take a while. Have a seat in the reception area, and I'll have a look-see. Oh, I see you already know Private Wells. Nice girl—I mean, *soldier.* And one other item—she has something for you." With that, the captain nodded and smiled at Todd.

"Thank you, sir!" As Todd returned to the reception area, Terry was standing at her desk with an envelope.

Terry said, "Todd, this mail has been forwarded to you from Fort Dix. I think you'll be *very* interested in the letters. I'm sure Sally Anderson is pining for an answer from you."

"Great!" exclaimed Todd. "I was wondering where all my mail was. Sally's my girlfriend in California."

Terry glanced around to see if anyone was listening, then asked, "If I can get a pass, can we meet off base?"

"I guess we can," replied Todd. A moment later, he was called back into the captain's office. As he walked past Terry, she said, "See ya!"

The captain said, "Sit down, Private. I see what you mean. A spot of trouble, was it? Well, the army may not be commissioning you right now. But later, with your abilities, it could happen. Right now, I'm going to do you a favor and move you up to the advanced unit. I'm also putting you on notice that you may be called on to do more. As I said, the army needs your skills. Good luck, Private. You're dismissed."

As Todd left, the captain gave him that smile again.

~

Before Todd even got across the headquarters porch, he was already opening the first letter. By the time he reached his barracks, he'd read all three of them. The letters were confusing, filled with pleading mixed with a bit of anger. In each letter, Sally wrote about desperately wanting him to come home, no matter what. In one letter, there were blemishes on the page—Sally's tears, as she explained.

Todd read the letters over and over again. He understood the "missing him" part, but the rest seemed disjointed. Why so much unhappiness? He concluded that there must be something more to Sally's ramblings that she hadn't put in the letters.

He didn't have much time to dwell on Sally's letters, because when he was posted to the more advanced training unit, the workload got even harder and more time consuming. Todd wondered, *If training to be a medic is this hard, how much harder will it be to train as a doctor?* The thought sobered him. His salvation was his knowledge of the periodic table. Time and again, he was able to find answers. The part about physical training and field dressing were the easiest. In fact, he became a leading student among a group of leading students, and he enjoyed the training.

Every night, Todd thought about Sally and her confusing situation. Two weeks later, he received another letter and hoped it would contain answers, but it didn't. It was just a short note that said she wasn't going back to school or cheer team. School had started, and she wasn't attending. No explanation was included. What was it? He decided to call her again.

Todd made an appointment to use a base phone, and he called at dinnertime. Although he let it ring a long time, no one answered. His curiosity and frustration increased.

The intense training continued, but the next weekend he was given a pass. Terry contacted him, and they agreed to get together in San Antonio at a popular restaurant on the River Walk. Todd pretty much knew what the result of their meeting would be. Did he feel guilty about Sally? A little bit, but his hormones easily overpowered his loyalty.

~

Todd and Terry met at a small Mexican café on the River Walk, had a bite to eat, and drank a few beers. Terry, a tall lean girl, had changed her short brown hair to medium length and bleached it blond, and wore pretty heavy makeup. She was kind of overdressed, with painted nails and a pedicure too. She wore a white, sleeveless blouse with black fringe, a short black skirt, and open-toed shoes—all combined with a new sense of self-confidence and flirtatious eyes.

After greeting each other, the first thing Terry said was, "I've got us a room for later."

"Why, Terry! I do believe you've got a one-track mind," teased Todd.

"Yes, I do when it concerns you. Maybe I can be your girl while we're here?"

Surprised, Todd said, "Wow, Terry, you don't let much grass grow under your feet, do you? You want to be my girl right off?"

"Yes, I do," she said, "and we can start by me proving that I'm a cut above your back-home girl."

"Terry, you saw the letters, didn't you? Sally's still in high school—well, she *should* be—and on the cheer team. So she's—"

"Holy cow! She's on the cheer team at San Luis Obispo High? We heard about them, even at our school. Is Sally one of the girls who, you know, do things besides cheering?"

Perplexed by the question, Todd said, "Well, yeah, she does lots of stuff besides that. They're very active, but what's that got to do with anything?"

Terry's eyes widened as she spotted an opening. "Haven't you heard that they go out with guys and do stuff to boost the team? You know what I mean by *stuff*, don't you?"

Suspecting something, Todd grew defensive. "No, I don't know. What *stuff*?"

Terry now retreated just a bit, and with some reluctance said softly, "Todd, I don't actually know whether Sally takes part in that stuff."

Todd was now visibly upset. "What do you mean by *stuff*? Come on, Terry. Out with it!"

"Todd, I only know what I've heard, so don't be upset. Maybe it's other girls, not Sally."

"You're friggin' right! What, Terry?" Todd exclaimed.

Terry said, "Well, they—I'm not saying it's her—put out for guys. You know, guys in the booster club and others. It's all over among the other cheer teams. The only name I've heard is a really stacked girl named Bonny or Bobby—something like that."

Todd said, "Brenda? Is the girl's name Brenda?"

"I think so," said Terry. "Yeah, that's it, Brenda! She's got some fantastic figure, or so I've heard."

"Holy shit! I suspected something was going on with Brenda. I know she put out, because ... But Sally? No, not my Sally."

Terry should have kept her mouth shut, but the temptation of sticking in a knife was just too strong. "Even if Sally *is* easy like that, it doesn't matter now. She's there, and I'm here with you."

Todd sat perplexed for a moment, searching for an answer. "Yeah, that's true, but I'm not going to ... Shit, let's just eat and then—"

Just then Captain Covert stepped up to their table and said, "Hello, you two! This is unexpected. Nice to see you. Renewing old friendships, are you? May I join you?"

Terry hesitated, but Todd said, "Why, sure, Captain! Can I buy you a drink? What's your poison?" Meanwhile Terry excused herself and went to the ladies' room.

As she disappeared among the crowd, Captain Covert said, "Remember that favor I did you the other day? You know, moving you to the advanced unit?

"I sure do," said Todd. "I appreciate that, sir. I sure do, and I guess I owe you one in return, don't I?"

"No *sir* here, okay? It's just two guys out on the town. And you could do me that favor by letting me have a shot at Terry today. What do you think? Would that work for you?"

Surprised, Todd said, "Uh, we'd planned to ... Well, maybe. Okay, why not? I could just get up and leave now, and let you make my excuses. Would that be the return favor you were looking for?"

"Perfect, Todd! I'll make sure Terry knows that you left to deal with an emergency."

"Yeah, Captain, that should do it. I'll just hit the bricks then, okay? Oh yeah, one more thing. I guess Terry's got a room booked someplace." He and the Captain stood and shook hands, and Todd left. He'd already decided that Terry wasn't in Sally's league anyway, or Miss Lady's either.

~

Back at Fort Sam Houston, training continued with an increasing sense of urgency, spurred on by bad news from the Far East. They'd heard rumors that the Cav, an air mobile division, was being trained. If that was true, this little faraway skirmish was about to get very serious. The Cav, a revolutionary new kind of unit, involved helicopter-deployed air assault with the latest equipment, personnel, tactics, and leadership. It was still being developed, but all the lifers were talking about it. Nothing happened, but rumors flew. Everyone wondered if the Cav would be deployed in 1962, but most thought it would take longer to fully train the units. Meanwhile the troops rotating back from Vietnam told lots of nasty stories.

Now that Todd knew what Brenda—and probably Sally—had been up to, his mixed feelings came into play. On the one hand, he saw Sally with Kenny, but on the other hand was the realization that he really did love her. Knowing what he now knew threw his emotions into turmoil. And most of all, what in the hell was going on that made her so erratic and fearful? No clues came to mind.

That afternoon, Todd was ordered to report to battalion headquarters with his records file. In the meantime, he wrote to Miss Lady and thanked her for the money, mailing the letter on his way to headquarters.

~

In the office, Todd stood before Terry again and said, "Private Wyrum, reporting as ordered."

"Hello, Private Wyrum. I'll tell the captain that you're here. Let's see your paperwork." Terry said this coldly, only briefly glancing up at him.

"Yes, ma'am. It's all here." He handed over his file and sat down. She was now just as cold as she'd been hot before, and it wasn't hard to guess why.

A couple of minutes later, the captain opened his door and said, "Come on in, Private Wyrum, and have a seat. Terry, will you get me his orders, please?"

Terry brought Todd's file to the captain, and as she sashayed back out, he gave her a long, admiring look. When the door was closed, he said to Todd, "Thanks again, Private. It all worked out."

"Oh, great, sir! I'm glad to hear that."

"Yes, indeed ... Well, on to business. I see from the record here that your training has been going very well! You're at the top of your class, and considering that you were jumped forward, that's some accomplishment. My compliments."

Todd said, "Thank you, sir. I work hard, and I'm glad it's paying off."

"You'll be finished with this part of your training in two weeks. To have completed this training in just twelve weeks, rather than the normal sixteen, is a real feat, Private—and at the head of your class, too!"

Todd nodded appreciatively, and the captain continued. "There's a posting available that would suit you. It would require you to volunteer for an advisory unit in Vietnam. You'd be deployed with a Vietnamese army unit in the field, along with other United States Army personnel. An advisory group is usually about ten men, and the medics needed to fill these slots are critically important and in short supply. Normally a more experienced medic is put into one of these positions, but because of the shortage, we've had to reach out beyond that. You, Private Wyrum, are just such a soldier. Would you consider volunteering for such a mission? It would mean promotion to E-5 right off."

Given all the rumors, Todd wasn't too surprised at this turn of events. He replied, "Yes, Captain, I would consider it, but I do have some questions."

The captain said, "I'm glad to hear that, Private. Go ahead, shoot!"

"What about leave first before deployment? Is there any?" asked Todd.

"Good question ... I have no way of knowing, but it could be Germany first. They're short of medics there, too. It could also be here in the States, or in fact any place the army has a presence. But my first guess is Germany. Is that a posting you'd feel better suited to, Private?"

"No, sir! I'll volunteer for Vietnam, but not Germany. When do I leave, sir?"

"Hold on, Private. You've still got two weeks left in your training, plus a ton of paperwork to wade through. But I'm very glad you've volunteered, and good luck to you. Terry—Private Wells, that is—will give you the forms to get started. You're dismissed, Private Wyrum."

Todd shook hands with the captain and left the office. As he walked out the door, he saw the captain and Terry standing close and talking intimately with each other. He thought to himself, *Go, Terry! That girl doesn't waste much time going for what she wants.*

On the way back to his training unit, Todd stopped and said to himself, "Oh shit, I completely forgot about my promise to see Sally after medic training!" Looking back at the HQ office, he considered returning to ask for reconsideration of his request. But surely he'd get leave after this, so he could return to Sally then. Yeah, that was the best bet. He'd go and visit her after his training, before deployment to Vietnam.

Todd felt confident that he'd made the best choice, which was *not* to go anywhere near his mother in Germany.

~

The two weeks passed quickly, and the paperwork wasn't such a grind either. On the day before he was to leave, Todd was again ordered to report to the HQ, but it wasn't Terry and the captain in his office this time. Instead, it was a major with medical corps insignia on his lapels, and two NCOs with first sergeant stripes.

"Private Wyrum reporting as ordered, sir."

"At ease, Private. I'm Major Neal, and these are Sergeants Koberg and Philips. There has been a change of plans regarding your deployment, and we thought we'd better let you know now. It will probably be a disappointment for you, but it's a change that's really necessary. You will be leaving with me and the sergeants here tomorrow at 0630 hours. We'll fly to Washington, and from there on to Vietnam. At Fort Lewis, we'll form up with the rest of a new advisory group of which I'm the head. The disappointment is that you'll have no time for home leave in—where was it?—California. I'm sorry to tell you this, but it's really quite necessary that we get there quickly. Is that clear, Private Wyrum?"

In the blink of an eye, Todd imagined the despair on Sally's face. Without requesting permission, he collapsed back into a straight-back wooden chair and quietly said, "Yes, sir, I understand."

Sergeant Koberg put his hand on Todd's shoulder, glanced at the other two men, and said, "Sorry about this, son. You've got a girl back there or something, don't you?"

Forgetting military protocol, Todd replied, "Yeah, but how did you know?"

The sergeant looked around and said, "We've been around this army a long time, Private. We're sorry about this, but it's got to be this way. And anyway, if she waits for you, then you'll know she's the right girl. On the other hand, if she doesn't, then you'll realize she was the wrong one. Understand?"

All Todd heard was a replay of what Terry had divulged. He simply said, "Yeah, I do."

Finally the sergeant said, "Don't worry, Private. Everything will turn out okay. And on the more positive side of things, Major Neal has something for you. Major?"

Todd was proud of his new stripes and being tops in his medic class. Before leaving the ceremony, he asked, "What's happened to the captain and Private Wells. Will they be going, too?"

Major Neal said, "No, they're off to a disciplinary hearing at Fort Hood. You'll not be dealing with them again. See you at 0630 in the morning, Private Wyrum. You're dismissed."

All the way back to his billet, Todd thought about Terry and the captain. What he'd seen was true. The captain, an officer, would get the shaft, while Terry, an enlisted woman, would be free as a bird.

The next morning Todd was at the HQ building with his gear and wearing his new stripes. They left a few minutes later. He hadn't written to Sally about the change, but he knew she'd be extremely disappointed. The anguish in her last few letters had conveyed something bad. He didn't know exactly what, but it was a pretty safe bet that it had something to do with what Terry had told him.

Nevertheless, the guilt of not having written to Sally about what was going on gnawed at Todd. His mixed feelings about her betrayal and his own less-than-honorable behavior whipsawed his emotions, so he wrote a letter to her during the flight. These last few weeks, he'd sent her only cards. She'd be shocked to get his next letter from Vietnam—really shocked.

At Fort Lewis, they joined up with other soldiers with various specialties. The trip lasted twenty-eight hours. Todd had heard lots of bad stuff about Vietnam, but nothing had prepared him for that first blast of wet, pungent heat and the smell of decay as they debarked the plane at Tan Son Nhut Air Base in Saigon. He was soaked in sweat within ten minutes. And something besides heat hung in the air—fear.

For Todd, the war had begun.

CHAPTER 28

Mrs. Sondheim

Brenda persuaded her mom to let Sally stay on if they cleaned, washed, and did other chores, but it was drudgery. Sally expected to hear any day now from Grandma and/or Deacon Jennings about banishing her to Paso Robles. She figured her best hope was that Mrs. Sondheim would come up with a plan.

On Tuesday, Brenda answered the phone and then shouted, "It's Mrs. Sondheim for you, Sally. Goody, maybe!"

With great anticipation, Sally picked up the phone and said, "Hello, it's Sally!"

"Good morning, Sally. This is Mrs. Sondheim, and I have some very good news. First, however, has your boyfriend decided to come home and marry you?"

"No, Mrs. Sondheim. I wrote to him—but no," Sally lied. She hadn't told Todd.

"Well, I'm so sorry that he's shirked his responsibilities. However, I'm not surprised, because I know what a one-track mind men can have. Okay, bear with me a minute while I explain. Mr. Hesselgren and I have worked out a plan that will give you a place to live, a job, and a little money to carry you along for a while. Does that sound like a plan you could accept? We're only three months away from the birth of your baby. Would this work for you?"

"Yes, yes, yes!" Sally yelled.

"Then here's the plan," continued Mrs. Sondheim. "I'll get your grandmother's approval first, but I'm sure she'll agree. If she does, we—Mr. Hesselgren and I—will pick you up tomorrow and take you to Paso Robles. He has an old, but nice, motel there called the Valley Inn. Are you aware of it?"

Sally said, "No, ma'am, I'm not."

"It will be free, and it's just off Spring Street. You'll have one big room, with a bath and kitchenette, at the back of the lot. How does that sound, Sally?"

"Okay, I guess."

Mrs. Sondheim said, "Good! There's more. I own a maternity shop—one of several that you might know of—called Once Upon a Baby. It's only a short walk from the Valley Inn, and it's a small, cozy place that carries a high-end line of cute things for women and girls like you. You'll have a job there for a few weeks, until the baby's time is near. After that, we'll have to figure out something else. Does that sound okay so far?"

"Oh yes, Mrs. Sondheim!" exclaimed Sally. "Thank you so much—and Mr. Hesselgren too. I didn't know he was a friend of yours, and I'm so grateful."

"Hold on, Sally," said Mrs. Sondheim. "There's more to consider. Have you considered the doctor or the hospital?" After a heavy silence on the other end of the line, she continued, "I thought not, but we'll deal with that too. Facilities in Paso aren't extensive, so we'll need to put some thought into it. I know several doctors there and a few nurses, and they could be a big help. After the baby comes, you'll need some help. Do you know anything about babies, Sally?"

After another long silence, Sally said, "No, nothing."

"As I expected. We'll get someone, a nurse probably, to come over to your new home and get you started on what you need to know. It's a lot—I can tell you that—but nothing an eternity of women haven't dealt with. You'll see! It will be easy. Oh yes, and we'll get you some cute new maternity clothes. It will be fun to do that together, don't you think? Any questions, Sally?"

Although she had lots of questions, Sally just replied, "No, Mrs. Sondheim, not right now anyway."

"Okay, with Grandma's approval, we'll pick you up about one o'clock, okay?"

Sally replied, "Yes!"

Mrs. Sondheim said, "Then you'll be off to a new life, new home, job, and most of all, your very own new baby. See you at one o'clock. Bye now!"

Sally hung up in some shock, but happier than she'd been in a while. She told Brenda the whole thing, and they hugged and cuddled down to talk it all through.

~

The next day Sally was packed and ready at one o'clock. The mason jar with its contents was the most important thing. She had had Brenda check the mailbox at Grandma's earlier, but there was nothing. It had been weeks since she'd gotten a letter from Todd. The cards were okay, but not what she wanted or needed.

In the backyard, Brenda's mom couldn't have cared less that Sally was leaving. Sally and Brenda sat on the front stoop in the summer sun, talking mostly about school and cheer team. When Mr. Hesselgren's big Cadillac swung into view, Brenda asked, "Hey, what about Todd's truck?"

Sally shrugged and said, "What about it? I've got no driver's license, and by now it might not even run. I'm for darn sure not going to call that Miss Lady person about it, you know?"

"I guess not!" Brenda replied.

When the big car pulled up at the curb, Mrs. Sondheim got out and waved at them. Mr. Hesselgren came around from the driver's side, and they walked up the sidewalk to the girls.

Mr. Hesselgren said, "It looks like you're all ready, Sally. Hello, Brenda! I'll bet she's been a big help, hasn't she, Sally?"

Sally held Brenda's hand and said, "Oh yes, she sure has. I don't know what I'd do without her."

An awkward moment passed as Mrs. Sondheim gave Brenda a hard look. Then she said, "Well, let's get this stuff in the trunk and be off."

Brenda's mom came out and stood on the front porch. "So it's you two coming to the rescue. I'd never have guessed. Well, I'm well rid of her. She's a pain. I wouldn't trust her with any man old enough to stand upright. The two of them strutting stuff around. Good riddance."

"That's enough, Gwyn," said Mr. Hesselgren. "Sally's a nice girl who got in trouble, that's all. You, of all people, shouldn't be throwing stones, considering some of your own antics."

"Shit, you listen to me, Hesselgren," said Gwyn. "I've been putting up with their crap for—"

Mrs. Sondheim reached out as if to slap Gwyn, but Mr. Hesselgren grabbed her arm and said, "She ain't worth the trouble. Let it go. We've got Sally to look after." Turning to Brenda's mom, he said, "Back in the house, Gwyn, or it will be me what gets after you, you hear? Go on now."

Gwyn turned sullenly and walked back to the front door. Then she pointed at Sally's bump and said in a nasty voice, "You got just what you deserved." Before any of them could respond, she went inside and slammed the door shut behind her.

Mrs. Sondheim put her arm around Sally and said, "Just ignore that old tart. She has no reason to insult you. Now, let's all cheer up! We're off to new beginnings, right? Hess, are we about ready to go?"

"You bet!" exclaimed Mr. Hesselgren. "Let's get in the car and head out. In fact, let's stop off and get some grub on the way. Brenda, do you want to come with us? We'll bring you back when we return from Paso. How about it? You hungry?"

Brenda perked up momentarily, but then she said, "I'd love to, but I've got cheer team stuff."

The three of them gave knowing nods to one another, then walked to the car.

Sally leaned out the window and took Brenda's hands. "I'll miss you something awful, Brenda. Will you come visit me, please? You're my best friend, and I can trust you too. Please?"

When Sally said the word *trust*, Mr. Hesselgren and Mrs. Sondheim smirked at each other.

Brenda replied, with tears in her eyes, "Yes, I'll visit whenever I can, though it's a long way. I'll miss you, Sally!"

Mr. Hesselgren put the big car in gear, pulled out into the street, and drove off toward the highway and Paso Robles.

Sally couldn't have felt more alone if she had been on her way to the moon. No Todd, no letter, no friend beside her, no cheer team—only a room, a job, and a baby on the way.

~

Just two blocks off Spring Street, the Valley Inn was two rustic, bungalow-type structures with parking in front. A wooden boardwalk connected up with the reception office. It was all wood, with a shake roof and forest-green trimmed windows looking out at the parking area. It was definitely old, but clean and well kept. The end unit was Sally's cozy new home.

The interior was decorated in a western theme with wooden chairs, table, and other bric-a-brac. It had rodeo-themed wallpaper, and the ceiling sloped to match the roof. There was one big double bed, a couch, and two chairs. The kitchenette was to one side, with a small table and three chairs in an adjacent alcove. The bathroom had a toilet, sink, shower, and window.

Mr. Hesselgren and Mrs. Sondheim helped Sally move in and even stocked the kitchen for her. An hour later, the three of them looked around and admired Sally's new home. As they prepared to leave, Sally tried to thank them. But just then her baby gave a bunch of kicks, and she sat down abruptly. "Wow, I guess he really likes his new home! Want to feel?"

"Ha ha!" exclaimed Mrs. Sondheim. "Sally, you seem to really be getting into motherhood. And yes, I do want to feel." She sat down on the armchair and put her hand on Sally's bump. "Want to give it a try, Hess? Pretty neat, I'd say!"

With a big smile, Mr. Hesselgren said, "No, thanks. I'll leave that to you experts, but we'd better get moving. Sally, sweet child, I'm at your beck and call. The phone's right there. Don't be afraid to use it. We're your friends. I'll make sure, if it's convenient, that Brenda gets a chance to visit, too."

Mrs. Sondheim said, "Well, Sally dear, we're off. I second everything that Mr. Hesselgren said, okay?"

"Yes, ma'am!" replied Sally. "I don't know how to thank you both. This is such a nice, cozy place, Mr. Hesselgren."

Mrs. Sondheim gave her a kiss on the cheek and walked out to the car. As they drove away, she asked, "Hess, why did you offer to get Brenda involved again? She's a wild one—and probably one reason that Sally's in this fix."

He replied, "I'm only a man, and you know how weak we are when tempted by the stronger sex."

"Give me a break, Hess! This isn't the war. We've got responsibilities," said Mrs. Sondheim.

"Well, Gwyn's just the same, so it's no wonder that Brenda's that way," said Mr. Hesselgren. "Did you see the tits on her? Jeez ..."

Mrs. Sondheim said, "Sally had best not sit around feeling sorry for herself. We've got to keep Mrs. V away from her. Do you think a word to Big Earl might be in order? Did you know that he's friends with that Todd kid who knocked Sally up?"

Mr. Hesselgren said, "We'll see. Maybe Todd will come back to her. One never knows."

~

They stepped off the plane to a sergeant's greeting: "Welcome to 'Nam, garden spot of the East."

Their trip through Saigon was an eye-opener. To call it *different* would have been a gross understatement. The city was filled with the chaos of bicycles, mopeds, honking horns, blaring music, and narrow streets packed with people hawking everything imaginable. The rumors of beautiful girls in provocative outfits, called *áo dià*, were true.

They spent two days in Saigon before being trucked off to their base, several worlds away. Their Deuce and a Half truck took them into an ancient labyrinth that seemed little changed since the nineteenth century. The dusty roads passed by rice paddies, water buffalo, fetid streams, a few motor vehicles, and lots of mopeds. It was primitive, yet cultured. There were also many signs of the country's French colonial past, and some people they met were bilingual.

The Vietnamese army was everywhere, as well as lots of paramilitary police whose job seemed to be talking to the pretty girls. Todd and his colleagues were told that there were some real good units in Vietnamese army, but also some really bad ones. Their assigned unit was an airborne formation.

Leaving a region of rice paddies, they moved into the hill country. An escort of Korean War–era armored vehicles joined the caravan as it snaked its way up into dense foliage. The farther they went, the fewer people they saw. Eventually they were engulfed in a triple-canopy jungle that bathed them in damp, oppressive heat. Five hours later, they were at the base, next to a small town in thick jungle.

The base was actually just a big clearing filled with every kind of military tent and gear imaginable. More than six hundred personnel were stationed there. Todd's Medical Corps section of eight was headed by Captain Bradshaw and paired up with a Vietnamese army platoon of forty.

The captain spoke fair Vietnamese, but many others didn't. Todd made a point of trying to learn the language as quickly as possible.

Todd enjoyed his team's camaraderie, but they had no time for anything but work. It was both physically and mentally demanding. The wet heat sapped their energy like a huge sponge. He quickly discovered that his level of expertise was far better than the others', so he concentrated on bringing them up to speed in the field and bivouac. His Vietnamese students learned quickly, and by the third week, everything was working smoothly. So they started patrols "outside the wire" for several days at a time.

The many stories he'd heard about bad stuff—bugs, spiders, snakes, centipedes, and so on—were true, and they got into everything. The Vietnamese took them for granted, but the Americans had a hard time with them. Several men were evacuated because of life-threatening bites, or just exhaustion.

Todd ran into new diseases, and old deadly ones too. Malaria, dengue, and dysentery were common among the local populations. The Americans were especially vulnerable to a form of athlete's foot that was ten times worse than usual, though it seemed to leave the locals alone. It started with the feet, but then it would work its way up the soldiers' legs. The itching, bleeding mess was untreatable in the field, so anyone who got it was sent to the rear.

On the fourth week of these long patrols, they first encountered the dreaded booby traps. "Bouncing Betty" got two men, and others scattered from the blast and stepped on punji sticks. This convinced the group commanders that there were bigger, well-armed groups in the area.

A week later, they ran into a Viet Cong group and had their first serious firefight. Several Vietnamese soldiers were wounded. Todd took care of some men, and instructed his trainees on treating the others. The wounds were bad, but everyone was treated and evacuated successfully.

Todd also did some training with the local population. When he got to know these civilians, they turned out to be polite, hospitable people who learned fast. He liked them, and they seemed to like and appreciate him too.

Todd had little time to write to Sally, and he felt guilty about that. He did write a short letter to her, but the truck carrying that mail was ambushed and everything on it lost. A second letter got ruined in a creek crossing. He hadn't received anything from Sally, either, but he did finally manage to get one off to her.

~

Letter #16

From: SPC-5 Todd Wyrum
c/o Bravo Co.
Fifth Special Forces Group
An Lộc, Republic of Vietnam

To: Sally Anderson
691 Mitchell Drive
San Luis Obispo, California

My sweet Sally,

Well, I guess you can see from the postmark on this letter that I'm in Vietnam. I know, too, how disappointed you are that I didn't get leave to see you. Sorry, but there wasn't anything I could do. As it was explained to me, it was either here or some other overseas base. I hope you'll get over it and see this in perspective. In the long run, it's best if I do this now.

I hope you noticed that I've been promoted to E-5. It was part of my agreeing to come to Vietnam. A little more money, too, doesn't hurt, and I get other extra pay for being here. Here's my first installment to help you out, and I'll try to send you some money each month.

I love you more than the whole world, Sally. But I can't change the army, and the army wants me here. The usual deployment is a year. You can handle that, can't you?

I'm still in Bravo Company. This is the Fifth Special Forces Group, an elite unit. Our main job is advising the South Vietnamese army. Because things are accelerating fast, I only spent a few days on "in-theater training" before I was deployed as an adviser to a Vietnamese army unit. They know very little about medical care, so I'm doing lots every day, both in the field and on base. We're near a place called An Loc, although I'm not sure that's how it's spelled.

We're seeing lots of enemy activity, but I'm usually behind the front area. There's stuff we can't tell folks back in "the world." (That's what we call the States while in 'Nam.)

I've got new friends, too, but we're so busy that we don't get to do anything but work. That means marching, instructing, eating, and sleeping, in that order. Lots of the first two. Not so much the last two. This is by far the hardest work I've ever done.

I know you cheer team girls are the leaders in the school, but I hope you don't get carried away. You can be social with Brenda, but don't let her—you know—wild side influence you.

When you and I were broken up that time, it sure wasn't me who went looking for her. She came on to me, posing as hurt and all. Ask her, and I hope she'll be truthful about it. Don't forget me now, amid all the cheer team fun and school dances. Again, sorry for not coming home to see you.

Your loving Todd

~

Mrs. Sondheim helped Sally settle in and purchased new clothes, food, cute curtains, and kitchen utensils for her. They also made plans to get things that Sally would need for the baby. The couple who ran the Valley Inn weren't very nice at first, but after Mr. Hesselgren had a talk with them, they were all smiles.

Sally mentioned Todd's truck and asked whether she should get a license and drive it up to Paso Robles, but neither of her newfound saviors thought that was a good idea. Grandma called a couple of times, and she and Sally would talk briefly, but Grandma was obviously racked with guilt over abandoning Sally. She promised money, but it never came.

Ever since being rescued by Mr. Hesselgren, Sally had wondered about the connection between him, Mrs. Sondheim, Big Earl, Mrs. V, and others. It seemed to Sally that whatever it was lurked around the edges of everything they did. Was it some sort of collusion around small-town politics and under-the-table money? It seemed to involve, among other things, liquor licenses, building inspections, traffic fines, underage drinking, gambling, and girls.

There was much more, but it was all shrouded in that long-ago past of wild times, of which they seldom spoke. During World War II, minor corruption had thrived in small towns. In the case of San Luis Obispo County and these old friends, that corruption had just continued under the radar after the wild times faded. Each of them had their own area of interest, they all made money, and nobody got hurt. Sally's condition was just one of the occasional rough patches to be smoothed out.

If there was any risk in this back-scratching arrangement, it was Mrs. V's greed and ambition. Mrs. Sondheim and Mr. Hesselgren weren't helping Sally just to be nice. It was in everyone's best interest that her condition and the circumstances under which she'd gotten that way be hushed up.

When Sally told Mrs. Sondheim that she had written to Todd about the baby, she had been lying—and that lie caused her to lose sleep. She knew that if her untruthfulness was found out, the help she needed might disappear. The only way around this was to tell Todd, but fear and guilt held her back. She struggled with this every day, and as time passed, it got worse and worse. One afternoon, when she was in the office at the shop, Judy, the proprietor, eyed the bump and said, with an edge in her voice, "Your guy coming back anytime soon to help out, or are you on your own?"

"I don't know," admitted Sally. "He's in the army over there in Vietnam, so …" The desk phone rang and Judy picked it up. Sally was relieved to leave the office.

That was the last straw. With no idea what she'd say, she began to write *the letter*.

~

Letter #17

From: Sally Anderson
c/o Valley Inn
1919 Spring Street Circle
Paso Robles, California

To: SPC-5 Todd Wyrum
c/o Bravo Co.
Training Unit B-22
Fort Dix, New Jersey

Dearest, darling Todd,

See the new address? I'm not home anymore. I read your letter over and over and still can't quite believe it. You're in another country far away, and I'm here without you.

Now I must tell you what I should have told you that day at the courthouse, or at the bus depot, or in a letter, or just sometime. I feel so stupid, and I'm so sorry. You have every right to know this.

How do I start? What will you think of me? Why did I wait so very long? Will you still love me? Will you come back to me? I'm so alone, Todd. I'm crying now as I write this.

Oh Todd, I'm going to have our baby. Yes, our baby—your baby. It was that last day up by the creek. I thought I was safe, but obviously I wasn't. Now our little child, our baby, will be here in three more months.

There's more bad news! Mrs. V got me kicked out of school, and Grandma sent me away. I stayed at Brenda's house for a while, but then her awful mom kicked me out. I had to do something, so Mr. Hesselgren—you know him from the booster club—has given me a nice, cozy room in his motel in Paso Robles for free. Mrs. Sondheim has given me a job at her maternity shop on Spring Street. So now I live in Paso. See my new address on the top of this letter? My only friend is Brenda, and she can't even get up here very often.

Now do you understand how much I need you? Our little baby is coming, and he or she—it could be a girl—wants to see their daddy. Please come home to us, okay? Tell the army bosses that you've got a more important thing to do. Be safe, Todd! I hear bad things about that place on the radio.

There is so much more to all this, but I'm exhausted just from writing this little bit. I love you, and I hope you still love me. Your baby and I are waiting. Please come home and marry me.

Your loving Sally, and our little baby too

~

Sally waited a week before mailing this call for help. Little Todd, as she was calling the life growing inside her, was acting up constantly.

Judy, who ran the motel, asked, "What are you gonna name the kid? You know, your baby? What name are you gonna give him or her?"

Sally immediately blurted out something that had been rattling around in her head for weeks. "Todd Wyrum is my baby's name, after his father. I'm Sally Wyrum, and I'm married to Todd, you see? So all the teasing about my *boyfriend* doesn't matter. We're married, and I'm Sally Wyrum."

~

The next Monday, Sally started working at Once Upon a Baby, a few blocks from her new home. The building stood alone just off the sidewalk. It was a 1940s nondescript style with big picture windows in front displaying maternity clothes. A soft bell rang as Sally entered the shop.

Inside was all powder blue and pastel pink, done in an eclectic but attractive style. There was a big open space in the middle with tables covered with dolls wearing baby outfits. The ceiling was raised with lighting in a coffered recess, and the carpet, too, was pink and blue. There were three dressing rooms plus an office, and photos of babies and their mothers lined the walls. Soft music played in the background, and the whole place was quite feminine.

An attractive, slightly overweight, middle-aged women appeared and said, "Hello, and how do you do? May I help you?"

A bit nervous, Sally took a step forward and said, "Oh, hi! I'm Sally Wyrum. Mrs. Sondheim told me to report to you for work today. I hope I'm not late."

"Oh no, Sally, you're just fine. I've been expecting you, but I wasn't quite sure when. I'm Mrs. Jacks, Mrs. Sondheim's partner and manager. It's so nice to finally meet you!"

"Nice to meet you, too," said Sally. "I wasn't sure about the time."

"Not to worry, Sally. We've a small specialty shop here, and I hope you'll enjoy working here. And by the way, you can call me Dotty. Everyone else does."

"Thank you, Dotty. I hope my baby won't be a problem." The name *Dotty* rang a bell for Sally. It was something that Mr. Hesselgren had said. Images of the 1940s—clothes, partying with soldiers—flitted through Sally's thoughts.

Dotty replied, "No, of course not. It's the business we're in. No explanation necessary. Mrs. Sondheim has explained everything to me. These things do happen."

Sally said, "That's really nice of you. I could pay or work it off if you—"

"Now Sally, none of that! Like I said, it's all covered. Let's get started, okay?"

Dotty was quite nice, and the "getting started" took the rest of the week. Once Upon a Baby carried only the best merchandise. One thing that Dotty covered carefully with Sally was how to record sales. Almost all transactions were cash, and they billed all customers separately. Dotty clearly indicated that no questions should be asked about the money and where it went, so Sally quickly dropped that subject.

Almost all the customers were women, and Sally grew to love talking about her baby, with a few untruths about Todd thrown in. All in all, she liked the job, and the Valley Inn was okay too.

Late one morning the following week, Mr. Hesselgren, Big Earl, and Mrs. Sondheim stopped by. Dotty welcomed them nervously and showed them into her office. Then she told Sally, "They are not to be disturbed. Why don't you and I pick out some new outfits for you? Would you like that?"

"Sure, but I can't afford to buy much," said Sally.

Dotty said, "Sally, let's have none of that. As I said before, it's all taken care of. Now, let's have some fun!"

That broke the ice for Sally. "That's okay with me, Dotty. I'd love to wear some of these cute outfits!"

"How about this one? Want to try it?" Dotty held up a top with little yellow flowers on a white background, pearl buttons, and a sash collar tied in a big bow at the neck.

"Oh yes, that's so cute!" exclaimed Sally, practically skipping into the dressing room. She came out beaming a few minutes later and danced around with a twirl. For the first time in weeks, she felt pretty and proud.

Dotty said, "Sally, you look gorgeous. You could be Expectant Mother of the Year, I'm sure."

"I hope so, Dotty. I want to look my best while I help you."

Sally and Dotty went on with the mini modeling session for half an hour. Then the bell on the front door rang, and a tall, handsome man, slightly balding, entered. Sally had seen him in the shop before, but just to pick up an envelope or box from Dotty and then quickly leave. This time he stopped and introduced himself as Wesley Warren—he said everyone called him Wes.

From the moment he entered the shop, Wes exuded self-confidence, talking at length about his new car dealership in Bakersfield. Sally couldn't help noticing that he wasn't wearing a wedding ring. Wes had been a partner of Mr. Hesselgren and Mrs. Sondheim for many years, and he asked several questions about the shop, including details about Sally. Between chatting with Wes and wearing her new outfit, Sally became so relaxed that she forgot about Todd, the baby, and her wall of worry. An attractive, rich, confident man was, it seemed, flirting with her.

After several minutes of small talk, Wes excused himself and joined the meeting in Dotty's office. A half hour later, he come out, looked at his watch, and said, "Well, it looks like this meeting will go on longer than I anticipated. Can I take you to lunch, Sally? I know of a nice little place nearby. How about it?"

It all sounded so grown-up, and Sally thought, *A lunch date with a business executive? My, my!* She was so taken by his offer that she fell back into her flirtatious mode so recently put aside. She even batted her eyes a bit and bent over to give him a shot of her cleavage. When she looked up, she noticed that his eyes had hit the mark and even widened a bit.

"Yes, Wes, I'd love to—if that's okay with Dotty," she said.

Wes stuck his head in Dotty's office and said, "Back in a few. I'm taking Sally to lunch. Bye!" He helped Sally into her coat and escorted her outside to his big Buick, then drove a few blocks to a small, romantic Italian place with tables overlooking a patio garden.

Lunch was even more than Sally had hoped for, with excellent food and service. In fact, she enjoyed it so much that she almost forgot about her predicament. The waiter didn't ask her age, and she got a little tipsy on the wine, which she was not accustomed to drinking. Wes had wine too, plus a few martinis before and after the food. Had Sally been her former self, and her condition not been so apparent, she might have wished that the afternoon would develop into something else. Little Todd kicked to remind her.

By the time they left the restaurant, Sally knew a great deal about Wes and his business. He also knew a lot about Sally, though most of it was untrue, especially regarding Todd. Mrs. Sally Wyrum, as he now knew her, had conflicting emotions. By the time they were back at the shop, her reality was back in full swing, but Wes hardly noticed. He'd seen lots of cleavage and was pretty drunk.

A month passed, and all she got from Todd was three cards with exotic Asian themes. She received no reply to her baby letter. Everything in her life was focused on Little Todd. "One month to go," said the doctor at Sierra Vista Hospital.

Sally's new home and fake name cheered her up, but mostly she took care of Little Todd.

CHAPTER 28

The Pink Cloud

Right after Todd returned from a three-day deployment, a Vietnamese colonel showed up at camp in a new car escorted by jeeps carrying machine guns. Handsomely dressed in a crisp tiger-striped uniform, he was accompanied by an entourage of similarly attired officers and a couple of beautiful women. After consulting with the local unit commanders and Captain Bradshaw, he left without contacting any of the locals. Todd knew this was not a good sign.

After the colonel and his carnival sideshow left, a camp meeting was held. As usual, the weather was hot and humid, and everyone sat under a big World War II–era olive drab tent. Todd drank a Coke, took off his boots, and poured lukewarm water over his head. He looked up through the dense triple-canopy jungle, trying to ignore the slightly putrid smell. Catching a glimpse of the deep blue sky, he longed to be at Avila Beach.

Todd's calm was broken when a Vietnamese officer walked up and addressed the assembled unit. The attitude among the Vietnamese soldiers immediately turned to nervous hostility.

Next, Captain Bradshaw addressed the group. "Soldiers, we've been reassigned to the rice paddy area east of here. Don't ask me why, because the higher-ups haven't told me. I do know that there's been lots of bad shit going on around there, so I guess we've been selected to clean it up—and we will. There won't be any new replacements to go with us. We'll draw supplies and be off in choppers in the morning at 0700. We assemble at 0630. Any questions?"

Todd said, "Yeah, Captain, I've got one."

"Okay, go ahead," said Captain Bradshaw.

"I think the army, in its infinite wisdom, should issue us an escort unit like the one that just left with those muckety-mucks. I could sure use an issue like that. Those 'she soldiers' look like they could conquer the VC in no time. I mean, who'd fight if you could R&R with that? I'd say I speak for us all in that regard, Captain." Raucous laughter and agreement ensued even before the sergeant ended his request.

"I'm in complete agreement with you, Sergeant, though my wife would put up a roadblock that even Charlie couldn't get through. But in consideration of your request, I'll forward it to Saigon as a rush order. How's that? I bet it'll be approved before your *next* tour is over."

"Fucked again!" exclaimed Todd. More laughter.

After several more jokes, the captain said, "I don't know whether we'll land at a fire base, an HQ, or a hot landing site. So be ready, locked, and loaded when we saddle up, okay? We've got mail call, but we won't get to that before we leave. See Sergeant Strite after we land. Clear? Dismissed!"

~

At 0700, they were in the air. The *bananas*, as the old choppers were called, clanked along over jungle and scrub hills, then approached an area of rice paddies interspersed by broken tree lines. For the first time, Todd got really nervous, his chest tightened up, and he broke out in a cold sweat. The choppers descended and slowed down at about two hundred feet above the trees. Off in the distance, clouds of smoke from mortar rounds could be seen, but little could be heard over the noise of the old helicopter. The light on the bulkhead was red.

Todd picked up the helmet he'd been sitting on, placed it on his head, and grabbed his medical kit. The other men slung weapons (LAW) and M-79 grenade launchers over their shoulders. Radio frequencies were checked. The gunners at each door cocked their M-60 machine guns. Ammo boxes were readied. The captain, a former airborne trooper, yelled, "In the door!"

Todd sat with his legs hanging out, ready to jump to the ground. The copilot yelled in broken English, "The landing zone is hot. Thirty seconds!" The chopper descended, just skimming the paddies as the ground rushed by. The impact of mortar rounds could now be heard, and shrapnel zinged through the chopper, causing Todd to duck.

They slowed, nose down, at the edge of a raised embankment by a water-filled paddy, then stopped abruptly just a few feet above the ground. Todd jumped out, landing in knee-deep water, and sprinted for a nearby tree line. The Vietnamese officers and Captain Bradshaw shouted commands as they ran, hunched over, the fifty yards to the trees, which seemed like miles. Off in the distance, Todd saw soldiers from previously deployed units hunkered down and firing at the unseen enemy. Gunfire caused the water to splash up around Todd as he ran.

Several mortar rounds hit nearby, slamming into the dirt of an embankment and sending up huge clouds of earth and vegetation. Todd's entire unit was covered in mud that stuck to their boots and made every step an effort, as lines of machine-gun rounds laced past them. Todd saw the captain's mouth move as he shouted commands, but Todd could hear nothing over the deafening noise interspersed with the cries of injured soldiers.

Light arms fire crackled throughout the mortar barrage, and Todd saw several soldiers out front go down. He ran forward, zigzagging back and forth, to the first of the wounded men and turned him over. Lying in the slime of a rice paddy, the man had been hit in the face. He briefly babbled something in Vietnamese through a mess of blood, bone, and teeth, then fell silent.

Off to his right, Todd saw Captain Bradshaw make the cut throat motion, indicating that the man was dead. The captain sprinted over to Todd and shouted, "He's done! Get the fuck outta here, Wyrum. Now!"

But Todd couldn't move, and his hand shook as it rested on his medical gear. Through the thunder of more explosions, he looked up at Captain Bradshaw, whose mouth was moving but making no sound. The captain lifted Todd to his feet, and they ran across the rice paddy toward the berm.

Halfway there, Todd hit the ground just as a mortar round exploded on top of the soldier running in front of him. Todd was thrown backward by the detonation, landing flat on his back in the mud. He was covered in blood, bone, and scraps of uniform, and a pink haze enveloped him. The other soldier had simply disappeared. Todd struggled to his feet and sprinted forward. Fifty steps later, he collapsed on the embankment next to the Captain.

Captain Bradshaw calmly said, "Don't worry, it isn't your blood.

That's what happens when a round hits a guy. He's just disintegrated, gone instantly, completely, no pain. This is just vaporized blood. We call it the pink cloud. It happens a lot, but you'll never get used to it."

The captain pointed to a downed man nearby, and Todd crouched down and crab-walked over to administer to his leg wound. As he worked, his mind dwelled on the captain's words, "the pink cloud."

Pretty soon, his unit's mortars found the range of the enemy's position, and the fire began to fall off. Captain Bradshaw and most of the unit had moved off to assault the enemy, and Todd and the Vietnamese medics were left to tend the eight wounded men. Two had died and were left to be placed in body bags later. For the next twenty minutes or so, the firefight moved off into the denser vegetation just west of the paddy fields.

Within an hour, all firing had stopped, and Todd's unit began to reassemble on the big dike behind the last paddy field. It was by far the most intense encounter they'd had with the Viet Cong, and it had proved costly. Out of the forty-five men who'd begun the assault, ten were down.

Then they scouted the area position and established a perimeter defense. They also found the bodies of several dead VC and took one wounded prisoner. Todd took care of the man, who had shrapnel wounds on his legs and torso. He was obviously in great pain, though he was trying not to show it. He was slight of build, and his eyes shone bright and unafraid. It was the face of Todd's new, hard enemy.

Orders came down to hold their position until further notice. Todd and the other Americans could hear the captain on the radio as he objected to this order. "We're sitting ducks here, sir," said Captain Bradshaw. "Let's move up to the hills out west, a raised area with some open space around. That's a better defensive position, sir, and it's only a short hump away."

After listening for a moment, the captain put down the radio, looked around uncomfortably, and said, "We stay put. Everyone go around and make sure we're as tight as possible, understood?" Several of the men looked at him with questions on their faces, but Captain Bradshaw barked, "Orders are orders. Now get cracking!"

They hunkered down for the rest of the day, and Todd's shaking stopped, but not his fear. They made their position as strong as possible with claymore mines all around. They also sighted in the mortars on locations they thought might be good enemy cover.

Todd and the other medics took the best possible care of the wounded. He amputated a Vietnamese soldier's arm that had been hanging on by some skin and tendons. It was a by-the-book procedure, and when Todd finished stitching it up, the wounded man smiled and gave him a thumbs-up. Two soldiers died, and a chopper picked up the remaining wounded men.

They sent out patrols far and wide, discovering lots of evidence of a Viet Cong presence, but they made no contact. Morale among the Vietnamese soldiers was low. There was a feeling of being forgotten out on the fringe, exposed to the enemy without support. The unease seeped into Todd too. The lifers back at Fort Hood had been right—1962 was going to be a rough year.

As time wore on, Todd and his fellow advisers began to see a different Vietnam. Their allies, the South Vietnamese, didn't seem all that serious about the war, whereas the enemy was very engaged. The Viet Cong were well armed, brave, resourceful, and tactically proficient. In contrast, the South Vietnamese army wasn't aggressive and fell into trap after trap laid for them. The advice offered by Captain Bradshaw and the other officers wasn't being followed.

At Todd's level, the training went well, but it didn't filter up to the higher echelon. This lack of progress was a constant topic of complaint among his fellow advisers. The most stunning realization was that some of the Viet Cong had AK-47s, which was a better weapon that their own. Their RPGs were also effective, along with their use of mortars and the greatly feared booby traps. The wait-a-minute vines that constantly tripped them up were no fun either.

A patrol came back and reported signs of enemy activity but no actual soldiers. The sense of uneasiness grew as night fell. Everyone knew that night was the Viet Cong's favorite time to attack. Getting ready to take up his night position, Todd cleaned up so that if he had to deal with wounded men, he wouldn't contaminate them. He instructed the Vietnamese medics to do the same, and then sat and waited with his fellow American advisers.

Their position, which sat about six feet above the surrounding paddy fields, was thirty feet wide and stretched out in an east-west direction for fifty yards plus. A raised edge surrounded the area at about table height, with scrub bushes growing along the inclined sides. It was like a long, raised, shallow bowl. The mortar holes were placed at the center of this mound, and four M-60 machine gun positions were spaced out along the perimeter. Two-man foxholes were being dug. The area for the medics, covered with a tarp, was at the north edge of the bowl. A tree line was off about three hundred yards on the west and north sides, with flooded paddy fields on the other two sides. The air was wet, hot, and still. Not a sound could be heard.

As he cleaned up, Todd said, "What a morning's work, Captain! And the VC—wow!"

"No shit, Sherlock! Fuckin' A, right? Why the hell didn't they deploy us to a site in those hills? It's calm over there." Jones pointed at the hills, and Todd agreed.

With little conviction in his voice, Captain Bradshaw said, "Woulda, coulda, shoulda! That's war, boys. Maybe they didn't know, so knock it off and let's get back to prepping for tonight."

Todd took off his helmet and liner and set them on his pack. For just a moment, he looked longingly at his most treasured position, a lock of Sally's hair wrapped in plastic. Then he filled the helmet with clean water from his canteen. He placed his dog tags and wallet, Miss Lady's gift bracelet, Sally's lock of hair, and a few other personal things in his helmet liner and set it on the raised edge of the bowl. Removing his wet boots, he stripped down to his shorts, placing his other gear, including his name tag, on top of his boots and weapon. Other guys were doing much the same. All was calm.

Before washing up, Todd decided to write a few more lines to Sally.

~

Letter #18

From: SPC-5 Todd Wyrum
c/o Bravo Co.
Fifth Special Forces Group
An Lộc, Republic of Vietnam

To: Sally Anderson
691 Mitchell Drive
San Luis Obispo, California

Darling Sally,

Well, we finally had close combat with the VC, but all went well, so don't worry. We've moved by helicopter down into the rice-growing areas just east of where we had been. It's different here. There are lots of small hamlets and villages nearby, but we haven't visited any of them yet.

Captain Bradshaw says we'll get a short leave soon, and I sure hope so. It would be nice to visit some of the interesting temples and monasteries that we've heard so much about.

I'm picking up some of the local lingo, too. It's a big help that I took French at school, since that's the second language here. In fact, it's the first language among the higher-ups, or so it seems. I'm slowly making friends with the medics, but the officers don't interact much. Don't know why.

There's a big national holiday coming up here. The locals call it some unpronounceable name, but we just call it Lunar New Year. We're all hoping for some R&R for it. We'll see.

Bye for now. Got to clean up. I'll write more later.

Your Todd

~

"Hey Todd, you think she'll wait for you?" This drew a derisive laugh from everyone. It was his devotion to writing to Sally that provoked the question. They'd all seen her picture, too.

Todd said, "Yeah, I do. So cut the shit on that score, okay?" More general guffawing ensued. Todd put down the letter, dipped his hands in the lukewarm water, and doused his face and hair.

All around him, the others were doing much the same. A few minutes of cleaning up and general BS passed among the soldiers. The whole area, from tree line to paddy fields, glowed in the late-afternoon hour before sunset. Everyone was relaxed, servicing their weapons or cleaning up. While they relaxed, the sergeant handed out the mail, and Todd had a letter from Sally. He started to open it, but then decided to finish cleaning up first.

Suddenly, off in the distance, the distinctive *crump, crump* of mortar rounds being dropped into tubes echoed from the tree line west of their position. Then the staccato rip of heavy machine-gun fire punctuated the still air, and Todd yelled, "Incoming!"

Everyone dived for a foxhole. Todd had missed getting his gear, but he crouched low in his half-dug hole. The first impact was deafeningly loud and jerked him around. The mind-numbing explosions continued for a minute or two, then let up briefly. Men were screaming in pain all around him, with yells of "Medic!" coming from every direction. Crouching, Todd rushed toward a wounded man, then paused and raised his head to survey the area. More *crump, crump* sounds came from afar. The impacts inched closer and closer with gigantic crashes. Suddenly Todd had the sensation of flying ... and then he was enveloped in a pink cloud.

~

Seventy-five hundred miles away, it was raining heavily on the Carrizo Plain. Sheets of water poured down on the ranch, while a rare lightning storm danced overhead. The rain beating on the roof woke Miss Lady, and she sat up in the pitch dark with a feeling of foreboding. At intervals lightning flashes lit the room, lending a ghostly feel to the night. Her mind was blank, but her feelings swam off with the noise of the torrent.

Getting out of bed, she slipped into her beautiful old dressing gown and walked to the bedroom door. She opened it and saw, at the far end of the hall, the faint glimmer of the TV test pattern throwing its light across the rec room. She pictured the Boss sprawled on the couch, boots off, head thrown back, snoring, drunk, an empty bottle of Jim Beam his only companion.

Miss Lady walked down the dark hall, lightly running her hand across the pictures hanging there. A memory was attached to each one. She pulled at the big oak door, which slowly creaked open. The sky was inky black, and she walked out onto the porch, oblivious to the puddle of rain that she stepped in.

She couldn't see anything, but she felt something—deeply, profoundly. A lightning strike, followed by rolling thunder, lit the yard. There in front of her, for an instant, stood the water trough. Minutes passed and nothing happened, except the soaking rain cascading off the roof and onto her. She was wet through and through in just a moment, but she felt none of it. Something was welling up inside her. She took two steps forward. Another lightning strike!

And there, in the faintest of outlines, was her boy, her man, her Todd, standing in the water trough as on that day an eternity ago. She breathed deeply, stepped forward, and reached out to the image. Another strike, and that lock of hair fell across his forehead and a wide, innocent smile appeared. Another step, and she reached toward the outline, which was growing bolder. "Oh, my Todd, come to your Miss Lady. Oh my ... Please, Todd, I love you so."

For the briefest of seconds, that might have been a lifetime, her Todd of old was there with her—tall, lean, sensual, and smiling. The mirage spoke softly, "I love you, too, Miss Lady." Then it receded in a wisp and was gone.

Miss Lady stood in the downpour for a long time, but Todd never returned. Finally she went inside and back to bed. Wet and exhausted, she slept with a sense of foreboding in her heart.

~

Little Todd kicked Sally awake, harder than she'd ever felt before. The storm was raging outside. She sat up abruptly and said aloud, "Oh, you naughty boy, stop that. Why'd you wake me, my little boy? Is it the storm? It can't hurt you or get you wet or anything, so calm down."

Sally got up and walked to the window. It was indeed a big storm, such as they seldom experienced. She pushed back the curtains and watched the river of water cascade off the roof and flow down toward Spring Street. A far-off lightning strike lit the room, and rolling thunder cracked soon after. After a few minutes, Little Todd kicked hard again and moved around. Without the slightest thought, she put her hands to her huge belly and said to him, "Now behave, or I'll have to tell your father about this. So there!"

Looking around the dark room, she said, "Are you here, Todd, my love?"

She stood at the window, surrounded by the dark, thinking of their ravenous lovemaking during the storm at Avila Beach. Their desperate desire in the shack was also vivid in her mind. The wind-driven rain, the waves smacking up between the planks, the creaking pier, the slamming door, the rough boards of the old shed wall as Todd pounded her as she clawed his back. Vivid were these images. Their desperate, animal need for each other was primeval. She curled up around her craving and love for him wondering, *Where are you, Todd? Where?*

~

That February day dawned clear, still, and warm on the ranch. Breakfast was over, and the Boss had gone to town. Mrs. Cruz was cleaning up, and the cowboys were down the hill at the corral, working the stock. At the front porch, Cruz stood next to the trough holding Todd's horse, Splash, who seemed jittery.

Miss Lady was dressed, made-up, and looking forward to a ride to the high pasture. She walked out the door and said, "Oh my, Cruz, doesn't Splash look great? She's ready for her weekly ride."

"Miss Lady, she does—and you look ready, too."

"Indeed I am, Cruz, indeed I am!" Just as she stepped up to mount Splash, Miss Lady noticed a black car approaching down the entry road at the second bridge. As the car drew nearer, she could make out two men in it. The car pulled up three car lengths in front of them, and after a moment the two men got out. Miss Lady waved and said, "Good morning! Can we help you?"

Standing beside the car, the two men waved back. Then they put on their hats and walked toward Cruz and Miss Lady. Their faces were serious. Only then did Miss Lady notice that they were army officers.

As they approached Miss Lady, Cruz reached out and put his hand on her arm to steady her. It was the only time he'd ever touched her.

Miss Lady's warm smile faded into a frown of recognition. One of the men held a briefcase. She gasped, and her legs buckled. Only Cruz's firm grip kept her from collapsing.

As they stood in front of her, eyes sad, the officer carrying the briefcase said, "Good morning, ma'am. I'm Major Simpson, and this is Lieutenant Phelps. Are you BonnieWyrum, mother of SPC-5 Todd Wyrum?"

Barely able to stand, Miss Lady looked up at the obviously uncomfortable visitors with the look of a forlorn child on her face. Cruz said in a heavy accent, "This is Mrs. Wyrum, but she's Todd's guardian, not his mother. Do you understand me, sirs?"

Lieutenant Phelps quickly helped Cruz steady Miss Lady. They backed her up to sit on the edge of the water trough. Miss Lady stared at Major Simpson, her chin quivering and her body hunching farther over with each word.

The major drew a deep breath and said, "I have some unpleasant news for you. I must also apologize for our delay in getting here to see you. Perhaps we can go inside?"

Miss Lady hesitated a moment, then shook her head.

The briefcase was opened, and a sheaf of papers was taken out. The major read from one of them, "Mrs. Bonnie Wyrum, it is my unpleasant duty to inform you that your son, SPC-5 Todd Wyrum, was killed in action last month in Vietnam. For acts of bravery in carrying out his duties during an action in that country, he has been posthumously awarded the Silver Star."

Lieutenant Phelps took out a flat blue box, opened it, showed the Silver Star to Miss Lady, and then handed it to Cruz. Both officers then took a step back, came to attention, and saluted crisply. Then the lieutenant read several award comments and instructions for a future burial ceremony at the national cemetery in San Bruno, California. He also read a page of official information, including death benefits. He asked Miss Lady to sign a form, which she was barely able to do.

It was obvious that the two officers were uncomfortable standing outside in the sun to perform this duty. When the paperwork was completed, a heavy silence fell over the small group. Miss Lady stared at the officers, not fully comprehending what had just happened. Cruz awkwardly held her hand. In a strained voice, the major said, "Mrs. Wyrum, do you have any questions?"

Following a long moment of hesitation, Miss Lady again shook her head.

"I'm so sorry to bring you this news. So very sorry. I wish we could do more." Major Simpson's words trailed off, and he looked away for a moment. "Well, we'd better go now," he said. "Again, I'm so sorry to bring you this news."

Tears streamed down Miss Lady's sorrowful face as she looked back at him without saying a word. Finally Cruz said, "I'll take care of her. Thank you, sirs."

The two officers sadly walked back to their car and drove away.

A long silence shrouded Miss Lady and Cruz. They watched the car until it disappeared around a bend. Then Cruz helped Miss Lady to her feet, and they went inside.

~

It was a slow afternoon, and the radio played in the background as Sally and Dotty did some odds and ends around the shop. The announcer said, "We hope you've all had a great weekend along the central coast. This weather was pretty good for the season. We'll have more music coming up right after the local news."

Sally considered turning off the radio until the music returned, but she knew that Dotty liked having it on. Ignoring the general monotony of the broadcast, Sally occasionally perked up at some interesting subject. She was preparing a box of maternity clothes for a woman who was going to have twins. One item in the broadcast that did interest Sally was the local sports roundup. She knew that her high school cheer team would be performing at the games, and she was eager to hear any commentary about them. She really missed Brenda, the rest of the team, and, of course, the attention.

At the end of the sports roundup, the announcer said, "All of you San Luis Obispo High School boxing fans will be sorry to hear this news. Todd Wyrum, a former team member, has been killed in action in Vietnam. Todd was awarded the Silver Star for his actions. Sad news indeed! Our condolences go out to his family and friends. The school will have a remembrance ceremony for him later, we're told. We'll announce those details later. Sad, very sad!"

Sally hadn't been listening closely—until the announcer said the words "Todd Wyrum" and "killed in action." Then she went into convulsions and screamed, "Killed? Killed in ... Todd is dead?"

Her deafening, anguished scream jolted Dotty out of her chair. "Good God, what in the world? Sally dear, what in the blazes is so wrong?"

Sally sprawled across the big table, screaming as Dotty ran up to her. "Oh no, Todd! Oh no, not my Todd. It can't be! Oh, Todd!"

Dotty tried to comfort her, but Sally cried uncontrollably, throwing her bloated body around in a dangerous way. It was so bad that Dotty called the local doctor whom Sally had been seeing in Paso Robles. He was only a few blocks away, and he came right over. While he attended to Sally and gave her a sedative, Dotty called the newspaper and confirmed Todd's death. She also called Mrs. Sondheim, who was there within an hour. That was Sally's last day of work. The baby's birth was ten days away.

It was February 12, 1963.

BOOK IV

Ten Years Later

CHAPTER 30

Little Todd

Sally stalked from the rec room into the kitchen, trying to avoid the news—something about Vietnam, a subject she hated. She yelled at the top of her voice, "Wes, for God's sake, will you turn that infernal racket down, please? Even the football game is better than that."

Wes's voice rang out above the TV. "Get with it, Sally! It's basketball season. It's the news and just an update on Vietnam stuff, not about the war. It's over soon, and then the game's on."

"My Lord, must we relive that nightmare endlessly?" exclaimed Sally. "Vietnam was ten years ago, and it's over! Find something else to watch—anything. You know how I hate that war stuff. Let's not dwell on the past, okay? And anyway, it's too loud."

All the wives were busy preparing food. The TV was on here in the kitchen, too, but it was a pregame program that featured college cheerleaders. Sally and the other wives liked this program because it was sometimes about local high school cheer teams. It was the happy camaraderie of homemakers cooking and gossiping, distracting them from dealing with the men in the other room.

Sally waited for her husband of nine years to change the program—but he didn't, which was typical of him. Every year it got harder and harder to be around him. The booze, the unexplained absences, and his impatience with Little Todd caused lots of family friction.

Ten minutes later, a basketball hit the kitchen window with a loud bang. Wes came charging through and onto the back porch, where Little

Todd and some of his friends had been throwing the ball around. The window wasn't broken.

Wes stumbled past the other boys and snarled at Little Todd, "What the hell are you doing out here? I told you to play your goddamn games on the court. That's why I put it there. You break that fuckin' window, boy, and there will be a whipping coming your way, understand? Damn kids these day. Shit!"

"Yeah, yeah ... Okay, I got it! No balls on the porch." Little Todd's answer to his stepfather was a mixture of disrespect and fear.

Wes rounded on him and yelled, "What was that, kid?"

Little Todd stepped back from Wes and exclaimed, "Yes, sir!"

"You're damn right, sir!" exclaimed Wes. "And I don't need to tell you again, do I?"

"No, sir!"

Standing at the window, Sally spoke up and said, "Wes, you're not setting a good example by yelling at the boy and using language like that. We talked about this before, didn't we? Now please stop."

Wes said dismissively, "It's the same at the dealership. The young kids got no respect."

Sally knew when to stop. The car dealership was a sour subject. Things hadn't been going well lately, which made his moods even harder to predict. Where was the money going?

Wes's mention of a whipping put a degree of fear in Sally. Little Todd was ten now, and he was a confident, raw-boned kid just like his dad had been. As the boys moved off the porch, she noticed that the girls, even at such young ages, had noticed Little Todd. Her own young life's path—including Todd—flashed through her mind.

There was also some degree of guilt in Sally's attitude. Little Todd had grown up hearing glowing tales of his father, killed a hero in Vietnam. But that hadn't always sat well with Wes, who hadn't served. Sally's efforts to curb her pride in Little Todd's father weren't too convincing, and she knew that was her fault.

Also, Wes was aware that Sally and Todd hadn't been married, and he knew about her wild times with Brenda. When Wes and Sally got married, she hadn't wanted to change her son's last name from Wyrum, and that had stuck in Wes's craw. He had never said anything to Little Todd, or anyone else that she knew of, but the subject hung in the air anytime they quarreled. And quarrel they did lately, over everything.

Within their marriage, the car dealership, politics, friendships, the big house, money, booze, frequent absences, and most pointedly, Wes's attitude toward his stepson were all constant points of friction. This last item, for Sally, overshadowed everything else.

But Sally pushed this confrontation aside, bucked up her attitude, and pressed on with the party and having fun with her girlfriends. They were a great bunch of involved women from Bakersfield's younger families. Coaching the local girls' cheer teams was the most fun of their many shared interests, and their husbands had interests in coaching the city's sports teams.

Sally had her other friends too. A few minutes later, Brenda showed up at the party, causing a brief lull in all activities. She was the same Brenda of Sally's adventure days, just updated, with as much pride as ever. She wore a short, tight black skirt, wide pink belt, white scoop-neck blouse, and white sneakers with pink laces. Her hair cascaded off her head, and she was still the showstopper that she'd always been. She jiggled through the room like a bowl of Jell-O, every move choreographed to draw attention. The TV didn't stand a chance. With all the attention now directed at her, Brenda exclaimed, in a theatrical way, "Ooh, can I help out?"

Another woman spoke up condescendingly, "I think we've got everything ready here, dear. I guess you can set the table—that is, if you have time among your other duties."

Brenda slid up next to Sally and asked, "Can I help you, Sally, please?"

None of the women in Sally's group much liked Brenda, but because of the unwritten rules among women, she was tolerated as Sally's friend. "Oh sure, Brenda! I didn't see you come in. You set the table, okay? I'll only be a few more minutes here."

"Okay, dear!" Brenda sashayed out into the dining room and went to work.

Sally went back to preparing the salad, but she overheard Brenda say, "Oh, hi, Wes! How nice to see you. Rooting for USC or the cheerleaders? Ha ha!" This drew comments and a cheer from the men watching the pregame show.

Wes and Sally's big suburban house was now filled with friends, business associates, and their many kids. The game got underway with beer, wine, and hard liquor drinks, plus tons of food everywhere. It was a happy and raucous gathering. Last month's Super Bowl was another topic of conversation. There had been heavy betting among the group on that game, and Wes hadn't done well.

During halftime, Sally was coming out of the bathroom upstairs when she turned toward the side hall. She heard low talking, interspaced with soft laughter, coming from the alcove off the second bathroom, so she walked down the hall and looked around the corner.

Standing there with her back to the end wall, one leg half raised, arms pushed back, and head tilted provocatively, was Brenda. Wes was leaning over her, one arm over her head, looking down the front of her blouse. They were both smiling, but Wes looked intense, whereas Brenda was completely relaxed and in control.

Surprised, Sally said, "Oh, I didn't know you two were up here. What's ..."

Upon hearing Sally's voice, Wes jerked up straight, lowered his arm, and turned to look at his wife.

Brenda didn't move, but shifted her big black eyes in Sally's direction. "Why, Sally," she said, "we've just been talking about you. Haven't we, Wes?"

"Well, kinda!" said Wes. "Brenda's been filling me in on what's happening out on the coast. You know, in the old neighborhood? Your old cheer team is still going strong, Sally. Right, Brenda?"

Brenda said, "Right, Wes! You're so right. The old cheer team, right! Well, I'm outta here. See you downstairs, Sally." Brenda brushed past Sally, giving her an odd look, and rejoined the party downstairs.

Sally stood in the doorway, as she and Wes looked at each other. It was an awkward moment. Finally Wes said forcefully, "What? We were just talking."

"I didn't say anything," said Sally snidely. "So you were talking. It surely couldn't have been about our old bouncing boobies, right? Or could it be an update?"

Feeling trapped, Wes pushed past her and said, "Talking, that's all!"

Sally followed him downstairs, where she saw Brenda standing off to one side. As Wes walked by her, Brenda gave Sally a look that she generally reserved for uninteresting men and said, under her breath, "I always thought Wes was a jerk."

Sally replied, "Now, Brenda, let's not get off on that subject now. It's a party."

"Oh yeah? Do I have to remind you why you got hitched to him?" asked Brenda. They both rolled their eyes and looked over at Wes.

Sally said, "What else could I do? I had a baby, no money, no home, and a dead-end job! At the time he seemed like—well, a catch."

"But it's not that way now, is it?" said Brenda. "And what do you think he might've been getting at upstairs? He had his face almost on them. You saw him! A few more minutes, and what do you think he might've proposed? And another thing—why has he been out of town so much lately? Where's he been, Sally? The man is a jerk."

Sally nodded, and they walked back into the kitchen.

~

The party was a big success, and a few women stayed afterward to help Sally clean up. Their husbands were out in the yard drinking beer, discussing the game, and speculating about who could win it all. UCLA had won today's game. The TVs were still on and tuned to the news.

To everyone's surprise, the program was preempted by a special report on the Vietnam POW release. The women continued cleaning the kitchen while the men assembled in the game room. There was a long introduction by an announcer about the circumstances surrounding this much-anticipated event, and then the feed cut to Clark Field in the Philippines.

The women stopped working to watch. Sally didn't want to watch, but since it was a big event and all the other wives were staying, she did too. Brenda stood next to her.

The announcer said, "Welcome to all our viewers from the USA and around the world. We are only moments away from seeing the POWs returning just today—February 12, 1973—from captivity in Vietnam. The plane is just beginning to taxi up to our location in front of the terminal, and the crowd here is huge. There's a big assembly of military brass and, of course, family members gathered near where the ramp will lead down. It's just a few minutes now."

It was a long few minutes while the plane got into position and the stairs were rolled up to the plane. The cameras panned the crowd as the commentator continued. The door to the plane opened, and the first man appeared, frail but smiling. He waved at the crowd and started down the stairs.

"Ladies and gentlemen, we now see our first POW deplane. He is descending the ramp. He has now reached the bottom. The crowd is waving at him, and he's saluting a general who is welcoming him. My friends, this is very dramatic. Cries of joy are coming from the people gathered here, and honestly I can hardly contain myself. Other POWs are exiting the plane and descending now. Oh my, friends, this is wonderful. I'm sorry that I'm so choked up."

Minutes passed as the POWs came down the stairs, lined up on the tarmac, and greeted a row of waiting dignitaries. The camera panned down the line, showing faces haggard but smiling.

In the kitchen some women had tears in their eyes as everyone stared silently at the procession. The camera spent only about ten seconds on each face, and this went on for several minutes.

Sally wanted to look away, but she couldn't. Then, in one corner of the TV picture, a new face appeared faintly as the camera approached. Something was familiar about it. As the camera drew closer, a strange choking sound came out of Sally's gaping mouth. "It's ... It's Todd ... My Todd!"

The other women turned to look at her, and someone shouted, "Oh my God! What is it, Sally?"

Then the man's entire face showed on the screen. Sally reached for the TV, her fingers splayed and hands trembling. On shaky legs, she moved toward that face—touching the screen, clawing at it, with sobs breaking from her mouth. She staggered, and the other women struggled to hold her up. Broken words spilled out of her mouth, "It's my ... Please, oh please, let it be him!"

Holding on to her friend, Brenda screamed, "This is impossible, Sally! But it's him—it's Todd!"

Sally's eyes rolled back in her head, and she fainted dead away, limp as a rag.

Little Todd walked into the kitchen, and seeing his mother on the floor, he quickly bent over and cradled her in his arms. "Mom, what's the matter? Please, speak to me. Please, Mom!"

At the back of the room, Wes said derisively, "Shit, she's just had one too many."

Brenda heard him and snapped, "Why don't you just shut up, Wes? Sally's in shock. It's Todd—he's alive. Todd's one of the returning POWs. Now do you understand? You're such an ass sometimes!"

"Screw you, Brenda! Like hell it's Todd. He died over there. It was official." Wes walked up to the group assembled around Sally.

Little Todd looked up at him and said "It's my mom, and you leave her alone. She's my mom!"

Wes's face contorted in rage, and he drew back to slap Todd. Brenda pushed herself between them and cried, "Don't, Wes! He's just a boy—even if he's not *your* boy!"

Another man in the crowd pulled Wes away. But as he backed off, Wes said to Little Todd, "Okay, but you're gonna get yours, kid. Oh yeah, you're gonna get yours. You just wait!"

Sally was still lying on the floor in her son's arms, so the other women went into action. One woman got a cool washcloth and applied it to Sally's face. A second woman got towels and put them under her head, while still another woman took off Sally's shoes. Looking for smelling salts in her purse, one woman said, "What in the world? My word, Brenda, do you know what's going on?"

Little Todd looked at Brenda with questioning eyes, incomprehension written all over his face. "Brenda, what did you say? Was it about my ... my dad?"

Brenda touched his cheek and said, in a most motherly way, "Todd, it's true. It's your dad, and he's not dead! He's there on the screen, alive and coming home to you and your mom. She saw him on TV and was just overcome. I can hardly believe it myself, but it's true. I saw him, too. He's real! Oh, this is wonderful, just wonderful. I'm so happy for you and your mom. Yes, and I'm happy for me, too!"

Sally was coming around now, and everyone was smiling, crying, or both. Her blinking, helpless, childlike stare asked the question that her mouth couldn't form.

Brenda put her face close to Sally's and said softly, "It's true, my darling. Todd's alive and coming home to you and your son."

Sally smiled and asked, "Is it really Todd, my sweet loving Todd?"

Little Todd said, "Yeah, Mom, I guess it's true. It's Dad—my *real* dad!"

Sally was helped to her feet, and they continued watching the broadcast. The announcer read a list of the POWs released and said more would be coming later, but when Todd's name was not among them, a shadow of doubt rippled through the group.

Then he began another list, plus explanations. "Ladies and gentlemen, we have more information for you about some of the other POWs on this second list. Many POWs who weren't in the Hanoi Hilton were not known of until quite recently. These men were held in various places in outlying areas of the country and even other countries. Most of them were soldiers and marines who were captured in the ground war portion of this long fight. And as you know, most of those held in Hanoi were from air crews shot down over the north. These others, whose names I'll read off in a moment, were held in much worse conditions."

The announcer read the list. When he got to Todd's name, he made this comment: "Enlisted United States Army 1962—age seventeen. Awarded a Bronze Star during training. Deployed, Republic of Vietnam, late in 1962. Received Silver Star in early '63. He was confined, unknown to the army, in Cambodia until a short time ago. Today—February 12, 1973—is his first day in the States since 1962. My God, that's ten years!"

Sally sobbed uncontrollably, and Todd and Brenda held her as she almost collapsed again. All the wives around were helpful and conciliatory with much congratulations spreading among them. Wes didn't reenter the kitchen.

The party finally broke up, and Sally, Todd, and Brenda were left alone in the big house. Wes had left with the others. The three of them sat together long into the night, talking about the joy of it all and their plans. The further they got, the more questions Little Todd had about every facet of Sally's life and how all this had happened. How come his name was Wyrum and Sally's name was Warren? How did Sally get from a Wyrum to a Warren?

As Sally and Brenda tried to explain it all to the smart and inquisitive boy, an obvious problem arose. Little Todd was figuring out that it didn't all fit together. Sally either had to tell the full truth or get caught in a lie later, and that wouldn't do. She'd been living with half-truths for too long. As hard as it would be, she had to tell Little Todd the whole story—except for her adventures with Brenda, of course. Deciding what to tell Big Todd would be equally difficult.

~

Since it was the weekend, Sally couldn't find out much of anything about Todd or the POW release. The TV station had some information, but nothing much, so Sally decided to go see the local army brass on Monday. Little Todd was brimming with questions—very *adult* questions.

He followed her around the house asking questions nonstop, and he was beginning to get frustrated at her lack of answers. She knew she'd have to tell him a degree of truth, but how to start and what to tell him?

"Mom, when are we going to see Dad? Don't you think we'd better find out some stuff first? Holy cow, there are lots of things to consider, like what does this mean for Wes? Aunt Brenda might be able to help. She knew Dad pretty well, didn't she?"

Sally replied, "Yes, she surely did. Don't worry, Todd. It's going to work out okay. We've just got to ... Well, there's just a lot to consider." Sally shuddered to think how she would explain things to Little Todd if, indeed, Brenda's role in past events came into consideration.

Looking across the dining table at her son, Sally wondered at his surprising level of maturity. "Todd, I want you to listen carefully and not interrupt me too much. You might find some things confusing or even upsetting. Just remember that your name is still Wyrum, in honor of your dad. I had a hard time persuading Wes not to change it, but you're Todd Wyrum and that's what matters."

"Sure, Mom, it's okay. I just want to know everything!" said Little Todd.

Sally looked at her jubilant, expectant son, but when she opened her mouth to begin, nothing came out. If it was this hard to square events with Little Todd, how much harder was it going to be with Big Todd? The situation was just too much for her, and she began to cry.

Little Todd's face dropped, and he quickly came around the table and hugged Sally. She said, "Oh, Todd, I love you so much, and I love your dad too. But even things that are wonderful, loving, and nurturing aren't always easy to explain. Love is—well, complicated, especially when it gets mixed in with growing up and other stuff. Oh, I'm going about this all wrong, aren't I?"

"No, Mom, you're doing it okay, really! Just tell me about you and Dad and love and how you—well, how you fell in love and stuff. That's not hard, is it? I sorta know how babies are made, so you can do that."

Sally dropped her head into her hands and exclaimed, "Oh God, I can't do this now. I need something. Excuse me for just a minute, Todd." She got up from the table, her face flushed, and went to a cupboard in the kitchen. Todd followed her in.

Sally got out the footstool, climbed up, and reached into an upper cabinet. She pulled out Wes's "emergency rations," as he called it—a half-empty bottle of Bushmills Irish whiskey. To Todd's surprise, she then got out a shot glass and poured it full. "I know you don't see me do this often, maybe never, but every once in a while it's necessary. So bear with me a moment, okay?"

"Sure, Mom!"

Sally gulped the shot down and said, "That's better. You may need to indulge in some of this stuff someday, Todd. Not all of Wes's ideas are bad ones."

Little Todd said, "Sure, Mom, I understand ... I guess."

"Okay, let me start by saying that I wasn't always your good old mom and a homemaker. When your dad was a boy—and oh, what a boy he was!—I fell in love with him in an instant, and I told your grandma, right then and there, that I was going to marry him someday. Can you believe that?"

Sally took a deep breath and poured herself another shot, and Todd's face looked a bit more calm. Knowing that if she stopped now, she'd chicken out for sure, Sally plowed ahead. "We met at Grandma's house on Mitchell Drive, when I was just beginning to grow up. Todd was a bit older than me."

"How old were you, Mom? How old was Dad?" asked Little Todd.

Looking at her son, Sally realized that in four years, he'd be as old as she was on that day. She looked at him in wonder, and then gazed off into the distance and said, "Oh my God, it's, it's been ... ten, ten years!"

The age thing and its connection to him didn't register. "Okay, Mom, what happened?"

Sally paused as her mind raced for an answer. "Todd, this is something I think we should talk about with your dad—your *real* dad, okay? We'll find him and go to him and talk then. That will be the best, don't you think?"

"Sure, Mom, that's great! When are we going? I mean, can we go tomorrow?"

Sally almost collapsed with relief at this chance to delay the inevitable. "It might take a bit longer, but soon. Yes, soon. After all, he is far away in the Philippines."

"That's kinda far, isn't it? Yes, let's do that, Mom!"

~

That evening, Sally and Brenda talked long into the night. Sally lay on the bed, and Brenda sat on the floor next to her in a pile of pillows. With their faces close, as in the old days, they hatched a plan for Sally, Little Todd, Wes, and divorce, but many questions remained unanswered. At the top of that list was the question of how Todd would react after ten years of captivity. In fact, they didn't even know how to find him. This talking and planning went on until they were exhausted and fell asleep. After years of seeing each other only occasionally, it felt good to be close again.

As Brenda was leaving the next morning, Sally said, "One more thing. Little Todd's growing up now, and as we both know so well, boys will be boys. So you might consider slightly less revealing clothing when you're around him. Yesterday in the kitchen, I noticed that his attention wasn't completely on my well-being. Understand, just a little, okay?"

Brenda picked up her overnight bag, gave Sally a big parting smile, and replied, "Why, of course. I didn't even notice. Bye, Sally. I'll see you in a few days, okay? Love you."

"Oh sure, you didn't notice, really?" said Sally, smiling. "Next week. Drive carefully. Love you, too!" They kissed as they parted. She knew full well that Brenda was aware of the impression she made on everyone, even Little Todd. Brenda was still Brenda.

Sally and Little Todd had a long talk and decided to keep everything regarding Dad to themselves. Todd resumed his usual life with school and friends. He was a happy kid.

Wes returned home that evening, but he had nothing to say to Sally or Little Todd. He had obviously been carousing out of town, but Sally knew better than to ask for details. Hungover and grumpy, he soon went up to bed and slept until late the next morning.

Two days later, Wes said that he needed to go to Las Vegas to see about a new potential dealership. Sally was suspicious, but she had bigger fish to fry.

Part of Sally and Brenda's plan was that Sally would get Todd's 1940 truck out of storage at the dealership and restore it. She wasn't even sure exactly where it was. She hadn't seen or driven the truck since way back in San Luis Obispo, a lifetime ago.

Sally knew almost nothing about cars, despite being part-owner of a dealership. Her own car was a Chrysler station wagon owned by the dealership. She got a new one every other year, and this was her year to do so. She would do the trade when she went down to see about the truck.

There were several other parts to the plan that she and Brenda had conjured up—and *conjured* was the right word. Everything was mixed in with the towering emotions of it all. Item number one was to find Todd, and item number two was to contact a lawyer about a divorce. Everything else was a confused jumble of fear, joy, and love.

Right after Wes left for Vegas, Sally took the first step. She called someone whom she hadn't seen in years, Todd's old lawyer, Victor Pearson. He was still practicing in, of all places, Bakersfield, and they agreed to meet the next day. She'd go by the dealership right after that.

Victor Pearson was still a no-nonsense, right-to-the-point lawyer who had handled every kind of case imaginable. Sally paid him a retainer of $1,000 and proceeded to tell him the whole story. When she tried to avoid certain awkward topics, such as cheer team stuff, he sensed right away that she wasn't being up front with him.

At one point he said, "Mrs. Warren, I need it all, even the stuff from a past you'd rather not reveal. I'm your lawyer. Nothing—and I mean *nothing*—gets out about any of this, period. Your personal activities are safe with me. But if I'm going to represent you properly, I need to hear it all, okay? It's what I *don't* know that can hurt you."

It took the better part of two hours to lay it all out. Sally was quite embarrassed, but Mr. Pearson didn't even blink. She even went into her cheer team adventures, and when she got really red in the face and started stammering, he said calmly, "Go on, Mrs. Warren. Don't forget, I was young once, too. Please continue. You're doing just fine!"

After the consultation, she was more exhausted than after a cheer team halftime routine. Mr. Pearson ushered her into a private room and got her a Coke. "Why don't you sit in here for a few minutes while I make a couple of calls? It's tiring, isn't it, going through a part of one's life that presents some challenges. Don't be upset. Just relax, and I'll be with you in a few minutes."

"Okay, thanks, Mr. Pearson. I do feel better now, but you're right—it is quite tiring."

When he returned, he had some papers for Sally to sign and a list of things he needed from her. He said, "Mrs. Warren, I've made an appointment for you with a friend of mine who's an army officer. He might be very helpful to you in finding and making contact with Todd Wyrum. You know, I do remember him well from our court appearance a ways back. He seemed like a very nice boy. I do hope this all works out for the best, for both of you."

Sally said, "Oh, Mr. Pearson, I so appreciate your help. I feel much better knowing you're on my side, and it's reassuring that you remember Todd, too. Thanks so much for helping."

"Mrs. Warren, I look forward to representing you. However, having said that, let me offer you a cautionary note. Todd has undergone a horrific experience, and he may be damaged both physically and emotionally. I was in the war, and I saw lots of damaged friends come home to a long rehabilitation period. I don't say this to alarm you, but to prepare you. Understand?"

"Oh yes, I do. I want to take care of Todd. I love him, Mr. Pearson. I've loved him all this time, and now he has a son—a wonderful, loving son—to get to know. I'm so hopeful, especially after talking with you. You know, Mr. Pearson, I feel a lot like I did that day, long ago, at court. Like a young girl with all my love and tomorrows ahead. Thank you very much!"

"It's all going to work out," said Mr. Pearson. "Now, you go tend to the things on that list, and see Colonel Beckett too. I'm pretty sure he'll be helpful. Goodbye now."

~

Sally drove to the dealership, buoyed up and ready, and headed into the office. As she greeted everyone, she noticed that they were polite but unusually reserved. When she was ushered into Mr. Williams's office, he said, "Nice to see you again so soon. That was a great party you put on. Mrs. Williams is going to be challenged to do as well at the next one, which will be at our ranch next month. Sit down. Can I get you some refreshment? Is Wes with you?"

Sally replied, "No, he's not. And thanks, but nothing for me. Please do say hi to Millie for me, and I know she'll have no trouble matching my success ... Well, on to business? I need to retrieve that old Ford truck of ours that you've had in storage for years. I'll need it fixed up and ready to drive. I'll need the license updated too, if that's not too much trouble. Also, my trade-off for a new wagon is due, so I guess I'll take care of that while I'm here."

Mr. Williams had an uncomfortable look on his face. "Have you and Wes talked lately—I mean, about the dealership and things?" he asked.

"No, he's been away a lot. Mostly, I assume, in Nevada, looking into your new dealership out that way. Is there a problem?"

Mr. Williams looked away, now appearing even more uncomfortable. He pressed a button on the office intercom and said, "Mrs. Gorman, can you come in here? And bring those notes I gave you. This will only take a minute."

Mrs. Gorman greeted Sally, sat next to the desk, and handed the notes to Mr. Williams.

After a moment of silence, Sally asked, "Is something wrong? All I need is the truck and to exchange my wagon."

Mr. Williams now looked like he was actually in some pain. "I'd hoped that you would talk with Wes before coming in. That would have been very helpful. As it is, I'm going to have to lay it all out for you and ... Well, Mrs. Gorman has the figures to prove it. Here goes, and I'm really sorry to have to tell you all this. You're a very nice person and—"

"My word, Mr. Williams, just spit it out," said Sally. "You look like a little boy who has to pee."

"Okay, well, there isn't any new dealership in Nevada—or anyplace else. We're in some pretty serious financial straits because of Wes's, uh ... irresponsibility. The truth is that he's been gambling heavily lately and using company assets to do it. All his stock is mortgaged to the hilt, and your house too as far as we know. He even borrowed money against his car, which is owned by the dealership, and those payments are behind by six months. We'll need to take back your car to cover ourselves during inventory, and we can't give you a new one. If you want me to go over this in more detail, I've got the figures right here. mmm ....!"

Sally interrupted, "Why, that's impossible! Wes hasn't said a word to me about any of this!"

Mrs. Gorman got up and put her hand on Sally's shoulder. "We've spent the last couple of weeks trying to resolve this with Wes, but just this morning a couple of lawyers showed up to serve us. Wes told us he'd have this all cleared up yesterday with a really big infusion of cash, but he didn't show up, and we can't find him. And Sally—I mean, Mrs. Warren—I'm sorry to say that as far as any assets in the dealership are concerned, you're broke. In fact, you're more than broke, because Wes owes us a lot of money."

Sally's buoyant mood was completely shattered. She just sat there for a minute, and then looked away and asked, "How could this happen without me knowing? Just a few weeks ago, we were considering having a pool installed. I don't understand. And what about my car? I can't manage without a car."

Mr. Williams said, "Wes kept us in the dark, too. We can't even help you with the car. Like I said, we have to have your wagon back today, so I need to ask you for the keys. We're really sorry about this, Mrs. Warren, but it's Wes's fault. He's hurt us all deeply with the losses he's incurred. Again, I'm so sorry, but I need those keys now."

The keys sat on Sally's handbag, which was on the desk in front of her. As he picked them up, Mr. Williams said, "The truck is still here someplace. I'll have one of the boys go find it. That is at least some good news, isn't it?"

Completely numb, Sally just nodded. Mr. Williams and Mrs. Gorman left the office and called the repair shop about finding the truck. Ten minutes later, Sally was asked if she wanted to see it. Sally, Mr. Williams, and two big mechanics walked to the back of the lot, to a run-down metal building in the storage yard. It took another ten minutes to find the keys, but finally the doors opened and there sat Todd's Ford truck, behind a pile of junk. It was dirty but undamaged.

Sally forced a smile. *What else could go wrong?* "I love it. Can you get it out so I can drive it home? It's all I have."

Mr. Williams hung his head and said, "As God is my witness, I can't authorize anymore of anything for Wes or you without prepayment. Sorry, but those are the partners' orders."

"What? I can't even get home!" exclaimed Sally. "You'd make me walk five miles? And I've got to pick up Todd in an hour. This truck, which belongs to me, is more than thirty years old, and you won't let me have it? Shame on you, Mr. Williams. Shame on the bunch of you!" Sally's mouth quivered, and a sob escaped her lips as she leaned back against the junk pile.

One of the young mechanics said, "Oh shit, boss, you can't do that. We'll fix it up for her. We didn't even know this gem was back here. Wow, a 1940 pinhead Ford pickup! Hell, it's probably worth lots more than some of the used clunkers we've got on the lot. We can fix it up, Mrs. Warren, in just a couple of days. Will that work for you?"

"I don't know about that," insisted Mr. Williams. "I can't authorize anything that costs even a dime, so we'd better not do—"

The other big mechanic leaned over and put one arm around Mr. Williams's shoulders in a rather intimidating manner. "Boss, we're gonna do this gratis," he said, "after we close up, you know? We've got them brought-back tires almost new, so we'll use them and a wire package and hoses. Won't be no problem at all. A couple hours on the engine, then the interior stuff and a car wash. You ain't gonna begrudge the little lady a few gallons of water, are you? You ain't the kind of guy to say no to this little lady, are you? I don't think so. We'll do it for you, little lady. Give us two days. Okay, boss?"

Mr. Williams said reluctantly, "Okay, but keep this quiet. If it gets out, we'll all get the ax!"

Sally gave the two grease monkeys a huge smile and said, "Oh, thank you! I'll be back the day after tomorrow. Can I get a ride home?"

By the time Sally got home, she'd almost—but not quite—forgotten that she was dead broke. She had $600 in her checking account, but when she called the bank, she was told that less than $10 remained in the savings account. Just weeks earlier it had held more than $20,000. Sally figured she could raise several thousand dollars by selling her jewelry. Brenda's idea to raise money, however, was *definitely* out.

Two days later, a neighbor drove Sally to the dealership. She almost jumped for joy when she saw the truck. It was just like Todd had left it years earlier. It took the mechanics an hour to teach her to drive a three-speed, floor-shift truck, but finally she drove it home—broke, but happy. On the upside, she got lots of looks from high school and college guys who saw her in the cool truck. After all, a girl's ego is important too.

~

Sally thought she had until the end of the month to figure it all out, because that's when the bills came due. Wes usually paid the major bills, but he still hadn't come home. When she looked through the stack of overdue bills, however, she discovered that they were in a deep financial hole to the tune of thousands of dollars.

Sally didn't want Little Todd to know about this. He was overjoyed riding in the truck, which made quite an impression when she drove him to and from school. All of Sally's many girlfriends were shocked, but she hardly cared anymore. Todd, her true love, was somewhere in her future. It was as if Wes and the money problems were completely disconnected from her emotions. Her heart soared, and she slept soundly with joyous, erotic dreams.

Sally contacted Colonel Beckett, as Mr. Pearson had recommended, and he agreed to help. A few days later he called back and said he had the information, but that he wouldn't be comfortable giving it to Sally over the phone. Instead, he mailed it to her, and it arrived three days later.

The packet provided Sally with all the information she needed. In fact, it was more than she really wanted, but now that she had it, she couldn't stop reading. A few photographs were also included. It was shocking, distressing, but Sally read it all in one long, emotion-filled night.

Todd had mistakenly been reported KIA after his gear, including his dog tags and personal effects, had been found at the scene among the dead. The event itself had been one of the first full-scale assaults in the war, and Todd had suffered minor wounds and been captured by the Viet Cong. He was then taken to a jungle prison camp and held under horrific conditions for most of his captivity, along with several other prisoners whose names were blacked out in the report. Todd was confined underground in "tiger cages" and later shackled in a hut at night. Upon his release, he was suffering badly from several diseases and malnutrition. He'd lost some teeth and weighed less than ninety pounds. Sally avoided the paragraph about torture, which was just too disturbing. The final summary greatly buoyed her feelings. Todd would need a period of convalescence, but there was, miraculously, no permanent damage.

Todd's convalescence, which was described in another report, would take place first at Clark Field and later in Lettermen Hospital in San Francisco. Then he would be flown home to Travis Air Force Base, outside Sacramento, on June 3. When Sally finished reading, she cried herself to sleep.

One thing the report didn't explain was how to contact Todd. Sally's efforts were thwarted by army regulations that forbade giving information to nonfamily members. Colonel Beckett didn't know either, although he said that if he found out, he'd call her.

During this three-month wait for Todd's return, Sally was kept busy dealing with the fallout from Wes's gambling debts. He'd finally come home, but his usual grumpy self had been replaced by a depressed, almost paranoid shell. He apologized profusely and tried half-heartedly to explain how his life had spiraled downward into gambling debt—and there were debts aplenty. His partners at the dealership had managed to save the company, but he was asked not to return. The company lawyers would contact him. His car was repossessed, the utility companies threatened to cut off service, and foreclosure notices were served on the house and a boat they'd recently bought. Payment checks for Little Todd's music lessons and the cleaners bounced and were returned, the golf and country club canceled their membership, and a crew from a furniture company showed up one morning to repossess the TV and other stuff. Without even asking, a landscaping company stopped by to dig up and remove two trees from the front yard.

The Mexican yard crew came to the door after finishing up and wanted to be paid, so Sally scraped together what she could, paying them partly in spare change. She told them not to come back. Her girlfriends wanted her share of the money for the upcoming party at Millie's house, but Sally didn't have it, and they didn't volunteer to help her out. Word had gotten around. This situation spelled *outcast* in Sally's world of suburban women.

Wes moped around the house, watching old sport films and going to Gamblers Anonymous almost every day. Some woman called a few times asking for him in a rather desperate-sounding voice, but he didn't want to talk with her. He gave Sally all the money he had left, which was less than two hundred dollars. She asked him about getting a job selling used cars, which is how he'd gotten started, but he just shrugged and walked off.

Sally had money for food and gas, plus a little extra that Brenda had sent her. She volunteered to coach a girls' cheer team part-time at a local high school.

Then Mr. Pearson called and asked her to come by. They needed to talk, he explained, which sounded a bit ominous to Sally. While Todd was in school, she drove downtown. Mr. Pearson ushered her into the office in his usual polite but cool manner.

He said, "The things necessary to proceed with filing for divorce are ready. They're marked where you need to sign, so you can go ahead."

Sally signed the papers and said, "Thank you, Mr. Pearson. I'm glad we're about to do this. You said on the phone that there were some other things we need to discuss. I'm ready!"

"I've discovered some information that you need to be aware of," he began. "For starters, your husband is being investigated for fraud. Also I've learned that some people from Nevada are looking for him regarding unpaid gambling debts. The fraud investigation is serious, and the gambling debt is dangerous. I strongly suggest that either Wes leaves your home or you and Todd move out—and I mean today. The people looking for him aren't nice business folks. As I said, this could be dangerous."

Sally's heart was pounding, but she was much tougher than she'd been even a month earlier. She said, "I'll get him out, Mr. Pearson."

"On the brighter side, you've gotten some useful information from the colonel, right?"

"Oh my, yes! But you were right to warn me. My Todd's been through a lot, and he'll need a long time to recover from his ordeal. I'm ready for that."

Mr. Pearson said, "There's one other thing that you'll need to deal with. How is your financial situation?"

At the mention of money, Sally's face fell noticeably and she said softly, "I'm not in very good shape. In fact, I have only a few dollars left. I can't even pay you now. Little Todd and I have enough for food and his school, plus gas, but that's it. In two weeks, I'll be broke."

"I thought so, and I'm prepared for that. You need to declare bankruptcy immediately. If you agree, we can do this today. It will not—I repeat, *not*—help you with any money right now, but it will protect you in the future. And we hope that future will be spent with your two Todds, right?"

Sally said, "Yes, Mr. Pearson, if you think that's best, I'll do it. Are these the papers?"

"Yes, they are, Mrs. Warren. You can sign as indicated."

Sally signed them, then sat back and asked, "Mr. Pearson, what about the money to pay you? I don't have it, but you've been the key to us going forward to happiness. How am I going to—"

"That's enough now. Don't be upset. I've more news for you. Let's go out on my garden porch for a moment. It's my favorite spot for informal business dealings."

They walked outside, and he said, "I'm sure you recall, from long ago, Mr. Hesselgren and Mrs. Sondheim?"

Sally's mouth dropped open, and she said nothing.

"Yes, I thought so," he said "Well, they are also my clients. In the course of looking into all this, I made contact with them—unofficially—and mentioned your predicament, in the course of other dealings. They both mentioned that they had helped you before, as friends, and it seems that they're still your friends. In any case, it's in their best interest, even beyond friendship, that you and your returning Todd go smoothly into the next phase of your lives. So they authorized me to give you this, and to tell you 'good luck' from them." With that, he handed Sally a thick, unmarked envelope. "Don't open it here. It's best that I not know what it contains."

Sally nodded and took the envelope. "Mrs. Sondheim and Mr.

Hesselgren? I can't believe it. They did help me very much, but that was ... I don't know what to say."

Mr. Pearson said, "Nothing needs be said. Just move on with your life. Now on to other things. It seems that your Todd will be paid, with interest, for his time spent in captivity. This will be a considerable sum. He has also been promoted two army ranks in consideration of whatever the service does in these cases. I don't know much about that, but Colonel Beckett may be able to shed some light on it if you choose to ask him. Todd will also receive a continuing partial disability check each month for life. So you see, Mrs. Warren, you'll not be in such bad financial straits as you may have thought!"

"But what about your fee, Mr. Pearson?"

"It's all taken care of—all of it!" he assured her.

When Sally got to the truck, she opened the envelope and found two thousand dollars inside. For a few minutes, she sat in the truck and considered the relationship between her benefactors, Brenda, cheer team, Little Todd, and herself. Finally she decided that it was a subject best left unexplored. She had a short cry, and then drove home in her really cool truck and got some more looks on the way. The truck scene was growing on her.

CHAPTER 31

Truckin'

Wes wasn't all bad. When Sally explained it all to him, he threw no tantrum, did no yelling, leveled no threats, and agreed to the divorce. He was apologetic and said he'd do what he could to help her and Little Todd. He said it was all about the gambling, and it had always been.

When Sally told Wes that Todd would be home from Vietnam and she wanted to marry him, he said, "I always knew. The way you acted, carrying on about how great he was. Yeah, I knew." He signed the divorce papers and was gone the next day. He said goodbye to Little Todd also.

Sally was free, and the love of her life would be with her forever and ever. Almost hourly, she mulled over what would happen when they met. The more she thought about her reunion with Todd, the more questions arose—where, when, what to wear, dress up or down, hair, makeup, shoes, skirt or shorts or pants, lingerie, sexy or demure, happy or serious, hugs, kisses, shake hands. It went on and on.

One morning she looked too long at the bathroom scale, which she hadn't stood on in years, and a terrible thought sprang into her head: *Have I gotten fat?* It took her two days to work up the courage to weigh herself, and when she did, it showed 110 pounds. She'd been five pounds less her sophomore year in high school. She spent a half hour looking in the full-length mirror until she finally found herself acceptable, though just barely.

How would Todd be? Would he want her? What about Little Todd? That part was easy. Her love for Todd covered it all. She wanted him in any way, shape, or form—and she wanted him to still love her. She and Brenda spent hours on the phone. No item was too minor to obsess over.

The last thing Sally did was have the nice mechanics at the dealership secretly get the truck in the best shape possible. They were happy to do it.

~

Finally the big day approached—June 3, 10:00 a.m. at Travis Air Force Base. Sally and Little Todd were ready. He was excited, though a bit worried, but Sally was happy enough for both of them.

Sally found out, through Colonel Beckett, that only immediate family members would be allowed passes to greet the returnees. After much thought and more talk with Brenda, she came up with a plan to pose as Todd's sister whose married name was Warren. It would be no problem to pass Little Todd off as who he really was, her son. She still had her old Sally Wyrum driver's license from her days back in Paso Robles, so she could use that to prove her former name, and she had Todd's birth certificate in case she needed it. The only remaining unknown was whether Major Wyrum or that Miss Lady person would be there. Of all Sally's concerns, that was the worst one.

The next morning, Sally and Little Todd packed, got in the truck, and headed north on Highway 99. They would stay in a motel near the base so they would be fresh when Todd's plane landed the next day.

The drive was fun, and Sally let Little Todd take the wheel wherever they stopped, usually at a Big Orange. She showed him how to work the floor shift, back up, and turn around. He caught on right away and wanted to do the actual driving. They sang their favorite songs, and the truck ran like new. He even inspected the engine. He reminded Sally so much of her big Todd.

They tried several motels in and around Fairfield, but everything was full. Finally they found a place in Vacaville. Sally reserved one room for that night and two adjoining rooms for the next night. Every time she opened her purse, she thanked God for her old friends and Mr. Pearson.

Sally and Little Todd both got a good night's sleep and were up early the next morning. The day that she and Brenda had discussed a hundred times had finally arrived. Part of her wished that Brenda was there to help, though she was also glad not to have to worry about her oh-so-competitive friend.

Sally had been to the salon two days earlier, and now her hair was a huge pile of blond and red ribboned curls. She and Brenda had decided to go the whole nine yards on makeup, which took hours. When they argued about "the look" they wanted, Brenda finally carried the day: "You do want him to pick you out in the crowd, don't you? And Sally, what's your best asset?"

"Well, I guess. But I don't want it to be, you know, *too* much," Sally said.

"Sally, the guy's been in prison for ten years. Get with it! What in the hell do you think he's gonna want? Yeah, and even before food, I'd guess. Remember what he was like before he left? And those big hands?"

Sally replied, half joking, "Well, I guess."

"You'll probably walk bowlegged and be unable to wear a bra, I'd venture," said Brenda.

Sally did a little cheer routine, hands in the air, and spun around while rolling her eyes mischievously. "Oh yeah, I can hardly wait!"

Brenda asked, "So it's a yes?"

Sally smiled slyly, now convinced. "Yes, dramatic it is!"

Sally started with soft pink lipstick with liner. She did her eyes dramatically with lots of mascara and two shades of eye shadow, and then she plucked and touched up her eyebrows one last time. Before Little Todd woke up, she quietly got into her most sexy lingerie. Her bra was a cutaway with blue trim and panties to match, and she had nylons and a garter belt with the same trim. Her stockings were white with patterned tops. Brenda had lent her a revealing dressing gown.

The dress was the most important part—low cut, sleeveless, bright pink with blue trim and frills at a deep neck. The skirt was short and flared with pink-and-blue petticoat. She wore a necklace and bracelets that Todd had given her long ago. She had on pink satin low-heeled shoes.

When Little Todd saw her, he exclaimed, "Wow, Mom, what did you do? Jeez!"

Sally did a proud pirouette for him and asked, "Do you think Dad will like it?"

"I guess Aunt Brenda sure did help out and everything," Little Todd said. "Well, gotta go fix up the truck. See you downstairs!" He quickly turned and bolted out the door, leaving Sally to ponder what he had just said.

The mirror posed the question: Was Brenda's influence too much?

But Sally decided, *Too late now. This will have to do. Hope you like the new me, Todd. I'll love you, no matter what!* She put the finishing touches to her outfit, slipped into her old cheer team jacket, and had a last look in the mirror. Confident that she was ready, Sally left the room.

As she walked up to the elevator, two men got off and both did double takes. In fact, they even looked back at her as she got in. One guy stood outside the doors as they closed and said admiringly, "Wow, lady, just wow! I sure hope he appreciates you!"

When Sally got to the truck and Little Todd saw her in the cheer jacket, he said, "I like that, Mom. Can we go now? It's almost nine." He seemed completely at ease, without a single misgiving about what might happen. His handsome, open, innocent boy's face saw only happiness ahead.

Sally was in an upbeat mood, though somewhat nervous. "Yes, let's get going, my handsome man."

~

During the twenty-minute drive to Travis Air Force Base, Sally got even more nervous. She turned on the radio, and she and Little Todd sang along to help calm her nerves.

At the guard post, an enlisted woman asked, "Pass?"

Feigning surprise, Sally exclaimed, "I didn't know I needed a pass. We're related to Todd Wyrum, so can we go in?"

"No, ma'am, you need a pass. You can park over there and get one at the security office."

Sally parked the car, took off her cheer coat, and walked over to the security office with her son. Before they went inside, she said to Little Todd, "I'll bet if it was a man guard, he'd have let us in. What do you think?"

Little Todd said, "Ha ha! For sure, Mom. You look great!"

"Now Todd, just make sure you go along with anything I say. I'm going to have to fib a little bit."

Todd nodded.

After a short wait, Sally and Little Todd stood at the reception desk. A woman sergeant eyeballed Sally critically and asked, "Ma'am, can I help you?"

"Yes, I'm Sally Warren, and this is Todd Wyrum. We're here to pick up Todd Wyrum, who's getting back from Clark Field today. I'm told we need some kind of pass."

"Yes, ma'am, you do need a pass. Are you related to Mr. Wyrum?"

"Yes, I'm his sister," replied Sally, "and this is my son, Todd Wyrum. My name now is Warren, but I was Sally Wyrum before I married."

"Can I see some identification for you both, please?" Sally dug out her ID and handed them to the sergeant, who looked them over and asked, "Do you have anything proving you're his sister?"

"Why, yes, I do." Sally produced the driver's license from 1963.

"Well, this doesn't prove that you're his sister."

The woman's tone made Sally suspect that this wasn't really about credentials. This was a woman-to-woman challenge. They argued back and forth for a few minutes, but finally the sergeant shrugged and said, "I'm sorry, but this doesn't prove anything."

Meanwhile Sally had noticed a captain sitting in an adjoining office. She decided to make a fuss, hoping to draw his attention. "This is outrageous," she exclaimed. "How dare you address me in that unprofessional way. I want to see your superior officer."

The captain stuck his head out from the office and asked, "Sergeant, is there a problem?"

Sally spoke up, "There certainly is, sir. My brother is coming in from Clark Field shortly, and this sergeant won't let us in. We're quite upset! We've come so far, and this isn't fair. I'm his sister!"

The captain said, "Now, let's hold on here a minute. Sergeant Smith, what's the problem? Does she have the required documentation?"

"I'm not really sure, sir. She doesn't have any documentation that proves that she's his sister. Instead, this is what she's got."

The captain took the things, looking Sally over in a very manly way, and examined them carefully. Then he said politely, "Mrs. Warren, I'm Captain Goodrich. Let me go pull the file on this Todd Wyrum, and that may shed some light on our problem. In the meantime, the sergeant here will get you some refreshment. Sergeant! Sorry, Mrs. Warren. I'm sure we can fix this."

Sally leaned over the desk and said, in the sexiest voice that the circumstances allowed, "Thank you, Captain Goodrich. I so appreciate your personal attention to my problem. I'm sure *you* can straighten this out as no one else can."

Sally's response was not wasted on the sergeant, who glared at Sally and then walked out.

The captain called after her, "The refreshments, Sergeant—now, not tomorrow."

Brenda's strategy was working. A couple of minutes later, the sergeant came back and handed Cokes to Sally and Todd without comment.

A few moments later, the captain reappeared. "There's nothing in the file, Mrs. Warren, about him having a sister. The only people mentioned are his mother—that's Lieutenant Colonel Wyrum, if I'm not mistaken—and Barbara Wyrum, his guardian. There are sure a lot of Wyrums around, but no one else is on Todd Wyrum's attendance sheet."

Sally sat down, giving the captain a good opportunity to survey her dress, and said, "Well, we are a big family. Aren't we, Todd?"

"Yeah, and I want to see my uncle!" said Little Todd, who went along with the fib perfectly.

Five minutes later, they left the guard post. Sally looked back at the captain, who was still standing in the door. He yelled after them, "Wow, great truck. A 1940 pinhead Ford, right?"

Little Todd yelled back at him, "That's right! Pretty cool, huh?"

With a last nod from the captain, Sally drove off toward the receiving area.

~

They parked and walked to a ramp area where the returning POWs would be. It was a big crowd of family members and military brass, plus medical vehicles and personnel. A few minutes later, a loudspeaker announced that the plane was on approach. There was great excitement among the crowd.

The plane landed and taxied slowly—it seemed an eternity to Sally—to the reception area. A set of stairs was wheeled to the plane, and finally the door opened. Expectation in the crowd was electric. A woman near them fainted. A couple in the front fell to their knees and prayed. Couples hugged and wept openly. Even several military officers could be seen crying. Entire groups of people, including Sally and Little Todd, held hands.

The first POW appeared in the door, waved, and walked down the stairs. A woman screamed and ran forward, throwing herself on him as he reached the bottom step. He saluted the welcoming officer even as they embraced. The crowd surged forward.

More men came out the door and down the stairs. Sally's control slipped, and she began to cry. Little Todd hugged her. They were quite near the bottom of the stairs now.

Suddenly there he was, unmistakable, the lock of hair falling across his forehead. Sally's knees buckled, and she yelled, "Todd! We're here, Todd!"

Little Todd jumped, waved, and yelled even louder, "Dad! Dad, we're here!"

Halfway down the stairs, Todd lifted his head. As his eyes scanned the milling crowd, his gaze fell on Sally and Little Todd. He stopped, swaying slightly, with a blank expression on his face. Then a small smile broke through, and he grabbed the rail to steady himself and waved with his other arm. As other POWs pushed past him, his smile broadened and tears rolled down his face. He shook his head, then took a few more faltering steps forward. At the bottom step, he half-heartedly saluted the receiving military officer.

Standing there was a ravaged but recovering warrior of 130 pounds, with skin stretched and parched. His uniform hung on his wiry frame, his hair had thinned, and he stooped just a little. His hands had been broken, his neck was scarred, and his color was washed out. But Todd's eyes shone through, unbroken! He was still the boy Sally remembered and loved.

Little Todd broke free of Sally's embrace and raced forward. Sally followed, pushing through the surging crowd as best she could. Little Todd threw his arms around his father, and pressing his face to Todd's chest, yelled, "Dad!" And so the father, though somewhat bewildered, embraced his son for the first time.

At just that instant Sally reached Todd, her face flushed with a girlish smile. Standing just a few inches from him, she said with a sobbing voice, "I love you, my darling Todd."

"Oh Sally, is it you? I can't believe it! Oh, my darling, I live only because of you. Oh God, I love you!"

Sally threw herself at him and said, "This is our son, Todd. Yes, Todd, just like you."

Todd pushed his son back and held him at arm's length, studying him closely.

"Say hi to your son, Todd Wyrum. Our son!" exclaimed Sally.

Todd and Sally then kissed the kiss of more than thirty-five hundred days of missing, of dreams and nightmares. It was a kiss of reborn love and expectant passion. It went on and on, with gushing words of devotion. It was a hunger of heart and body, begging to be quenched. Ten minutes of this passed as many other people around also were consumed with joy.

When they finally drew breath, Todd asked, "How did all this happen?"

"Oh, Todd, we've got time for me to explain everything later. For now, let's just go! Remember our last day up by the creek at our place? Remember how safe we thought we were?"

Todd shook his head and said, "Well, I'm beyond words. Our son?"

Little Todd chimed in. "Dad, Dad, Dad ... my dad!" Sally and Todd pulled back and laughed heartily. Little Todd added cheerfully, "Oh yeah, just wait until you see the truck. Wow! Mom had it all fixed up, and I've kept it clean for you. It's the coolest—you'll see."

"Son, I can hardly wait," Todd said. "Let's go see it and get a big breakfast. Yummy American food!"

Little Todd ran ahead as they walked to the truck. About halfway through the parking lot, Todd stopped, stood back from Sally, and gave her a good look. "Wow, that dress, your body—all of it! You're even more beautiful in person than in my fantasies. Dreams of you kept me going, Sally. I lived on my love for you."

"No less for me, Todd. I never stopped loving you, but there is a lot to tell about these last ten years!"

Todd laughed and said, "You think you've got lots to tell? You don't know the half of it!"

Little Todd spent the next half hour showing off the truck to his dad. As Sally drove them to breakfast, Little Todd sat in the middle, and they were probably the happiest people in the world. They went to the same place on Highway 12 where Sally and Little Todd had eaten on the previous day. When the waitress came to take their order, Sally spoke for Todd: "My husband will have chicken-fried steak, cottage-fried potatoes, crispy, and eggs over easy. Cereal for us, two plus orange juices. And, of course, coffee. Thank you!"

Todd threw his head back and gave a huge laugh. "Oh, Sally, you remember so well—and exactly right too. Remember out by the train station, at Dave's Lunch, that night after the storm in Avila Beach? My favorite breakfast! Oh my, Little Todd, isn't your mom a kick? What a woman! My girl still, even after all these years!"

"Yeah, Dad, Mom's great—the best mom anywhere. And Mom, show him the pictures, please? And don't forget the ring. You know, *ping, ping, ping!*"

Sally said, "Todd, I brought along some of our history, so that you'd feel a part of what we did. You were always here with us. Isn't that right, son? And this too!" Sally pulled the chain at her neck, and the fifty-cent-piece ring that Todd had given her long ago came out of her cleavage. She put it in his hand.

"Yeah, Dad, see? Mom told me about the *ping, ping, ping* stuff!"

Todd said, "I'd almost forgotten. And you're right—Grandma used to complain so much."

Sally hugged both her guys and said, "I've worn it all this time, and I've had to tell Little Todd the story many times."

Todd grasped the ring and said, "Well, *ping, ping, ping* it is! Let's see about this history, Sally."

"I've got the photos right here in my purse," said Sally.

Little Todd spoke up. "It's more like a suitcase, Dad, see?"

They all laughed when Sally brought out the album, which contained a complete record including Little Todd's birth, baseball games, riding a horse in a cowboy outfit, Halloween, and so on. As Todd looked on, the memory of Miss Lady and Splash briefly cast a shadow across his mind. Wes was in some photos, but Sally passed over them. Others included Brenda and her son, Charles.

"Good old Brenda! Hasn't changed much, I see." Todd said this in a nonjudgmental way.

The food came, and while they ate, they continued to look at the photos. Todd said, "I love that one with you two at Avila Beach. Can I have it for my wallet? It's both of you at your best."

Sally gave Todd a sidelong come-hither look and batted her eyes. The photo showed Little Todd building a sand castle, and Sally kneeling next to him in a very revealing bikini. Sally said, "Why yes, Mr. Wyrum, you can have this one. It seems your taste hasn't changed much."

When they left the diner, Little Todd asked, "Can I show Dad how I can drive?"

Sally replied, "Well, okay, but stay in this gravel parking area."

"Yeah, Mom!" Little Todd exclaimed excitedly.

"I'm looking forward to this, son. Go ahead. I can hardly wait," said Todd.

While Little Todd drove around, their touching grew bolder. Todd's hands searched out Sally's bust as she aroused him to erection. By the time Little Todd finished his driving exhibition, they were both quivering with anticipation. When he pulled up and stopped, Sally said with a shaking voice, "Why don't you let your dad drive now? After all, it's his truck."

"Yeah, Dad, you drive," said Little Todd.

"Okay, but remember that I haven't driven in ten years, and I no longer have a license. Nevertheless, here goes!" Todd drove around the gravel lot to the hoots, laughter, and comic instructions of his family. "Now I've got everything, and I'm truckin' along in style. I can't believe you two kept it in such great condition all these years. I love you both with all my heart."

~

It was a fine day of reminiscing as Sally and Todd drew closer during a picnic at a hilltop park. They snuck touches under each other's clothes when Little Todd wasn't looking. By evening, Little Todd's energy was played out. He dozed on Sally's lap, and she relished holding him.

Meanwhile she was memorizing every detail of her returned Todd. No detail was too small, not even the scars on his broken hands. She didn't want to waste a minute, and as her hands explored him sensually, her desire grew. He woke somewhat under her touch, but then dozed again.

After the picnic, they went to a drive-in. Todd had always enjoyed a big appetite, but this was ridiculous. He ate a cheeseburger, French fries, onion rings, a milkshake, and pie.

After the movie, they returned to the motel. The day had been filled with the events of the past ten years, except for the things they couldn't divulge in front of Little Todd.

Little Todd was exhausted, and he went straight to bed in an adjoining room. In the fading light, his parents sat on his bed and told him about high school and the secret spot on the creek. He wanted to hear again how they had met. They even sang, "I'm gonna sit right down and write myself a letter" for him. Before the song was over, however, he was asleep. His parents sat there a few minutes longer, watching Little Todd sleep, all the while beginning to arouse each other with gentle kisses, caresses, and soft words.

Finally they went into the adjoining room and shut the door. The embers of their lust, which had been building all day, finally burst into flame. The instant the door closed, they were in each other's arms. In the semidarkness, they stumbled over a chair and fell against the wall, then the bed.

"Oh, Todd, I've dreamed about—" Todd's mouth crushed her words. Sally's body pressed against him, and clothes flew asunder. She pivoted him to his back and sat astride his loins, putting his big hands to her breasts. Her fingers wouldn't wrap around the girth of him, as she placed him between the crimson lips of her pussy. His fingers teased her hypersensitive nipples, then he raised his mouth to them, licking and sucking her cherries. Slowly Sally relaxed, and he parted her softness to exquisite pain. "Oh, Todd, fuck me!

It was driven, clawing, biting, consuming sex, with every place explored. As he went deeper, she felt like a huge flowering tree filled her. Finally the tree erupted, and a long cobra-headed white snake lanced into the depths of her pussy. She flowed around him as they came together, once, then again, and Todd growled, "Sally, I love you!

A moment of loving rest, then more! His erection fit perfectly between her breasts, which were now even bigger, and she looked into his eyes as he gushed up into her mouth and over her face, everywhere. They lay head to toe, and tongues and lips took their fill of each other's honeyed juices, with shared spasms racking their bodies. Finally they lay there in exhaustion amid the shambles of the bed, bedding and mattress askew on its frame. Todd said, "Oh Sally, you still taste like cotton candy."

Sally laughed and hit him with a pillow.

Their carnal pleasures abated, but the loving went on. Todd said, "Remembering and wanting this is what kept me alive and sane. You. Without you, I wouldn't have come back. Many times you kept me from giving up. The only other thing was the periodic table, if you can believe that. I memorized and worked it, drawing it on the dirt floor."

"Oh, Todd! When I thought you were gone, I still felt you there, deep in me, as I dreamed. Only those dreams and Little Todd kept me from despair."

An hour of soft romance followed. Finally Sally said, "I have one more surprise."

"Go for it, kid!"

Sally grabbed a bottle of champagne and two glasses from the mini-fridge. She poured two glasses, and they drank. "My darling, how do you like my new haystack hairstyle?"

"I love it, and the smeared makeup too," said Todd.

"Oh, you're so mean! Let's catch up. You must have lots of questions, and me too."

Todd nodded and said, "True. You want to go first?"

"Okay, but I'm a little scared. I've got to tell you some stuff. Well, here goes! I was pregnant with Little Todd when you want off to boot camp. I intended to tell you the night of the graduation dance, but we both know how that went. I kept meaning to write you, but I chickened out every time. Finally I did write, but the letter came back after—well, you know. Now I hate just the mention of Vietnam. They hurt my Todd, and I hate them and that place!"

"Sally, I'm okay. They damaged me, but in other ways. My body is mostly healed, and I'll get counseling for the stuff that really matters. It's the nightmares that I need help overcoming, but I think your love and attention will heal me the most. And even the worst of experiences yields some good. I had to have that attitude to survive. See, I learned Vietnamese! It's the one percent that was good."

"Okay, I think I understand, so I'll go now. When Brenda and I were on cheer team, we got kind of mixed up. Mrs. V got us to do stuff that—"

"Stop, Sally. I know all about the adventures that you and Brenda did. It wasn't your fault. Mrs. V was an exploiter, and you were a victim. I met a girl who told me all about it. She'd been on a cheer team at a different school and heard rumors of your exploits. But I did stuff, too. Miss Lady even had a name for it. She called it 'pimping you out' for money."

Sally looked away in shame. "Oh yes, Todd, bad things ... but that was back then. I don't care about all that, if you don't. We've got each other again."

"That's right, Sally. That's all in the past."

They hugged and kissed for a few minutes. Then Sally said, "I'd better keep going, because if I don't, I'll never get it out. I married Wes because you were gone and I had Little Todd and no money and no job and nothing. Back then Wes was a successful car sales guy, but I never loved him. And as time went on, he wasn't very nice to Little Todd."

Next Todd started to tell her what happened to him after he was reported KIA, but Sally didn't want to hear it. "Stop, Todd. It's enough that you're home. Like I said, I don't want to ever know about that place. I read the report, and that was way too much."

They talked the night through, and a couple of times they looked in on Little Todd.

At one point, Todd mentioned that he needed to take care of some business on the ranch. There was a long silence, and then Sally said, "I guess you don't know that they—Mr. and Mrs. Wyrum—passed on a while back. I don't know the circumstances. Mr. Pearson told me."

Todd looked away forlornly and went to the window. After a heavy silence, he just said, "Oh."

"If you want, Todd, we can go—"

"No, that's okay. I guess it's not important now."

More talk, and then they made love again.

"Todd, darling, I need to tell you this. I don't have any money except a few dollars that I brought on this trip. Wes's gambling drove me into bankruptcy."

"Oh, I never even knew him before the fight. It was Miss Lady's lawyer. I guess I'd better tell you about that, too. You see, I'd been working on the ranch since I was a kid, and my mom kinda farmed me out to them. Then that year you and I met, I was out there and she—"

"Stop, Todd. She took advantage of you. It wasn't your fault. I suspected that."

Todd froze, but Sally couldn't see in the dim room. "I wasn't exactly taken advan—"

"No, Todd. Women can be really mean and catty. Let's leave that, too, okay? I don't want to know how she—well, you know. I mean, a slutty older woman."

"Sally, it wasn't like—"

"I don't want to know any of it. None, do you hear?"

Sally was awake the rest of the night, just watching Todd sleep. They made love again in the dim morning—a softer love, but no less rapturous. It ended only when they heard Little Todd knocking on the adjoining door and calling out, "What's the matter, Mom? Dad, is everything all right?"

After taking a moment to gather their wits, Sally yelled, "Yes, darling, everything's okay. It's just Mommy and Daddy catching up on things. Sorry we woke you."

Todd looked at Sally with a big smile. "That won't be the last time he's woken up in the night, I expect." They put on robes, laughed, and let him in.

Little Todd looked at them and said, "You sure have lots of noisy catching up to do."

"We've been apart a long time," Todd explained, "so yeah, we've got a lot of catching up to do."

Sally put her arms around big Todd and said, "Yes, my darling son, your father and I do have lots of *that* to catch up on."

Todd continued the thought. "And a lifetime to do it. Don't you agree, Mrs. Wyrum?"

Little Todd yelled, "That means you're gonna get married, right?"

Sally said, "Yes, we will, Todd. And then your dad and I will have a nice long honeymoon. Isn't that right, Mr. Wyrum?"

Todd was standing at the window in quiet contemplation. He pulled back the curtains as though he was looking out at something far, far away, over the rolling hills marching off in the distance. A few horses and cattle grazed way off on a far hill. A shadow crossed his eyes, and a specter sat on the scene that only a memory could capture. A long moment hung in the air, and then his face changed. He said, "Well, yes, I expect so. But we've had a hundred honeymoons already, haven't we?"

CHAPTER 32

Postscript

Grandma Julia Anderson

Grandma eventually forgave Sally for her indiscretions, but she got to know Sally's new family only briefly. She passed away in 1977 at the age of seventy-six.

Gail and Zoe

Gail stayed close to Grandma's church teachings and became a devoted Pentecostal minister, traveling widely and teaching the word of God. She never married, nor did she reconcile with Sally. She's now a pastor and lives in Del Rio, Texas. Zoe married right out of high school, had a family, and still lives in town.

Kenny

Kenny went into medicine and later managed a hospital. However, he became addicted to prescription drugs, which led to his forced retirement. His whereabouts are unknown.

Mr. Hesselgren

Mr. Hesselgren remained on the margins of San Luis Obispo County affairs for the rest of his life. He was investigated by the sheriff several times, but charges were never brought against him. He ran his string of motels until his death in 2001 at the age of eighty-three.

Mrs. Sondheim

Mrs. Sondheim was the queen bee of the county for the rest of her life, despite being found guilty of tax evasion and fined heavily. She, Sally, and Todd remained friends. She died in 2008 while playing bridge at the Monday Club. She was ninety-four.

Big Earl and Gwyn

Earl became under-sheriff, in which capacity he steered issues, inquiries, and investigations away from certain of his acquaintances and allowed the local unofficial business community to prosper. He and Gwyn married when he retired in 1982. They live in a mobile home park outside Paso Robles. Gwyn and her daughter, Brenda, aren't close.

Principal Jennings

Principal Jennings left San Luis Obispo High School in 1965 to become superintendent of schools for Kern County. He retired in 1985 and now lives in Wickenburg, Arizona.

Flo

Flo closed her shop when a high-end store opened nearby. Her whereabouts are unknown.

Deacon Jennings

Deacon Jennings continued with church until his inappropriate behavior with high school girls was discovered. Then he was forced out, his wife divorced him, and he had a nervous breakdown. He now lives in an assisted living facility for the mentally impaired in Oregon.

Bea

Bea worked the bars in Bakersfield until she married the owner of the Rodeo Cantina. She managed it until they lost their liquor license for serving minors. She died in 1999.

Wes (Wesley Warren)

Wes remained in Bakersfield after he and Sally divorced. He has worked successfully in several auto dealerships, though his gambling addiction is ongoing. He is a prominent organizing member of AA in the area. He remarried and has two children.

Coach Charles

Coach left the high school in 1966 to take over as football coach at a community college program in Solano County, where he has won several championships. He retired in 1986 to a ranch in that county, where he continues to volunteer as a coach and official.

The Boss (Myron Wyrum)

The Boss died of sunstroke complicated by acute alcohol poisoning in 1970. He was found slumped to the ground, near the high pasture, an empty bottle of Jim Beam next to him. Whether he'd gotten off or fallen off his horse could not be determined. He's buried in the family plot behind the big house under the live oak tree. He was sixty-four years old.

Major Wyrum

Major Wyrum served in the Army Nurse Corps until 1981, when she retired a full colonel. After the Boss passed away, she tried to take what she reasoned to be her portion of the ranch. A court fight ensued, after which she got nothing except the everlasting hate of Miss Lady. She never became close to Todd, Sally, or her grandson, and she saw them infrequently. She died in 2005 and is buried at a national cemetery in San Bruno, California. She was eighty-five years old.

Mrs. V (Valery Valverte)

Mrs. V continued to work her cheer team adventures with other girls until suspicions were raised. Then she promptly resigned from coaching and teaching, and left town. Nurse Jones left at the same time. Efforts were made to bring charges against Mrs. V, but these were thwarted by a murky trail of supposed misdeeds, the reluctance of past adventure girls to come forward, and people in high places hoping it would all be swept under the table. There were later rumors of her running a dominatrix house in Santa Barbara. Her whereabouts are unknown.

The House in Pismo Beach

The house burned to the ground about the same time Mrs. V left the county. Arson was suspected but never proved. The insurance company refused to pay out anything. It sat, a pile of burned-out junk, until a new home was built there years later.

Zeke and the Bar J

In 1969, the owner of the Bar J died. At that time, Zeke left the Rocking W and married the widow, with whom he'd had a long secret liaison. They made peace with the other ranchers on the Carrizo and turned the whole plain into a much more cooperative ranching endeavor. Now quite old, they still live on and work the Bar J.

Splash

Todd's well-loved horse lived a long, fruitful life on the ranch. She was well cared for and ridden often. Zeke and all the cowboys appreciated her hard work and calm demeanor. She died up on the high pasture one hot summer day at the age of seventeen.

Miss Lady

Only two months before Todd was released from confinement in Vietnam, Miss Lady died on the ranch. All that time since Todd's presumed death, she'd kept herself up and the ranch, too, but the light had gone out of her eyes.

One Sunday evening, when the cowboys returned from a wild weekend, they found her in the bunkhouse in front of Todd's old locker. Wearing a rodeo outfit, she sat leaning on his bunk. Her hair and makeup were as perfect as ever. Todd's old chaps, lariat, boots, gloves, spurs, and other stuff were spread out around her. In her hand were dog-eared pictures of her and Todd at a rodeo. Her face was relaxed and showed a tiny smile. The cowboys all cried.

Her will said that she didn't want to be interred in the family plot, but up among the rocks under a big live oak tree in the high pasture. She wanted a plain white headstone with her small turquoise ring embedded in it. She wanted the ground next to her left undisturbed, in case someone else might someday wish to rest next to her. She didn't say who. She was just fifty-three years old.

The Ranch, Jackie, Joan, and the Cruzes

When Miss Lady died, the ranch passed to her daughter Joan. Jackie had died in an auto accident the previous year. Joan has since married into a wealthy family in the horse country of Maryland. She kept the ranch, but she had Cruz and his wife manage it. When they passed on some years later, their son, Jose, took over. He still lives in the big house and has made a prosperous business of it. It looks pretty much the same as when Todd worked there in the 1950s.

Brenda

Brenda graduated on time from high school and kept up with Mrs. V's adventures while she finished. A year later, she had a baby boy whom she named Charles. She worked as a cocktail waitress all along the central coast, until she was able to buy into a funky restaurant/club in Avila Beach. Over time and the renovation of the town when Union Oil Company departed, the place has prospered. She is now the manager, and if you're ever in Blix, you're sure to recognize her. She's the same girl she always was, and with the same interests, too.

Brenda's son, Charles, completed college and law school. He then took over the law practice of Mr. Pearson when he was disbarred in 1992.

Brenda and Sally are still friends. She lives in Shell Beach, California, overlooking the ocean. She never identified Charles's father or married.

San Luis Obispo

SLO is now a big-time college town, having long since transitioned from the mission village founded by the Spanish in the 1770s. From the late nineteenth to mid-twentieth century, it was an important stop on the Southern Pacific Railroad, and then a slightly seedy college town at the time of our story. It's now the home of Cal

Poly State University, one of the best architecture, engineering, and agricultural schools in the world.

Scrubby and Lloyd's, the El Morocco Club, Dave's Lunch, the Irishman, Mission Bar, the Surf Motel, and Barbara by the Sea are gone now, and some character left with them. The town is now prosperous, however, with the best weather anywhere.

Todd and Sally

Three happy people returned to Bakersfield and picked up the broken pieces of Sally's life. They stayed there for only a couple of weeks, however, and then moved to San Luis Obispo, where they began to build life anew. In the autumn, Todd enrolled at Cal Poly, where he completed a double major in chemistry and psychology. Little Todd was signed up at the local school in See Canyon. They rented a quaint house in Avila Beach, up the hill from the old school. Sally got a waitressing job in the area, sometimes working with Brenda.

Todd and Sally kept to themselves and spent lots of time exploring the central coast in a boat they often borrowed from the yacht club. They were very happy.

During Todd's time at Cal Poly, he became involved with ROTC and returning veterans from Vietnam. His final term paper for his psychology class was on PTSD, a pretty new field at the time. This led to a book on the subject that had similarities to a twelve-step AA program. Titled *Winning Yourself Back*, it was quite successful. Upon graduation, and on the strength his book, Todd was offered a job as a professor at UCLA.

Sally took a job managing a local restaurant and did volunteer work, too. Little Todd got a new nickname—Todd 2. After a few years they were able to buy a dilapidated home by the famous California architect Rudolph Schindler. It was in the Westwood section of Los Angeles near the university. They restored the house to its original design, but what they loved most was the big back porch and yard. As the years passed, Todd's focus became more and more on PTSD and all its ramifications. He traveled to many places to lecture, coach, and mentor. They prospered and were very happy. As time passed, they became even more devoted to each other and Todd 2.

It turned out that Todd was more badly injured than first diagnosed. He was unable to conceive more children, but that didn't bother them. Todd 2 was plenty.

Todd never went back to the ranch. The memories were just too overwhelming, and Sally didn't want to look into those old experiences either.

At eighteen, Todd 2 went off to college. He eventually became the doctor Todd had always wanted to be. He's in private practice in LA, doing pediatrics. He's married and has three children.

Todd and Sally almost always hold hands when together. Sally still wears his *ping, ping, ping* fifty-cent-piece ring at her neck. The mason jar sits on the bay windowsill of their kitchen, where it catches the morning light.

They still have the truck, and Todd drives it to work most days.